hearts fire

A HEARTSTRUCK NOVEL

LARA BRUNI

PB ISBN: 979-8-9928796-1-2

Copyright © 2025 by Lara Bruni

Cover Design: Lara Bruni

Ryder & Noia character art: @hazelbronartist

 Formatted with Vellum

also by lara bruni

heads up

Even though this is book a spicy rom-com, there are some serious themes in regard to PTSD, addiction and a brief dream sequence with mentions of blood and gore.
Your mental health matters.

playlist

Waiting For Superman — **Daughtry**

Flaws — **Vancouver Sleep Clinic**

If Only — **Tiffany**

Houses — **Great Northern**

Morphine — **Digital Summer**

Pieces Of Me — **Tiffany**

"Have I gone mad?"
"I'm afraid so. You're entirely bonkers. But I'll tell you a secret, all the best people are."

— ALICE IN WONDERLAND

For those of us who dream of having their own book boyfriend

NOIA

"I NEED ANOTHER MONTH." BALANCING MY COFFEE IN ONE hand, I press my phone against my ear with the other as I deftly dodge a puddle in the middle of the sidewalk.

Portland in October shouldn't be this hot, but I'm already starting to sweat through the pits of my blouse. "It's not like I'm asking for an effing kidney, Amanda."

"We can't push the deadline again, Noia. Your readers have been waiting long enough."

"You know I have a wedding coming up. I know it's last minute, but..." I sidestep a tourist who has stopped right in the middle of the sidewalk to take a photo of a massive mural painted on the side of the building across the street.

Fuck's sake.

"Noia, we've already pushed this deadline twice." My agent's voice has that clipped, I'm-trying-not-to-lose-my-shit tone that I've become all too familiar with over the past few years. "Besides, the release date is set in stone. The publisher has already—"

Something slams into my back and my coffee goes flying. My phone slips out of my hand, clattering to the sidewalk as my ankles wobble in a pair of ridiculous four-inch heels Sasha convinced me would "make a statement" at today's meeting.

I pinwheel my arms, but it's no use. Unable to catch myself, I fall backward, my head slamming against the concrete.

Gravity is such a bitch.

ONE

THE ONE THING NO ONE TELLS YOU ABOUT WEDDINGS IS how goddamn itchy and traumatic everything is.

The dress. The fake eyelashes. Not to mention the ridiculous expectations.

"Are you sure about this?" my mom asks again, her smile not quite reaching her eyes as she hands me a flute of champagne. "How's your head feeling? It's been a week and you still have a bump."

"Tish," Sasha cuts in sharply. "It's her wedding day. Maybe don't interrogate her while she's being stuffed into a straight jacket made of statin and lace."

I smirk. My best friend Sasha is a badass. We've known each other since we were in the sixth grade, and she's always had my back. Shit, we even got our periods the same fucking week.

We first met when I was twelve. I was sitting on a bench, nose buried in a book, trying to blend into my surroundings over by the basketball court, when Lexi Carter and her crew cornered me.

Keeping my nose in my book, I hoped if I ignored them, they'd get bored and just go away.

But Lexi was having none of it. She snatched my book out of my hands, dangling it just out of reach.

"Give it back," I mumbled, wishing I had the courage to punch her in her smug little upturned nose.

"Or what, freak?" Lexi sneered, flipping through the pages. "God, this is so lame."

It was at that moment when a blur of red hair and righteous fury showed up out of nowhere. Sasha—a girl I barely knew from math class—stormed over like a pint-sized hurricane and stepped between us.

"Back off, Lexi, or I swear to god I'll tell everyone about what happened at camp last summer," Sasha growled, green eyes flashing.

All the color drained from Lexi's face before she dropped the book on the ground and she and her posse scattered.

Then Sasha sat down next to me, handed me half her smashed PB&J, and said, "You like books? Cool. Me too." And from that day forward? Best friends for life.

"Earth to Noia," Sasha grins, snapping her fingers in front of my face.

I grab the glass from my mother's hand and down half of it in one gulp.

"I'm fine," I murmur, mostly to myself. "Eric is a good guy. A little narcissistic, but he doesn't snore and he gets along with Goonie. That's gotta count for something, right?"

They look at me, both of them slowly shaking their heads.

"We'll support you no matter what, you know that," Sasha smiles.

Music floats through the church walls from outside the bridal suite. Inside, it smells like flowers and anxiety, which, for some reason, suddenly feels wildly ironic.

I sit in front of the vanity mirror, staring at a version of myself I never would have been able to put together on my own

—I'm more of a stretch pants and sweatshirt kind of girl. The perfect up sweep of my blond hair, the shimmery shadow and glossy lips, sure as shit doesn't feel like me. Not for a second.

"God, I look like a freaking cupcake."

Sasha steps behind me to fluff my veil. "You look beautiful."

I study her as she stands behind me in the mirror. With a ride or die soul and a smart-ass mouth, she's always been there for me. Just like she is now, wearing her deep green maid-of-honor dress like a badge of honor.

My mom, Tish, is pacing over by the window, setting my nerves even more on edge.

"Mom," I sigh, shaking my head. "Can you stop acting like someone just ran over your dog? Marrying Eric isn't such a bad thing."

Mouth twitching, my mom crosses her arms. "You've only known him for six months."

"Seven," I correct.

"You're only doing this because your manager said it would be good for your image," she volleys back.

"Incorrect," I say, pointing at her with my champagne glass. "I'm doing it because I'm thirty-two and tired of explaining at every family gathering why I'm not married yet. And because I can't make one of my fictional book boyfriends come to life so I can bring him to Thanksgiving dinner."

Sasha snorts. "He'd just burn the turkey and flirt with your grandma."

"You both know Gram's can give as much as she gets."

We laugh, and for a second the air in the room feels lighter—like maybe I'm not making the biggest mistake of my life.

But that second is short-lived.

There's a knock on the door, followed by a deep, hesitant male voice. "Uh, Sasha? Can I talk to you a sec?"

Sean, Eric's best man, is a cinnamon roll of a guy. Eric met him in college and they have been best friends ever since.

Sasha's brows pull tight. "Just a sec. I'll be right back."

Heels clicking against the tiled floor, she slips out, closing the door softly behind her.

Taking a seat, my mom crosses her legs, aiming a look at me over the rim of her glass. "Sugar... If something feels off, it would be better to back out now. Other than in your books, you don't owe anyone a happily ever after."

"Mom..."

She shrugs a shoulder. "Just trying to keep you from doing something stupid."

Just as I open my mouth to fire back, I hear Sasha's raised voice coming from the other side of the door.

"You'd better find out where that motherfucker is, or so help me—"

I sit up straight.

My mom looks up sharply. "What the hell—?"

I stand from my chair, heart thumping in my chest.

A second later, Sasha storms in, cheeks flushed and fists clenched.

"What's going on?" I ask, blood pounding in my ears.

She pauses, almost as if she wants to soften the blow, but when she sees my face, she lets out a defeated sigh.

"Noia..."

"Spit it out."

"Sean can't find Eric," she explains. "He's not answering his phone and he's not here at the church. No one has actually seen or talked to him since last night."

My mom gasps, hand flying to her chest. "I *knew* that guy was no good. I *knew* it. There was something twitchy in his eyes, always smiling like a politician."

Fuck, I don't even feel like crying. I'm just... stunned.

The silence in the room is so heavy, I can almost feel it in my bones.

"Maybe he got stuck in traffic?" I offer a little too brightly. "Or maybe his phone died. Maybe he's trying to find a parking spot?"

Sasha shakes her head slowly. "Noia. He was supposed to be here an hour ago. Sean checked with the hotel. His car is gone."

"I always said you should've stuck with that fireman with the motorcycle," my mother grouses. "What was his name? Lucas?"

"Luca," Sasha and I say together.

"He was crazy. He set my mailbox on fire after I broke up with him," I mumble.

"Well, at least he *showed up*," my mom snaps.

Not trusting my legs to keep me upright, I sink back onto my chair.

"I don't understand," I whisper. "He told me he really wanted this. He helped choose the cake, said he couldn't wait to see me walk down the aisle—"

Sasha kneels in front of me and grabs my hands.

"Noia. Listen to me. This is not about *you*. This is about him." She stands up with a huff. "That asshole, douchebag, piece of shit, coward."

My throat burns, but for some reason, I can't bring myself to cry. I'm too numb and way too fucking pissed.

My mom hands me her champagne and I take it, draining the glass.

"I need to get out of this fucking dress," I finally say.

"You want me to get the scissors?" Sasha asks, reaching for her purse.

"Yes," I growl. "Then I want a fucking bonfire."

Sasha's mouth twitches and my mom nods.

I look at myself in the mirror one last time.

If there's one thing I *do* know for sure? It's that Ryder Blackwood would never do this shit to me.

TWO

A WEEK AFTER BEING LEFT AT THE ALTAR, I REALIZE MY condo has become a mausoleum of empty wine bottles, fast food containers and unanswered questions.

Aside from the rain it's pretty quiet.

It hasn't stopped for days. It's the kind of steady, droning drizzle that quickly soaks the city to the bone, painting the skyline in grey watercolors, and turning headlights into blurry stars.

I used to love this kind of weather, all moody and cinematic. But now it feels like the universe is sighing right alongside me.

Curled up on my couch in one of Eric's old hoodies, I refuse to admit it still smells like him. Oversized and swamp green, I've matched it with a pair of threadbare boy shorts that used to be sexy, but now just scream: *Emotionally Damaged*.

The city sprawls beyond the floor-to-ceiling windows set between glass and steel with a thousand lives humming along on the other side.

My condo sits on the twenty-fourth floor. All sleek white walls, brushed gold fixtures, high ceilings and way too much curated art. It looks like it belongs to someone who actually has their life together.

I haven't washed my hair in three days and there's an entire bottle of Sauvignon Blanc sweating on the coffee table. My laptop is sitting on my thighs like a lead weight, open to a blinking cursor on a half-finished chapter I've rewritten so many times it doesn't even make sense anymore.

I stare at the name on the screen and want to scream.

Ryder Blackwood

My newest fictional god is a brooding, leather-jacket-wearing, sinfully hot former-Marine-turned-tattoo artist with a heart of gold buried under ten layers of emotional damage.

He's my latest blue print of a book-boyfriend that women across the world will thirst for by the time I'm done with him.

But there's a problem. I can't write about him anymore.

He won't talk to me. He just... sits in my head, arms crossed, silently judging my lack of brain power. And the worst kind of writer's block? Is when a figment of your own imagination starts ghosting *you*.

I've texted Eric once. Just once.

I don't even know what the hell I want to say. I just want to understand. I deserve at least that much.

That was four days ago, and the asshole left me on READ.

I never imagined I'd be the woman staring at her phone, rereading a text she regrets sending, but here we are.

A hard knock breaks through my reverie.

Dragging myself to the door, I toe aside a stack of unopened mail spread across the floor and crack it open to find Sasha, holding up a giant canvas tote bag with a bright smile on her face.

She's in high-waisted black leggings, an oversized lilac sweater that slips off one shoulder, combat boots, and a messy top knot that makes her look effortlessly cool. Her skin is dewy from the rain, but her eyeliner's still intact.

"You look like shit," she says, brushing by me to step inside.

"Great," I mumble. "That was the look I was going for."

She sets the bag on the kitchen island with a thunk. "I brought supplies. Wine, stuff to make a charcuterie, trashy tabloids and bottle of tequila. And also—because I love you—a discounted cake from the bakery down the street that says 'Sorry Your Life Is Trash' in black frosting."

That actually makes me snort.

"I also brought these," she adds, digging out a pair of fuzzy socks with middle fingers stitched into them. "Because mood."

"Not only are you my bestie, you are an icon."

"Tell me something I don't know."

We settle onto the couch with a spread fit for two queens. We don't talk much for the first hour. We don't have to.

She flips through a tabloid reporting a rumor I've ghosted the wedding on purpose to drum up publicity. There's even a blurry photo of me looking haunted outside a grocery store.

Jesus. I had no idea I looked *that* rough.

"You need to leave," Sasha says out of nowhere.

My eyebrows shoot up. "Excuse me?"

"Eventually," she says around a bite of brie. "But preferably now. You've got this look about you. You know—the one where your hair's about to join a cult and your laptop is planning a murder-suicide."

"I've been working," I lie.

"No, you've been pretending to write while watching twelve-year-old baking competition reruns on HGTV and stalking Eric's Insta."

I open my mouth to argue.

"You're also out of clean underwear and have been wearing the same hoodie for five days."

"I washed it," I mutter.

She gives me a look.

"Fine. I *Febreezed* it."

Sasha leans forward, grabbing my knee and giving it a shake. "Babe. You need a reset. A real one. Not the kind where you sage your living room and end up crying into a pint of Chunky Monkey."

I sigh. "And where exactly do you propose I reset my shattered emotional soul?"

She lifts her brows. "Lakeside."

I blink. "You mean my writer's cottage?"

"It's perfect. No distractions. No press. No memories of an ex-fiancé lurking in every corner."

It's true. I haven't been there for over a year. My writer's cottage is about an hour outside of the city, nestled next to a lake in a quiet, isolated area near a small town called Lakeside, surrounded by woods, fog and the occasional moose.

I bought it after my second book hit the bestseller list. It's always been a place I can run to when deadlines loom or the world gets too loud.

"Think about it," Sasha says gently, pulling her feet onto the couch. "No expectations. No social media. Just you, your writing, and a chance to figure out what the hell comes next."

I tip my head back and stare at the ceiling as the rain drums against the windows.

"Fine," I finally say. "But only if you come with me."

She smirks. "I thought you'd never ask."

The lake house smells like cedar and dust.

It's a two-story, three bedroom cottage tucked beneath a

canopy of evergreens, with light wood siding and a wide front porch that creaks under our feet. The air up here is different —crisp, damp, and laced with pine. No more car horns or people. No more of my mom calling to "check in" and casually remind me that she always knew Eric was a spineless coward.

Sasha pushes open the door and breathes in deep.

"God, I missed this place."

Inside, everything is as I left it: cozy and cluttered. Bookshelves sag under the weight of hardcovers, paperbacks and fake plants. A macrame wall hanging is tacked up above the stone fireplace. There's a mismatched velvet armchair by the window and a navy blue typewriter I don't use resting on the antique writer's desk I bought because I thought it made me look old school bookish.

"I had the fridge stocked a couple of days ago," Sasha says, tossing her purse on the couch. "Wine, pasta, pop tarts. All the essentials."

"I knew I kept you around for a reason," I grin, setting Goonie down on the floor.

Sasha rolls her eyes, but I can still see the concern lingering in the expression on her face. She's been doing that a lot lately— watching me like a hawk—like she's waiting for me to crack.

"Go ahead and judge," I huff as I hang my jacket on one of the hooks by the door.

"Nope." She kicks off her boots. "You're getting none of that from me."

Once Sasha leaves, not only will I be alone with my self-deprecating thoughts, but my unfinished manuscript, and a stupidly hot fictional hero who refuses to cooperate—my skin feels itchy just thinking about it.

At least my cat, Goonie, will be here for impromptu cuddles.

Sasha plops onto the couch and drags the couch blanket over her lap.

"Remember when we stayed up all night here binge-writing book three?" she asks, her eyes going soft with the memory. "You were eating chips with chopsticks to keep your fingers clean."

"Best system I ever invented."

"Back then, you were unstoppable."

I stare out the big picture window that faces the lake. The water is slick and grey under low-hanging mist, while trees stand sentinel on the opposite bank like watchful shadows.

"I used to know how to get lost in the story," I say quietly. "Now I can't even fake it."

Standing from the couch, my bestie steps over and pulls me into a hug. Warm, tight and familiar, she smells like vanilla and fabric softener.

"You're gonna be okay," she whispers into my hair.

"Even if I never write again?"

She pulls back, grips my shoulders and gives me a hard look. "*Especially* if you never write again. You're more than just your books, Noia. It's important for you to remember that."

She stays long enough to unpack the extra groceries we bought and build me a cheese plate I don't feel like eating. She makes the bed with clean sheets and lights a lavender candle in the kitchen.

When she finally zips up her bag and shrugs on her coat, the setting sun is painting everything in amber and gold burning off some of the mist. But that won't last long.

"You sure you're good?" she asks as she stands in the doorway.

I wave her off. "Go. Take your tight yoga ass and leave me here to rot."

She snorts. "You've got Goonie to protect you." She grins at my fat calico as he jumps onto the couch and spins a couple of times before claiming his spot. "Call me if the woods try to murder you."

"I'll scream your name into the trees and hope for the best."

Pulling me into another quick hug, she turns and heads to her car. I stand at the door and watch until her taillights disappear down the gravel road and get swallowed by the fog.

And just like that—I'm alone.

When I realize I've been holding my breath, I blow it out in a whoosh.

After pouring myself a glass of wine, I change into an old thermal and a pair of fleece leggings, and light every candle I own. Less musty now, the house smells more like lavender, citrus, and sage.

I crack open the windows to air out the house, just enough to hear the lake lapping softly at the shore as the stars, one by one, slowly start winking into existence against the night sky.

Grabbing my suitcase, I go upstairs to my bedroom, sit at my desk and open my laptop to a blank page. The cursor blinks back at me until after a few minutes, I reluctantly start to type.

Ryder Blackwood stepped out of the dark. Leather jacket soaked in blood and rain, his eyes were full of—

Ugh. I stop, backspace and try again.

Ryder leaned against the doorframe, smirking like—

Delete.

Delete.

Delete.

I slam the laptop shut.

Resting my head in my hands, I groan. "Come on. Talk to me, you stupid, sexy figment of my imagination."

All I can hear is silence—the kind of silence where the only sound you can hear is the ringing in your ears.

I push away from the desk and pour another glass of wine.

The night stretches on as I scroll on my phone. I listen to old voicemails and delete Eric's number—again.

By the time midnight rolls around, I'm back downstairs, lying on the couch under a fleece blanket with my laptop open, page still blank.

I close my eyes and whisper, "Damn, I wish you were real, Rye. You'd know what to do."

Waking up in someone else's house isn't new—but waking up in one that smells like lavender and chaos?

Definitely a first.

I'm standing in the middle of a living room, barefoot, shirtless, and hella confused.

It's still dark outside, or maybe it's early. I can't really tell because the windows sitting across from me have a wall of mist pressing up against the glass. The air is heavy with something... familiar. This isn't a place I recognize, but there's this feeling I can't quite put my finger on.

The room is cozy and cluttered. A couple of soft throw blankets are draped over the back of a dark green velvet couch, and there's a stack of paperbacks on the coffee table, next to a candle.

A record player is sitting in the corner with a stack of vinyl leaning next to it.

And there are books. *Everywhere.*

Stacked on the shelves, piled under the coffee table, crammed into wicker baskets by the fireplace.

I walk past a framed cover of a novel hung as art on the wall.

Heartstruck: by Noia Wilde

Stunned, all I can do is blink.

Noia. That name stirs something to life inside me—deep and electric—making my spine stiffen.

I spot another copy of the same book lying on an armchair, spine cracked and covered in Post-Its. Plucking it up, I flip through it.

Scribbled in pencil every few pages are notes and rewrites.

Author notes?

More books are stacked underneath, each with a different title, but all written by the same author.

Noia Wilde

Tension itching between my shoulder blades, I sit on the couch. As I skim, flipping through the pages, the words start to become awfully familiar.

Wait. These are *my* stories, my military brothers' stories—or at least some version of them.

What the *fuck*.

A chirrup cuts through my spiraling train of thoughts, and I glance up to see a fat calico cat strolling into the room like he owns the place. With one torn ear, his squished, smug face looks like it's seen better days. Rubbing against my leg with a low purr, he gives me a judgmental look.

I stare, judging right back. "Bet you're a little menace, aren't you...?" I take a look at his name tag. "Goonie."

When I snort out his name, he gives me a loud, indignant meow.

"Right. That tracks."

Tossing the book down on the table, I stand up from the couch. My head feels a little foggy, which is weird. I take pride in keeping a clear head, and right now that is *not* what's happening.

I take another look around. The space is warm, lived in, and full of personality. I wander into the kitchen. Although the deep green cabinets, white farmhouse sink, and copper pots and pans hanging above the stove aren't my taste, the kitchen is still rather nice.

On the fridge, there's a magnet shaped like a typewriter that says: **Writers do it between the lines.**

I shake my head.

A corkboard hangs beside the pantry door riddled with scraps of paper—quotes, deadlines, and a grocery list pinned to it.

Wine
Cat food
Wine
Goddamn printer ink
Tums
~~Cat food~~

Unopened mail and what looks to be a planner with the words **'KILL HIM OFF???'** written in angry red pen, are sitting on a kitchen island covered in crumbs.

Off to the right, a hallway leads to a small guest bedroom with a queen sized bed and a fluffy light blue duvet.

The attached bathroom is spotless and bare, except for a box of tissues sitting on top of the tank, and shampoo bottles in the walk-in shower that smell like spicy vanilla and sex.

The door next to the bathroom opens into a closet, but aside from a couple of plastic bins filled with men's clothing, it's empty.

Leaving the bedroom, I walk back down the hall, pausing at

the foot of the stairs as the cat saunters up the steps past me like he means business, so I follow.

The second floor has two bedrooms and a bathroom.

When I come to the second door, I glance inside and see a rumpled queen sized bed against one wall, with a big desk tucked in front of the window on the other.

Slumped over the desk, dead asleep with her head buried in her arms, hair a messy halo of blonde curls, is a woman that I can only assume is the one who wrote me into existence.

Noia Wilde

Lips parted, she's snoring softly. Ink smudges her fingertips, and her laptop, still open beside her, is glowing like a beacon.

Dumbfounded, all I can do is stare.

I don't know what the fuck I expected, but it wasn't *this*.

She's beautiful in a chaotic, soft-around-the-edges kind of way.

Wearing a robe that's hanging off one shoulder, her skin is pale and I can see a light scattering of freckles across her nose, highlighted in the glow of her desk lamp. One foot is bare, while the other has a sock hanging half on, half off.

I should be furious. And in a way, I kind of feel violated. It's not like I had a choice in being here.

Instead, I just feel... unsettled. Like something inside of me has been tilted on its axis.

"Christ," I mutter, scrubbing a hand down my face.

Not wanting to disturb her quite yet, I turn away and head back downstairs.

I take a seat on the couch and flip on the TV—she's got way too many streaming subscriptions, by the way—and choose something mind numbing.

Goonie hops up beside me, kneading the cushion as he gives me his best resting murder face impression, then hops into my lap.

His purring soothes my nerves, and within minutes, I'm out like a light.

WHEN I WAKE UP, SUNLIGHT IS POURING THROUGH THE windows, and Goonie is sitting on my chest staring down at me.

Gently shoving him off, I stretch and shuffle to the bathroom. After I take the longest piss of my life, I go to wash my hands and see the mirror above the sink has a Post-It stuck to it.

You got this, babe—Sasha

Back in the kitchen, I dig through the freezer until I find a pack of bacon. I toss it into the microwave to defrost and search for a pan.

Goonie yowls dramatically, making me jump.

"Alright, alright," I mutter, opening random cupboards until I find a tub labeled: **GOONIE'S SHIT**.

Popping it open, I scoop some food into his bowl, which he proceeds to devour like he hasn't been fed in days.

The microwave beeps and I get to work.

As I turn the bacon over in the pan, there's a creak from the floorboards above, followed by a soft thud.

Cocking my head, I listen close, just as Goonie lifts his head and bolts up the stairs.

I narrow my eyes... and wait.

FOUR

noia

I WAKE UP TO THE SMELL OF BACON—WHICH IS WEIRD because I'm pretty sure I haven't bought bacon in I don't know how long. All I've been living off of the past few days is wine, Pop-Tarts, and existential dread.

It's been a week since Sasha dropped me off and I haven't ventured out of the house the entire time.

I'm a wreck.

Not only do I smell bacon, but someone is singing. The sound, low and deep, isn't bad, it's just a little off-key.

I bolt upright, and immediately regret it. My robe is slumping off one shoulder, and my head is throbbing like a goddamn drum line is marching through it. And my mouth? It tastes like cheap wine, jalapeño flavored Cheetos and regret.

So. Much. Regret.

Goonie yowls at me from my bedroom doorway, making me cringe. It feels like my head is going to explode.

Fuck. Me. Running.

"Yeah, yeah. I smell it too," I mutter.

Swinging my legs over the edge of the bed, I nearly trip over an empty bottle of merlot.

Barefoot, sans the one sock still clinging for dear life to the top half of my left foot, I yank it off and toss it on the floor.

Trudging down the stairs and into the kitchen, I turn the corner and freeze.

There is a *man* in my kitchen.

And not just any man. A shirtless man.

Broad shoulders flex seductively as he reaches for the coffeepot. His dark hair is a little long and messy, like he's just rolled out of bed after doing wild, sexy, unspeakable things. Tattoos curl around brawny arms and across a chiseled chest. And that *ass*. God has definitely taken her time on that tight, I-would-give-my-left-tit-to-bite, sexy as sin ass.

Standing in my kitchen like he owns it, he's humming and flipping bacon in my Hell's Kitchen frying pan like he's the star of some goddamn Food Network cooking show.

There's something familiar about him I can't quite place, but before I can put together some semblance of a coherent thought, something along the lines of a gasp and a squeak escapes my throat.

Without bothering to look up, he growls, calm as can be, "Took you long enough. Hope you like your eggs scrambled. Oh, and I slept in the guest room last night. You know, since I have nowhere else to go?"

What in the fresh, ever-loving hell?

"Who the *fuck* are you, and what the hell are you doing in my kitchen?" I snap, grabbing the nearest weapon I can find. My favorite spatula is bright pink and made of silicone, and not even close to lethal, but it's all I've got.

Still not quite ready to come to terms with what I'm seeing, when he finally turns to look at me, it hits me, and I feel like I could die.

Not literally, obviously. But if a cardiac event were to strike me down in this moment, I would go out looking at the sexiest face I'd ever created.

"I'm Ryder."

Ryder Blackwood, the newest bad boy hero from my best-selling romance series, Heartstruck, is standing half-naked in my kitchen.

Cooking bacon.

He's looking at me with smoky gray eyes, flashing a sexy crooked smirk above a jaw that could cut some serious glass.

"You know... the guy you've left hanging mid-scene for the past week?" He quirks an eyebrow. "Appreciate that, by the way. Real cool."

I blink and my robe slips further off my shoulder.

His eyes flick from my face to my bare shoulder, then drop to my chest, which happens to only be covered by a thin, cropped white tank top.

The only other piece of clothing, other than that and my robe, is a tiny pair of sleep shorts and what I have no doubt is a partial camel-toe, completing the ensemble.

I gasp, pulling my robe closed. "Don't stare at me, you perv!"

He snorts. "Kinda hard not to when you're flashing me like you're the entire cast of *Magic Mike*."

Clutching my robe with one hand, I wave the spatula in his face with the other. "This is not happening. You are not real. You're fictional. I made you up!"

He points to himself. "Do I *look* fictional to you?"

I'm not about to answer that. Mostly because he seems to be real. More than, actually. Not to mention annoyingly smug about it.

I back up a step, my heart tap dancing against my ribs.

"Okay. Okay," I whisper-mutter to myself. "I'm dreaming.

Or maybe I'm still drunk. Maybe both. This has got to be some sort of weird stress-induced hallucination."

Walking toward me slowly, he holds out a mug filled with coffee like a peace offering. "You're not dreaming. I'm here. I don't know why or how. But it seems I'm stuck in your world and I'm pretty sure you're the only one who can send me back to mine."

I look down at the coffee. Then up at him. Then back down at the mug.

The mug has a cartoon cat painted on its side and a caption that reads:

'Be Nice To Me... Or You Could End Up Dead In My Novel.'

"Jesus. I've finally lost my fucking mind," I mumble as I take the mug.

He tilts his head. "You don't remember writing this scene, do you? The one where I'm in your kitchen shirtless, cooking bacon? With plenty of banter and sexual tension. Page ninety-eight, kitten."

The cup of coffee almost slips out of my hand. "That was never... I never actually..." I stammer, shaking my head hard enough to bring back my hangover headache with a vengeance. "I only *thought* about writing it. It was just an *idea*."

Raising a brow, his beautiful, full mouth twitches up at one corner. "I guess we're living it now."

"Okay." I drag in a shaky breath and wave the spatula in the air between us. "You. This. Me. None of this is really happening."

Ryder moves to lean one hip against the counter looking like something out of a fucking Calvin Klein ad, watching me unravel with way too much amusement for my liking.

"I mean, this isn't *real*. I don't care how hot you are, you're fictional. A figment of my overcooked imagination and unresolved emotional trauma."

"You forgot 'devastatingly charming,'" he rumbles around a mouthful of crispy pork perfection.

I hold up a finger. "Shut up. Just—shut up and stay right there."

Carefully setting the mug on the counter, I turn and bolt back upstairs to my bedroom.

Whatever. I'm a woman on a mission—a very panicked, half-dressed woman on the verge of a nervous breakdown—but on a mission nonetheless.

Crashing into my desk chair, I grab my laptop and open the document file faster than a gremlin on Red Bull, fingers flying across the keys.

Suddenly, Ryder Blackwood disappeared, never to be seen again. Poof. Gone. Goodbye forever. Insert explosion sound. The end.

I hit SAVE with dramatic flourish, slam the lid shut, and exhale.

Silence.

I stand up slowly, heart thudding, chest tight, and walk back down to the kitchen, where he's still standing, effing shirtless, smirking bigger than before.

"What in the actual fuck?" I whisper.

"You know." He picks up another piece of bacon and points it at me. "You're underestimating how stubborn I am. It's how you wrote me, remember?"

Grabbing the spatula off the counter again, I storm over and slap the flat side of the flipper against his chest.

He quirks a sexy eyebrow. Does this guy *ever* flinch?

"You don't belong here," I bite out. "You're not *real*."

Slowly, he leans in, pushing his chest against the spatula.

He smells like... I take a deep breath in. Sandalwood... Another deep breath... Leather.

Holy hell.

"Then why," he murmurs, "do you look like you can't decide whether you want to slap the shit outta me or kiss me?"

I swallow. Hard.

"Definitely leaning towards *slap*."

Tilting his head, his gaze drops to my mouth. "You sure 'bout that?"

I step back, trip over Goonie, who yowls in protest, and nearly topple to the floor before Ryder catches me.

Of course he does. Isn't that what leading men do?

Warm, rough hands with fingers curling just a little too perfectly around my waist, hold me tight.

I shove at his chest. "Let go of me, you fucked up figment of my imagination."

He looks down his nose at me, and has the audacity to smirk —again. "You're the one who brought me into your world, *kitten*. And the only problem I can see? Is that you're way too overdressed for this scene."

I shove at his chest again.

He still doesn't move. Not even a twitch.

Jesus, he has more muscle than one man should legally possess, fictional or not.

"You need to go. *Now*. Back to Novel Never Land. Or wherever it is my overworked subconscious dragged you from."

"I tried." Ryder shrugs like he doesn't have a care in the world. "Obviously, it didn't work. Believe me, I'd love more than anything to get back to that shower scene you never finished. Which means *I* didn't get to finish. Just so you know—I prefer my balls flesh colored, by the way, not blue."

Making a strangled noise somewhere between a screech and a sob, I scramble away.

I lunge for my phone on the counter and hit speed dial. There is only one person I know who can talk me down from this level of literary delusion.

"Come on, come on. Pick up, pick up—"

"Hey, girl!"

Relief flares in my chest when I hear my bestie's voice. "Sasha! Thank god!"

"You okay?" she asks. "You sound funny."

"Something's wrong," I whisper-hiss as I duck and crouch behind the kitchen island. "Like, *seriously* wrong. I think I've finally cracked. Snapped like a fucking twig."

There's a beat of silence before she responds. "Okaaay... What and how much exactly did you drink last night?"

"Um..." I peek over the top of the counter. Ryder is still standing there all smug and shit, licking bacon grease off his fingers like he isn't the literal cause of my current existential spiral. "It's Ryder."

"Ryder *who*?"

"*Ryder Blackwood*," I whisper-yell into the phone.

"Wait—*the* Ryder Blackwood? The new hero from your current WIP? The broody, emotionally constipated, tattooed bad boy with the motorcycle?"

"Yes!" I hiss.

"Oh! I see. Did you finally write the smutty kitchen scene?" she asks, way too interested.

"NO! I mean—*he's in my actual kitchen*, Sash! Cooking bacon, handing me coffee and talking to me like he's a real person. I tried to delete him, but it didn't work! I rewrote his exit! I used the dramatic wind explosion and everything!"

She goes quiet.

"Sash?"

"You need a nap. Or drugs. Wait. Maybe not drugs. Did you start doing drugs?"

"Damn it, Sash. I swear to God, he's *real*. He's a living, breathing man standing in my kitchen. And he has abs—*so many abs*," I groan. "Pretty sure his abs have abs."

I stand from my crouch, lean against the island, letting my guard down for half a second.

Big mistake.

Reaching across the island, Ryder snatches the fucking phone right out of my hand and winks at me before he speaks.

"Hey, Sasha." His voice is all sex and liquid silk. *Jesus.* "Quick question. Ever wonder what it would be like to talk to someone your best friend wrote into existence with an enemies-to-lovers trope?"

"*WHAT THE SHIT?!*" I hear Sasha shriek.

I dive over the counter like a female version of Jason Bourne, tackling him with all the force my robe-clad, chaos-fueled self can muster, crashing both of us against the fridge.

"Give. Me. My phone!" I growl, right before it drops with a clunk to the floor.

"Only if you say please," he growls back, leaning in close, eyes bright with challenge.

"God! You've got to be the biggest asshole I've ever written."

Grinning the biggest shit-eating grin I've ever seen, he spreads his arms wide. "Your doing, not mine."

Snatching the phone off the floor, I scramble back across the tile like I've seen the devil himself, and put it back to my ear.

Sasha is laughing so hard I can barely understand her. "I *told* you the steam in your books was gonna bite you in the ass one of these days," she gasps. "You better call your editor. Tell her you manifested a shirtless, sex fueled menace with perfect pecs and no off switch whatsoever."

This bitch.

"I hate you so much right now."

"And I love this for you. *Bye-eee.*"

After she hangs up on me, I drop the phone onto the counter.

When I turn around, Ryder's gaze is zeroed in on me like I'm some kind of crazy puzzle he can't figure out.

"What?" I snap.

Keeping my arms crossed, I do my best to keep my robe from falling open again. For some reason, every inanimate object I own is doing its best to betray me this morning. "Are you waiting for a standing ovation? Maybe a 'World's Sexiest Hallucination' trophy?"

His eyes go from soft gray to full on storm before he pushes off the counter with lazy grace. With the easy confidence of a cat stalking its prey, he starts walking toward me.

My pulse picks up, skin tingling with heat under his steely gaze. I back up, heart thudding against my ribs, until the smooth kitchen wall meets my spine, halting any further retreat.

Stopping just a breath away, Ryder's dark and stormy eyes trace every inch of my face. My lips, my throat—the spot where I know my robe is gaping open—again. I can almost feel it, like a fingertip sliding across my skin.

I can't move. Can't breathe.

My skin flushes and nerves dance in my veins as my entire body tightens in anticipation, waiting for him to pounce.

He leans in, brushing his lips along the shell of my ear, making me shiver so hard, I want to scream. Or come. Coming would be nice.

Shut. Up. Noia.

His voice is a low growl as he whispers, "You should really go take a shower."

I blink and my heart drops.

"What?"

"Your hair is a rat's nest, and you smell like booze and desperation."

I gape at him, and he gives me a smarmy grin.

Shoving him in the chest, I stomp past him before I turn and flip him off. "You're such dick, Ryder Blackwood!"

"Correction," he calls after me. "I'm *your* dick."

Turning on my heel, I run upstairs to my bathroom, slam the door and turn the shower on full blast.

The water is a little too hot, but I don't care. I stand under the spray in an attempt to boil the memory of his smug face out of my brain.

"Yeah, well. You smell like a dark forest and every bad decision I've ever made," I mutter-whine to myself, scrubbing shampoo into my scalp with way too much force. "And you're acting like you own the place. Which you don't. Because this is *my* house. My life. *My story.*"

I yank the conditioner bottle open with a vengeance.

"And you think you can just waltz in here, shirtless, self-righteous, and entirely too sexy for someone I *created*, and try throwing me off *my* game? Nope. Nuh-uh. Not gonna happen."

Steam swirls around me as I slap a handful of conditioner into my hair, scowling at the wall of white subway tile.

"You're not even that hot," I lie to myself as the water beats against my back and my brain buzzes.

And then, mid-conditioner, it hits me.

My eyes widen, and I stop frantically running my hands through my wet hair. "Oh, my god."

I have an idea. A brilliant, devious, chaos-fueled idea.

"If I can't delete you," I whisper, my voice full of malice. "Maybe I can *distract* you."

A wicked grin curls at my lips.

Squeaky clean and fully alert, I wrap myself in a towel, and storm out of the bathroom full of pure, unadulterated spite.

Water drips from my hair and runs down my shoulders, leaving a trail of water on the floor in my wake.

Fuck it. I have a purpose, a goal, a loophole in the very laws of fictional physics.

If I can't write Ryder Blackwood out of my world? I'll write him into a corner.

A very *erotic*, tongue-filled corner.

Making a beeline for my desk, I open my laptop.

So he wants to play games? Fine. Let's see how he likes kissing someone *else*.

Hands still damp from the shower, I crack my knuckles and type like my life depends on it.

Ryder stepped into the sunlit bookstore, eyes scanning the quiet corners of the shop until they landed on Lexi.

The barista-bookworm with legs for days and a mouth made for sucking his cock, turned, her eyes going wide when she spotted him. "You came back," she breathed.

He took one step forward, then another, their chemistry igniting like sparks on gasoline. "I couldn't stay away," he said, voice low and rough.

And then he kissed her, slow and deep, devouring every inch of her mouth.

My lips twist into a satisfied smirk. Take that, Ryder Blackwood.

As soon as I hit SAVE, the air shifts and a static hum crawls across my skin much like the moment right before lightning strikes.

A floorboard creaks behind me.

No. Nope.

I spin in my chair and—

Mother fucker.

Leaning against the door jamb—still shirtless by the way—his arms are folded across his chiseled, tattooed chest, jaw twitching at his temple, eyes locked on my laptop. And his signature smirk? Gone.

His growl is low and dangerous. "Lexi? Really?"

My stomach drops somewhere between the keyboard and the entrance to hell.

"Oh," I squeak. "Hey. Fancy seeing you here."

"You wrote in *Lexi*?"

I lift my chin in defiance. "She's a fully developed love interest with a mysterious past and great bone structure. She's a sexy smart-ass, loves coffee, and—"

"You made me *kiss* her."

"Well, *yeah*," I snark, pushing a strand of damp hair away from my face. "You were getting a little too comfortable in *my* house. Figured you could use a distraction."

Pushing off the door, he moves into the room, one slow, stalking step at a time.

"Let me get this straight," he rumbles, voice full of danger and—god help me—sex. "You conjure me out of thin air—into a world where I don't belong—and your first move is to pimp me out to some literary NPC with *espresso breath*?"

"I wasn't *pimping* you out," I snap. "I was creatively redirecting your attention."

"To who?"

"Lexi!"

My heart jack hammers against my ribs as he keeps moving further into the room.

"To a woman who, technically, doesn't even exist?"

"Well, technically *you* didn't exist until I typed you into existence, so—"

He takes another step closer and I shrink back into my chair, heart racing as I glare up at him.

Then, to my shock, my towel slides open between my legs.

His eyes drop to my thighs. "Careful," he murmur-growls. "Pretty sure that thing is hanging on by sheer willpower alone."

My hands fly down to adjust the towel. "Eyes up, Casanova."

"Not a chance. Believe me when I say, watching you try to outmaneuver me in your bath towel is the highlight of my strange new reality."

I try to stand, but he's so much faster.

Now towering over me, his hands land on the desk, caging me in. Heat radiates off his body, and I can smell the mix of sandalwood, leather, and midnight clinging to his skin.

Fuck me.

"You don't get to control me like that." His voice is quiet, edged with something primal. "Not anymore."

I swallow, tilting my chin up to meet his eyes in defiance. "I'm a writer. It's my job to control the narrative."

"Once upon a time." His gaze finds my mouth. "But I think something broke inside me when I showed up. I don't want *her*, Noia."

My breath catches.

"I want *you*."

His words burn like a brand on my skin, searing through every nerve ending straight to my core. I'm surprised I don't come just from the look in his eyes alone.

"I don't—" But the words get stuck in my throat.

His face is so close, I can see the tiny flecks of blue in the gray of his irises.

My eyes track his tongue as it slowly drags across his full bottom lip. The tension between us tightens and coils like a live wire ready to blow into a million sparks.

Then he pushes away.

Just like that. No mind-blowing kiss. No heat-sparking

climax. Just empty space and another smug-as-shit grin splitting across his handsome face.

"What the hell?" I gasp, breathless and flustered.

Reaching across me, he gently closes the laptop. "Try writing me into another woman's mouth again," he says softly. "And I'll start *rewriting* the rules myself."

"What the fuck is that supposed to mean?"

His wink makes my clit pulse. "Guess you'll have to wait and find out."

And then he walks out of the room like he didn't just steamroll my brain and body all at the same time.

I stare up at the ceiling and groan, "I'm so *fucked*."

FLINGING OPEN THE BEDROOM DOOR, I MARCH INTO THE living room like I'm storming onto a battlefield.

Dressed in a baggy hoodie, leggings, and enough eyeliner to scare off a raccoon—I'm more than ready for a fight to the fictional death.

But what I'm not prepared for?

Ryder sitting on my couch like a centerfold in a writer's retreat brochure. He's reading *my book*, writing notes in the margins, in red pen, all while Goonie—the little furry traitor—lays curled up next to him on the couch purring away.

"Are you editing my novel?" I ask incredulously.

Keeping his eyes on the book, he casually licks his thumb and turns a page. "Technically, I'm critiquing your dialogue—the early stuff. You got much better later on."

Anger flashes through my veins. "You're marking up my best-seller with a red pen like it's a fucking *term paper?*"

"You repeated the word 'breathless' six times in chapter three," he volleys back, still flipping. "We get it. He takes her breath away. Maybe let her *breathe* once in a while."

"I'm going to *murder you.*"

Finally, he looks up. "You already tried. Remember? The Lexi smooch scene? I barely survived *that* cliché," he huffs, giving me an over-the-top shudder.

With a groan, I flop onto the loveseat and dramatically shove my face in my hands. My next words come out a muffled, "Why are you being like this?"

"Because. I'm a creation of your deepest, darkest fantasies. And, because you imagined me this way, you're just going to have to deal with it."

Silence fills the air between us. The only sound is the gentle rasp of Ryder turning another page and Goonie purring as my fragile ego bleeds out somewhere between chapters six and seven.

Then softly, he asks, "Why has it been so hard for you to write lately?"

Flopping my arms into my lap with a sigh, I drop my head against the back of the couch and stare up at the ceiling.

"I was supposed to get married."

The sound of flipping stops.

"I had the dress, a violin quartet and the cake. It was all planned perfectly." I swallow against the lump attempting to crawl its way up my throat and roll my head to look at him. "And he didn't show."

Ryder doesn't speak; he just looks at me. For once, his expression isn't smug or smirky. It's a look that makes my chest pull tight.

"What a fucking asshole."

"Yeah." I shift and lift my head to stare down at my finger-nails. The black nail polish I applied a week ago in an attempt to clear the cobwebs from my brain is already starting to chip.

"Still doesn't explain why I ended up here. How you somehow summoned me into your world."

I let out a snort. "I didn't *mean* to summon you."

"Well." Setting the book aside, he leans forward, resting his forearms on his knees. "You did. And maybe the universe—or your messed-up, anxiety fueled imagination—brought me here for a reason."

I look at him. "To fuck with my head?"

"To *help* you," he corrects, pointing a long, thick finger at me.

I wonder what sort of dirty things those can get up to?

I shake off the fantasy as he continues. "You want to finish your book, and I want you to finish my story. We can help each other. Win-win."

I frown. "And how exactly do you propose we do that?"

He grins his signature slow, panty-melting grin—one that should be illegal in twenty-seven countries by the way.

"Simple. You write me a proper ending, and I help you get your mojo back. But there's a catch."

"Of course there is."

"I want the full experience. The real deal. I want to *live* while I'm here. Have some fun. We could eat great food, listen to music, and go dancing. Maybe even fuck with your ex. Make him regret ever leaving you at the altar."

My eyebrows lift high enough to fondle my nine-foot ceiling. "You want to... fake date me?"

His eyes drop to my mouth. "No, kitten. I want to *actually* date you. While I'm here, I want it all. The full experience."

Heat crawls along my sex, making me squirm. "Exactly what do you mean by *all*?"

Glancing up from where he definitely watched me squeeze my thighs together, he leans in, his voice a low purr. "You. Me. A little revenge. A lot of fun. And eventually... every single orgasm you've ever imagined me giving someone else? I'll give to *you*."

My breath hitches. "You're serious?"

"As a heart attack," he says, mouth so close it almost feels like a dare. "We're not going to half-ass this, Noia. You want to fix your writer's block? Then we're going to have some wild, crazy fun to help inspire you. Then, you'll write out everything we do after we act out the story in real life."

Taking a step back, he holds out his hand. The contract he's offering me has sex and danger written all over it.

"What do you say? Deal?"

I stare at his big, beautiful hand. A hand that could grip my throat, while his fingers from the other pump furiously inside me. It's a thought that has my heart racing and my brain short-circuiting.

And my ovaries? Those traitors are signing right on the dotted line.

Fuck it.

I reach out and shake his hand. "Deal."

ryder

WHAT THE *HELL* HAD I JUST AGREED TO?

I watch as Noia's warm, soft fingers slide out of mine after we shake on our twisted little deal, and all I can think is—where the hell did I come up with *that*?

It wasn't just some casual suggestion. It was a goddamn mission statement. One that involves real-dating my creator, seducing her, helping her write, and basically making her life better all while figuring out how the hell I'm going to help her finish my story.

I lean back against the couch and drag a hand through my hair.

The words had just... tumbled out. And it surprises me how much I actually *meant* them.

I should be pissed at her.

One second I'm on the brink of a climactic moment—the kind that usually ends in blood, sex or both—and the next, I wake up here. In her world. In her house.

It was jarring.

But what throws me the most? I'm not mad. Not *really*.

Beneath the frustration, and the weird, tangled confusion of being fictional and suddenly not... there's something else.

Curiosity and... need. A need that curls low in my stomach every time I look at her.

Noia Wilde, the prolific author dubbed 'The Queen of Steam', has a tragic backstory and a stubborn, sexy mouth. Chaos in a bun, she's all sharp, snarky comebacks and soft, full lips, swearing under her breath while she stomps around the house like a pissed-off cat.

And now she is sitting next to me, flustered and fidgety, pretending like she doesn't notice the way I'm eye fucking her.

Why hide it?

She's *hella* sexy.

Not in the over-processed, Instagram-filtered kind of way. The real kind of sexy. The kind that creeps up on you. The kind that makes your mind go blank and your dick stand painfully at rock-hard attention.

With messy dark blond hair and a hoodie that clings to her curves, her lips are a little puffy and red from biting them while she pouted in her room.

She doesn't even realize how beautiful she is. Which, of course, makes it even worse.

And hell, I know exactly how she wrote me.

I'm supposed to be broody and dangerous with a little redemption buried under all the trauma and smirks. But despite everything she plotted out, none of it prepared me for how real this would feel. Or how drawn I would be to her.

I sit back and watch her turn on her heel and stalk toward the kitchen, muttering about needing more caffeine.

My gaze follows her hips as they sway, attitude cranked up to eleven.

I smirk.

Yeah. I want to do this. Not just because I want her to finish my story—but because of her.

Deep down, I know she didn't mean to summon me here. She doesn't even believe I am real. I'm pretty sure she's just playing along, seeing how all this is going to play out—or if she might wake up tomorrow morning in the looney-bin.

Her life is unraveling, words jammed up inside her like the Hoover Dam, heart still wrecked because of some douchebag who didn't even have the balls to show up to his own wedding.

And, even after all the bullshit she's been through, she hasn't completely broken down.

Noia is strong and stubborn, cussing and fighting me with a fire in her eyes that says she's ready to take on not only me, but the whole goddamn world.

So yeah. I'm going to help her.

She needs help finishing her story. And maybe, just maybe... so do I. Even if it means seducing her—and especially if it means watching her squirm every time I get too close.

"I'm gonna more than make it worth your while, kitten," I murmur to myself.

Grabbing her book from the coffee table, I flip through it again. My notes are scribbled along the margins, but instead of going back to correct the dialogue, this time I distract myself by imagining how the next scene should play out *off the page*.

So, I'm going to take her out on a real date—one filled with pure, unadulterated sexual tension.

I look up as she reappears, cradling a mug and side-eyeing me like she regrets every life decision she's ever made leading up to this very moment.

She looks delicious.

I shoot her a grin. "You should wear something that would make your ex cry," I say.

She blinks slowly before her eyes widen. "What?"

"For tonight. We're going out. If we're going to do this, we're doing it *right*."

A look of panic flashes across her face for about half a second before her eyes narrow in suspicion. "Tell me what you mean exactly by *out*."

I stand, stretching like a cat who ate the canary, and stalk over to her.

"We're going to a bar," I answer. "A very public, loud, rowdy bar full of people who'll see you glowing like the goddess you are. No one will be able to take their eyes off of you. I guarantee it."

"Goddess?" she scoffs, rolling her eyes. "That's a stretch."

I lean in, brushing past her shoulder, letting my breath graze the shell of her ear. "Oh, kitten. You have no idea how *god damned* gorgeous you really are, do you?"

She sucks in a breath and stills.

Good.

Because this story? This story is about to get *really* interesting.

IF YOU EVER WANT TO TRULY GET UNDER A WOMAN'S SKIN— you know, dig down to her nerves and start building a summer home there? Just start tossing her clothes over your shoulder while you stand in her walk-in closet half-naked.

Trust me. Works like a charm.

"No. Nope. What even *is* this? A wool onesie?" I mutter to myself, flinging another piece of clothing over my shoulder onto the growing pile on the floor behind me.

"Ryder!"

"I told you we're going out. Think of it like a special occasion. If you're going to make your public debut as my girlfriend, you gotta wear something that makes men choke on their drinks and rethink all their fucked up life choices."

"I swear to god, if you stretch out my crop top—"

Stretching the garment taut between my hands, I raise a brow and smirk. "This tiny thing? Kitten, I could fucking floss with it and it wouldn't lose its shape."

She muffles her scream into a pillow before chucking at my head.

It bounces off my back, landing next to the heap of shirts, skirts, and what I'm pretty sure is an angry pair of shiny faux leather pants.

I glance over my shoulder, and yep, there it is. That flustered thing she does where she crosses her arms, face flushed as she tries to decide whether she wants to throttle me to death or let me throw her on the bed and throttle her—*with my cock.*

My way would be much more fun.

She hasn't made up her mind yet. But I'm hoping for option B.

"You are a walking disaster, Ryder."

"Pot. Kettle, kitten," I wink before turning back to the closet, a man on a mission.

"I said I've got it," she snaps, swatting at my hand as I reach for a hanger.

"You clearly *don't*," I say, tossing a wrinkled cardigan over my shoulder. "This is a fashion emergency, and I refuse to be seen in public with a woman wearing sad librarian beige."

"That's *cashmere,* you dick."

"Cashmere's not bulletproof against frump."

The sound she makes at my come back is akin to a half-gasp, half-growl as she tries to push past me.

Hooking my arm out to block her path, I dive deeper into the racks of cotton and chaos.

It not just about finding her an outfit anymore. This clothing war, is now based on principle.

Also... the view is well worth the trouble.

Ducking under my arm, she bends over to yank a top out of a bottom drawer, and I lose my train of thought for at least thirty seconds.

Long, toned legs, and the curve of her plump, round ass are staring me right in the face.

Jesus.

Already shirtless, I'm dangerously close to losing more than just my shirt, so instead, I turn away, cough, and launch another dress over my shoulder. "Too pink."

"That's *raspberry!*"

"It's one sequin short of a Barbie Dreamhouse."

Noia huffs behind me, her voice growing sharp. "Why are you like this?"

"Um... How many times do I have to tell you? You wrote me this way. Or did you forget already?"

"Shit. I must be some sort of masochist," she mutters. "Pretty sure I'm gonna need years of therapy."

"Little late for that, kitten," I grin.

It takes another ten minutes of glorious chaos—me flinging every fashion offense over my shoulder, while Noia curses like a sailor trying to stop me—before I finally find it. A little red number buried between a tragic bridesmaid dress and an old tattered hoodie.

The top is off the shoulder with long, flowing sleeves. The red fabric whispers danger and confidence. It's the kind of top that'll make any man want to unbutton not just his pants, but his morals—if he has any to begin with.

Holding it up like a trophy, I crow, "Found it!"

Mouth open, Noia stares, eyes wide with shock. "I haven't worn that since—"

"Well, you're wearing it tonight."

She hesitates, lips parting as her fingers brush the fabric. "It's too dressy."

I take a step closer and lower my voice. "No. It's *perfect*."

Her gaze lifts to mine and silence pulses, thick and electric in the air between us.

Tearing her gaze away, she swipes the top from my hand and spins around, muttering something about needing at least ten minutes and threatening me with violence if I so much as peek.

Fair enough.

While I wait, I take some time to look around.

Her bedroom smells like lavender and paper, and the walls are a grayish-blue, kind of like the sky right before a storm breaks it wide open.

One wall has floor-to-ceiling bookshelves, overflowing with romance novels, poetry, old journals, even a few vintage fairy tales with cracked leather spines.

The queen-sized bed is a mess of rumpled cream colored sheets, a mountain of pillows tucked into mismatched cases and covered in a quilt that looks handmade.

One side of the bed is clearly more lived-in than the other, with an open notebook and a pen half-tucked underneath a pillow.

A copy of the popular vampire novel *Dark In Blood* lies face-down on the nightstand next to a salt lamp and half a glass of water.

Her desk sits in the corner under a large picture window that looks out at the woods, with a chunky yellow throw draped over the back of the chair tucked underneath it.

A wire photo board with clipped snapshots hangs on the wall next to the window, with a picture of Noia and a cute redhead laughing with their heads thrown back, and a few other pictures tacked up haphazardly around it.

Done with my tour, I flop back onto the bed and tuck my arms behind my head.

I feel *good*. Energized. Like the adrenaline high you'd get from a perfect heist.

Fifteen minutes later, the bathroom door creaks open.

I sit up and promptly forget how to breathe.

Noia steps through the doorway like a slow-motion dream. Black skinny jeans hug every curve like they've been stitched to her thighs. Red hooker heels give her legs for *days*, and that red top? It drapes off one shoulder, revealing just enough collarbone to short-circuit every rational thought I've ever had.

My gaze takes all of her in as I stare and lick my lips.

"Stop looking at me like that," she mumbles, fidgeting with her hair.

"Holy shit, you're stunning," I murmur.

Her flush is bright crimson and gorgeous.

"Wait a second." She narrows her eyes at me. "You can't go out like that."

Confused, all I can do is blink. "What?"

"You're not wearing a shirt and you're barefoot."

I shrug. "Not my fault."

"In your last scene, you were supposed to be dressed for the gala."

"Well, you never got around to writing that part did you? So, technically, this is *your* fault."

"You're not walking into a bar looking like the goddamn cover of a Highland romance novel."

"Why not?" I shrug again. "Could be good marketing."

She groans, pinching the bridge of her nose. "You're impossible."

I get up and give her my best faux-innocent smirk. "I could always borrow one of your sweaters."

Noia snaps her head up so fast it's a miracle her neck doesn't break. "Touch my cashmere and die."

"Noted. But, seriously. You actually think I would wear *cashmere*?"

A long, thoughtful pause hangs in the air before her expression slowly shifts into something that can only be described as devious.

Uh-oh.

"Wait a second," she whispers.

"What?" I deadpan.

"What if... I *write* you into a shirt and shoes?"

Okay. That doesn't sound so bad.

I raise an eyebrow, waiting for her to come to terms with what she'd just said. "What're you gonna do? Manifest it with your mind? Or do I just sit here while you narrate it?"

But she's already on the move.

Rushing over to her laptop sitting on the desk, she opens it up like a woman possessed.

Focused and determined, her tongue pokes out between her lips as she stares at the screen.

Fuck. Why is that so goddamn hot? I wonder what else she can do with that tongue?

Down boy.

Tapping her finger on the desk, she mutters under her breath before she starts to type, speaking the words out loud as she goes.

"Ryder is wearing a black button-down shirt, its soft fabric clinging to him like a second skin. His sleeves are rolled up, and his collar is open, with a black pair of motorcycle boots completing the ensemble."

A weird tingle that feels a lot like static travels across my shoulders, down my arms and across my feet.

I look down, and sure enough, a black, fitted button-up with the top two buttons undone, cuffs rolled halfway up my forearms and a pair of motorcycle boots are now covering my upper torso and feet.

"Well, shit," I whisper.

Noia looks up, triumphant. "Ha! I did it. I actually—" Her eyes flick over me as she bites her lip.

"Oh no," I smirk. "You wrote it sexy, didn't you?"

"I didn't mean to—" she starts, her face turning beet red.

"You said, and I quote: '*clinging to him like a second skin.*'"

"I was trying to be *descriptive*!"

Stepping into her personal space, I stare down at her. She's at least six inches shorter than me. "You're picturing me without it now, aren't you?"

Her cheeks flame.

I lean in and whisper low. "Don't worry, kitten. I remember how you wrote *that* part, too. Not that I'm going to need you to write it for me again. I've got my own ideas too, you know. And I can't *wait* to make those ideas come to fruition."

Her strangled shriek makes me chuckle as she stomps out of the room and down the hall, yelling something about 'never giving a fictional man this much power again.'

Grinning like the devil, I shove my hands in my pockets and watch her go.

She can run and hide behind her sass, sarcasm and writer's block all she wants, but I'm part of her world now.

And believe me—I'm just getting started.

noia

A WALL OF HEAT AND SOUND HIT ME FULL ON AS I FOLLOW Ryder into the bar.

Music pulses against cracked wood floors and exposed brick walls, the scent of beer, leather, and sweat almost overwhelming —and it's packed.

Bodies press together, swaying in slow, sinful rhythms as laughter, rough and loud, fills the air. And underneath it all? The rapid, insistent beating of my heart.

Maybe it's the music.

Maybe it's my nerves.

Maybe it's the way Ryder lightly brushes his hand against my lower back as he steers me through the crowd toward the bar, that makes me tuck in close to him as we push our way through the crowd.

As we saddle up behind some people waiting in line, he leans in, his voice a warm growl in my ear over the pounding bass. "What do you want?"

I suck in a breath and shiver.

"Whiskey sour," I answer, raising my voice over the din,

ignoring the smug glint in his eyes like he knows *exactly* what the night has in store for me—what *he* has in store for me.

Elbowing our way between two groups of girls squealing over tequila shots, we squeeze up close to the bar. Behind me, Ryder plants his hands firmly on either side of the bar, caging me in, and orders our drinks.

And God help me, I *like* it.

The bartender sets our glasses down as Ryder tosses a bill onto the counter. Handing me my drink, his fingers brush mine, making my stomach flip.

"Drink up, so we can dance."

I take a sip, and he raises an eyebrow before he downs his glass of whiskey in one shot.

Setting his empty glass on the bar with a thunk, he takes a finger and lifts my glass so I have no choice but to gulp it down or it will end up all over the front of my top.

Shaking off the brain freeze, I slam the glass on the bar. "What the fuck, Ryder?"

"C'mon," he says, jerking his head toward the dance floor.

Glancing nervously at the writhing bodies, I'm only able to hesitate for a second before Ryder snags my hand and pulls me into the middle of the crowd. The bass beats against my chest and the crowd swallows us whole as lights strobe overhead, heat rolling off the dancing bodies in waves.

Moving like he doesn't give a damn who's watching, Ryder dances like he *is* the music.

And it's *killing* me.

I want to mold my body against his, lose myself in his eyes, and run my hands along the hard planes of his chest. Instead, I force myself to stand back and match his rhythm.

Closing my eyes, I sway my hips and lift my arms, letting the music take over and flow through my veins.

When I open them, he's watching me with so much hunger, I almost trip over my feet.

Tension coils in the air between us. Every brush of his arm, every tilt of his body as it leans against mine, is building a pressure in my chest so deep it almost hurts to breathe.

So, rather than meet his gaze, I turn my back on him and dance.

He moves in, lining his body up against mine. The heat coming off his body soaks through the thin fabric of my top as his scent, dark, rich and intoxicating, assaults my nose.

One wrong move, one inch closer, and I could easily come completely and totally undone.

I suck in a breath and swallow it whole, dancing like my life depends on not turning around and dragging him into the darkest corner of the bar and letting him have his way with me.

An hour slips by in a blur. We take a couple of breaks, but we mostly stick to dancing and drinking.

He buys me a couple of shots, and they burn down my throat, loosening my limbs. I can't think about anything else except the way his eyes track my every move until he leans in, his voice a low rumble in my ear.

"Stay here. I need to hit the head. You want another drink?"

"Sure."

My head is dizzy, and my clit throbs a staccato rhythm between my thighs as I watch him disappear into the crowd toward the back.

I'm still catching my breath when a guy with blond, greasy hair slinks up next to me. Wearing a leather jacket that has seen better decades, his breath smells like cheap beer and cigarettes.

"Hey, sexy," he slurs, leaning in way too close. "Wanna dance?"

"No." I step back, giving him a firm shake of my head. "I'm waiting for someone."

His grin flashes me a chipped front tooth. "You can do better, babe. Dance with me."

I give him another sharp, shake of my head. "Not interested."

Ignoring me, he reaches out, fingers digging into my upper arm as he tries to drag me onto the dance floor.

I jerk my arm away. "I said *no*."

Dancing bodies blur in my peripheral, the music warping and spinning, just as Ryder materializes out of the crowd.

Slamming our drinks down on a nearby table, he shoves his body between me and Greasy Guy.

With a growl, Ryder's eyes flash in warning. "She said no, asshole."

"What's it to you, pretty boy?" Greasy Guy sneers.

Ryder's answering smile is so close to deadly, it's a wonder the other guy doesn't drop dead on the spot. "You sure you wanna find out?"

It happens so fast, I don't have time to blink.

The other guy moves to shove Ryder, but Ryder is much faster.

Crack!

One punch lands square across the other guy's jaw. Greasy Guy staggers back into another table, knocking over the occupants drinks with a crash.

Shouts erupt all around us and someone screams as drinks start to fly.

Greasy Guy lunges, his swing flying wild when Ryder ducks. Grabbing the bastard by the jacket, Ryder throws him against the bricks. The asshole lands with a thud, rattling the framed photos hanging on the wall as he slides to the floor.

Then two of the guys' friends come running and try to jump in.

Big mistake. Huge.

Whirling around, Ryder drops one guy with an elbow to the sternum while deftly dodging the other's wild swing. The crowd scatters, forming a circle around the brawl as someone yells for security.

"Ryder!" I shout over the chaos, but he's in the zone, moving methodically. Lethal and cunning, his practiced moves make my stomach flip.

The second guy catches him with a glancing blow to the cheek. Ryder barely flinches, responding with a lightning-fast combination of fists that sends the man stumbling backward into the crowd.

Blood roars in my ears as I watch him fight, defending me with all the deadly grace I imagined he would have—it's terrifying and thrilling all at once.

As Ryder catches one of them with a brutal right hook to the ribs, the second guy seizes his arm, and that's when I see red.

Without thinking, I snatch my empty glass from the table and smash it over the second guy's head.

With a howl, he clutches his bleeding forehead as he stumbles away.

Finally, the bouncers barrel in, dragging bodies apart, yelling about calling the cops. People scramble across overturned chairs, sliding through pools of alcohol strewn across the floor.

Taking my hand, Ryder yanks me against his side.

"Time to go, kitten."

Muscling us toward the door, he weaves us through the chaos. He's obviously done this before, turning his body into a wall between me and everyone else trying to escape.

We burst out into the cool night air, panting as the door slams behind us.

I stare up at him and grin, heart hammering as adrenaline screams through my veins.

Lip split and bleeding, he looks down at me, returning my grin.

I should be scared, but instead? I'm *wrecked* for him.

"You okay?" he asks, voice rough.

Speechless, I can only nod.

He cups my face in one big, warm hand, thumb brushing gently along my jaw.

Without another thought, I rise onto my toes and kiss him. Hard.

He freezes for only half a second before he kisses me back like he's been waiting his whole damn life to do it. Mouth hot and demanding, he tastes like whiskey and danger.

I melt into him, my hands fisting in his shirt as he backs me up against the brick wall of the bar.

The kiss is everything—desperate and consuming. His tongue sweeps into my mouth, claiming and coaxing as he slides a hand up to tangle in my hair. My body arches against his, seeking more of that delicious friction as he presses against me.

I jerk back first, gasping, the taste of whiskey, blood, and adrenaline on my tongue.

Stunned, Ryder blinks down at me. The look on his face says I've hit him with a two-by-four and he's not sure what to do about it.

Dragging his knuckles across his split lip, he smirks. "If that's how you say thank you, I'll have to save your sexy ass more often," he says, voice hoarse.

I shove him hard in the chest. "Don't push your luck, Roadhouse."

Backing up a step, his laugh is a low, rough sound that rumbles through my body, straight to my core.

The cool night breeze nips at my bare shoulder, slapping me back to reality. Turning on my heel, I stalk through the parking lot, my heels clicking against the cracked pavement.

Ryder follows at a leisurely pace, acting like we didn't just start a full on bar fight.

Typical.

I yank open the passenger door of my beat-up SUV for him, but he ignores me. Instead, he walks around the front of the car and makes himself at home in the driver's seat.

Glaring at him, I climb in.

Cocky as hell, he throws me side-eye, tapping the steering wheel with two bruised knuckles. "What? You're shaking, so I'm driving."

I'm not shaking, I'm still effing buzzing from that kiss.

I slam the door closed, yank my seatbelt across my lap and cross my arms, stewing as he fires up the engine.

We peel out of the parking lot, tires squealing, silence stretching tight in the air as he drives.

Finally, mouth twitching, he cuts me a glance. "You gonna thank me for saving you, kitten?"

"You're insufferable," I mutter, staring hard out the window. "Wasn't the kiss enough?"

He just laughs.

We drive the next few miles in silence, streetlights flashing in staccato bursts. My heart is still hammering against my ribs. My lips are still tingling, my body way too aware of every damn bruised, bloodied inch of him sitting across from me, grinning like the devil himself.

God, he's beautiful. And *infuriating*.

I hate how good he looks, all bruised up—like he could tear the world apart with his bare hands, then laugh in its face when all is said and done as we ride into the sunset.

"You didn't have to hit that guy so hard," I mutter, knowing damn well he absolutely did.

Ryder snorts. "You're welcome for saving your pretty ass. Again."

"I had it under control," I pout primly.

"Sure you did," he drawls. "Right before you smashed a glass over that guy's head like a feral little hellcat."

I open my mouth, then close it and lift my chin. The last thing I would ever admit is that I did it for him. Nobody touches my man, fictional or not—not that he *is* my man.

Gah! You know what I mean.

"Just trying to pull my own weight."

"It was fucking hot," he says without missing a beat.

I turn in my seat, ready to bite back with something clever. But the words die a quick death on my tongue, because he's not looking at me like he's teasing anymore—he's *smoldering* like he wants to gobble me up.

My heart skids sideways.

Fuck.

After we pull into my driveway and park, neither of us moves a muscle as the engine hums, the sound of my labored breathing too loud in the small cab.

Finally, Ryder turns off the engine. Tossing the keys into the cupholder, he shifts in his seat, knee brushing mine. "You still owe me."

"Owe you what?" I rasp.

He leans in, close enough the scent of leather and sandalwood swirls around my head, making it hard to think.

His smile is slow and wicked. "The story. Remember?"

Right. *The story.* The reason he's here. The reason I'm not alone anymore.

Jesus, my throat is dry. "You're not gonna let me forget, are you?"

"Not a chance."

He brushes a knuckle lightly along my jaw.

"You want to finish it?" he murmurs. "Find out how it ends?"

Before I can stop myself, I nod.

His wolfish grin widens. "Good."

Popping the door open, he hops out.

Every sane thought I thought I had is completely obliterated and I sit for a second, gripping the seatbelt, struggling to breathe.

What the hell am I doing?

Before I could talk myself out of it, I grab the keys, kick the door open and follow him up the steps.

Lips quirked, he waits for me on the porch, hands stuffed in his pockets.

Brushing past him, I unlock the door, and step into the dark, quiet house. Suddenly, it hits me with terrifying clarity—whatever story this is we're acting out—it feels nothing even close to fiction.

It feels real. It feels sexy and dangerous.

The door clicks shut, and I throw the lock.

Dropping my keys on the console table, they hit the wood with a clatter much too loud for my rattled nerves.

Ryder's heavy boots thud behind me, and I spin, heart jack hammering against my ribs. "Don't you have an ice pack you need to shove against your face or something?"

He grins, swiping at a smear of blood on his lip again before slowly licking it off his thumb. "I'd be grateful if you helped me out with that, kitten."

My pussy pulses as I track the way his tongue slides over his thumb. With a scowl, I shove past him and head into the kitchen. "You're impossible."

"And you're adorable when you're homicidal. Guess we're both winning tonight."

I flip him off and rummage through the freezer until I find a frozen bag of peas and toss it over my shoulder.

Without so much as a flinch, he catches it one-handed.

Show-off.

"You're lucky I didn't smash that glass over *your* head," I mutter.

"Sweetheart, you could punch me in the nuts, and I'd still say thank you."

I whirl to glare at him and suck in a breath.

Shirtless and sprawled out on the couch, Ryder has his head tipped back, bag of frozen peas pressed against his jaw.

Dark bruises bloom across his ribs under tattoos twisting over muscle.

Rolling his head to the side, he gives me a once-over before locking eyes with mine.

Heat licks down my spine, and my mouth goes dry.

"You're staring," he rumbles, smug smirk breaking across his face.

"No, I am not."

"Yup. You are."

"Your face looks like it got stomped on by a horse," I growl.

His laugh is rough and stupidly sexy as he stretches his arms over the back of the couch, flexing his abs.

Fuck me sideways.

Cheeks burning, I look away, pretending to be *very* interested in organizing the mail on the counter.

His voice drifts across the room as a lazy tease. "You realize you picked your first bar fight tonight, right?"

"I didn't *pick* anything," I mumble, tossing an envelope to the side.

"You smashed a glass over a guy's head. That's pretty badass."

I glance up at him from beneath my lashes. "You're impressed by that? Seriously?"

He grins. "Kitten, I'm half in love."

I snort, shaking my head. "And I'm sure you're half brain-dead from all those hits you took to the head."

"Meh." He drops his head back against the couch and closes his eyes. "Only the good half."

Unable to stop myself, I laugh.

It's the kind of laugh that sneaks up on you, yanking a real smile right out from under me, cracking something loose in my chest that has been stuck there for months.

And, God help me, it feels good. And terrifying. And addictive.

I shove a hand through my hair, suddenly feeling restless. Like I need to move or scream or do *something*.

"You're staring again," he says, not even bothering to open his eyes.

"Shut up."

The quirk of his lips is slow and relaxed. "Why don't you come over here and make me."

My pulse skitters, right before I grab a throw pillow and whip it at his head.

He catches it midair, laughing as he tosses it aside.

"You fight dirty, kitten."

"You have no idea," I grumble, spinning away before I do something stupid.

Like crawl into his lap and shove my tongue in his mouth. Or gently run my fingers over his abs, before leaning in to kiss the dark bruises marring his ribs while I dry hump him till we both come in our pants.

Clearing my throat, I force some air into my lungs. "You should, uh... probably clean yourself up."

Peeling one eye open, he grins. "You worried about me?"

"More worried about you getting bloodstains on my couch," I retort as I move to hover above him.

His laugh is deeper this time as he stands in one smooth

move to tower over me. So close I can feel the heat radiating off his skin—again.

I stumble back a few steps and bump into the counter.

Moving in close, he dips his head and braces his hands against the marble, caging me in.

"You're gonna have to stop looking at me like that, *kitten*," he murmurs.

I swallow hard, hating how my body reacts. How my skin prickles in response to his proximity. How my pulse flutters like a frightened bird against the side of my neck.

"Like what?" I rasp.

"Like you want to run your hands all over my body."

I lift my chin in defiance. "In your dreams."

Tilting his head, he leans in another inch and narrows his eyes. "All. Damn. Night."

We stare at each other, breathing the same air, hearts hammering out two chaotic, reckless beats.

And then—mercifully—he pushes off the counter and steps away, breaking the spell.

"I'm gonna take a shower," he growls, slowly sweeping his gaze from my toes to my tits, before locking his eyes with mine. "You're welcome to join me."

Scandalized, my mouth drops open.

With a wink, he saunters down the hall and into the guest bedroom without another word, leaving me standing alone, vibrating with adrenaline and need.

"Arrogant, cocky, gorgeous jackass. Why couldn't I have written you with a smaller ego?"

My head falls back, and I groan.

What the hell was I thinking when I imagined him?

Okay, yeah. I'd needed an outlet after my heart was broken. So I created Ryder, hoping it would take my mind off of how fucked up my life really is.

My intention had been to write about what I believed my fantasy man should be, all while weaving pieces of myself into the story as a way to fill the void of my own fucked up life.

I can lie to myself all I want, but deep down, I know the truth—whether I want him to or not—Ryder Blackwood has picked his girl.

And that girl is *me*.

I sigh as I walk down the hall to the guest room and fling open the door. Ignoring the sound of running water coming from the adjoining bathroom, I rummage through the closet and pull out a pair of my dad's old sweats and a T-shirt and throw them on the bed.

There is no way I'm going to let Ryder Blackwood get under my skin, or in my pants.

No matter how much I want him too.

THE SHOWER TURNS OUT TO BE A BIG MISTAKE.

Standing under the hot spray, I scrub the blood from my knuckles and try to forget how Noia was looking at me—like she wanted me to devour her body and soul.

Every drop of water hitting my skin reminds me of how her tongue felt dancing with mine outside the bar.

Fuck.

I lean my forehead against the tile wall and let the water beat against my shoulders. This isn't how any of this was supposed to happen. I'm supposed to be helping her so she can finish the book, so I can get back to my world, my story, my life— or whatever the hell you want to call it—*I'm* not even sure what to call it anymore.

But when a memory hits of how her body felt pressed against mine on the dance floor, and the way she kissed me like her life depended on it—those are the moments when I feel like I might not want to go back.

Which is insane, of course.

Supposably, I'm a fictional character who somehow got yanked into this reality by my creator. There's no way something this bat-shit crazy can last forever. Hell, it probably won't even last another week without some sort of cosmic consequence we don't even know about yet.

But Christ on a cracker, the way she looked tonight. The red top I chose sliding off her shoulder, black jeans hugging every curve, the fire in her eyes when she smashed a glass over that asshole's head...

I've never wanted anyone more.

The water beats against my back and I brace my hands against the tile wall, letting the heat work out the knots. The fight tonight was nothing, just a few bruises and a split lip. I've had much worse.

What's eating at me is the way Noia looked when that asshole grabbed her. The flash of fear in her eyes before it turned to fury. The way she stepped up and fought back. Fought for me.

Fuck me, that was hot.

I'm a guy who knows how to read between the lines. And right now, Noia is screaming everything she's not saying with just her body language. The way she fidgets with her sleeves. How she keeps glancing at me when she thinks I'm not looking. The way her breathing gets shallow every time I get close.

She wants me. And as much as I want her, too—I don't know if I should do anything about it.

Not yet, at least.

I shut the water off, grab a towel and wrap it around my waist. Bruised and battered, my reflection grins back at me in the foggy mirror like a fucking idiot.

Something shifted between us tonight. That kiss? It wasn't just the adrenaline talking. That was real—raw—and all I've wanted since I first saw her passed out on her desk the night I showed up.

When I open the bathroom door, I find a pair of sweats and

an old faded T-shirt with the comforting scent of fabric softener laid out on the guest bed.

I pull them on and walk back into the living room, where I find her curled up on the couch with her laptop. Having changed into flannel pajama pants covered in tiny cats and an oversized T-shirt, she's typing furiously, hair twisted up in a messy bun held together by a pencil, glasses perched on her nose.

I sit down beside her. "Whatcha writing?"

She gestures at the screen. "I'm trying to figure out what happens next."

I peek over her shoulder. The title reads 'Chapter 8' but the page is mostly blank except for a few false starts.

"What's the problem?"

"I don't know how to write you anymore."

"What do you mean?"

Finally, she glances at me, and I can see the exhaustion in her eyes before something vulnerable flickers across her face and she looks away. "When I wrote about you before, it was all fantasy. I could control everything—what you said, what you did, how you made the heroine feel."

"And now?"

"Now you're here, making your own decisions, saying things I've never even thought about writing." She closes the laptop with a soft click. "It's confusing and scary."

I reach over and tuck a strand of hair behind her ear. Visibly shivering at the contact, she doesn't pull away.

"Scary isn't always bad," I murmur.

"Says the man who started a bar fight."

"Says the woman who finished it."

That earns me a small smile, and something loosens in my chest.

"How do you feel?"

Her question throws me off. "About what?"

"I mean, you've gotta be pretty pissed about being pulled away from everything you know."

I sit back and consider her question. It's the first time she's actually asked me how I feel about being ripped from my world and dropped into hers like some sort of cosmic joke.

"Honestly?" I run a hand through my damp hair. "I should be furious. But the weird thing is... now I'm not sure I had much of a life to be pulled away from."

She frowns, turning to face me fully. "Explain."

"I keep trying to remember what I was doing before I ended up here. What my apartment looked like, what I ate for breakfast, who I talked to." I shake my head. "It's all fuzzy. Like trying to remember a dream after you wake up."

"That's because I haven't written those parts," she says softly. "Your backstory is mostly trauma and angst. I haven't gotten around to the mundane details yet."

"So what you're telling me is that my entire existence was basically one long, dramatic monologue punctuated by motorcycle rides and a brooding attitude?"

She winces. "Well, when you put that way..."

"Kitten, it sounds like I was one leather jacket away from being a walking cliché." I grin at her horrified expression. "But you know what I'm not mad about? Tonight. The bar, the fight, that fucking kiss..." I lean closer. "It felt real. More real than anything I can remember."

Her cheeks flush a beautiful shade of pink. "Ryder..."

"I'm not done." I reach for her hand and thread our fingers together. "You want to know how I feel? I feel alive. For the first time since I can remember, I feel like I'm actually living instead of just existing on a page."

"But what happens when the story ends? When I figure out how to send you back?"

"Maybe that's not the right question."

She looks away and I reach over and tilt her chin up, forcing her to meet my eyes. "Maybe the right question is: What if you don't want to send me back?"

Her breath catches. "That's not... I can't just..."

"Can't what? Be happy?" My thumb traces the line of her jaw. "When was the last time you felt this alive, Noia? The last time someone made you laugh? Made you feel beautiful? Made you feel like you had to smash a glass over some asshole's head for them?"

"You're not real," she whispers.

"I'm real enough to kiss you. Real enough to fight for you. Real enough to fall for you." The words slip out before I can stop them, hanging heavy in the air between us. "And hopefully, sometime very soon, real enough to *fuck* you."

"No." She pulls her hand from mine.

I try to reach for her again, but she shoves my hands away and pushes herself up from the couch. "I think it's time for me to go to bed. *Alone.* Maybe when I wake up in the morning, this will all have been just a crazy dream."

For some reason, her words hit me hard and when her face falls, the vulnerability in her eyes makes my chest ache.

"Noia—"

"Good night, Ryder."

noia

THE SOUND OF RYDER'S HEAVY SIGH FOLLOWS ME UP THE stairs. Part of me wants to turn back and see what would happen if I just let myself fall.

But I can't. This isn't real—there's no way *he* is real.

I close my bedroom door and lean against it. Sliding down until I'm sitting on the floor with my knees pulled to my chest, I press my palms into my eyes until I see swirls of light.

"Get it together," I whisper. "He's not real. This isn't happening. You'll probably wake up tomorrow and find yourself in a freaking loony bin."

The memory of his lips on mine, the way his tongue swept into my mouth, makes my thighs clench together.

Crawling into bed, I pull the covers over my head and hope that when morning comes, I'll wake up alone. That my life will go back to being simple, predictable, and safe.

But sleep doesn't come. I toss and turn, replaying the events from tonight in my head. Dancing with him. The fight. The kiss. The last thing he'd said to me before I ran away.

'Hopefully, sometime very soon, real enough to fuck *you.'*

When I finally drift off, I dream of large hands, stormy gray eyes and writhing tattoos in a world where fiction and reality blur, until I can't tell where one world ends, and the other begins.

I WAKE TO SUNLIGHT STREAMING THROUGH MY CURTAINS and the smell of coffee drifting under my nose.

For one blissful moment, I forget everything. Then it all comes crashing back—the bar, the fight, Ryder's unexpected confession.

The floorboards creak outside my door, followed by a soft knock.

Groaning, I bury my face in my pillow. He's still here.

Damn it.

"Go 'way," I mumble.

Despite my command, the door opens.

"Rise and shine." Ryder's voice is infuriatingly cheerful. "I made coffee."

I peek out from under my pillow to see him standing in the doorway, looking hot as fuck in the morning light. His hair is tousled, the bruises from last night already starting to fade to a dull purple. The T-shirt I lent him stretches across his shoulders, sweats hanging low on his hips and he's holding two mugs of coffee.

"I hate that you're so cheerful. You're not a morning person, remember?"

He lowers his chin and narrows his eyes at me. "Oh, I can go all broody and gruff in a matter of seconds, kitten. Just say the word."

His voice skitters across my skin and shoots straight to my core.

What the fuck?

I push myself up to sit against the headboard and pull the covers up to my chest like a shield. "My dad's T-shirt is almost too tight."

He grins, walks over to the bed and hands me a steaming mug. "It works. And it smells nice. Like you."

The way he says it—all husky and warm—makes me want to dive back under the covers and never come out.

"Don't you have somewhere else to be? Like, I don't know, back in the pages of my manuscript?" I grumble, taking a cautious sip. The coffee is perfect—just the right amount of cream and sugar.

Damn him.

"Nope." He sits on the edge of my bed, making the mattress dip. "I'm all yours today."

I narrow my eyes at him over the rim of my mug. "What's that supposed to mean?"

"It means we're going on another date."

I choke on my coffee. "Excuse me?"

"You heard me." His eyes gleam with mischief. "We made a deal, remember? I help you write, you help me live. And today, we're going to have some fun."

"I have work to do," I protest weakly.

"Yeah, you do. On me." He winks, and I feel my face flame. "Besides, I've been thinking about our story problem."

"*Our* story problem?"

"You can't write because you're blocked. And I think I know why." He leans forward, elbows on his knees. "You're afraid."

"I am not—"

"You're afraid to let yourself feel anything real after what that dickwad did to you." His voice softens. "So you're hiding, trying to write about passion and love and happily ever-after's without actually experiencing any of it for yourself."

I stare at him, speechless.

"So here's an amendment to my previous proposal." He takes the mug from my hands and sets it on the nightstand. "Every day we do something different. Live out the storyline. We do all the things you've been afraid to do. We have fun, take risks. And hopefully you can start to feel happy and inspired again."

"And then what?"

He gives me a slow, devastating smile. "Then, as we already discussed, every night after we get home, you write it all down."

I want to say no, kick him out of my room and barricade the door. But the challenge in his eyes—warm and alive—makes me hesitate.

"What exactly did you have in mind for today?"

His grin widens. "That's my girl. Dress in something comfortable and bring a swimsuit."

"A swimsuit? It's barely sixty degrees outside!"

"Trust me, kitten," he says, already heading for the door. You're going to love what I have planned for us today."

The door closes behind him with a click, leaving me alone with my racing thoughts and half-empty cup of coffee sitting on my nightstand.

ryder

I DON'T THINK I'VE BEEN THIS EXCITED ABOUT SOMETHING since...

Shit. I can't remember.

Luckily, I know how to use the internet, so when I woke up this morning, I researched some tourist attractions in the area and found an underground hot spring not too far from here.

And not just any hot spring—one with secluded natural pools nestled in caves, with steam rising through cracks in ancient rock formations. The website promised 'a transcendent experience.' Perfect for breaking down the walls of a grumpy romance novelist with writer's block.

While I wait for Noia to get ready, I rummage through her kitchen and pack a small cooler I found in the back of a closet with snacks. There's not much food in the house, but I manage to find some fruit and cheese in the back of the fridge.

I check my watch—which was mysteriously sitting on the nightstand when I woke up this morning. It feels like the longer I'm here, the more real things are starting to become. Like the universe is filling in the blanks of my existence, one small detail at a time.

Maybe my wallet will show up next. I had to use Noia's credit card to book today's little excursion. I was only able to pay for our drinks at the bar because I'd found a fifty in my pocket.

I can hear her stomping around upstairs, muttering to herself and, for some reason, it makes me smile. For someone who writes about emotion for a living, she sure is terrible at controlling hers.

Goonie winds between my legs, meowing impatiently. I scoop some food into his bowl and scratch behind his ears.

"You're on my side, right, buddy?"

He chirrups, then immediately abandons me for his breakfast.

The sound of footsteps on the stairs makes me look up. Noia is wearing black leggings, an oversized sweater that hangs off one shoulder and a scowl that could curdle milk. She's piled her hair on top of her head in a messy bun, and she's clutching a small bag to her chest like a shield.

"This better be worth it," she grumbles.

I can't help but grin. "Good morning, sunshine."

"Don't push it." She drops her bag on the counter. "I packed a swimsuit, but I can't promise you I'll wear it."

"We'll see about that."

She narrows her eyes before reluctantly following me outside. "Where are we going, exactly?"

"It's a surprise."

"I hate surprises."

"No," I correct her, shoving the cooler into the trunk of the car. "You hate not being in control. Big difference."

Her mouth opens, then closes. She knows I've got her pegged.

"Come on," I say, softening my tone. "When was the last time you did something spontaneous?"

She fidgets with the strap of her bag. "I spontaneously agreed to go on this mystery date with you, didn't I?"

"Okay. I'll take that."

As I close the trunk, I can feel her watching me. The weight of her gaze makes my skin tingle and my cock twitch.

"I'm driving," she announces, holding out her hand for the keys.

"As long as you follow my directions," I say, dropping them into her palm.

"I'm already regretting this," she growls, a hint of a smile playing at the corners of her sexy lips as she slides into the driver's seat.

The drive takes about an hour, winding through forests and past other small mountain towns. Noia keeps the radio tuned to a classic rock station, occasionally humming along.

When we finally pull into the Earth & Fire Hot Spring parking lot, her eyebrows shoot up to her hairline.

"A hot spring?" she asks, her voice sounding somewhere along the lines between surprise and suspicion. "This was your big plan?"

"Not just any hot spring," I correct, grabbing our bags from the back seat. "The most exclusive natural hot spring in the state. Private caves, mineral pools, the works."

She eyes the rustic wooden building skeptically. "How did you even know about this place?"

"I have my ways," I answer mysteriously, shooting her a lopsided grin.

Inside, the lobby is all natural wood and stone, with ambient wooden flute music playing softly and the scent of eucalyptus floating in the air.

A woman with silver hair greets us from behind a bamboo counter. "Welcome to Earth & Fire Hot Spring. What's the name on your reservation?"

"Blackwood," I say smoothly. "Two for the private grotto experience."

The woman smiles knowingly as she types something into her computer. "Ah, yes. The couples package. Follow me."

"Couples package?" Noia whisper-hisses under her breath as we trail behind our guide.

I shrug innocently. "Best value for the money. Especially since I used your credit card. I, unfortunately, don't have mine."

She looks like she wants to strangle me, but curiosity seems to be winning out over irritation as the hostess leads us through a series of dimly lit corridors. The air grows warmer and mistier, the smell of mineral water getting stronger the deeper we go.

After a couple of minutes, our guide stops in front of a heavy wooden door.

"This is your private grotto. There are three connecting pools of varying temperatures. Towels and robes are provided. The natural minerals in these waters are known for their healing properties—both physical and spiritual." She winks at Noia. "Enjoy your experience. You have one hour to yourselves. If you require refreshments, just ring the bell."

As soon as the door closes behind us, Noia turns and looks at me with wide eyes.

"Exactly how much did this cost me?"

"Does it really matter?" I set our bags down on a bench carved into the stone wall. "Small price to pay to help with our current dilemma."

The grotto is breathtaking. The natural cave has pools of steaming turquoise water illuminated by soft, recessed lighting. Candles flicker in small alcoves, and a small waterfall trickles between two of the pools.

"This is..." she trails off, taking it all in.

"Awesome?" I finish.

She nods, a reluctant smile tugging at her lips. "It's beautiful. I already feel more relaxed just standing here."

"Then let's get to it." Reaching behind me, I pull my shirt over my head and toss it aside.

Her eyes widen as they dart over my chest before quickly looking away. "Um, where's the changing room?"

I point to a small alcove behind a bamboo screen. "There." Raising an eyebrow, I let my gaze slowly drag up her body as I lick my lips. "Unless you'd prefer to change out here."

She shoots me a look that could melt the polar icecaps in all of a second. "In your dreams, Blackwood."

"All day and all night, kitten."

ELEVEN

noia

I DUCK BEHIND THE BAMBOO SCREEN TO CHANGE INTO MY bathing suit, trying not to get excited about what the next hour might bring.

My hands shake a little as I get undressed. This is insane. I'm about to get half-naked with a fictional character who somehow materialized in my house, and charged a spa experience to my credit card.

The black bikini I packed suddenly feels too small and revealing. It's a simple two-piece, nothing too scandalous, but when I catch my reflection in the full length mirror tucked into the alcove, I realize it shows more skin than I've revealed to anyone in months.

"You okay in there?" Ryder's voice carries over the sound of water lapping against stone.

"Fine," I answer, sounding unsure even to myself. Wrapping one of the plush robes tightly around my body, I clear my throat. "Just... need a minute."

When I step out from behind the screen, Ryder is already lounging in the largest pool, arms stretched across the stone ledge, water lapping at his chest. Head tilted toward the ceiling, his dark hair is slicked back. Steam rises around him as rivulets run down his shoulders and the tattoos covering his torso, like he's some sort of mythical sex god.

He looks up at me and his eyes go molten. "You planning to swim in that robe?"

"Maybe." I clutch the terry cloth tight. "This was your idea, remember? I never agreed to getting in the water."

"Come on, kitten," he growls, voice low and coaxing. "The water's perfect. And those mineral properties our guide told us about? They're supposed to ease tension."

"I don't have any tension."

He snorts. "Right. And I'm not sitting here waiting with bated breath to see what you're hiding from me underneath that fluffy robe."

Heat floods my cheeks. "Ryder..."

"Just get in the damn water, Noia. I promise to behave."

His gruff but gentle tone makes me pause. When was the last time I actually did something that scared me? Or let myself be vulnerable with someone?

Before I lose my nerve, I drop the robe.

Ryder goes completely still, his eyes traveling slowly from my face down to my toes and back up again, lingering on the curves of my hips, and the swell of my breasts barely contained by the tiny swatch of black fabric.

"Fuck me," he breathes before squeezing his eyes shut and shaking his head as if to clear it.

I quickly slip into the water, grateful when the hot mineral-rich liquid covers me up to my shoulders. The temperature is perfect—hot enough to make my muscles relax instantly, but not so hot I can't breathe.

"Better?" Ryder asks, his voice sounding strained.

I nod, not trusting myself to speak. The pool is smaller than it looked from the outside, and even though we're sitting on opposite sides, it feels almost as if the heat is radiating from his body alone.

We sit in silence, relaxing, for about ten minutes before I speak up.

"So," I say, desperate to break the tension. "What happens now? Do we just... sit here?"

"We could talk." He leans back against the stone edge, arms spread wide. "Get to know each other better." His eyes are hooded but focused, like a predator stalking its prey. "Ask me anything."

I raise an eyebrow. "Anything?"

"Yup. I'm an open book."

"Ha, ha. Okay..." I take a deep breath, the steam making my head feel a little fuzzy. "What's it feel like? Being fictional and then suddenly... not?"

He considers, jaw working as he thinks. "It's like waking up from a dream you didn't know you were having. Everything that happened before feels... hazy. Like memories that aren't quite mine. But every moment since I showed up in your living room? Crystal clear."

I watch the water ripple around his shoulders as he shifts, moving a fraction closer to me, then he pauses, running a hand through his wet hair. "I'm starting to remember things. Things you didn't write."

My heart skips a beat. "Like what?"

"Like my apartment above a tattoo shop and the smell of coffee from the café next door. My motorcycle—a 1976 Triumph Bonneville that I rebuilt myself." His eyes grow distant. "I remember a woman named Claire who taught me how to ink my first tattoo. A dog named Rookie I had as a kid."

"That sounds impossible," I whisper. "I never wrote any of that."

"I know." He looks at me intently. "My turn," he says. "Why romance novels?"

"That's your question? Really?"

He shrugs. "I want to know why you chose to write about love when you're so terrified of it yourself."

The question hits deeper than I expected it to. I sink lower into the water, letting the heat seep into my bones while I consider how to answer.

"Because in books, love always wins," I finally say. "The hero shows up and fights for the heroine. He doesn't just... disappear."

"Like Eric did."

I nod, throat tight. "In my books, the guy who says he loves you won't leave you behind in a thousand-dollar dress while three hundred people wait as your life implodes all around you."

Ryder's expression turns dark. "Tell me about him."

"Why?"

"Because I want to understand what kind of asshole has the balls to break someone like you."

He says those words like I'm something precious that shouldn't have been damaged, and it makes my heart skip a beat.

"He was... perfect on paper," I admit. "Good job, nice family. My mom loved him at first. My agent really loved him. Hell, even Goonie tolerated him, which is saying something."

"But?"

I trace patterns in the water with my hands. "But he never looked at me the way you're looking at me right now."

Ryder goes still. "How am I looking at you?"

"Like you can see straight into my soul. Like you actually want to be here with me." Our gazes lock. "Eric always seemed like he was somewhere else, even when we were together. Like I was just another item on his to-do list."

"Fuck him," Ryder says, the venom in his tone soft and lethal.

"Want to know the worst part? I knew. Deep down, I knew he wasn't the one. But I convinced myself that fairy tale love was just fiction. That settling for someone who showed up and paid half the bills was enough."

"You're terrified of love, aren't you, kitten?"

"I'm not terrified of love," I protest weakly.

"Bullshit," he counters. "You write these incredible, passionate love stories where people risk life and limb for each other. But in real life? You were going to marry some guy who didn't even bother to show up."

"Eric wasn't—" He's right. Eric was safe. Predictable. The kind of guy who remembered to put the toilet seat down and never surprised me with anything more adventurous than maybe a new flavor of yogurt.

"He wasn't what?" Ryder presses, sliding even closer.

"He wasn't you," I whisper, the words falling from my lips before I can stop them.

The admission hangs in the steamy air. Ryder goes still, gray eyes searching my face.

"What do you mean, he wasn't me?" he asks, floating closer.

My laugh comes out shaky. "I mean, he wasn't passionate or dangerous. He was... comfortable. And after my dad died and my mom went through her whole breakdown, comfortable felt like enough."

"But it wasn't."

"No," I answer, the word barely audible. "It wasn't. I kept waiting to feel something—anything—for him. But every time he touched me, I just felt... empty."

Ryder is close enough now that I can see the water droplets clinging to his dark eyelashes. "And when I touch you?"

My breath catches. "I—"

"When I touch you..." he continues, his voice dropping an octave into a rough whisper. "...what do you feel?"

Everything.

Fire.

Need.

Terror.

Fucking alive.

Rather than answer, I duck under the water, hoping the water will mask the heat burning in my cheeks. When I resurface, Ryder is still close enough for our knees to brush under the water.

"Running away again?" he asks softly.

"I wasn't running. I was... ducking."

His laugh is low and rough. "Same thing."

As much as I want to argue, I know he's right. I've been running from real feelings my entire adult life. It's easier to write about passion than to let yourself feel it. Safer to create fictional men who can't disappoint me than to risk my heart with someone real.

"You know what I think?" Ryder reaches up and pushes a wet strand of hair away from my forehead before grazing his knuckles against my cheek.

"What?" I can barely breathe.

"I think, somehow, you brought me here because you were tired of playing it safe. Your subconscious knew what you needed, even if you aren't ready to admit it."

"And what's that?"

He reaches up and traces his thumb along my bottom lip, making me shiver despite the heat. "Someone who won't run. Someone who'll fight for you. Someone who will make you feel everything you've ever been afraid to feel."

The air between us crackles with electricity. His thumb

continues to trace my bottom lip slowly back and forth, making every nerve ending in my body scream for more.

"This is crazy," I murmur. "You're just a character from my barely written book."

"And yet." His eyes drop to my mouth. "Here we are."

I should move away. Slide back to my side of the pool and put some distance between us. But my body refuses to listen to reason.

Instead, I find myself drifting closer, drawn by some magnetic force I can't explain.

He breathes my name like a prayer. "Noia."

"Yes?"

"Tell me you want this."

"Honestly?" I swallow hard. "I think I do."

TWELVE

ryder

Her words hit me like a bolt of lightning, lighting up my veins, sending all the blood in my head rushing straight to my cock. I can see the way her pulse flutters at the base of her throat, pupils dilating as she holds my gaze.

"That's not good enough, kitten," I murmur, my thumb still tracing the curve of her bottom lip. "I need you to be sure."

Her swallow is audible and I feel her body tremble. "I'm not sure of anything anymore—not since you showed up."

I lean in close, my mouth hovering above hers. "Then let me help you figure it out."

Closing the distance, I capture her lips with mine.

The kiss is much different from the frantic, adrenaline-fueled one from outside the bar. I make this one slow and deliberate. I can taste her hesitation, the slight resistance as her mind battles with her body. But then she melts into me, her lips parting on a sigh that I swallow with a brush of my tongue.

My hands grasp her waist under the water, pulling her so close, she's practically sitting in my lap.

Mouth tasting like vanilla-mint and desire, her hands slide

up my chest to tangle in my hair as I back her against the smooth stone edge of the pool.

Bracing one hand against the rock beside her head, I slide the other down to squeeze her tight round ass beneath the water.

"Fuck," I breathe into her mouth. "I've wanted to do this since the first time I saw you passed out on your desk."

She pulls back slightly, eyes wide and dazed.

"Tell me," I murmur, my forehead resting against hers.

"This is... insane." Her voice is breathless, shaky. "I should push you away, pretend this never happened."

"But?"

"But I can't stop thinking about how you make me feel." Her hands are still tangled in my hair and I'm loving it way more than I should.

I brush my lips along her jaw, tasting the sweet mineral water on her skin. "You deserve someone who looks at you like you're the fucking sun and moon. Someone who can't breathe when you're not in the room."

Her pupils dilate as I cup her face in my hands. "Someone who wants to memorize every inch of your body with their tongue."

I shift, shoving my hands beneath the thin fabric of her bikini bottoms, fingers digging into the soft flesh of her ass as I claim her mouth. When she gasps against my lips, I seize the opportunity, deepening the kiss as I slide my tongue against hers, exploring every inch of her mouth.

The water swirls around us as I lift her onto my lap and she straddles my thighs. Her wet skin slides against mine, creating a delicious friction that makes both of us groan into each other's mouths.

My hands wander, tracing the curve of her ass before sliding between her legs from behind. When my finger glides up her center, she breaks the kiss with a gasp, her head falling back. Even underwater, I can feel how hot and slick she is for me.

She whimpers, her hips instinctively rocking against my touch. "Oh, god."

"Eyes on me," I command softly, and her eyes flutter open. The sight of her pupils blown wide, lips swollen from my kiss nearly undoes me.

Her thighs tighten around my waist as I continue to stroke, slowly circling my finger at her entrance.

"Ryder," she moans, nails digging into my shoulders. "I can't—"

"Yes, you can," I growl.

When I increase the pressure, her eyes fly open, panic replacing the haze of desire as she shoves against my chest and I slide away, too stunned to stop her from climbing out of the water.

"Where are you going?"

"I write slow-burn romance, and I just realized what we were about to do wouldn't happen until at least halfway through the book."

"Seriously? We have at least thirty minutes left."

"Seriously. You really want to help me write, clear my writer's block? Then you need to take it slow. Make me burn for you."

"Right. Kind of like what you just did to me."

"What did I do to you?"

I grab my cock under the water and squeeze, hoping the pain will somehow make the blood rush back to the head on my shoulders. "Well, for starters," I say, my voice strangled. "You left me hanging with a raging hard on."

"And what an impressive one it is," she calls out from behind the bamboo screen.

"How do you know?" I scoff.

"*Duh.* Not only was I just sitting in your lap, but I wrote you into existence, didn't I?"

I scrub my hands over my face and groan. "You're killing me."

"Thought about that, too."

What the fuck?

"Are you messing with me?"

A snicker filters from behind the screen as I pull myself out of the water.

"Careful what you wish for, kitten."

The rustling sounds stop abruptly.

I grab a towel, wrapping it around my waist as I stalk over to lean against the wall, close enough I can hear her labored breathing.

"Are you going to answer me?"

"About what?" she asks, her voice carrying a teasing lilt that makes my blood simmer.

"Were you seriously thinking about killing me off? Or not writing about me at all?"

Silence sits heavily in the air. Then she steps out from behind the screen fully dressed, hair damp and curling around her shoulders. The vulnerability in her eyes nearly knocks me off my feet.

"Of course not. Why the hell would I kill off one of the leading men in a series, silly? My readers would cancel me for sure." She shrugs. "Besides, why do you care? I'm still not convinced you're real."

I let out a frustrated breath. "You, know. I'm starting to think you're using the whole 'you're not real, just fictional' line as a bullshit excuse to keep me at arm's length."

"Maybe I am," she admits quietly.

"Why?"

"Because, in just the past couple of days, you've made me feel more than Eric did in our entire relationship."

"How long were you together?"

"Seven months."

Folding my arms across my chest, I cock my head. "That's not very long."

She stomps over and jabs her finger into my chest. "Don't be a dick. It's still longer than I've known you."

Completely closing the distance between us, I back her against the cool stone wall. "Your mouth is saying one thing, but your eyes..." I trace the line of her jaw with my knuckle. "Your eyes tell me you're scared shitless."

Her breath hitches. "I'm not scared of you."

"Maybe not," I agree, leaning in until my lips brush her ear. "But you're sure as shit scared of how I make you feel."

She shivers and I can feel her pulse racing beneath my fingertips as I gently wrap my hand around her neck, tilt her head back, and squeeze.

"You can run all you want, kitten," I whisper-growl. "But we both know that our story... is just getting started."

Stepping back, I give her space to breathe. "I brought snacks, but how about we go home and make some lunch instead? I'm starving."

The relief on her face is almost comical. "Food. Yes. That's... Um... a great idea."

Knowing I've thrown her completely off balance, I grin. Good. That's exactly how I want her.

THE DRIVE BACK IS TENSE. RYDER FIDDLES WITH THE radio, stopping on a hard rock station playing 'You Give Love A Bad Name' and turns it up, drumming his fingers against his thigh.

I can't help but steal glances at his full lips, and the shadow of stubble darkening the line of his jaw. His damp hair is curling slightly at the nape of his neck, and I have to grip the steering wheel tight to keep myself from reaching out to touch it.

What the hell is happening to me?

When we pull into the driveway, the sun is high in the sky.

Ryder hops out before I have a chance to cut the engine and stretches his arms over his head. His shirt rides up, revealing a strip of tanned skin and a trail of dark hair that disappears into the waistband of his jeans.

My clit throbs in response, and I force myself to look away. How I managed to push myself away while he was on the verge of fingering me, I have no idea.

"Still hungry?" he asks as I follow him up the porch steps.

"Yes," I admit, fumbling with my keys.

Inside, Goonie greets us with an indignant meow, winding between my legs like he's been abandoned for weeks instead of hours.

"I'll feed him," Ryder says, already moving into the kitchen. "You want a sandwich?"

"Sure," I nod, suddenly feeling awkward in my own home.

The tension from what almost happened at the hot spring clings to me like a ghost, lingering in every tentative glance at his muscular back and bulging biceps.

While Ryder rummages through the fridge, I slip upstairs to change, peeling off my damp clothes and pulling on a soft oversized sweater and shorts. When I come back down, he's laid out a spread on the kitchen island—turkey, cheese, avocado, and some chips he probably found in the back of the pantry.

"This okay?" he asks, looking strangely domestic as he slices tomatoes.

"Perfect, thank you," I murmur, sliding onto a stool.

We eat in companionable silence as Goonie purrs, winding between our feet, begging for scraps, until Ryder clears his throat and wipes his mouth with a napkin.

"Are you going to write about what we did today?"

I take a sip of water. "Actually, yeah. Today was... inspiring."

He gives me a slow smile as he puffs up his chest. "Good."

Trying not to squirm in my seat, I ask, "What's next on your 'Help Noia Get Her Mojo Back' agenda?"

He takes another bite of his sandwich, chewing thoughtfully. "I'm thinking we should—" His eyes narrow as he fixes his gaze on something outside the window.

Spinning around, I follow his line of sight. "What is it?"

He stands so abruptly his chair nearly topples over. "What the fuck?"

Sandwich forgotten, he strides over to the window and presses a palm against the glass.

"What?" I ask, hurrying over to stand beside him.

His voice is filled with disbelief. "That's my truck."

I follow his gaze. A massive black pickup is sitting in my driveway. It wasn't there when we pulled in—I'm certain of it.

"How—?"

But Ryder is already at the door.

I follow him out onto the porch, watching as he approaches the sleek black truck. It's a beast of a machine—a black Ford F-150 with tinted windows and oversized tires, towering over my mid-sized SUV.

"This is my truck," he says again, voice tinged with disbelief as he runs his hand along the hood. "My fucking baby."

"There's no way," I gasp.

"But it is," he insists. "I recognize every scratch, every dent."

Ryder circles it slowly, trailing his fingers along the glossy paint. "The custom exhaust, the aftermarket rims I installed myself." He peers through the driver's side window. "Even the air freshener I hung from the rear view mirror."

My voice is barely above a whisper when I finally speak. "I never wrote about any of that."

When he reaches the driver's side, he tugs on the handle and opens the door.

"Keys are in the ignition," he says, looking back at me with wide, excited eyes.

"Shut. Up." But even as I say the words, I can't deny what's right in front of me. Just like waking up to Ryder cooking breakfast in my kitchen and him kissing me in the hot spring.

I walk over to take a peek inside as he slides into the driver's seat like he's done it a thousand times before, hands caressing the steering wheel. When he turns the key, the engine roars to life, the deep, powerful rumble vibrating its metal frame.

"Holy shit," he breathes, reverently running his hands over the dashboard.

My mind is racing. This can't be happening. First Ryder shows up out of nowhere, and now his truck appears out of thin air in my driveway? The boundaries between fiction and reality are crumbling faster than I can put them back together.

"Get in!" he yells, revving the engine.

"What? No!" I yell back over the ferocious rumble, crossing my arms. "I'm not wearing any shoes!"

"So? We won't go far." His eyes are wild with excitement. "Come on, kitten. Live a little."

"Where would we even go, anyway?"

His grin is wild and dangerous. "Anywhere. Everywhere. Come *on*. Aren't you excited to see what happens next?"

The rational part of my brain is screaming at me to go back inside, lock the door and call a freaking psychiatrist. But there's another part of me—the part that writes romance novels about risk, passion and adventure—already urging me around to the passenger side.

"Just a quick drive," I tell him firmly as I climb inside. "I gotta get some writing done."

The interior smells like him, all leather and sandalwood. The seats are worn in all the right places, and there's a small tear in the upholstery near the gearshift. It feels lived in and very... real.

"Buckle up buttercup, and hold on," he orders as he throws the truck into reverse.

We tear down the gravel driveway, stones pinging against the undercarriage. Ryder handles the massive vehicle like a pro and when we hit the main road, he guns it, the force of the acceleration pressing me back against the seat.

"Jesus!" I shriek as I grab the oh-shit handle. "Are you trying to kill us?"

"Just enjoying being behind the wheel again, kitten," he laughs, easing off the gas a little. "You have no idea how good this feels."

I watch his profile as he drives—the way his hands clench the steering wheel, the feral glint in his eyes as he peers happily through the windshield with a slight smile playing at the corners of his mouth.

He looks... content. Like a puzzle that's finally found its missing piece.

"This is insane," I murmur, more to myself than him. "First you show up outta nowhere, and now your truck materializes itself in my driveway?"

"I told you I was remembering things," he says, shooting me a glance. "Things you didn't write. Like this truck. I rebuilt the engine myself after I got back from my last tour."

"Tour? Like, military?"

"Afghanistan. Two tours."

I frown. "I never actually wrote that either. It was just an idea."

His knuckles go white as he grips the steering wheel. "But I still remember all of it. The heat, the dust, the way the air smelled right before a sandstorm hit."

We drive in silence for a few minutes, the radio playing softly in the background. I watch his face and wonder what else he remembers.

"What else?"

Unclenching his hands, he taps his thumb against the steering wheel, thinking for a few moments before he answers. "I remember the shop where I bought this truck and the first time I took it off-roading. Oh! And the dent I put in the tailgate? It's from when I backed into a light pole outside my tattoo parlor."

My stomach does a somersault. "*Your* tattoo parlor?"

He nods. "Skin & Ink."

"Never heard of it."

He shrugs. "Not yet. But who knows what tomorrow will bring?"

I PULL OFF ONTO A NARROW DIRT ROAD LEADING UP TO A ridge overlooking the lake and cut the engine.

The silence that follows is broken only by the sound of our breathing. The lake stretches out like a mirror, reflecting the stars as they start winking to life in the darkening sky.

"This is beautiful," Noia breathes, voice soft with wonder.

When I look at her, the dashboard lights are casting shadows across her face. "Yeah, it is."

Her lips part slightly as she takes in the scenery. I lick my lips, my heart rate speeding up at the sight of the gentle curve of her neck as she leans forward to peer out the windshield.

"How did you know about this place?"

"I didn't," I admit. "I just... drove? It felt like I already knew where I was going."

Releasing the seatbelt, she turns to face me, tucking one leg under the other. "This is all so fucking weird, Ryder. Your truck appearing out of nowhere, you remembering things I never wrote. What's happening to us?"

"I think the real question should be: What's happening to you?"

Her brow furrows.

"Think about it. The longer I'm here the more I remember about a life I didn't have before. But what if it's not just about me being real? What if it's about you finally letting yourself *believe* in something real?"

She goes quiet, chewing on her bottom lip—a habit I find incredibly distracting.

"You think I'm making this happen somehow?"

"I think you're a powerful woman who has spent years writing about passion and connection, all while denying yourself both. Maybe your subconscious finally got tired of the bullshit and decided to take matters into its own hands."

"By manifesting a fictional book-boyfriend?"

"By manifesting what you actually want instead of settling for what you think you deserve."

Noia stares out at the water, her reflection ghostlike in the glass.

"Eric never would have brought me somewhere like this," she says quietly. "He would've made reservations at some trendy restaurant where we'd sit across from each other making small talk about what happened to him at work while he checked his phone every five minutes." The laugh she huffs out sounds bitter. "I used to think real-life romance was about being with someone reliable."

"What about now?"

Her blue eyes are luminous when she turns to look at me. "Now I'm sitting in a truck that shouldn't exist with a man who shouldn't either, and I've never felt more alive."

She presses her fingers to her lips. The admission seems to surprise her as much as it does me.

"Noia—"

"We should go back," she says quickly, reaching for her seatbelt. "I really do need to write tonight and my feet are getting cold."

With a sigh, I turn the key and the engine roars to life. Leaning over, I turn on the heat and adjust it so it blows onto her bare feet.

"Thank you," she says with a sigh.

"Anything for you, kitten."

I hear her take a breath in as she shifts to rest her elbow next to the window. Resting her head in her hand, she keeps her gaze focused outside.

Shifting into reverse, I stretch my arm across the seat behind her as I back up, my fingers grazing the soft curls at the nape of her neck. She shivers under my touch, and I glance down to see her nipples are hard beneath her sweater.

The smell of vanilla and mineral water brushes softly under my nose, making my cock twitch and my jeans feel tight.

Despite the charge in the air, we both keep silent on the drive back. My nerves are on edge, like the calm before a storm.

When we pull into her driveway, I kill the engine.

The moonlight spills through the windshield, painting her skin in silver and shadow. "So you want me to write about today and see where it goes from there?"

"Yes."

"What if..." she starts, then stops, swallowing hard.

I wait silently, giving her a chance to gather her thoughts.

"What if I write something, and it changes you? Makes you different?"

I reach across the center console and take her hand. Her skin is soft against my calloused palm. "I'm not worried."

"You're not?"

"No. I trust you," I say simply. "I trust that whatever you write will be what needs to happen."

She stares down at our joined hands as my thumb traces

absentminded circles on her wrist. "I don't know if I trust myself. Not anymore."

"Then I guess you'll just have to let my trust be enough."

Her eyes flick up to meet mine and I feel something shift—a kind of understanding, an acceptance—between us. She nods once, then slips her hand from mine and opens the door.

I follow her inside, watching as she immediately starts to head upstairs.

"I'll be down here if you need me."

She turns slightly and nods before she disappears.

I sit on the couch, and Goonie immediately comes over to curl up next to me. I flip on the TV, keeping the volume low, but I can't seem to focus on the screen.

My attention keeps drifting to the sexy way Noia bites her lip, and the little furrow between her brows when she's concentrating too hard. How her nipples hardened when my fingers brushed against the back of her neck in the cab of the truck.

The shower turns on upstairs.

My hand moves to shift my cock, but I can't get comfortable knowing she's up there naked with water sluicing over her soft, creamy skin.

"Fuck."

Needing a different type of distraction, I shove up from the couch and head to the kitchen to make something for dinner.

I rummage through the freezer and cupboards, surprised to find it better stocked than I thought it was. There's chicken, pasta, and an assortment of veggies. Whoever stocked this place before she arrived knew what they were doing.

Forty-five minutes later, I take a plate of garlic butter pasta with grilled chicken and a glass of white wine upstairs. The shower stopped running a while ago, and I can hear the rapid-fire tapping of keys coming from her room.

The door is partially open and a sliver of golden light spills into the hallway. I tap gently with my knuckle before pushing it open.

I pause in the doorway and take her in. She's sitting cross-legged in her chair, hair piled messily on top of her head, wearing an oversized T-shirt. Her glasses are perched on the end of her nose, and she's completely lost in whatever world she's creating. Her fingers fly across the keyboard, pausing only when she bites her lower lip in concentration.

Taking a deep breath, I will my dick to behave.

I set the plate down on the corner of her desk, careful not to disturb the organized chaos of sticky notes and reference books. Her laptop screen glows with words from my story—our story.

I catch glimpses of phrases: "mineral water slick on his skin" and "the truck appeared like some kind of phantom," my name flashing randomly before my eyes.

She's good. Really good. The way she captures our tension, the heat simmering beneath every interaction—it's all right there on the page—raw, honest and sexy as hell.

"You gonna eat that or let it get cold?" I ask, leaning against the edge of her desk.

Startled, Noia jumps, her hands flying to her chest. "Jesus, Rye! How long have you been standing there?"

Did she just give me a nickname?

Brushing off the thrill it gives me, I chuckle. "Long enough to read that I apparently have eyes 'the color of storm clouds gathering over a restless ocean.'" I smirk. "Kind of poetic if you ask me."

Her cheeks flush that beautiful shade of pink and she quickly minimizes the document. "It's a first draft," she mumbles, adjusting her glasses. "And you weren't supposed to read it yet."

"Why not? It's my story too."

She eyes the plate, steam still rising from the perfectly seared chicken. "You cooked?"

"Found some stuff in your freezer that wasn't completely fossilized." I push the plate closer to her. "Eat."

She stretches, arching her back in a way that makes her breasts push against the thin fabric of her T-shirt.

Forcing myself to look away, I clear my throat.

"Thanks." She picks up the fork and takes a tentative bite. Her eyes widen. "Holy shit, this is really good."

"Don't sound so surprised," I snort.

"Sorry. It's just... Eric couldn't boil water without burning it."

Annoyance flares. "How about we not talk about him right now," I growl.

Her irises go wide as she swallows, eyes bouncing between mine. "Okaaay..."

"I just..." Huffing out a sigh, I rake my hands through my hair. "I'm sorry, it's just that—" I clench my fists at my sides, trying to keep my voice steady. "Do you have any idea how fucking hard it is to be around you?"

Her fork pauses halfway to her mouth. "What?"

I take a step closer, my voice dropping to a dangerous rumble. "You have no idea how fucking hard it is for me right now. Standing here, watching you stretch like that, knowing you're wearing nothing under your shirt."

Her fork clatters onto the plate.

"Do you know what I really want to do?" I lean forward, gripping the edge of her desk, caging her in. "I want to grab you, throw you on the bed, and fuck you until neither of us can remember our own names. It's taking everything I have—every ounce of self-control—not to do exactly that."

Her lips part, eyes going wide and dark as she stares up at me.

My gaze flicks to the line of her throat, where her pulse flutters wildly and I push away from the desk, needing some distance before I lose what little restraint I have left.

"I'm going to bed," I announce, my voice rough. "Make sure to get some sleep. After breakfast tomorrow, we're going out. I have a day trip planned."

Without waiting for a response, I turn and stalk out of the room, closing the door behind me with more force than necessary.

I stalk back downstairs to the guest room, strip down and fall onto the bed, staring at the ceiling. My body is tense, cock hard as a rock, skin hot.

What the hell is happening to me? I've never felt this way about anyone before. This desperate, all consuming need. It's not just physical—although fuck knows I want her body—it's more than that.

I want all of her. Her smile, her sass, her stubborn determination. I want to be the reason she laughs, the reason she writes, the reason she believes in love again.

And that terrifies me more than the possibility I could disappear at any moment.

Shifting on the bed, I readjust my dick, then freeze. Something feels different. I glance down and a jolt of recognition hits me—I'm wearing boxer briefs—black cotton briefs with a tiny tear near the waistband.

Wait a minute. These are mine.

When I first appeared in Noia's living room, I was commando under my pants. I know this because I only wear boxers to bed, if at all.

But these—these aren't just any boxers—they're *my* boxers. The ones I specifically remember buying at a small shop in San Diego after my last deployment.

I bolt upright, heart hammering against my ribs. Throwing

off the covers, I swing my legs over the side of the bed. Crossing the room in three long strides, I yank the closet door open so hard it bangs against the wall.

"What the fuck?"

The closet is filled with clothes. Henley shirts, faded and new, hang on plastic hangers and my worn leather jacket is hanging on a hook. My favorite boots are sitting lined up like soldiers on the floor against the wall. Even my old Marine Corps T-shirt with the hole in the sleeve that I can't bring myself to throw away stares back at me.

"Holy shit," I mutter.

I reach out, fingers trembling slightly as I touch the familiar fabric.

Grabbing the leather jacket, I bring it to my nose and inhale. It smells like me, like motor oil and the cologne I've worn for years. The worn patches at the elbows, the slight tear in the inner pocket where I once stored a switchblade, are all exactly as I remember.

Every piece feels like a memory. The more I touch, the more I remember. The gray T-shirt I was wearing when I first met Claire at the tattoo shop. The jeans I had on when I drove my bike cross-country after being honorably discharged.

An entire life I didn't have before is starting to form around me, piece by piece, memory by memory.

Pulling on a pair of jeans and a black Henley, I pace the room, trying to make sense of it all. My truck showing up was one thing, but this? This is something else entirely.

I'm about to head upstairs to tell Noia when I spot something on the nightstand that definitely wasn't there before—a wallet and a set of keys.

Snatching them up, I flip the wallet open. There's my driver's license with my face scowling back at me. Credit cards.

A faded photo of my unit in Afghanistan. Cash. Even my goddamn library card.

The keys feel familiar in my palm—the key to my motorcycle, my apartment key, and the distinctive skull-shaped key that unlocks the door to my tattoo shop.

My heart is racing. It's like the cosmos is anchoring me into this world more firmly with each passing hour. The universe seems to be filling in all the gaps, creating a complete life for me outside of Noia's manuscript.

I need to see her. Now.

noia

FROZEN, I SIT AT MY DESK, STARING AT THE CLOSED DOOR.

Holy. Shit.

My heart is hammering so hard I can feel it everywhere—in my throat, between my legs. Ryder's words echo in my head, each syllable vibrating through me.

"I want to grab you, throw you on the bed, and fuck you until neither of us can remember our own names."

Damn.

I squeeze my thighs together, trying to ease the ache. This is insane. He's insane. *I'm* insane for even entertaining the idea of...

Of what? Sleeping with a fictional character? Having mind-blowing sex with the most gorgeous man I've ever seen, who also just happens to be a figment of my imagination?

I stare at my laptop screen, trying to focus on the words I had been writing before Ryder interrupted me. But all I can see is the intensity in his storm-gray eyes, the barely restrained hunger in them as he glared at me.

Taking a deep breath, I force myself to focus on the words and lose myself in the story. I describe the look on Ryder's face when he saw his truck—a mix of shock, joy and pure, unadulterated excitement—the way his whole body seemed to vibrate as he slid behind the wheel.

After a while, I stop typing long enough to take another bite of his amazing chicken. Then, fingers back on the keyboard, I start typing again.

Ryder's hands trailed down her spine, leaving goosebumps in their wake. "I've been waiting for this,"he whispered against her neck, "since the moment I first laid eyes on you."

I pause, chewing my lip. No, that's not right. Deleting the line, I try again.

Ryder stepped back, creating some distance between them. "We should take this slow," he said, though his body was tense with need.

A little better? Slow-burn is what I'm good at. It's what—

Thundering footsteps pound up the stairs, and before I can react, my door flies open with a bang that nearly has me tumbling out of my chair.

"Fuck's sake! Don't you know how to knock? I could've been naked!" I screech, heart racing as I clutch the arms of the chair.

Ryder is breathing hard, eyes wild, dressed in jeans and a black Henley I've never seen before.

"My clothes...," he pants. "...all of them..." Still panting. "...in the closet downstairs."

"Say again?"

"My clothes. My wallet." He holds up a set of keys, jangling them for emphasis. "The keys to my apartment. To my shop."

"Your... shop?"

"Skin & Ink. My tattoo parlor? The one I told you about earlier."

Legs shaking, I stand up slowly. "That's impossible."

"More impossible than my truck just showing up out of the ether?"

Suddenly, the laptop chimes with an email notification. I turn to check it, and gasp.

Immediately on alert, Ryder comes over to look.

"It's from Skin & Ink Tattoo," I say, voice barely above a whisper. "Confirming my appointment for tomorrow at two p.m."

Ryder goes still. "Holy shit."

"But it doesn't exist!"

"Apparently it does now." He pulls out his phone—another item that must have materialized out of nowhere—and taps the screen. "Oh, fuck."

He turns the phone toward me. On the screen is a website for Skin & Ink, featuring photos of intricate tattoos and a staff page with Ryder's brooding face, front and center.

"This is getting too weird."

"Tell me something I don't know." He grabs my hand. "Come on. Come see."

Next thing I know, he's pulling me down the stairs to the guest room. When I step through the open door, my jaw drops.

The closet that was nearly empty this morning is now stuffed with men's clothing. Dark shirts, worn jeans, boots and a leather jacket that looks like it's seen better days.

"You sure all of this is yours?" I whisper.

"Every last piece." He runs his hand along a sleeve of the leather jacket. "I got this after my first tour. The zipper sticks sometimes."

I move closer, touching the fabric. It feels real. It smells real —like sandalwood and leather and something unmistakably... Ryder.

"This is nuts."

He paces the room, running his hands through his hair. "I'm

telling you, Noia. My life here in your world is becoming more real by the minute." He grabs my shoulders, turning me to face him. "I have more memories—real memories."

His eyes are so intense, so sincere, I can't look away.

Reaching into his back pocket, he pulls out a wallet and flips it open. "Look!"

I take it with shaking hands. Inside, there's a driver's license with his face glaring back at me, credit cards and a few hundred dollars in cash.

I stare at the wallet, then back at him. "What do you think this all means?"

"I don't know," he admits, dropping onto the edge of his bed. "But it feels like the universe is trying to tell us something."

I shift in my feet. "What are you going to do?"

Leaning forward, forearms on his knees, he puts his head in his hands. "I need to go see it for myself. Are you cool with putting off our date tomorrow?"

I move to sit beside him on the bed, hesitating only a moment before placing my hand on his back, tracing small circles between his shoulder blades. Breath catching, he stiffens, but after a moment, he relaxes, leaning into my touch.

"Of course," I say softly. "This is important. Do you want me to go with you?"

Ryder shakes his head and flexes his jaw. "No. This is something I need to do on my own." He runs his hands through his hair again, leaving it sexily disheveled. "I need to see if it's real. If they know me. If I have clients, a history there."

My hand stills on his back. "I understand."

When he turns to look at me, our faces are inches apart. His eyes drop to my lips, and for a breathless moment, I think he might kiss me.

But then he pulls away and stands. "You should go get some sleep," he says, voice gruff. "It's been a weird day."

I let my hand fall to the bed, feeling oddly dejected. "Yeah. Weird doesn't even begin to cover it."

"I'll see you in the morning," he says, backing toward the door. His eyes never leave mine and then something flashes in them—Regret? Desire? Fear?—that makes my heart stutter. "I'm gonna a go for a drive. Clear my head."

"Okay. Goodnight," I whisper.

He pauses at the threshold, turning back with a half-smile that doesn't quite reach his eyes. "Goodnight, Noia. And thanks. For understanding."

Then he's gone, leaving me alone, sitting on his bed, the ghost of his warmth still lingering beside me.

Goonie appears in the doorway, meowing softly as he pads over to rub against my ankles.

"You saw that, right?" I ask as I pick him up, cradling him in my arms like a baby. "I'm not going crazy?"

Unconcerned with my existential crisis, he blinks up at me and starts to purr.

Rising from the bed, I make my way back up to my room. I can't help feeling that with each passing day, and with every new item that materializes, Ryder is becoming more firmly anchored in this world.

My world.

And the scariest part? I'm starting to think that not only could he be real—but I might actually want him to stay.

THE NEXT MORNING, I WAKE TO THE SMELL OF COFFEE AND bacon again. Some things, at least, are becoming routine.

I pull on my robe and pad downstairs to find Ryder fully dressed in dark jeans and a charcoal Henley that hugs his broad shoulders and arms perfectly. Hair still damp from the shower, he's pacing the kitchen like a caged animal.

"Morning," I mumble, making a beeline for the coffeepot.

"Hey." His voice sounds tight and distracted as he glances at his watch and then back at me. "I'm heading out soon."

"Alright. Are you okay?"

He nods, jaw ticking away. "My appointment's at noon. Apparently, I have a client coming in for a full sleeve."

"A client you've never met?"

"Technically. But I remember meeting her. Not only that, I somehow remember designing the tattoo of a dragon, too."

I take a sip of my coffee, thankful for the much needed jolt of caffeine. "Her?"

He tilts his head at me and grins, transforming the nervous expression on his face to one of mischief.

"Jealous?"

"What? No." I scoff, hiding behind my mug. "Don't flatter yourself."

His grin widens as he reaches for his leather jacket, shrugging it on with that effortless grace that makes my stomach flip. The worn leather stretches across his shoulders like it was made for him—because, apparently, it was.

"So what are your plans for today?" he asks, adjusting the collar.

I lean against the counter, trying to look casual when there's nothing casual about any of this whatsoever. "All the fun stuff. Clean the house, go food shopping since we've pretty much demolished most of what was here. Oh, and I need to call Sasha. She's been texting me non-stop, wanting updates."

"Updates on what?" he asks, popping an eyebrow.

"On you, obviously." I take another sip to hide my blush. "She thinks I've either gone completely insane or hit the jackpot."

He chuckles, checking his pockets for his keys. "What do you figure?"

"Jury's still out," I mutter, a small smile tugging at my lips. "When will you be home?" The question slips out before I can stop it, and I immediately want to take it back.

Home. Like this is his home now, too?

He pulls his keys from his pocket, jingling them thoughtfully.

"Probably not till late," he says, pocketing his wallet. "Depending on what happens when I get there. Just starting a full sleeve can take a few hours, at least."

I nod, trying to appear casual even as my stomach knots with anxiety. What if he leaves and never comes back? What if this is where our story ends?

"Well... good luck."

He moves toward the door, then pauses, turning back to look at me. In three long strides, he's standing before me. Before I can react, his hands come up to firmly cup my face.

"I'll text you." His eyes lock with mine. "Try not to miss me too much, kitten," he murmurs, his voice like gravel and honey.

Then he's gone, the door closing behind him with a soft click.

Frozen, I stand in the middle of the kitchen, coffee cooling in my hands, my face tingling from his touch.

"Well, shit." I look over at Goonie, his cat eyes judging me from his perch on the counter. "I'm in trouble, aren't I?"

Outside, Ryder's truck rumbles to life.

My cat looks at me and chirrups, which I take as a definitive yes.

With a sigh, I head upstairs to shower and get dressed, trying to ignore the hollow feeling in my chest. Is it ridiculous to miss someone who's been gone less than a minute, especially when that certain someone shouldn't even exist?

As I step into my panties, my phone buzzes with a text.

SASHA: *CALL ME IMMEDIATELY YOU TRAITOR. I NEED DETAILS. ASAP.*

Rolling my eyes, I tap the call button.

She answers on the first ring. "It's about damn time!" she huffs in my ear. "I've been dying over here!"

"Good morning to you too," I chuckle, wedging the phone between my ear and shoulder as I pull on my jeans.

"Oh no, don't you 'good morning' me, missy. You have a hot fictional guy in your house who just happened to materialize in your kitchen, not to mention you've ghosted me for days!"

"Hey. As I recall, after I called and told you what happened, I asked for your help and all you did was laugh and hang up on me!"

"And I stand by that decision!" Sasha cackles. "But seriously. In my defense, it was either laugh or call the paddy wagon. I figured laughing was the safer option for our friendship. Now. I need all the juicy details. Have you slept with him? Please tell me you at least made out."

Putting the phone on speaker, I tug my sweater over my head, and check my reflection in the mirror. "We've kissed. Twice."

"TWICE? And you didn't call me *immediately* after? What kind of best friend *are* you?"

"The kind who's probably having a complete mental breakdown," I mutter as I grab my phone and head back downstairs. "Sash, things are getting weird. Like, really weird."

"Good weird or bad weird?"

I pour myself another cup of coffee and take a seat on the couch. "His truck showed up in my driveway yesterday, out of nowhere. And now he has an entire closet full of clothes, his wallet, keys to an apartment and a tattoo shop he owns that actually, before last night, never existed."

Silence.

"Sash?"

"I'm... processing," she answers slowly. "So you're telling me that not only did you manifest your fictional book boyfriend, but now you're manifesting pieces of his life?"

"That's exactly what I'm telling you."

"Holy shit, Noia. That's either the most romantic thing I've ever heard or the most terrifying."

"How about both?" I groan, flopping onto my side against the cushions. "He left this morning to go to his tattoo shop—which again, shouldn't even exist—to work on a client he's technically never met but somehow remembers designing the tattoo for."

"And how do you feel about all this?"

I turn onto my back and stare at the ceiling. "Scared," I sigh after thinking about it a moment. "Excited. Confused. I'm starting to fall for someone who, for all I know, could disappear at any moment."

"Sounds to me like you're finally letting yourself feel something real for the first time in years."

"Don't."

"Don't what? Tell you the truth? Noia, when's the last time you talked about a guy the way you're talking about him right now? Or the last time someone made you this excited?"

I shut my eyes in defeat. "Never."

"Exactly. So maybe stop overthinking it and just... see where it goes."

"Easy for you to say. You're not the one falling for a fictional character."

"Honey, from what you've told me, he doesn't sound so fictional anymore. In fact, he sounds pretty damn real to me."

My phone buzzes with a text and my heart skips.

RYDER: *I made it. You were right—this is fucking surreal.*

Everyone here knows who I am, and apparently, I have appointments booked out for the next three weeks!

I read the message to Sasha and I can hear the smile in her voice when she says, "Noia, I think you need to accept that whatever this is, it's happening. So. What are you going to do?"

"What am I supposed to do, Sash?" I stare at the text. "Write him a happy ending? Write myself into his story and hope for the best?"

"First of all, you *are* his story. And second, I'm coming to see this hottie for myself."

I nearly drop my phone. "What? No!"

"Yes. I've got some vacation days saved up. I'll be there Friday."

"But—"

"No buts! My best friend manifested a hot book boyfriend into existence. I need to see him with my own eyes, make sure he's treating you right, and ask him about any other fictional hotties he might know. Maybe he has a friend."

I groan, pressing my palm to my forehead. "You're impossible."

"And you love me for it. Text him back, clean up whatever disaster zone I know you're living in, and prepare the other guest room."

My voice sounds small when I ask, "What if he's gone by the time you get here?"

Sasha's voice softens. "Then we'll figure it out together. But I have a feeling he's not going anywhere."

After we hang up, I text Ryder back.

ME: *That's incredible. How do you feel?*

Three dots appear, disappear, then reappear.

RYDER: *Better than expected. Gotta go. TTYL.*

I toss the phone on the coffee table and lie back on the couch.

Goonie saunters in, meows, leaps onto the couch with a grunt and pads his way up my body, kneading his paws against my stomach before making himself at home on my chest.

"Oof! Damn, fur ball. You're getting heavy," I grumble. Sliding my hand over his soft fur, he starts to purr and I begin to relax.

I stare up at the ceiling, watching the patterns of sunlight shift across the plaster.

"Guess we're running with the punches from now on, huh, boy? And between you and me? I sure hope it's going to be a bumpy ride."

SIXTEEN

THE TRUCK ROARS WHEN I PRESS THE ACCELERATOR A little too hard, but the familiar rumble does little to calm my nerves.

I glance in the rearview mirror as Noia's cottage grows smaller behind me, guilt twisting in my gut. Leaving her home alone feels wrong somehow, like I'm abandoning her.

My chest aches at the memory of the look on her face before I left. I could've asked her to come with me, but I know this is something I need to do on my own. Not just for me, but for our story to progress in the right direction.

Taking the road that winds through dense forest, opens up to reveal a small lakeside town. The '**Welcome to Lakeside**' sign flashes by as I take the exit.

Quaint storefronts and café's line Main Street, with people strolling the sidewalks enjoying the morning sun. It all looks so normal, so real.

But what if I'm not? What if I walk into my shop and no one recognizes me?

My palms start to sweat.

Fuck, I've faced gunfire and IEDs with less anxiety than I'm feeling about what I'm about to do.

"Get it together, Blackwood."

According to the GPS on my phone—another item that conveniently materialized in my room—Skin & Ink is located just off Main Street, sandwiched between a coffee shop and a vintage record store.

As I drive through town, things start to look vaguely familiar. It's like having the strangest case of déjà vu.

I approach the address, slowing my truck down to a crawl as a storefront with a black awning and bold red letters that reads "Skin & Ink" in gothic script comes into view. My heart pounds as I back the truck up into a parking spot across the street.

The building looks exactly like I remember. Can I really call these fragmented flashes memories, though? With its red brick façade, the building's large windows display different styles of artwork and a flashing neon *OPEN* sign.

I sit, staring in disbelief as my hands grip the steering wheel so tight my knuckles turn white. I can see movement inside. People. Real people who supposedly know me.

"Fuck it," I mutter, killing the engine.

The bell above the door chimes as I step inside, and the familiar scent of antiseptic, ink, and leather hits me smack in the face. The walls are covered with flash art—skulls, roses, pin-ups, and intricate Celtic knots. There's a counter display full of jewelry and aftercare products, and the steady buzz of tattoo machines fills the air.

"Ryder! There you are, man," a deep male voice calls out.

I turn and see a guy about my age with a full sleeve of tattoos on each arm and gauged ears grinning at me like we've known each other for years standing behind the counter. My mind scrambles, and then—like a key freeing a lock—recognition clicks solidly into place.

"Jax." The name falls from my lips without a thought. "Sorry I'm late."

Jax Riley is my business partner and best friend. He's not only the guy who taught me how to clean a tattoo machine, but the one who got my name tattooed on his ass after losing a drunken bet.

"No worries, brother. Your client's already here. She's in the back with Lizzy, filling out paperwork." He tosses me a binder. "Here's the final design you worked up for her dragon sleeve. Fucking sick, by the way."

I catch it and flip it open. Detailed sketches of a Japanese-style dragon designed to wind from shoulder to wrist jump out at me from the page.

Not only do I recognize the sketch as mine, but my handwriting with abbreviations about shading and color—notes only I know how to interpret—line the margins.

"Yeah, thanks."

This is beyond fucking weird.

He cocks his head and studies me. "You don't look so good. Late night?"

"Something like that," I mutter, glancing around.

The shop is exactly as I remember.

Leather couches sit in the waiting area, with framed photos displaying our best pieces gracing the wall behind them. A row of stations for the other artists' are along the wall to the right.

It's all so familiar, yet I've never actually been here before. At least, not in any reality I know of.

Jax claps me on the shoulder. "You good, man? You look like you've seen a ghost."

Dude. You have no fucking idea.

"Just... didn't sleep much," I manage, which isn't entirely a lie.

"When do you ever?" He laughs, turning to help a customer

looking at display jewelry before he turns back to me. "Let me guess. Another nightmare?"

The casual way he asks tells me he knows about my PTSD and night terrors. The cold sweats that sometimes leave me gasping for air at three a.m.

"Oh, and Claire called. Said she's bringing lunch for everyone around one."

Claire. The name hits me like a punch to the gut. Suddenly, I can see her in my mind—tall, with short purple hair and tattoos sleeved down one arm. A few years older than me, she's the one who gave me my first real job after I was discharged from the Marines. The woman who believed in me when no one else did, now manages my shop.

He brushes off my silence by clearing his throat.

"So... Your station's all set up. I cleaned your machines this morning since you were running late." He tosses me a set of keys. "You left these in the back room again."

Snatching them out of the air, I turn them over in my hand. They're different than the ones that appeared last night.

"Thanks."

As I walk toward the back, it feels like I'm in a dream. Muscle memory guides me past the reception area, over to where multiple tattooing stations are set up. Each one is spotless, with different artwork and personal touches, making them unique to the artists that work there.

I pass two other artists working on clients who smile and nod.

The station in the far corner has my name etched on a small plaque. The walls surrounding it are covered with both dark and colorful, intricate designs—all of them mine. A framed Marines emblem hangs next to a worn Megadeath poster, and a small desk holds a sketchpad, various pens, and a black coffee mug with *Fuck Off* printed in blue on the side.

"There he is," a bright female voice calls out.

When I turn around, a petite woman sporting long black hair with blue tips and colorful tattoos covering almost every visible inch of skin is standing behind me smiling.

"Hey, Lizzy," I nod as more memories start clicking into place. Lizzy Cade was my first hire and is the best portrait artist in the county. She loves whiskey and has a pet iguana named Slash.

"This is Allie." She gestures to a woman with long blond hair, who looks nervous, standing beside her. "She's ready for you. Oh. And I got her paperwork sorted for you, too."

"Thanks, Liz," I say as she walks away.

Stepping forward with a shy smile, Allie holds out her hand. "I've been looking forward to this for months," she says, smiling shyly. "Ever since I saw your work at the tattoo convention in Denver."

Denver? I've never been to Denver. Except... Flashes of memories from that weekend suddenly flood my mind.

Jesus. This is starting to get disorienting.

"Good to see you again," I say, taking her hand and giving it a quick squeeze. "Ready to get started?"

She nods enthusiastically and follows me over to my station, where I signal for her to have a seat.

Everything feels surreal as I adjust the height of my stool. I set up my equipment, prepare the stencil, and mix the ink.

When I remove the stencil from Allie's arm, she grins in the mirror. "It's perfect. Exactly how I imagined it."

"Great. Then let's get started."

The moment my needle touches her skin, everything fades away. The buzzing of the machine is like meditation, and I lose myself in the rhythm of doing line work. The outline of the dragon slowly begins to take shape—scales and claws emerging from her skin like they were always meant to be there.

A couple of hours go by, but it feels like minutes. My back aches from hunching over, but I barely notice. Creating art on a living canvas feels right, like it's a part of me.

"Hey, Ride. Got your favorite."

Claire's nickname for me hits me with a case of nostalgia, and I grin up at her.

Her purple hair is streaked with silver at the temples, and she's holding a paper bag that smells like heaven. She seems older than I remember. Her laugh lines are a little deeper and she has a nose piercing she didn't have before.

"Hey, Cee Cee." I sit up straight to stretch my back.

"Lunchtime, folks," she announces, setting down the bags of food on the break table. "I got those protein wraps you like, Ride."

I wipe my brow with the back of my arm. "Thanks. Almost finished."

Claire winks at Allie. "He gets like this—too focused for his own good. You doing okay, honey? He treating you right?"

Allie nods enthusiastically. "It hurts a lot less than I thought it would."

"That's because he's one of the best," Claire says with unmistakable pride in her voice. "Other than me, of course. I taught him everything he knows."

"Except humility," I mutter at Allie's arm as Claire's laugh rings through the shop.

"Never claimed to have that," she retorts, ruffling my hair as she passes. "Food's getting cold, ya'll. Wrap it up."

I finish the last scale I'm working on and sit back to admire my work. The outline of the dragon is complete, with some preliminary shading along the spine. It's good—better than good. It's exactly what I envisioned when I designed it.

"We need to stop here for today," I say, wiping away the excess ink. "How do you feel?"

"Like I could keep going," she answers. But the slight tremor in her hand tells me she's reached her limit.

"First session's always the hardest," I say, applying some protection cream to the fresh tattoo. "We've got three more sessions before it'll be complete. Just remember, this is a marathon, not a sprint, okay?"

She nods as she examines her arm in the mirror, eyes wide with excitement. "It's already so bad ass. I can't wait to see it when it's finished."

After she leaves, I pull out my phone to see a text from Noia asking how everything is going. I text her back to give her an update and shove it back into my pocket.

A few minutes later, with my lunch wrap halfway to my mouth, I get an alert.

KITTEN: *That's incredible. How do you feel?*

Not ready to talk about it yet, I go with blunt.

ME: *Better than expected. Gotta go. TTYL*

Finished with lunch, I toss the wrapper in the trash and wipe my hands on my jeans.

"I'm going to head upstairs for a bit," I tell Jax, who's sitting at the front counter sketching.

He barely looks up. "Sure, man. Your two o'clock cancelled and your next appointment's not until four."

My two o'clock was Noia. I grin and shake my head.

I grab my jacket and head toward the back of the shop where a narrow staircase leads to the second floor, my heart pounding nervously against my ribs as I climb.

Sliding the key into the lock, I open the door, and step inside.

The apartment is completely empty. There's no furniture, not even a light bulb in the ceiling fixture—just white walls and the afternoon sun streaking through uncovered windows across bare scuffed hardwood floors.

"What the hell?" I mutter, my voice a lonely echo in the vacant space.

I take my time walking through each room. There's a living area that connects to a small kitchen, a bathroom with a decent-sized shower, toilet and sink, and a bedroom with built-in closets standing open and empty.

Running my hand along the wall, I test the texture of the paint beneath my fingertips. It's real. The apartment exists, but for some reason it's not furnished or lived in.

And then it hits me—maybe it's not time yet. Maybe, like everything else that has been randomly materializing around me, it'll show up when I need it.

I lean against the window frame and look down at the street below, watching the people going about their normal lives, completely unaware of my existential crisis happening two stories above them.

My phone buzzes in my pocket.

KITTEN: *Okay, it's later. How is your day going?*

My heart skips.

ME: *Checked out my apartment above the shop, but it's empty.*

The dots dance as she types.

KITTEN: *Are you okay?*

ME: *I guess. Seems I'm only getting pieces of this life as I need them.*

KITTEN: *Makes sense.*

I feel another flash of guilt when I remember my promise we'd do something every day to help with inspiration.

Then I have an idea. I wasn't planning on doing this date yet, but I think it's the right time.

ME: *Hey. I'm gonna need you to be dressed up and ready for our blind date tonight when I get home.*

KITTEN: *Blind date?*

ME: *Yup. You got a red dress?*

The dots appear and disappear several times before her reply comes through.

KITTEN: *I think so... Why red?*

I can almost hear the skepticism as I read her words, and it makes me chuckle.

ME: *Because I know you'll look fucking hot in it, that's why. I'll text you when I'm on my way home with further instructions.*

KITTEN: *You're getting bossier by the day.*

"Oh, kitten," I murmur to myself. "You have no idea."

With a Cheshire grin, I pocket my phone and take one last look around the empty space. I guess I'll know when the time is right to check again.

Locking the door behind me, I head back downstairs.

Claire catches my eye as I reach the bottom. "Everything okay up there?"

My voice sounds overly incredulous when I answer, "Of course."

She studies my face with the same penetrating gaze she's always used that tells me she sees through my bullshit. "You seem off today. Anything you want to talk about?"

"Not really," I shrug. "Just got some personal shit that came up I'm trying to figure out. I'm good."

Seeing the look in her eye, I brace myself for what I suddenly know is coming. She steps forward and wraps her arms around me, giving me a squeeze.

Man, the woman is strong.

"You know I'm always here if you need to talk."

"I know. Thanks, Cee Cee."

noia

I SPEND THE NEXT HOUR CLEANING MY HOUSE LIKE I'M preparing for a military inspection. Scrubbing countertops, dusting shelves, and vacuuming every corner until the place looks better than it has in months.

"Sasha would be so proud," I mutter to Goonie, who watches me from atop the bookshelf. "Don't give me that look. This is for my sanity, not to impress Ryder."

Goonie blinks at me, clearly unconvinced.

After grabbing my purse and keys, I head for the door. "I'm going to the grocery store. Try not to destroy anything while I'm gone."

The cool air hits my face as I step outside, and I take a deep breath in. Maybe some time alone will help clear my head. I need groceries anyway—my fridge is practically empty except for condiments and that questionable yogurt that's been there since... Well, probably since before Eric left me at the altar.

The local supermarket is only ten minutes away, and I crank up the radio, singing along to distract myself from thoughts of Ryder and how he's doing at the tattoo shop. By the time I pull into the parking lot, I've almost convinced myself that everything will make sense, eventually.

Inside, I grab a cart and methodically work my way through the aisles. Real food this time—not just the frozen dinners and ramen that have barely managed to sustain me over the past couple of weeks. I toss in some fresh vegetables, a couple of chicken breasts, pasta, and enough coffee to fuel a small army.

As I'm debating between two different brands of pasta sauce, my phone buzzes.

RYDER: *Make sure you get beer. And steak.*

I nearly drop my phone. How did he—

RYDER: *And ice cream. You're almost out.*

ME: *Are you spying on me?*

RYDER: *Just a lucky guess. I saw the empty carton in your freezer. You should really throw things out when you're done.*

Unable to stop the smile spreading across my face, I shake my head.

ME: *Anything else, your highness?*

RYDER: *That's sir to you, kitten. And something for breakfast tomorrow that doesn't involve pop tarts.*

Rolling my eyes against the shiver caused by his 'sir' comment, I head to the ice cream aisle.

When I reach the checkout counter, I park myself in line behind a young couple. Pressed close together, the guy has his arm draped casually around the woman's shoulders while they debate which kind of chips to buy. There's something about their easy going affection that makes my chest ache just a little.

"That'll be $127.42," the cashier states, yanking me from my thoughts.

I pay and wheel my cart out to the parking lot and load the bags into the trunk. Just as I settle into the front seat, I get another text.

RYDER: *Wear your hair down tonight. I'll text you with further instructions when I'm on my way home.*

His simple command sends a tingle of excitement up my spine.

ME: *Bossy.*

RYDER: *Kitten, you have no idea. See you tonight.*

A SHARP KNOCK AT THE FRONT DOOR, MAKES ME NEARLY jump out of the red dress Ryder basically ordered me to wear.

When I open it, I almost forget how to breathe.

Ryder is standing before me in a blue button-down, sleeves rolled just high enough to show off his muscular forearms and the thick veins running from wrist to elbow. His hair is styled in its signature chaotic dark and messy and he's wearing cologne that should come with a warning label.

Warning: *This scent is designed to make your panties drop within seconds. Proceed with caution.*

Holding a single white daisy, he flashes me a smirk.

"Hey," he says, voice smooth. "I'm here for my blind date. You must be Noia."

My brain short-circuits. "What?"

He lifts a brow. "You agreed to have dinner with me tonight, said you'd be wearing a red dress?"

The flowy, red wrap around dress with the too high slit and the seriously low neckline actually makes me feel alive again—sexy. But the way he's eyeing me right now, I feel exposed—like he can read my thoughts through every visible inch of my skin—but in all the best ways.

"I understand you're a writer," he adds, brushing by me as he steps inside. "Romance novels, right? Bet you've got a thing for slow-burn and broody, dangerous, complicated men."

"Oh. My. God," I mutter, closing the door. "You're being serious right now, aren't you?"

Ryder texted me when he was on his way home and told me to wait upstairs until he texted me to come down, surprising me when he knocked on the front door.

He shrugs and walks into the candlelit living room like he didn't light all those damn candles himself.

There's soft jazz playing in the background and a couple of plates and wine glasses have been set out on the small table by the window. He even laid out cloth napkins. Where he managed to find those, I have no fucking clue.

This guy has this wooing thing pretty down pat.

"I figured we might as well make the most of what we're doing. Make it fun."

"You're deranged."

He flashes a grin. "Tell me something I don't know."

I cross my arms under my breasts, which pushes them up even more. "And what is the goal tonight exactly?"

Ryder's gaze flicks down to my chest and he slowly licks his lips before quickly looking away. He shrugs again, uncorking the chilled bottle and pouring the wine. "We're at a crossroads with your writer's block. So tonight, we're going to pretend we're strangers."

He hands me a glass.

I hesitate. "What if I don't want to play along?"

He takes a slow sip from his glass. "Then I sit here and snuggle with Goonie all night instead. He's way less emotionally constipated."

Goonie meows loudly from the kitchen in agreement.

Traitor.

My eyes volley between the wine, Ryder, and the flicker of candlelight dancing across his face.

Screw it.

"Fine." I take the glass and down half of it. "Let's play."

We sit across from each other and he makes small talk asking me what I do for a living other than writing. I play along and make up a story about how I design greeting cards for emotionally repressed men. He pretends to be a retired stunt double who teaches yoga to senior citizens.

Our knees bump under the table and we laugh as we talk. At one point, he reaches out to brush a crumb from the corner of my mouth with his thumb.

"So, Noia," he says, tilting his head, keeping his voice low and full of warmth. "Tell me something you've never told anyone before."

I twirl my wine glass, trying not to drown in the way he's looking at me and make up some more shit. I mean, it's a fake date after all.

AFTER DINNER, WE CLEAR THE TABLE AND HE CHANGES THE music. With the candles half-melted, he holds out his hand.

"Dance with me?"

I hesitate.

"Come on," he says, crooking his fingers.

There's no way he's going to let this go, so I let him pull me into his arms.

My world narrows to the feel of his chest against my cheek, the way his thumb strokes slow circles at the small of my back, and how our hips sway together like we've done this a thousand times before.

After a few minutes, I get nervous and back away, putting a few inches between us. When I finally look up, he's watching me.

"What?" I whisper.

"You're so beautiful."

My heart skips and he gives me a small smile. "And based on how quickly you just pulled away, I'm pretty sure you're doing everything in your power not to fall for me."

"How do you know?" I volley back.

He leans in close, his mouth a breath away from mine.

"Because if you had," he murmurs, "you'd let me kiss you right now."

My lips part in surprise and I take another step back, forcing out a laugh as I wipe my sweaty palms on my dress. "This is getting a little too intense for a fake date."

He doesn't respond, just looks at me with those intense gray eyes.

Then his smile fades into something darker, more dangerous. In two strides, he's in my space again, crowding me backward until my back hits the wall.

"What are you doing?" I gasp, my voice catching as his body heat surrounds me.

"Pretend time is over," he says, planting his hands on either side of my head. "I'm tired of all this slow-burn bullshit," he growls roughly. "It's time we take whatever it is we're doing to the next level."

My heart hammers against my ribs. "And what level is that?"

His only answer is to by capture my mouth with his. It's not the gentle kiss from the hot spring or even the adrenaline-fueled one from outside the bar. This is hunger and need and desperation all rolled into one devastating assault, switching my senses to high alert.

Sliding his hands down my sides, he finds the hem of my dress. Shoving the fabric up, he palms my ass and squeezes, pulling me against him as he deepens the kiss. I gasp into his mouth, which he takes advantage of, swiping his tongue against mine, making me weak in the knees.

I should stop this before it goes any further, push him away. But when his teeth graze my bottom lip, all rational thought flies out the window. My hands find their way into his hair, tugging him closer as heat pools low in my belly.

"Fuck," he breathes against my lips, his voice rough with desire. "You taste good."

His fingers dig into my flesh, lifting me to press his rock hard length against my center. A moan escapes my lips, and I feel him smile against my mouth.

"That's it, kitten," he murmurs, trailing kisses along my jaw to my ear. "Let me hear you."

When his teeth nip gently at my earlobe, I can't hold back my whimper. My head falls back against the wall, giving him better access to my neck, to which he then trails his lips along my skin down to my collarbone.

"Ryder," I gasp, my fingers tightening in his hair. "We shouldn't—"

"We *absolutely* should," he growls, his breath hot against my skin. He slides a hand up, thumb brushing the underside of my breast through the thin fabric of my dress. "Tell me to stop, and I will. But I know that's the last thing you want right now."

The challenge in his eyes makes my pulse race and I hate that he's right.

"I—" My words cut off when he kicks my legs farther apart and uses his other hand to graze a finger up my center over my panties.

"Holy fuck," he moans. "You're wet for me."

Pushing the delicate fabric of my underwear aside, he slides two thick fingers deep inside, making me gasp and arch against the wall.

"Oh my god," I whimper as his thumb finds my clit, pressing against it in tight, wet circles.

His fingers pump deeper, curling to hit the perfect spot inside as his eyes lock with mine. "You still think you're imagining me now, kitten?" He increases the pace, the delicious friction making me dizzy with need. "Does this feel real enough for you? Or do you need more proof?"

There's no way I can answer. I can barely breathe as he keeps working me with his thick, talented fingers. My hips buck against his hand, chasing the building pressure threatening to consume me.

"Answer me or I'll stop," he growls, fingers pumping faster, voice dark and commanding. "Am I real, Noia?"

"Yes," I gasp, clinging to his shoulders as my legs threaten to give out. "Yes, you're real."

His eyes are dark with hunger as he watches my face, gauging every reaction. "And this?" He presses harder against my clit, making me cry out. "Is this real too?"

"Yes, yes! Fuck—don't stop. Please!"

Capturing my mouth again, he swallows my cries as he works me closer to the edge. My entire body is trembling, teetering on the precipice of what is sure to be the biggest orgasm of my life.

When he pulls away, he flashes a victorious smile as he drops to his knees, shoving my dress up around my waist. "Good, girl. Now I'm going to devour you."

"Rye, wait—" My protest dies when his mouth replaces his thumb, his tongue flicking and circling my clit while his fingers continue their relentless assault.

My hands curl in his hair and he moans against me, the vibration sending shockwaves of pleasure throughout my body.

"Come on, kitten. Let yourself fall," he murmurs. "I'll be here to catch you."

The orgasm hits me like a tidal wave, crashing over me with so much intensity that I scream, my legs trembling as he works me through it, not letting up until I'm gasping and tugging at his hair.

When he finally pulls away, he looks up at me, mouth glistening with my arousal.

"That was..." Panting, unable to find the right words, I close my eyes.

"Just the beginning," he finishes, brushing a strand of hair from my face. "But only if you want it to be."

The vulnerability in his eyes catches me off guard. Despite his cocky exterior, he's giving me an out—a chance to slow things down.

"I—I'm sorry, Ryder. But I think we should call it a night."

His face goes from tender to hard in a span of seconds.

I WANT TO PULL HER BACK AGAINST ME AND FINISH WHAT we started. Slide my hands back under her little red dress, pin her back up against the wall and break down every one of her carefully constructed barriers.

But instead, I shove my hands deep in my pockets, giving her the out she so desperately needs.

"You know..." she says, adjusting her dress back into place. "You could just be a better actor than I thought."

I know she doesn't mean to gut me with those words, but they land anyway.

"We just talked about this and you agreed. Nothing about me or what I'm doing is fake." And that's the part that scares the shit out of me. "I promised I was going to do everything I can to help you, didn't I?"

I wasn't made to feel like this. I wasn't *written* for this. I'm the dirty fantasy. The fictional escape.

But there she is, standing before me in that goddamn red dress, looking like every ache I never knew I had, but now wanted.

So I do the only thing I can—drop the charm and let her see what's really underneath.

"You don't have to fall in love with me, Noia," I say with a soft growl. "Just try not to write us off before you give our story a decent ending."

She just looks at me.

"Fine," I say, low and controlled. "I'll clean up. You have a good night. It's been a blast."

Nodding once, I step away and start clearing the table in silence.

"Rye—"

"Don't sweat it. Just go write about today and I'll see you in the morning for breakfast."

She turns and heads up the stairs.

But just before she disappears at the top, I see the flushed look on her face as she touches her lips, as if she's second guessing herself.

I sigh as I move to rinse out the wine glasses.

She's not the only one.

I WAKE UP BEFORE DAWN WITH A RAGING HARD-ON AND THE taste of Noia still on my lips. Groaning, I throw an arm over my eyes and try to forget how she looked last night—all flushed and trembling against the wall, coming undone under my tongue, her pussy clenching my fingers tight.

"Fuck," I grumble, shoving off the covers.

After a cold shower—which does nothing to soften my cock, by the way—I pull on a pair of jeans and a Henley from my newly stocked closet. The house is silent as I pad into the kitchen, trying to be as quiet as possible.

I need coffee. And maybe a lobotomy to forget the way Noia looked at me last night. The desire and fear battling in those big, blue eyes of hers gives me the nagging feeling I might've pushed too hard, too fast.

The kitchen is filled with early morning light as I grind some coffee beans and measure them into the filter. The familiar routine soothes my rattled nerves. Leaning against the counter, I wait for the coffee to brew and stare out the window at the forest of trees.

What if I'm not what she wants after all? What if I'm just a temporary distraction, a character meant to be written out of her story as soon as her writer's block disappears? And then maybe I'll disappear.

The thought makes my heart sink with dread.

So, to distract myself, I decide to make breakfast. Grabbing some eggs, cheese, and vegetables from the fridge, I get to work, tossing together some omelets.

The sun is fully up by the time I hear movement upstairs—footsteps, a door closing, water running. My body goes on high alert, every sense tuned in to her presence.

When Noia finally comes downstairs, I'm sitting at the kitchen island, nursing my second cup of coffee.

Wearing jeans and a graphic movie T-shirt, her hair is damp from the shower and pulled back in a loose ponytail. The dark circles under her eyes tell me she didn't sleep much better than I did.

"Morning," I say, pushing a mug of coffee across the counter.

She takes the mug, not quite meeting my eyes. "Thanks."

I motion to the plate of food on the counter. "I made breakfast."

Glancing at the perfectly folded omelets and bowl of sliced fruit with mild surprise, she says, "You didn't have to do that."

"I wanted to."

She sits across from me, picking up a strawberry and turning it between her fingers.

Unable to bear it another second, I finally ask, "Are you okay?"

Glancing out the window, she nods.

"*Noia...*"

She finally raises her eyes to meet mine, and there's something in them I can't quite read.

"Do you regret it?" I ask, rougher than I mean to be. "What happened between us?"

Her cheeks flush, but she holds my gaze. "No," she says softly.

The knot in my chest loosens a little and then pings in surprise with what she says next.

"I'm the one who should be apologizing." She takes a deep breath. "I freaked out and pushed you away when things got too intense. It wasn't fair to you."

"You don't owe me anything, Noia. And you don't need to apologize."

"That's not true." She pushes her plate aside and leans forward. "I've been thinking about this all night. I stayed up writing about everything—how you make me feel, what I'm afraid of..." She takes a deep breath in. "I'm done running and I'm gonna be fully open going forward. Whatever happens between us..." She slowly breathes out. "I want to experience it. All of it."

I study her face, looking for any sign of hesitation. "Are you sure? Because I'm going to seriously take you out of your comfort zone."

"Yes." A small smile plays at her lips. "After last night, I realized it's what I need to do. What *we* need to do."

"What changed your mind?"

"I couldn't sleep," she admits. "So after I wrote about how I felt, I wrote about everything that happened yesterday. And the more I wrote, the more I realized you were right. I *have* been using fiction as a shield. You're not just words on a page anymore, Rye." Her finger brushes against one of mine. "You're here. You're real. And I'm tired of being afraid of the unknown."

I turn my hand over, palm up, and she slides her hand into mine, making my pulse ratchet into the stratosphere.

"So what now?" I ask.

She squeezes my hand. "Now we do what we agreed to do, continue to live out the story."

A huge grin spreads across my face. "Does this mean you'll stop freaking out every time I touch you?"

Her laughs melts something deep inside my chest. "All I can do is promise to try."

"Good enough." I pull her hand to my lips and kiss her wrist. "Finish your breakfast, kitten. You're going to need your strength for what I have planned today."

"Are you going to tell me this time, or is it another surprise?"

"A surprise." I wink at her. "But I promise it'll be worth it. I moved some appointments around, so we have all morning for the first half of the date. Then, after I get home from work, we'll finish the night out with the second half."

She grins and takes a bite of her omelet. "Sounds good."

I take my empty plate to the sink, smiling as I rinse, hopeful that maybe, just maybe, we're finally on the same page.

noia

Bookish Babe Books is super cozy. With creaky hardwood floors, mismatched armchairs, and shelves that tilt a little to the left. The air smells like fresh espresso, rain-soaked leaves from the open door, and old books that've been read too many times to count.

In fact, if bookstores were human, this one would wear vintage 80s ankle boots and drink a shit ton of whiskey.

Despite how much this place feels like home, I already feel off balance and overstimulated, and that was before Ryder crowded up behind me.

I shouldn't have let him bring me here.

His Henley hugs his arms and clings to his chest, and I'm not even close to convinced it wasn't sewn onto his body by some thirst trap witch. Wearing a snug pair of jeans, his smirk is dialed up to lethal.

"I'm regretting this already," I mutter, flicking my eyes to the door.

"Too late, kitten." His voice is low, cocky, and soaked in flirt as he rests his hand against my lower back. "We're already here.

And you promised to let me help you by bringing you to your natural habitat."

"My natural habitat is wine and solitude, dammit."

"True. But we're here to stir up your ecosystem."

I roll my eyes and stalk toward the romance section before my face betrays how much I want to lick him from bottom to top like a fucking cherry popsicle.

After what he said to me the other night about fucking me? I can't get that memory out of my head to save my life—pretty sure I'm already dead, though.

Wooden signs dangle above each aisle.

Horror. True Crime. Romance. Erotic Romance.

I make a hard left toward the aisle of my people, where pastel covers and shirtless men with tropes for days fill the shelves.

My veins throb with unresolved tension as Ryder's fingers trail along a shelf, his expression full of devilish curiosity. He picks up a book with a half-naked Highlander on the cover, raises a brow, and tucks it under his arm.

"For research," he says.

With a snort, I give him side-eye, trying to focus on the safety and familiarity of the books in front of me, and not on how his arm brushes against mine as he reaches for another book.

But he's too tall. The scent of sandalwood and rain is coming off him in waves, and he's so close, despite trying not to, that when I reach for a book, my arm brushes against his chest.

The contact sets off a fire in my belly that's a bitch to pretend doesn't exist.

"We're going to pick something specific," he says out of nowhere.

I glance at up him. "What?"

"A book. Find the one that wrecked you emotionally. One of

those 'stare-into-space-because-it-destroyed-you-forever' kind of reads."

"Why?"

"Because we are going to trade," he says, eyes dancing. "Forced vulnerability. Think of it as an emotional trust fall. You hand me your book trauma and I'll hand you mine."

"You're a menace."

"And you're deflecting."

"Fine." Already regretting what I'm about to do, I huff and pull *Flock* from the shelf. "Here. It's the first in a trilogy. If you think this one is intense, just wait until you read the second. It'll fuck you up for life."

He studies the cover, then reads the blurb, nodding in approval. "Bold choice. My turn."

Pivoting, he takes a couple of steps, snatches a book off a shelf, then turns and hands it to me.

When I check out the cover, my soul shrivels up and dies.

It's my book.

Heartstruck was my debut novel. It was the book that started everything. The book that brought Ryder Blackwood and his Marine buddies into fictional existence.

He smirks like he's already won. "Most transformative read of my life."

"You're ridiculous. You didn't read it, you lived it."

"Semantics."

"You cannot seriously expect me to read this to you."

Entering my personal space, he lowers his voice. "Page one-forty-seven."

"No."

"Read it."

"I will not."

He shrugs, unbothered. "Coward."

I glare and flip to the page, scanning it quickly.

No. No way. Nope.

It's the 'up-against-the-wall-in-the-library' scene. The one where the MMC says things that require a trigger warning. I can't breathe, let alone say any of it out loud.

"I was in a vulnerable place when I wrote this," I mutter.

"So wild," he murmurs, grinning. "And so fucking hot."

"I seriously hate you right now."

"*Kitten.*" He gives me a stern look. "You promised to be open-minded, remember?"

Rolling my eyes, I blow out a sigh. "Fine."

"Here." Gently taking the book out of my hands, he brushes his thumb against mine, and his tone instantly turns deep and sultry. "Let me."

And then he starts to read—*out loud.*

"She was trembling under his touch, her back pressed against the ancient library shelf as his fingers trailed like fire up her thigh."

I try to grab the book, but he holds it out of reach, slightly turning away. As he continues to read, his voice drops even lower, into a sensual growl that makes every hair on my body stand on end.

"I need to taste you," he whispered against her neck. "Right here. Right now."

Oh god. Did I actually write this? My face burns as I glance around, thankful we're alone in the aisle.

"Ryder, *stop,*" I whisper-hiss, but he just smirks and keeps on reading.

"Dropping to his knees, he pushes her skirt up around her waist. Hooking his fingers into the delicate lace of her panties, he drags them down her trembling legs. The sight of her pussy glistening for him makes his cock throb in anticipation."

My heart is hammering so hard against my ribs I can hear it in my ears. Ryder's eyes flick up to lock with mine over the top of the book, dark with heat as his voice caresses each explicit word.

"The first taste of her was like coming home. Sweet and smoky and so fucking perfect, making him groan against her slick folds."

Low, steady and sinful, his voice curls around every syllable, drawing it out, turning words that are already hot enough into full-blown bodily weapons. By the time he gets to the part where the heroine moans his name, I'm sweating through the pits of my T-shirt.

"Moaning his name, she bucked against his mouth, her fingers tangling in his hair as he licked a slow path from her entrance to her swollen, throbbing clit—"

Devising a sneak attack, I snatch the book out of his hands and shut it with a definitive slap.

He laughs, genuinely delighted.

"You're seriously evil, you know that?" I snap, lips twitching.

"And you, my beautiful kitten... are now sexually frustrated."

His beautiful kitten.

Those words hit too close to home.

"I'm walking out of here and never speaking to you again."

"You're just stalling." He brushes a finger down my cheek. "Tell me I don't live rent free in your head twenty-four seven."

I jerk away. "You don't."

"Liar."

Just as I open my mouth to tell him off, a voice comes from somewhere behind him.

"Excuse me—sorry—but... Oh my *God*, you're Noia Wilde!"

Caught off guard, I blink in surprise.

A woman, who looks to be in her early twenties, is cradling a stack of books in her arms, looking like she's trying not to vibrate out of her skin, staring at me like I'm made of magic or some shit.

"I am," I say carefully.

"I love your books so much," she gushes. "You're literally the reason why I started writing. I—oh my God—is this *him*? Is this the guy that inspired *Ryder Blackwood*?"

Ryder grins like he's signing autographs at the gates of hell. "I get that a lot."

The girl makes a noise that sounds like a cross between a squeal and a squeak and backs away. "I gotta go. Nice to meet you."

Turning slowly, I look up at Ryder. "What the hell was that?"

He just shrugs.

Shaking my head, I walk toward the front with my book under one arm and my dignity slowly dwindling away as it trails along the floor behind me, barely hanging on.

When we walk outside, the afternoon air feels blessedly cool against my heated skin.

He nudges my shoulder as we head toward his truck. "Did you have fun?"

I shrug.

"Later tonight, we're really going to test your boundaries," he says, opening the door for me.

"And how do you plan on doing that?"

"That, kitten, is also a surprise."

I climb up into the seat. Trying to ignore how incessantly my clit is throbbing, I deflect. "How about I throw a book at your head instead?"

"Plot twist," he growls, before shutting the door with a wink. "I like that kind of shit."

TWENTY

ryder

After dropping Noia off, I head to the shop. My body is still vibrating with energy from what went down in the bookstore. The way she blushed when I read that sex scene out loud —fuck, I almost took her right there between the stacks. Just the memory alone makes my cock twitch, and I have to adjust myself before climbing out of my truck.

The sights and sounds are even more familiar today when I push open the door to Skin & Ink. Claire waves at me from the front desk, and I return her greeting with a nod as I make my way to my station.

There's a client coming in at three for a cover-up—some ex-boyfriend's name that needs to disappear.

"You gonna tell me what's going on with you, or do I have to beat it out of you?"

I look up to find Jax leaning against the wall, arms crossed, eyes narrowed in suspicion.

A grunt is my only response as I start to gather my inks together for my afternoon appointment.

"Nothing's going on," I mutter, focusing on wiping down my station. "Just didn't get much sleep last night."

Jax snorts. "I've seen you work on three hours of sleep after multiple weekend benders and you were never *this* distracted."

Keeping my eyes on my work, I concentrate on laying out my equipment. "I'm fine."

"Bullshit." Pulling up a chair, he turns it around and sits, resting his arms across the back. "You've been acting weird for days. Showing up late, leaving early, walking around with this dopey-ass grin on your face."

I roll my eyes. "I don't know what the hell you're talking about."

"Claire thinks you're using again."

My head snaps up. "What? That's fucking ridiculous." My hands clench at my sides. "I've been clean for years and she knows it."

Jax raises his hands in defense. "Hey, I'm just telling you what she said. We're all worried about you, man."

"Well, don't be. Like I said, I'm fine."

"Then tell me what the hell is going on."

Setting down the machine, I run a hand through my hair and sigh. "Look, it's not a big deal. It's just... I met someone."

His eyes go wide, and a slow grin spreads across his face. "No shit? You're actually dating someone? Like, an actual woman who tolerates your cranky ass?"

"Very funny."

"Who is she? Where did you meet her? And why the hell haven't you mentioned her before?"

I hesitate, trying to figure out how much to say without sounding completely insane. "Her name is Noia and she's a writer." I clear my throat, knowing I'm going to catch shit for this one. "She writes spicy romance novels."

My best friend barks out a laugh. "A romance writer? Seriously?"

"What the hell is that supposed to mean?"

"Just that you're not exactly the hearts and flowers type." He leans forward, suddenly interested. "So how'd you meet her?"

"It's... complicated."

"I've got plenty of time." He glances at his watch. "My next appointment isn't for thirty minutes."

Knowing he won't let it go, I give in and lie my ass off. "Fine. She was parked on the side of the road, in the rain, trying to change a flat tire, and I stopped to help her out."

"And?"

"We started talking, and... I don't know. There was something about her."

"Wait, is this why you've been staying at that lake cottage instead of your apartment?"

I nod, relieved he was the one to come up with a reasonable explanation. "Yeah. My place is... getting renovated."

Jax eyes me suspiciously. "You never mentioned you're doing any renovations."

"It was a last-minute decision."

"So you're shacking up with some writer chick you just met? That doesn't sound like you at all."

"It's not like that," I say, even though it kind of is. "We're just... figuring things out."

"She must be pretty fuckin' special to have you this twisted up."

I can't help the smile that tugs at my lips. "Yeah, she is. Smart as hell. Stubborn as shit. Drives me crazy most of the time."

"Holy shit." Jax rests his chin on his arms. "You're actually into her. Like, *really* into her."

"Don't make a big deal out of it."

"This is a huge deal! You haven't been serious about anyone since Melissa, and that was what, over ten years ago?"

Suddenly, I remember. Melissa is my ex-fiancée. The one who left me for someone else before I came back from my second tour.

Jax's face falls when he sees my expression shift. "Shit, man. I'm sorry for bringing her up. That was a dick move."

I wave him off, trying to shake off the memory of the Dear John letter and the all months I drank myself stupid over it. "It's fine. Ancient history."

"No, it's not. I know better." He shifts in his seat, and quickly changes the subject. "So, when do we get to meet her? Claire's gonna want to give her the third degree, you know."

"Not happening," I say firmly, turning back to my station.

"Come on," Jax persists. "You can't keep her hidden forever. Bring her to the shop's anniversary party this weekend."

"I'm not hiding her. It's just..." My brain screeches to a halt. "Anniversary party?"

"Dude, seriously? The ten-year anniversary bash we've been planning for months? Saturday night? Ring any bells?" Jax looks at me like I've lost my mind. "We rented out The Brew for the whole night. Everyone's coming—clients, artists, friends. It's gonna be epic."

Another memory slams into me out of nowhere.

Shit.

"Right," I say, rubbing the back of my neck. "That party."

"So? Are you gonna bring her, or what?"

The idea of Noia in a room full of tattooed, hard-drinking shop regulars makes me hesitate. But the idea of showing her off? It makes something warm and possessive flare in my chest.

"I'll think about it," I finally say.

"That's not a no," Jax grins, clapping me on the shoulder as he stands, spinning the chair back around.

I pull my phone out of my pocket to check if there are any messages from Noia.

Nothing.

Disappointed but resigned to give her a chance to stew over what I might have planned for her after I get home from work, I slide my phone back into my pocket just as my client walks over, looking nervous.

"Hi," she says timidly. "I'm Jess. I have an appointment for a cover-up?"

"Hey, Jess," I smile and gesture at the chair. "I'm Ryder. Let's talk about what we're going to do with that name on your wrist."

As I work, I stress about Noia and bringing her to the party this weekend.

This could be a chance to see how she fits into this new part of my life that's becoming more real every day. It's also another chance to show her that what's happening between us is so much more than what goes down in some fictional romance novel.

TWENTY-ONE

"WELL, *THAT* JUST HAPPENED," I SAY TO GOONIE.

Leg in the air, he just gives me a low meow before he turns his attention back to cleaning his ass.

"Thanks for the pep talk, fur ball," I snort.

I grab my phone from my purse and collapse onto the couch. My heart is still hammering from what went down at the bookstore and I need to talk to someone before I spontaneously combust.

Sasha picks up on the second ring. "Hey!"

"I need help," I blurt out. "Serious, life-altering help."

"Did you kill him? Because I have muscles and a shovel."

"No, but I'm pretty sure *I'm* going to die of embarrassment." I groan and pull a pillow over my face. "He took me to a bookstore and read a sex scene to me out loud. From my own book!"

My bestie's cackling laughter fills my ear. "Oh my god, that's brilliant! Which scene?"

"Ironically, the library scene from Heartstruck." I let out an exasperated groan. "You know, the one where he goes down on her against the bookshelves?"

"Holy shit! The one where he's all..." She lowers her voice

in her best MMC impression. ...'I need to taste you'? That's one of the hottest scenes you've ever written!"

"Yes, and he read it in his deep, growly voice while staring into my eyes the entire time. In public!"

Sasha's laughter only escalates. "I think I'm in love with him already."

"This isn't funny!" I protest, trying to fight a smile. "A reader recognized me, too. And she recognized Ryder as *Ryder*! Well, as the guy that inspired him, but still."

"*Heartstruck* is about one of his military buddies, right? And he's mentioned in the story."

"I mean, technically, yes. Like that makes it any better? Ryder was never supposed to be real!"

Tossing the pillow aside, I get up and start pacing the living room. "And now he's planning some kind of boundary-pushing surprise for me tonight, and I'm kinda freaking out."

"Boundary-pushing how?" I picture her leaning in as she waits for me to tell her all the juicy details and sit back down on the couch in a huff.

"I don't know. But after what happened at the bookstore and last night when he..." I trail off, realizing I hadn't told her about our fake date.

"When he what?" Sasha pounces. "Noia Lynn Wilde, what are you not telling me?"

I sink deeper into the cushion. "Last night, he finger-banged me against the wall and then went down on me until I came so hard I nearly passed out."

"*Damn*. That good, huh?"

"Mind-blowing," I admit, heat creeping up my neck. "But then I panicked and all but ran away."

"Of course you did."

"But this morning I apologized and I told him I want to stop running. That I want to experience whatever this is that's happening between us." I stare up at the ceiling. "So he took me to the bookstore."

I sigh. "I must be losing my mind."

"Or maybe," Sasha says thoughtfully. "You finally get to live the life you've been writing about for years."

I groan. "That's what he keeps saying."

"Sounds like a smart man. I can't wait to meet him. So, what are you going to do about tonight?"

"I don't know. Just... try to be brave, I guess?" Nerves ratcheting up, I twist a strand of hair around my finger. "Maybe try not to overthink everything for once?"

"Good answer. I want every sordid detail when I come up this weekend."

"You're still coming Friday?"

"Try and stop me. I've already packed three bottles of wine and my good underwear. You know, just in case your man has any equally hot, single friends."

I laugh. "I'll let you know if any happen to materialize."

"Perfect. And Noia? Stop fighting this. You deserve a little magic in your life."

"I'll try. And I promise I'll tell you everything that happens between now and when you get here."

"You'd better. Love you like crazy, lady."

"Love you too."

After hanging up, I stare at the blank wall for a few minutes, trying to process everything that's happened so far. Then I grab my laptop and head to my room. If I'm going to come to terms with any of this, I need to get it all down.

For the next few hours, I lose myself in my words, describing every detail I can remember. The heat in Ryder's eyes as he read to me and the way my body responded to his deep, gravelly voice. About my growing certainty that whatever is happening between us is something I know I can't control and that maybe I don't want to.

The words flow easier than they have in months. I describe everything in vivid detail, not holding back on my conflicted feelings or the simmering attraction threatening to boil over. By the time I'm done, the sun is starting to set, casting long shadows across my desk.

My phone buzzes with a text, making my heart jump.

RYDER: *Be ready in 30. Wear something comfortable but sexy. I'm on my way.*

ME: *What exactly constitutes 'comfortable but sexy'?*

My heart trips when I read his reply.

RYDER: *Something easily accessible... *devil emoji* *eggplant emoji* *squirt emoji**

Now I'm even more nervous, but also very... aroused.

I save my work and shut my laptop, wondering what the hell he has planned. But if those emojis are any indication? I'm in for one wild night.

A shiver of anticipation slithers up my spine.

Twenty minutes later, I'm wearing a short black skirt paired with a soft blue cropped sweater. My hair is down in soft waves and I even put on a little makeup.

Glancing in the mirror one last time, I tuck a strand of hair behind my ear and take a deep breath and whisper, "You can do this."

The unmistakable rumble of an engine reverberates from outside.

Ryder's home.

My body instantly responds, a delicious warmth spreading between my thighs, knowing he's just outside.

When the door slams open, Goonie darts under the couch and I turn away from the hallway mirror just as Ryder strides in. His eyes, dark and intense, find mine immediately.

Shutting the door behind him with a decisive click, his leather jacket comes off in one fluid motion, revealing a tight black T-shirt that clings to every muscle. When he tosses his keys onto the counter, the metallic clatter makes me jump.

"I hope you're ready, kitten. We're going to have so much fun tonight," he growls, voice pure gravel and sex. "Where's the book?"

My mouth goes dry and I squeak, "Book?"

"The one you got at the bookstore today." His eyes travel slowly down my body, lingering on my bare legs before they travel back up to where my stomach is peeking out between my skirt and sweater.

"It's..." I swallow hard. "Upstairs... on my nightstand."

"Perfect." He crosses the room in three long strides and takes my hand. "Because we're going to need it."

"For what?" I ask, pulse racing as he tugs me toward the stairs.

"Part two of our date." His thumb strokes my wrist in slow, lazy circles, sending shivers up my arm. "Tonight is all about pushing boundaries, remember?"

"Right."

"Trust me," he murmurs. He leans in close, breath hot against my ear. "By the time I'm done with you tonight, you won't be thinking about anything except how good I made you feel."

"Oh," I whisper, heat flooding my face.

His eyes darken. "Unless you're not up for it. Say the word and we can just watch a movie instead."

I take a deep breath, remembering my promise to myself and to him. "No, I want this. I want... whatever you want."

His smile is slow and dangerous. "That's my girl."

The possessive edge in his voice makes my heart stutter and my body hum with anticipation.

One thing I do know for sure—whatever happens tonight—nothing between us will ever be the same again.

"Wait for me on the bed," Ryder instructs, voice low and commanding as he leads me into my bedroom. "I'm going to take a quick shower."

My heart hammers against my ribs as I perch awkwardly on the edge of my mattress with the book we bought sitting untouched beside me.

Through the bathroom door, I hear the water start running, and my imagination immediately conjures images of Ryder naked in my shower, water cascading down his tattooed chest.

Squeezing my thighs together does nothing to ease the ache pulsing between them.

I glance around my room, suddenly self-conscious about the rumpled sheets and the stack of romance novels sitting on my nightstand. There's even a half-empty wineglass from last night that I forgot to take downstairs.

God, he must think I'm a slob.

After what feels like an eternity, the water shuts off. I hold my breath, waiting, my fingers nervously toying with the hem of my skirt.

When the bathroom door finally opens, I nearly swallow my tongue.

Standing in the doorway with nothing but a white towel slung dangerously low on his hips, Ryder's hair is slicked back and wet. Droplets of water still cling to his chest, tracing paths over his tattoos and between the ridges of muscle before disappearing beneath the towel. Steam billows around him like some kind of sensual special effect.

Jeez, Louise.

"See something you like?" he asks, voice husky as he watches my eyes devour every inch of him.

I can't speak. Can barely even form a coherent thought. My eyes are fixed on a particular droplet making its leisurely way down his abs, following the dark trail of hair that disappears beneath the towel.

"I asked you a question, kitten."

My eyes dart up to meet his and his lips quirk up in an infuriating smirk as he takes a step closer.

"I—" My voice cracks. I clear my throat and try again. "Yes."

His eyes immediately go dark. "Good. Because you're going to love what I have planned."

The next thing I know, he's standing directly in front of me, so close I can smell the clean scent of my soap on his skin.

"Are you nervous?" he asks, reaching out to tuck a strand of hair behind my ear.

Not trusting my voice, I shake my head with the lie.

He moves over to my desk, pulls out the chair, and takes a seat. His legs are spread almost wide enough to see up the towel, stopping just short of heaven.

"Take off your top."

My breath catches and I hesitate at the command.

"*Now*," he says, voice dropping to a rough whisper.

Hands shaking slightly, I reach for the hem of my sweater.

ryder

"SLOWLY." I LEAN BACK IN THE CHAIR, DROPPING MY VOICE an octave.

Her fingers tremble as she lifts the hem, inch by agonizing inch, revealing the smooth skin of her stomach and the gentle curve of her ribs, until finally, the sweater comes off.

"Good girl," I murmur, my eyes locked on the black lace of her bra. "Eyes on me." They flick up. "Now the skirt."

Noia's eyes stay locked with mine. When her fingers find the zipper at her hip, the soft rasp of her sliding it down fills the charged silence hanging heavy in the room. With a gentle push, the fabric falls, pooling softly at her feet.

"Christ," I breathe, taking in the matching black lace panties that barely cover her pussy—she's fucking soaked already. "Show me that fine ass."

She obeys, slowly rotating to give me the full view. A strip of black lace is tucked up between those firm globes, and I have to grip the arms of the chair to keep from crossing the room and taking her right now.

"Turn around." When she does, I suck in a cleansing breath. "Now the bra," I order, voice rough.

Reaching behind her, she arches her back, breasts straining against the fabric as she unhooks the clasp. The straps slide down her shoulders to her elbows as she holds the cups in place.

"Don't make me ask twice," I warn.

When she lets the bra fall away, I'm rewarded with the sight of her full, perfect breasts, dusky pink nipples hard, begging for my touch.

"Now lie down on the bed," I command. "On your back."

She moves to the center of the mattress, golden hair fanning out across the pillows. The contrast of her pale skin against the darker sheets is enough to make my cock throb painfully to attention.

Rising from the chair, I grab the book from the end of the bed and flip it open, finding the page I'd marked earlier.

My fingers brush against hers as I hand it to her, sending a jolt of electricity up my arm and I have to clear my throat before I can speak again. "Read the highlighted section."

Her eyes widen slightly as she takes in what I've marked. It's one of the steamiest scenes in the book.

"Out loud?" she whispers.

"Every word," I confirm, climbing up onto the bed. "And don't stop until I tell you to."

She swallows hard and begins to read, her voice shaky.

"'His fingers traced a path up her inner thigh, making her tremble with anticipation. 'Please,' she begged, beyond caring how desperate she sounded. 'I need you to touch me.'"

As she reads, I trace the same path described in the book up her inner thigh, watching the goosebumps rise on her skin. Her voice falters when my fingers reach the edge of her panties.

"Keep going," I remind her gruffly.

She takes a shuddering breath and continues, *"'He smiled wickedly, knowing exactly what he was doing to her as his thumb* hooked the delicate fabric, slowly dragging her panties down her trembling legs.'"

I slide the black lace down her thighs as she reads, her voice catching when I toss them aside.

"'She was beautiful like this, spread out before him, completely at his mercy." Her voice is growing breathier by the second. "He could see how much she wanted him, could smell the sweet scent of her arousal.'"

I trail my fingers back up her legs, deliberately avoiding where I know she needs me most. "Keep reading, kitten."

"'When his mouth finally found her center, she cried out, her back arching off the bed. His tongue was relentless, alternating between gentle licks between her folds and sucking her clit until she was writhing beneath him.'"

Following the book's lead, I lower my head between her thighs. The first taste of her makes me groan against her slick heat.

"Oh god," she gasps, the book trembling in her hands.

"Don't stop," I command with my mouth against her pussy, the vibration making her hips buck.

As she struggles to focus on the words, I work her with my tongue. "'She could feel herself climbing higher, every nerve ending on fire. And when he slipped two fingers inside her, she nearly screamed.'"

I curl two fingers into her slick, tight heat, finding the perfect spot, pumping in and out, until her thighs start to shake.

"Ryder, I can't—" she pants.

"Finish the page," I growl, pulling back just enough to speak before diving back in.

Her voice is a shaky whisper as she reads the final line, "'The orgasm crashed over her like a tidal wave, leaving her gasping and boneless, completely wrecked from his touch.'"

As if on cue, she comes apart against my mouth, crying out

my name as her body convulses. The book falls from her hands as she fists the sheets, riding out wave after wave of pleasure as her inner muscles clutch at my pumping fingers.

When she finally comes down from the high, I grin, pressing gentle kisses to her inner thighs.

Moving up her body, I lean in close enough to brush my lips against her earlobe, inhaling her sweet scent as I go. "You smell delicious," I whisper against her skin. Her body shudders in response. "And you taste... God, you taste even better."

TWENTY-THREE

His words vibrate against my neck, sending aftershocks through my trembling body. I'm still trying to catch my breath from the first orgasm when his towel falls away. The sight of him—long, thick, and gloriously hard—makes my mouth water.

"Ryder," I whisper, reaching for him.

His powerful thighs nudge mine further apart as he moves between my legs, positioning his thick cock against my entrance.

"Are you ready? I'm going to fuck you so hard, kitten."

The raw need in his voice makes me whimper. I nod frantically, beyond words as I lift my hips.

"Tell me," he demands, eyes locked on mine as he pushes just the tip inside. "I need to hear you say it."

"Yes," I gasp, digging my fingers into his shoulders. "I need you inside me."

With a low, primal growl, he thrusts inside in one long, delicious stroke that makes both of us moan. The stretch and fullness of him seated inside me is almost overwhelming—almost too much—but perfect all at the same time.

"Fuck," he groans, dropping his forehead to mine as he stills, giving me time to adjust. His muscles tremble with the effort and I can feel his heartbeat through every inch of where our bodies connect. "You feel so good, Noia. So fucking tight."

Finally, he pulls back slowly before driving into me again, setting a rhythm that has me seeing stars. Each thrust is deeper, harder than the last, the headboard slamming against the wall as he takes me with an intensity that steals my breath away.

"Is this what you want?" he pants against my ear, hips snapping over and over as he drives into me. "To be fucked like this? So hard you won't be able to walk tomorrow?"

"Yes," I cry out as he suddenly hits a spot deep inside that makes my back arch off the bed. "Oh god, yes!"

Shifting the angle, he throws one of my legs over his shoulder, which allows him to fuck me even deeper, quickly spiraling me toward another peak.

"That's it, kitten," he encourages, his voice strained as he watches my face. "Let go for me again. I want to feel you squeeze my cock so hard."

Once his thumb finds my clit, circling it in time with his thrusts, I'm lost. The second orgasm hits me even harder than the first, tearing a scream from my throat as a tsunami of pleasure pulses through me.

Ryder's rhythm falters as my inner walls clench his cock. Voice hoarse, he shouts my name as he quickly follows me over the edge, body shuddering as he empties himself inside me.

For several long moments, we stay like that, tangled together, breathing hard, our sweat-slicked bodies pressed tightly together. Ryder's weight on me feels like an anchor, keeping me from completely floating away.

"Holy shit," I croak when I'm finally able to form words again.

He chuckles against my neck, the vibration sending pleasant aftershocks down my spine. "That's one way to put it."

Gently, he pulls out and rolls onto his back, tucking me against his chest. His heartbeat thunders in my ear, gradually slowing as we both catch our breath.

"Are you okay?" he asks, voice tender as he brushes my damp hair away from my forehead.

I nod, still too overwhelmed to speak. My body is boneless, utterly spent in the best possible way.

"Look at me," he murmurs, tilting my chin up.

When our eyes lock, something shifts in the atmosphere. Gaze soft, his earlier intensity has been replaced with something that makes my chest ache.

"That was..." I trail off, searching for the right words.

"Better than fiction?" he suggests, a small smirk playing on his lips.

"I was going to say incredible, but yes," I laugh, "definitely better than fiction."

His arms tighten around me as he presses a kiss to my temple. "Good. Because I've been wanting to do that since the moment I first saw you."

We lie in comfortable silence, his fingers tracing lazy patterns on my back. I feel myself drifting, content and sated, when he speaks again.

"There's a party this weekend," he says quietly. "For Skin & Ink's ten-year anniversary."

I lift my head to look at him. "Oh, yeah?"

"I want you to come with me." He's keeping his expression carefully neutral, but I can see the vulnerability lurking behind his eyes. "Meet the people I work with. My friends."

The meaning of what he's asking isn't lost on me. He's asking me to be a part of his new world in a very public way.

"Are you sure?" I ask, suddenly shy despite the fact that we're both gloriously naked.

"I wouldn't ask if I wasn't." His thumb traces my bottom lip. "Say yes."

How can I refuse when he's looking at me like that? Besides, I'm curious about the people in his life, the ones who somehow know him even though he's only existed in this reality for a short period of time. This journey we are on is more about him than it ever was about me. I realize that now.

"Okay," I agree softly. "I'd love to."

His answering smile is as brilliant as the sun before he captures my mouth in a kiss that quickly deepens, tongue lazily grazing mine as he slides a hand down to cup my breast and tweak a nipple.

"Again?" I gasp when we finally break apart.

"Got a problem with that?" he growls, rolling me beneath him and sliding back inside.

"God, no," I moan as he proceeds to fuck me into the mattress.

TWENTY-FOUR

I WAKE UP IN A TANGLE OF SHEETS TO SUNLIGHT PEAKING through the cracks in the curtains, painting golden stripes across my rumpled bed.

Reaching over, I find nothing but a cool empty space where Ryder's warm body should be.

"Ryder?" I sit up and wince at the delicious ache between my thighs.

Memories of his mouth on me, his body moving against mine, the way he grunted my name into my neck when he came. Heat floods my cheeks, and I bury my head in my hands with a groan.

After pulling on a T-shirt and shorts, I pad downstairs, following the scent of coffee and something sweet that makes my stomach growl.

Ryder is sitting at the kitchen island, scrolling through his phone. The muscles in his back flex as he reaches for his coffee mug, and I take a moment to appreciate the view—broad shoulders tapering to a narrow waist, his dark hair still damp from the shower.

The counter is covered with plates of steaming food—a stack of chocolate chip pancakes, a bowl of scrambled eggs with melted cheese, and a plate of crispy bacon.

"Wow. You really are a cook, aren't ya?" I say as I head toward the coffeepot. "What do you have planned for today?"

When he looks up at me, the heat in his eyes almost makes me drop my mug. He gives me a slow once-over, more than obvious he's remembering every detail from last night.

"My motorcycle was sitting next to my truck when I went outside this morning," he says, voice rough. "I have today off. So I figured we'd go for a ride."

I suck in a breath at the news, nearly choking on my coffee. "Your motorcycle?"

"Yep." He spears a piece of pancake with his fork.

"So first you, then your truck, then your clothes, and now your motorcycle. What's next, a pet tiger?"

He laughs, the sound warming me from the inside out. "God, I hope not. But I wouldn't put it past the universe at this point."

Taking a bite of pancake, I moan. "These are amazing."

"I know." His eyes darken. "Those are the same noises you made last night."

My cheeks flush. "Stop."

"Make me," he challenges, leaning close.

Setting down my fork, I reach over and grab a fistful of his shirt, pulling him in for a kiss. He tastes like maple syrup and coffee.

His hand cups the back of my neck, holding me in place as his tongue tangles with mine before he pulls back abruptly. "Guess you showed me, huh, kitten?"

Mortified, I pick my fork back up and take a bite of cheesy eggs.

"Hey, you okay?"

I shrug. "Why did you pull away so fast?"

Ryder shoves his empty plate aside and grins. "Because I can't have you distracting me. Or be out in public all day with a hard on."

"Oh." I smile and take another bite.

"We're going to take a road trip to the coast."

"It's too cold to go swimming."

"We are not going swimming," he says with a quick shake of his head. "Just riding up the coast to a great little seafood place where we can have lunch."

THIRTY MINUTES LATER, AFTER CHANGING INTO JEANS AND a light sweater, I'm standing in the driveway staring at a vintage black 1976 Triumph Bonneville gleaming in the sunlight.

Ryder runs his hand along the seat with such reverence, I almost feel a twinge of jealousy. "She's beautiful, isn't she?"

Okay, maybe not almost.

"I guess. If you're into potential organ donation."

"Put this on," he laughs as he hands me a helmet. "Safety first."

I eye the helmet dubiously before shoving it on. "Helmet head, my favorite."

"If you want, I can mess it up even more when we get back," he promises with a wink, sending a flash of liquid heat to my core.

"I found this in the closet, too," he says, handing me a small leather jacket.

"This was in your closet?"

He nods at me with a small smile as he puts on his helmet.

I shrug on the jacket. The leather is soft and it fits me perfectly.

"Ready?" he asks, patting the seat behind him.

I take a deep breath and climb on, wrapping my arms around his waist.

"Hold tight," he orders and kick-starts the engine. The bike roars to life, vibrating between my thighs in a way that's not at all unpleasant.

"I'm going to die," I mutter into his back.

Not only can I hear his chuckle, I can feel it vibrate deliciously against my breasts and it makes my nipples hard. "Trust me."

Before I can protest any further, we're on the move. The wind rushes past as he navigates the winding roads and after a few minutes, the initial terror fades, replaced by an exhilarating sense of freedom I've never felt before.

My world blurs as forests give way to rolling hills, then farmland, and finally, the first glimpse of the ocean in the distance.

I tighten my grip around Ryder's waist, pressing my cheek against his back.

When we finally pull into a small coastal town, my legs are numb and my lips are wind-chapped, but I'm grinning like an idiot.

"You good?" Ryder asks as he helps me off the bike, steadying me with his hands firmly on my waist.

"Surprisingly," I laugh, legs wobbly as I remove my helmet. "That was actually kind of amazing."

His answering smile is so bright it makes my heart skip. "I knew you'd love it."

We're parked in front of a weathered building with faded

blue paint. Letters peeling in the salty air, the large sign over the door reads: ***The Salty Dog***.

The scent of fried seafood and ocean air makes my stomach growl.

"Best seafood in the Pacific Northwest," Ryder says, taking my hand as he leads me toward the entrance. "You're going to love their lobster roll."

Inside the restaurant is exactly what you'd expect—rustic wooden tables covered in brown paper, fishing nets hanging from the ceiling, and the smell of garlic and butter thick in the air. It's packed, almost every seat taken.

The hostess has sun-bleached hair and freckles scattered across her nose. "Two?"

Ryder nods, and she leads us over to a corner table by a window overlooking the water. Waves crash against the rocks below, sending sprays of white foam into the air.

After we order a lobster roll for myself and a massive seafood platter for Ryder, he leans back in his chair and studies me.

"So," he says, taking a sip of his beer. "We've known each other for a few days now, and I still don't know much about your family."

I fiddle with my napkin. "Not much to tell. It's just me and my mom."

"What about your dad?" he asks softly.

Something in his tone tells me he already knows the answer.

"He died when I was nineteen." I look out the window at the crashing waves. "Heart attack. It was completely unexpected. He was only fifty-two and seemed healthy. He went for a run one morning and just... never came home."

"That's rough." His eyes soften as he reaches across the table to take my hand. "I'm sorry."

"It was," I admit. "But, of course, my mom took it even

harder. They were high school sweethearts. They had this epic love story that spanned almost three decades. After he died, she just... shut down."

"How so?"

I trace patterns into the condensation on my water glass. "She stopped eating and barely slept. I would come home from college on the weekends to find her sitting in his chair, wearing his sweater, staring at nothing. It was almost like she disappeared, too. So I moved back home for a while to take care of her."

I'm grateful for the interruption when the waitress brings our food. This isn't something I've talked about with anyone in a really long time.

"It took almost a year before she started acting like herself again," I continue after another bite of my lobster roll. "She joined a grief support group, started teaching again. She even dated a little, though nothing serious has come of it yet."

"Is that why you write romance?" Ryder asks. "Because of them?"

Surprised by his insight, I think about it for a minute. "Maybe, a little? I never thought about it that way, but yeah... I think seeing how they were together showed me what real love looks like. The kind worth writing about. I'd always wanted to be a writer, though. Since I was a kid. I was a voracious reader, too. Still am."

"And what about after college?" he asks gently. "How were you discovered as an author?"

"Okay." I pick up a fry from my plate and wave it in the air. "The truth is, I started out as a professional ghostwriter. I wrote dozens of love stories for other people before I was brave enough to admit I wanted my own name on the cover."

"Dozens?" He takes another sip of his beer.

"Yeah." My voice catches when I look up to see him looking

at me intently. "Writing has always been a way I could feel like I fit in without actually taking up space, you know?

"Growing up, I always felt kind of invisible. I got good grades, but I kept to myself. I didn't feel like I fit in anywhere. When I was twelve, we moved to Portland because of my dad's job, and I met Sasha. We've been best friends ever since."

"It's good that you have her in your life."

"It is."

He takes another sip of his beer, and I watch in awe. The memory of what that mouth touching the rim of his glass did to my pussy last night is making my inner walls flutter.

My next question almost comes out as a squeak. "What about you?"

"I don't really talk about my past."

"All I know is what I've already plotted out, which isn't much. So I'm just wondering if it's any different now from what I came up with before."

His brows furrow as he spins his nearly empty glass a couple of times before he speaks.

"My parents split when I was ten." Setting the glass aside, he leans back and crosses his arms over his chest. "Once I reached junior high, I got into a lot of fights. My mom told me that if I didn't get my shit together, I'd wind up in jail. So, I joined the Marines right out of high school. Figured if I wanted to fight, might as well pick something worth fighting for.

"I did two tours before I was honorably discharged. After my last deployment... shit got real messy. PTSD and anger issues basically took over my life. I met Claire at a meeting and she became my sponsor. Eventually she offered me an apprenticeship at a shop she was working at, told me I had a steady hand and a weird knack for listening to people's stories."

He glances up at me and the look on his face is so vulnerable I want to go over and wrap my whole body around him.

"That was the first time I felt like I belonged. Like maybe I was worth something outside of wearing a uniform."

"I'm so glad you found your place," I say softly.

"Kinda feels like maybe I'm still looking for it."

Those words hit me hard. It's my fault he's here. My fault he has to relive his past.

His gaze flicks toward the ocean, watching the waves as they crash against the shore.

"I'm sorry," I say, voice barely above a whisper. "It's my fault you're in this mess."

His sharp gaze snaps back to mine. "Don't be sorry for creating me, Noia. I'm not."

"But you were supposed to have a happy ending. That's my job, it's what I do—write happily ever after's. And instead, you're... stuck. In limbo. With me."

Ryder's expression turns dead serious. "Who says I'm not going to have a happy ending?"

The question, loaded with meaning I'm not ready to unpack, hangs in the air.

My cheeks flush as I fiddle with my napkin.

"Besides," he continues, a small smile playing at his lips. "I think we've established I'm not exactly 'stuck' anywhere."

I swallow hard. "What if all of this stops? What if tomorrow I wake up and—"

"And what? I've disappeared?" He shakes his head. "I honestly don't think that's how this is supposed to work. If anything, I'm becoming more anchored in this world, not less."

"But how can you be so sure?"

Reaching across the table, he takes my hand, tracing circles on my palm with his thumb. "I can't. But I'm not going to waste whatever time I have worrying about it. And neither should you."

The intensity in his eyes makes my heart stutter. Before I can respond, the waitress appears with our check.

"You two make such a cute couple," she says with a smile. "Been together long?"

Ryder's eyes never leave mine. "Feels like I've known her my whole life."

TWENTY-FIVE

THE RIDE HOME FEELS DIFFERENT. I PRESS MYSELF AGAINST Ryder's back, arms wrapped tightly around his waist, cheek resting between his shoulder blades. We take the coastal road home, the sound of the motorcycle a pleasant hum as the wind rushes past.

We pull into the driveway just as the sun is starting to set, painting the sky in brilliant oranges and pinks.

My legs are wobbly again as I climb off the bike.

"Did you have fun today?"

Ryder is looking down at me with those smoky gray eyes and I swear I could melt just from the intensity of his gaze.

"I did. Thank you."

"My pleasure."

The words hit low in my belly as he growls the words.

Clearing my throat, I hand him back the helmet and head toward the door. "I'm gonna take a shower and do some writing."

Hᴏᴛ ᴡᴀᴛᴇʀ ꜱʟᴜɪᴄᴇꜱ ᴏᴠᴇʀ ᴍʏ ʙᴏᴅʏ ᴀꜱ I ᴡᴀꜱʜ ᴀᴡᴀʏ ᴛʜᴇ lingering scent of ocean air from my skin. My mind keeps replaying the day on repeat—the exhilarating feeling of my first motorcycle ride, the way Ryder looked at me across the table at lunch, and the intensity in his eyes when he said he felt like he'd known me his whole life.

After toweling off, I slip into my comfiest pajama shorts and T-shirt before sitting down at my desk.

The words flow easily, my fingers flying across the keyboard as I describe the feeling of being pressed against Ryder's back on the motorcycle, the way the wind whipped through my hair and how the sense of freedom I experienced made me feel more alive than I've ever felt in my life.

I'm deep into our steamy scene from the night before when my phone buzzes. My mom's face lights up the screen, and I hesitate for a second before answering.

"Hey, Mom."

"Noia, sweetheart!" Her voice is warm and slightly breath-less. "I've been trying to reach you for days. How are you doing?"

I glance at my bedroom door. It's open just a crack, and I can hear Ryder moving around downstairs. "Everything's fine, Mom. I'm sorry I haven't returned your calls. I've been... writing."

"That's great! Your editor will be thrilled. I take it the change of scenery is helping?"

"Something like that," I murmur, biting back a smile. "It's definitely been... inspiring."

"You sound different," she says, her mom-radar kicking in.

I pinch the bridge of my nose and sigh. "Just tired from writing all day."

"Mmm-hmm." She doesn't sound convinced. "Well, I was calling to see if you wanted some company this weekend. I thought I might drive up, bring some of those cookies you love."

My heart jumps into my throat. "This weekend? Um, actually, Sasha's coming to visit. She'll be here Friday."

"Perfect! I can come on Saturday. I'd love to see Sasha too."

Panic flutters in my chest. "Mom, I don't think—"

"Nonsense. It's been too long since I've seen my baby girl. Besides, I want to make sure you're taking care of yourself after... well, you know."

"I'm fine, Mom. Really. Maybe another weekend, okay?"

"Oh, honey," she says, voice gentle. "I know you're still hurting from what Eric did, but hiding isn't going to—"

"I'm not hiding," I interrupt, voice sharp. Wincing, I soften my tone. "I'm working. And I'm... I'm actually doing really good."

There's a pause on the other end, and I can practically hear her processing the abrupt change in my tone.

"Mom." I take a deep breath. "I love you, and I appreciate you wanting to check on me. But I need you to trust that I'm okay. Better than okay, actually."

Another pause. "What aren't you telling me? Have you met someone?"

Jesus, mother's intuition is no joke.

My cheeks start to burn. "What makes you ask that?"

"Like I said, you sound... different, that's all."

Tears prick my eyes unexpectedly. "I'm just figuring some things out."

"Good things, I hope?"

I glance toward the door again, hearing Ryder's low chuckle from downstairs as he talks to Goonie. "Yeah, Mom. Really good things."

"Well, then I suppose I can wait to hear about them. But Noia? When you're ready to share, you know I'm here."

"I know. I love you."

"Love you too, sweetheart. And honey? Whatever else it is that's happening, don't let fear talk you out of it. You deserve to be happy, too."

After we hang up, I sit staring at my phone until a soft knock at my door makes me look up.

"Come in."

Ryder pushes the door open, holding two mugs. "Thought you might want some tea."

"Thanks." I accept the mug gratefully, wrapping my hands around its warmth.

"Who were you just talking to?"

"My mom."

He settles on the edge of my bed. "Everything okay?"

"She wanted to visit this weekend. I told her Sasha was coming and maybe she could come another weekend."

"You don't want her to meet me."

The quiet understanding in his voice makes me cringe inside.

"It's not that I don't want—" Frustrated, I let out a sigh. "God. You know our situation is complicated."

"Hey." He reaches out, brushing his fingers across my cheek. "Talk to me."

Despite my frustration, I lean into his touch. "How do I explain all of this... you, to her? 'Mom, this is Ryder. He used to be fictional, but now he's real. He's also helping me with my writer's block and now we're having amazing sex.'"

"You think the sex is amazing?"

I tsk and roll my eyes, making him chuckle. "Duh."

His gaze turns molten. "Wanna see how much more amazing it can be?"

ryder

NOIA'S EYES GO WIDE AND HER BREATH STARTS TO QUICKEN.

"I'll take that as a yes."

"I... I haven't finished writing about today."

I lean in and raise an eyebrow. "Just more fuel to stoke the fire, kitten." Taking the mug from her hands, I set it on the desk beside her laptop. "I think you've done enough writing for tonight."

Goosebumps rise along the smooth expanse of her skin as I trace my fingers up her bare arm, and it makes me grin.

I tug gently at the collar of her T-shirt, exposing more of her creamy skin.

"But I—"

"Shh." I move her hair out of the way, pressing my lips to the sensitive spot where her neck meets her shoulder. She melts against me with a soft sigh. "Your words will still be there tomorrow."

She nods, and I slide my hands under her thighs, lifting her up from the chair. Her legs wrap around my waist as I carry her to the bed.

Her soft weight feels perfect pressing against me.

"I can't stop thinking about last night," I confess, lowering her onto the mattress. "The way your pussy squeezed my cock. The sounds you made when I made you come."

Sliding my hand beneath her T-shirt, I trace my fingers up her ribs, reveling in the silky softness of her skin. "Take this off for me."

She sits up just enough to pull the shirt over her head, letting it fall onto the floor. The sight of her bare breasts in the soft lamplight makes my mouth go dry.

"You're so fucking beautiful," I breathe, cupping one breast, loving how it feels in my palm. Her nipple hardens beneath my thumb as I stroke it, drawing a soft gasp from her lips.

Lowering my head, I take the tight bud into my mouth, swirling my tongue before sucking hard. Her back arches off the bed as her fingers thread through my hair.

"Ryder," she sighs.

The sound of my name on her lips sends a thrill like I've never known straight to my cock.

I take my time, worshipping every inch of her body with my hands and mouth. When I finally slide her shorts and panties down her legs, she's trembling.

"Spread your legs so I can see you."

Slowly, she opens her legs and I suck in a breath at the sight. She's glistening.

"Holy fuck." I climb onto the bed and use my hands to press her thighs further apart. "I can't wait to taste you again."

The first stroke of my tongue against her center has her clutching at the sheets. She's already so wet, so ready for me.

I work her with my mouth and tongue until she's writhing, her pleas loud and desperate as she teeters on the edge. Only then do I slide up her body, pausing to shed my own clothes before rising above her.

"Look at me," I command softly.

Her eyes flutter open, dark with desire, and lock with mine. In that moment, something shifts between us—something deeper than physical attraction, more profound than lust.

Slowly, I push inside, watching her face as I fill her completely. The tight heat of her pussy gripping my dick nearly undoes me. Determined to make this last, I manage to keep myself in check—barely.

"You feel so good," she groans, wrapping her arms around my neck as I begin to thrust.

I set a slow, deliberate rhythm, wanting to memorize every sensation—the way she feels, the soft sounds she makes, how her body responds to what I do.

"Tell me what you need," I whisper against her ear, my voice rough with restraint.

"Harder," she breathes.

I don't hesitate for a second. Gripping her hips, I slam into her. Her gasps turn into moans, sending fire racing through my veins.

"Like this?" I growl, driving into her over and over, throwing a mental fist in the air when her eyes roll back in her head.

"Yes," she pants, digging crescents into my biceps with her nails. "Fuck, yes!"

When I pull out and flip her onto her stomach, she lets out a surprised yelp that turns into a moan when I yank her hips up and thrust back into her from behind.

"Fuck," I hiss. The new angle and the tight grip of her pussy nearly undoes me.

Pushing her down so she's lying flat on the bed, I slide one hand beneath her, finding her slick clit, circling it with my middle finger in time with my thrusts. Then I slide my other hand up between her breasts, to the elegant column of her throat, until I'm gripping her neck. The rapid flutter of her pulse against my fingers almost makes me lose it right then and there.

"You want more?" I grunt against her ear.

"Don't stop," she gasps.

Applying just enough pressure to let her know I'm the one in control, her entire body shudders beneath me as her inner walls start to clench.

"You like that, don't you?" I growl into her ear. "You like it when I take control."

"Yes," she whimpers, voice breaking as I increase the pressure on her clit.

Her body is trembling, back arched, half her face pressed into the pillow as I fuck into her with deep, long strokes. I can feel her getting close, her breathing growing more ragged with each savage thrust.

"Come on, kitten." My voice is rough with need. "I want to feel you."

And that's all it takes. One simple request and she shatters, crying out my name as her body convulses. The rhythmic pulsing of her walls around my dick is too much to resist, and I instantly follow her over the edge, burying myself deep as I come with a groan.

For several long moments, we stay locked together, breathing hard. Finally, I ease my grip on her neck and pull out.

Rolling her over, I press a gentle kiss to her neck and collapse beside her.

She rolls onto her side to face me, cheeks flushed, eyes bright.

"It wasn't too much, was it?"

"No," she says quickly, scooting over to rest her head over my heart. "I've never... no one's ever..."

At a loss for words, all I'm able to do in the moment is trace my fingers up and down her arm.

She's quiet for a while and when she finally speaks, her voice comes out soft and determined. "Ryder, I think we should sleep in separate beds tonight."

I go still. "What?"

She sits up, not quite meeting my eyes. "It's just... this is all happening so fast. I mean, a week ago you didn't even exist in my world, and now we're..." She gestures between us.

"Now we're what?" I ask, voice hard. "Having incredible sex? Getting to know each other? Living out our story?"

"That's just it." She runs a hand through her tangled hair. "I feel like we're rushing through chapters that need time to develop. We're skipping integral parts of the story."

Propping myself up on my elbow, I study her face. "What's this really about?"

She sighs. "It's about me needing to catch my breath. To process what's happening between us without getting lost in... this."

The rejection stings, taking me by surprise. "This being what, exactly?"

"The physical part." Her cheeks flush. "Don't get me wrong —it's amazing. But I write romance novels for a living, Ryder. I know that the most meaningful relationships build slowly. In my stories the characters need to develop trust and under-standing before jumping into bed."

"We've already jumped, kitten. Multiple times."

She shoots me a look. "You know what I mean."

I sit up fully with a sigh and drag a hand down my face. "So, what are you saying? You want to take a step back?"

"No. I'm saying I think we should slow down. Not have sex for a while."

"You said you'd let me take you out of your comfort zone."

"You definitely have," she nods. "But you also said we were going to do other things to help build inspiration. I can't just have inspiration based on sex, no matter how good it is."

"Okay. I see your point." I get out of bed and tug on my jeans. "If you want slow-burn, I'll give you slow-burn."

My eyes travel slowly over her naked body. She's still sprawled across the sheets, skin flushed, hair wild, looking thoroughly fucked and absolutely perfect.

"But just so we're clear," I say, dropping my voice into that low register I know makes her shiver. "This whole 'slow-burn' thing? It can go both ways."

She gets under the covers. "Explain."

I stand at the end of the bed, looking down at her with a smirk. "I can give you the bad boy, too. Give me a few days and you'll be *begging* me to fuck you again."

Her eyes widen, pupils dilating even as she scoffs. "If anyone is going to beg, it's gonna be you."

"Trust me, kitten." I lean forward, bracing my hands on the mattress. "It will be you."

She swallows hard. "Then I guess we'll just have to wait and see, won't we?"

"Yeah, we will." I straighten up and head for the door. "Sweet dreams, Noia."

"Ryder?"

I stop in the doorway and glance over my shoulder. "Yeah?"

"Why do you call me kitten?"

Her question catches me off guard and it takes me longer than I'd like to answer. "Because everything about you is soft in all the best ways. Soft curves. Soft, shiny hair. But when those claws come out..." I shake my head. "Let's just say it does something to me no one else has ever been able to do before."

I close her bedroom door behind me with a soft click, grinning when I hear her frustrated groan.

Downstairs, I pour myself a generous glass of whiskey and

collapse onto the couch with a sigh. Goonie hops up beside me, giving me his usual judgmental glare.

"Don't look at me like that," I mutter. "Your mom's the one who wants to slow things down."

He gives me a slow blink and a yawn before settling down next to my thigh, purring softly.

I take a long sip of my drink, the burn slowly easing its way down my throat. It's going to be a long, frustrating next few days.

Back in my bedroom, I collapse onto the bed and stare up at the ceiling.

So, Noia wants a slow-burn?

Fine. I'll make the burn so slow she'll combust from the inside out.

Game on, *kitten*.

TWENTY-SEVEN

noia

I WAKE UP TO AN EMPTY HOUSE AND A NOTE ON THE kitchen counter.

Gone to work. Made coffee. See you later. -R

That's it. No "Have a good morning, kitten"? The bare-bones note leaves me feeling oddly disappointed.

Pouring myself a cup of coffee, I sigh and lean against the counter. Maybe I made a mistake last night. Maybe I should have just let things continue as they were.

No. I was right to ask to slow things down. This thing between us is moving way too fast, spiraling out of control. I need to get my bearings before I completely lose myself.

Ryder's words echo in my head: *"Give me a few days and you'll be begging me to fuck you again."*

"Fat chance," I mutter to Goonie as he winds between my ankles. "I have more self-control than that."

Goonie's meow sounds skeptical.

Figures.

After breakfast, I sit down to write.

I'm deep in the zone when my phone buzzes with a text.

SASHA: *Just one more sleep and I'll be at your door!*

ME: *Can't wait! Fair warning though. Things have gotten…* complicated.

SASHA: *Good complicated or bad complicated?*

ME: *Both? I'll explain everything when you get here.*

SASHA: *Now I'm REALLY excited!*

I set my phone aside and try to focus on writing, but my mind keeps wandering. What will Sasha think of Ryder? What will she make of my crazy situation?

Around noon, my phone buzzes again.

RYDER: *How's the writing going?*

ME: *Good. Productive morning. How's work?*

RYDER: *Glad to hear it. Work is good.*

Then, a couple of minutes later:

RYDER: *What are you wearing?*

I nearly choke on my coffee. The nerve of this man.

ME: *Clothes.*

RYDER: *What a shame. I was hoping you'd still be naked.*

Heat floods my cheeks as images from the night before bounce around traitorously in my head—his big hand squeezing my throat, his hot mouth on my clit and the way he made me come completely apart.

ME: *I thought we agreed to slow things down.*

RYDER: *We agreed to slow-burn. And I never agreed to stop thinking about you. Or stop wanting you. This is me adding slow-burn into the mix.*

Despite my best efforts to remain unaffected, my pulse quickens.

ME: *You're really a pain in the ass, you know that?*

RYDER: *And you're avoiding my question. What are you wearing, kitten?*

I look down at my outfit and sigh.

ME: *Yoga pants and a T-shirt.*

RYDER: *The black ones that hug your ass?*

Dammit. Now my face is burning.

ME: *Yes?*

RYDER: *Fuck. Now all I can think about is peeling them off you with my teeth.*

I squeeze my thighs together, trying to suppress the pulse of heat between my legs.

ME: *Aren't you supposed to be working?*

RYDER: *I am working. Just finished a piece on a client's shoulder blade. But I keep thinking about last night and how your pussy felt fluttering around my cock just before I made you come.*

I stare at his words, my breathing growing shallow. This is exactly what I was afraid of—Ryder getting under my skin, making me lose focus.

ME: *STOP*

RYDER: *Stop what? Telling you how much I want to taste you again? How I'm already hard just thinking about the sounds you make when you come?*

"Holy shit." I fan myself with my hand.

ME: *You're seriously playing dirty, you know that?*

RYDER: *Don't say I didn't warn you. How's the slow-burn working out for you so far?*

I set the phone down, take a deep breath, and try to regain my composure. But the damage is done—my body is humming with need, and my concentration is completely shot.

This is going to be a very long day.

THE SOUND OF A MOTORCYCLE PULLING INTO THE
driveway makes my heart skip and I glance at the clock.

12:01 p.m.

Ryder is home early.

I hear his heavy footsteps on the porch, then the front door.
But instead of coming upstairs to find me, I hear him moving
around in the kitchen.

"Noia?" his rough, sexy voice floats up from downstairs. "I
brought lunch."

My stomach chooses that moment to growl. I've been so
absorbed in writing that I forgot to eat.

I go downstairs.

Ryder is leaning against the counter wearing dark jeans and
a tight black Henley. His hair is slightly disheveled, and there's a
smudge of ink on his forearm.

He looks good enough to eat.

"You're home early," I state, trying to keep my voice neutral.

"Slow day. Figured I'd come home and we could make
lunch together." He gestures to the counter where he's laid out
ingredients for what looks like gourmet sandwiches—thick slices
of bread, turkey, avocado, and some kind of fancy cheese.

"You didn't have to do that."

"I wanted to." His eyes meet mine, and there's something
different about them today. They seem more intense, more
focused. "Besides, I figured you'd be hungry. You tend to lose
track of time when you write and forget to take care of yourself."

His attention to detail makes a thrill shoot up my spine.

"We're going to make them together," he says, motioning for
me to join him. "I'm going to teach you how to make a proper
sandwich."

I roll my eyes. "I know how to make a sandwich."

"Not like this, you don't." His voice is authoritative and full
of swagger.

"Fine."

I move to stand next to him at the kitchen island and, side by side, we begin making lunch.

When I reach for the bread, our fingers brush, sending an electric jolt up my arm. I pull back quickly, but not before I see the slight twitch at the corner of his mouth.

"You okay there, kitten?" he asks, trying to act all innocent and shit.

"Yes," I mutter, focusing on spreading the mustard.

The length of his body brushes against mine as he reaches across me for the tomatoes. I know he's doing it on purpose—the subtle touches, the occasional casual brush of his body against mine—it's all part of his "slow-burn" plot.

Well, two can play at this game.

Instead of asking him to hand me the mayo, I lean across the marble, which puts my ass in the air.

When I straighten, he's behind me, his chest nearly touching my back, breath warm on my neck.

"Need help with that?" he murmurs, brushing his lips against my ear.

I freeze, knife suspended mid-air, my heart hammering loud enough against my ribs I wouldn't be surprised if he can hear it.

The heat of his body spreads over mine, and it takes all the power I've got to fight the urge to lean back against him.

My voice comes out embarrassingly breathy. "I—"

But before I can finish my thought, he steps away.

"I'll grab the plates," he announces casually.

When I exhale, it comes out shaky and my entire body is humming. The spot where his lips touched my ear is tingling, and I have to grip the counter for support.

Damn him and his big-dick energy.

When I look up, he's watching me with that infuriating smirk of his. The asshole knows *exactly* what he's doing to me.

He hands me the plates. "You good?"

"You're playing dirty," I accuse, setting the plates down with more force than necessary.

He pops an eyebrow. "I have no idea what you're talking about. We're just making lunch."

"Right." I cross my arms over my chest in an attempt to hide the fact that my nipples have pebbled beneath my T-shirt. "And I'm the Queen of England."

His eyes darken as they drop to my chest, then back to my face. "Okay, then, *your Majesty*," he says with a mock bow.

Despite myself, I laugh. "You're such a dick."

"And *you're* just as beautiful when you frown," he growls.

TWENTY-EIGHT

THE WAY HER FACE FLUSHES MAKES IT ALMOST IMPOSSIBLE for me to keep my distance. I want nothing more than to back her up against the counter and remind her exactly what she's missing, but I have a plan and I need to stick to it.

Mumbling something about getting back to work, she practically flees upstairs with her sandwich. I watch her go, enjoying the view as she takes the steps two at a time.

"Sure." I manage to keep my voice casual, even though every cell in my body is screaming to follow her up those stairs.

As soon as she disappears, I let out a long breath and adjust myself in my jeans. Fuck. This is going to be harder than I thought.

The plan was to make her want me so badly she'd break her own rule, but I didn't account for how fucking hard it would be on me, too.

When she bent over the counter to grab the mayo, my cock instantly went hard, straining painfully against my zipper.

Grabbing my plate, I grab a beer from the fridge, head to the living room and collapse onto the couch.

Goonie stares down at me from his perch on the bookcase.

"Don't look at me like that," I grunt.

He just keeps staring at me, swishing his tail back and forth. Then he shifts and I watch out of the corner of my eye as he paws at a stack of paperbacks on the shelf.

"Don't even think about it, pudge."

"*Chirrup.*"

Down go the books.

"Jesus. No wonder she calls you troublemaker."

I push up from the couch, pick up the books and set them back on the shelf, then grab Goonie and set him on the floor.

"Behave."

I turn on the TV, flipping through channels until I find an old action movie, hoping the mindless car chases might help to distract me.

But knowing Noia is just upstairs, probably still flushed and bothered by our slow-burn tête-à-tête, keeps me distracted.

Taking a long pull from my beer, I lean back and try to focus on the screen, but my mind keeps wandering.

This whole slow-burn game is torture, but I can't deny there's something intoxicating about the build-up of sexual frustration igniting the fire of anticipation.

My plan is to play this out over the next few days and into next week, then take her on a slow-burn overnight date.

The party at Skin & Ink is only a couple of days away, and the thought of showing her off makes something possessive and primal stir in my chest.

Setting my empty bottle on the coffee table, I grab the remote and turn up the volume, trying to drown out the sound of her keyboard clicking upstairs. Each tap is a reminder that she's up there probably writing about us.

About me.

I groan and adjust myself. "Fuck."

THIS KIND OF DRY, METALLIC HEAT DOESN'T COME FROM THE sun; it comes from the air itself, and it's boiling me from the inside out.

Sand scratches my throat when I breathe in, clinging to my skin as it works its way into the crevices of my gear.

My world is full of dust and beige as my boots crunch on the sand.

I know where I am, because I've been here before.

Afghanistan, 2009: Operation Tumbleweed.

I grip the handle of my M4, heart thudding low and hard in my chest. My vest is soaked in sweat and my hands are shaking.

Get it together, Blackwood.

"Ryder, move!" A voice shouts from behind me.

I spin around to see Kade, his face looking just the way it did before the mortar hit. He's waving me toward the Humvee, shouting something else I can't hear. His lips are moving, but the sounds in my head have gone muffled, almost as if I'm underwater.

He takes one step and my world explodes.

BOOM!

The sound hits me like a sledgehammer, flinging me backward to the ground. My ears are ringing and the air tastes like metal, burnt meat, and fire.

I scramble forward, my palms tearing open on the jagged rocks. Someone is screaming, but I can't tell if it's me or someone else.

Smoke curls around my face, and all I can see is what's left of a leg and other body parts strewn across the ground in bloody pieces.

My stomach lurches.

Kade is gone.

My lungs refuse to expand. I can't breathe.

My heartbeat is a loud drumming in my ears as I look around, searching for my gun, but it's gone.

Disoriented, I turn my head, and the desert landscape shifts, blurring to black.

Bolting upright, I immediately fall out of bed.

My chest stings and my eyes are wet as I push up from the floor onto my knees. I can still feel the heat, still hear the screams.

Dragging my hands through my hair, I give it a yank. I need the pain, something real to drag me back to the present.

A soft meow breaks through the chaos in my head, and I feel something warm and soft brush against my leg.

Goonie jumps into my lap, purring loudly as he headbutts my chin. His warm weight anchors me back to reality, pulling me away from the edge.

"Hey, pudge." My voice comes out in a rasp, hands shaking as I stroke his soft fur.

Rubbing firmly against me, his purr vibrates through my chest like a tiny engine. It's amazing how something so small can make such a difference, a steady presence helping to slow my racing heart.

"You're a good little man," I murmur, scratching behind his ears. "Just don't tell your mom I said that, okay?"

When my breathing finally evens out, I gently set Goonie on the floor and push myself up on unsteady legs. The night-mare has left me drenched in sweat.

Fuck. I need a drink.

Sweat slicking my skin, I leave my room and head straight for the liquor cabinet, pulling out the bottle of Jameson I bought last week.

Pouring three fingers into a tumbler, I down it in one burning gulp, then immediately pour another.

The warmth of the whiskey hits my veins, dulling the jagged edges of the dream and I head to the bathroom, taking the bottle with me.

Stripping off my sweat-soaked boxers, I leave them on the bathroom floor and turn on the shower.

Pressing my forehead against the cool tile, I let the water sluice away the remnants of my nightmare. By the time I step out, the whiskey has taken some of the edge off, leaving me exhausted but no longer trapped in the past.

I towel off and pull on a clean pair of boxers, not bothering with anything else, and I make my way into the living room.

The house is quiet and I'm thankful Noia is asleep and can't see this train wreck. Collapsing onto the couch, I stretch out my legs and glance at the clock on the mantle: 3:17 a.m.

Then, like a small ghost, Goonie appears and jumps up into my lap. He turns in three tight circles before settling down, his warm weight oddly comforting.

I sigh and stroke a hand down his back.

He blinks up at me, yellow-green eyes telling me he understands much more than he's letting on.

noia

The next morning, I wake up feeling a little groggy. After a quick shower, I head downstairs to make coffee and find Ryder already in the kitchen.

He's standing at the stove flipping pancakes. When he looks over at me, I notice a slight tinge of darkness under his eyes, and his face is a little pale. He looks exhausted, like he hasn't slept much at all.

"Morning." I study him with concern. "You okay?"

"Never better." Despite the smile he gives me, his eyes look... haunted. "Coffee's ready."

As I reach for a mug, his hand brushes mine, sending a shot of electricity up my arm. I chalk it up to an accident until it happens again when I'm pouring cream into my coffee. His fingers graze my wrist, lingering just long enough to make my pulse jump.

"How did you sleep?" I ask, trying to keep my voice steady as I take a seat at the island.

"Well enough." He slides a plate of pancakes in front of me, his chest pressing briefly against my back as he leans over me, breath warm against my neck. "You?"

"Fine, thanks," I squeak, nearly dropping my fork when he brushes his fingers across my lower back as he moves to sit beside me.

He's sitting so close our knees are touching. Every time I reach for something, he somehow manages to brush his fingers or arm against mine. Then, when I take a bite of pancake and a drop of syrup lands on my lip, he reaches over and swipes it away with his thumb, lingering an extra second.

"You have a little..." he murmurs, voice dropping into a low, gravelly register that makes me shiver.

"Thanks," I whisper, watching in awe as he slowly sucks the syrup off his thumb, eyes locked with mine.

My entire body flushes hot.

Fucking hell.

All through breakfast, he continues his subtle slow-burn assaults—resting a hand on my thigh, grazing his fingers along my collarbone when he points out Goonie doing something silly as his thigh presses firmly against mine.

By the time we're finished eating, I'm a fuck-all mess of nerves.

"Oops. Looks like it's time for me to go to work," he says suddenly as he gets up. "Big day ahead."

Thrown off by his sudden change in attitude, I stand and take our plates to the sink.

"Okay," I manage, trying not to sound as affected as I feel. "Will you be home for dinner?"

He pauses at the door, gray eyes dark as they sweep over me. "Actually, no. I'm meeting Claire and Jax after work to finalize details for the party tomorrow." His grin turns wicked. "But don't worry. I'll be thinking about you."

I nod. "Don't forget, Sasha's coming over today to spend the weekend. Try not to let her see you naked."

"Your wish is my command," he grins.

Then he's gone, leaving me flustered and frustrated.

"Sneaky bastard," I mutter under my breath.

Ryder might think he's going to win this little game, but I'm not going down without a fight. If he can touch and tease, then so can I. Two can play at this slow-burn torture.

With newfound determination, I head upstairs and get to work. The words flow, and by the time I look up, it's already past noon.

My phone pings.

SASHA: *Heading out now. Should be there in about an hour. Need me to pick anything up on the way?*

ME: *Wine. Lots of wine. And maybe some ice cream?*

SASHA: *That bad, huh?*

ME: *I'll explain when you get here. Drive safe.*

I close my laptop and head downstairs to tidy up. The house isn't messy, not since I scrubbed the shit out of it a few days ago.

There are signs of Ryder everywhere—a jacket thrown over a chair, a pair of boots sitting by the door and a half-empty glass sitting on the coffee table.

Picking up the glass, I take a sniff.

Whiskey.

I frown. Ryder doesn't usually leave his stuff lying around. There was something off about him this morning, but I was too distracted by his slow-burn flirting to ask him more about it.

After putting the glass in the dishwasher, I change the sheets in the guest room and make sure there are fresh towels in the guest bathroom. Just as I'm finishing up, I hear a car door slam outside.

Rushing to the front door, I throw it open to find Sasha struggling up the steps with what looks like enough luggage for a month-long vacation.

"Holy shit! Did you pack your entire apartment?" I laugh, hurrying to help her.

"You know it." She drops her bags and pulls me into a fierce hug. "God, I've missed you."

"Missed you too." I squeeze back, realizing just how much I've needed my best friend since she's been gone.

She pulls back, holding me at arm's length, and studies my face. "You look... different."

"Different how?"

"I don't know. Glow-y? Less like a depressed writer hermit and maybe more like someone who's been getting laid on the reg."

I feel my cheeks heat. "Sash!"

"Ha! I *knew* it!" She claps her hands together in delight. "I want all the steamy details. But first, let me get settled and then we'll pour some wine."

We gather her bags and head inside. After dropping them off upstairs, Sasha immediately makes herself at home, kicking off her shoes and heading straight for the kitchen, where she pulls a bottle of white wine from her tote.

"It's barely three in the afternoon," I protest weakly.

"As the old cliché goes... it's five o'clock somewhere." She grabs two glasses from the cabinet. "Besides, I've been driving for over an hour—traffic was a bitch, by the way—and I need to hear about this fictional man come to life who's got you all fucked and flustered."

Pouring myself a glass, I take a mouthful. "Okay. But it's complicated."

"The best stories always are." She settles onto the couch, tucking her legs beneath her. "Start from after you hung up with me that first day. And don't you dare leave out any of the good parts."

Taking a deep breath, I dive in. "Well, ever since he showed up, things have been... intense. And not just in the way you're thinking."

"So, you *are* sleeping with him?" Sasha's eyes go wide with delight.

"We *were*," I say, emphasizing the past tense. "But I put a stop to it."

Sasha almost chokes on her wine. "You did what? Why the hell would you do something like that?"

"Because it was all happening so fast!" I throw my hands in the air. "One minute he's magically materializing outta my manuscript, the next I'm—"

"Getting finger-banged up against a wall?" Sasha supplies helpfully.

"Eventually, yeah." I play with the hem of my shirt. "He offered to help me with my writer's block. And in order to do that, he's started taking me on dates he thinks will help give me inspiration. What we're doing started off as slow-burn, but then he got frustrated and told me we needed to get me out of my comfort zone."

I shrug and take another sip of wine. "Then we had sex, and it was fucking mind-blowing, but I write romance novels, Sash. You know and I know how this shit is supposed to work. The best relationships build slowly."

"So you're saying you want to go back to 'slow-burning' with the hot not-so-fictional tattoo artist who's already given you multiple orgasms?" she asks, shaking her head in disbelief. "Only you would come up with a shit idea like that, Noia."

"It's not that simple, Sash. I need to figure out what's actually happening between us. What if he's only here temporarily? What if once my writer's block is gone, he just... disappears?"

Sasha's expression softens. "That's what you're afraid of? Losing him?"

My heart twists. "Maybe."

"So, your solution is to *stop* having sex with him," she deadpans.

I groan and bury my face in a couch pillow. "I know how ridiculous it sounds."

"Yeah," she agrees, pouring more wine into my glass. "But I get it. You're protecting yourself."

"Exactly!" I point at her, grateful she understands. "But when I told him that, he turned it around on me and came up with this slow-burn idea. And now he's decided to torture me with it."

"Torture you?" Sasha's eyebrows shoot up. "How?"

"He's always finding ways to touch me—brushing by me, putting a hand on my thigh, standing close and talking low in my ear. This morning he wiped syrup off my lip with his thumb and then slowly sucked it off while locking eyes with me."

"Damn." Sasha groans, fanning herself dramatically with her hand. "That's so *hot*."

"He also told me that within a few days, I'll be begging him to fuck me again."

A slow, mischievous smile spreads across Sasha's face. "So turn that shit back on him."

"Actually, I did—by bending over the counter." I let out a frustrated breath. "But when I straightened up, he was standing right behind me!"

My best friend barks out a laugh. "Sounds like a game of 'slow-burn roulette.'"

I down the last of my second glass of wine and deadpan, "Don't I know it."

THE SHOP IS PACKED WITH CLIENTS WHEN I ARRIVE, AND I'm grateful for the distraction. But the steady buzz of idle chatter does little to drown out the memory of how Noia's pupils dilated and her breath caught when I swiped the syrup off her lip with my thumb this morning.

And the way her lips parted just enough that I could see the tip of her small pink tongue? She was practically begging to be kissed.

"Earth to Ryder." Jax waves a hand in front of my face. "You in there, man?"

I blink, realizing I've been staring at the same sketch for I don't know how long. "Yeah."

"You've been spacing out all day." He leans against my desk. "Is it that writer chick again?"

"Her name is Noia," I growl.

Jax holds up his hands in defense. "Whoa, easy there, Ride. Just asking."

I run a hand down my face and try to pull myself together. Last night's nightmare has left me drained, and this morning's slow-burn with Noia has my body wound tight—so yeah, not the best combination.

"Sorry," I mutter. "Didn't sleep much."

A flash of concern crosses Jax's face. "Nightmare?"

Even though Jax is one of the few people who stuck by me through the worst of my PTSD and pill addiction after I got out of the Marines, I just nod, not wanting to get into it.

"Have you talked to Claire about it yet?"

"No. It's fine. Just a rough night. It's the first in a long time, actually."

"If you say so." But he doesn't look convinced. "Anyway, we're meeting Claire at The Brew at six to finalize the party details. You still good with that?"

"Yeah, I'll be there."

Fuck. Even after talking with my best friend, my dick is still hard.

I adjust myself in my jeans and force my attention back to my work. I have two more clients today and a mountain of paperwork to get through before meeting up with Claire and Jax.

By the time six o'clock rolls around, I'm exhausted, but somewhat more focused.

The Brew is only a couple of blocks from the shop, so I walk, hoping the cool evening air will clear my head.

It looks exactly like I remember it. The converted warehouse has exposed brick walls and high ceilings. Decorated with oxblood leather booths, the rest of the place has wood and metal accents.

The building itself is split in two, with a restaurant on one side and a bar with a dance floor, pool tables, dartboards and a jukebox on the other. Warm amber light floods the space from Edison bulbs hanging from the ceiling.

Claire is sitting with Jax at a high-top table near the bar, nursing what looks like her typical drink of choice, a vodka soda. Her purple hair is pulled back in a messy bun, and she's wearing her usual black jeans and vintage band T-shirt. She's surrounded by paperwork and talking animatedly to a tall, bearded man I don't recognize until a memory slams into my brain.

Owen, owner of The Brew.

"Hey, Ride!" she grins.

"Hey, Cee Cee." I clasp her shoulder in greeting before nodding to Owen. "Appreciate you letting us take over tomorrow night."

"Are you kidding? You and your clientele are half my business most weeks." Owen's laugh is a deep rumble. "Plus, ten years is a big deal. You need to celebrate the right way."

I slide onto the stool next to Jax, who pushes a beer toward me.

"Already ordered for you," he says. "Figured you could use it."

"Thanks." I take a long pull from the bottle, the cold liquid soothing my dry throat.

"So," Claire slides a paper across the table. "Here's the final guest list. We're looking at about seventy people."

"Seventy?" I raise my eyebrows. "That's more than I expected."

"Well, we invited all the regulars, plus a bunch of former clients who moved away but said they'd come back for this." She taps her pen on the paper. "And, of course, everyone is allowed to bring a plus-one."

"Speaking of plus-ones," Jax smirks. "You gonna bring your writer girlfriend?"

Claire's head snaps up. "Girlfriend? What girlfriend?"

I shoot Jax a death glare. "She's not my girlfriend."

"Yet," Jax adds with a shit-eating grin.

"Hold up." Claire leans forward, eyes narrowed. "You're dating someone? And I'm just hearing about this *now*?"

"It's... complicated," I mutter, taking another swig of my beer.

"Her name is Noia," Jax supplies not so helpfully. "And she writes steamy romance novels."

Claire's eyebrows shoot up so high they nearly disappear into her hairline. "*You're* dating a romance novelist?"

"What the hell is that supposed to mean?" I growl.

"Just that she doesn't sound like your usual type," she says, echoing Jax's previous misconception. "But seriously, a writer? That's... unexpected."

"She's different," I say, feeling oddly defensive. "Super smart and talented."

Claire studies my face, her expression softening. "You really like this girl."

"Yeah. I do."

"Well, I can't wait," she says with a mischievous glint in her eyes. "I need to meet the woman who's finally managed to crack that titanium shell of yours."

"Don't go getting any ideas," I warn. "None of 'Claire's Third Degree.'"

"What? I would never," she says with mock innocence.

"Bullshit," Jax coughs into his fist.

We spend the next hour going over final details for the party —the food, drinks and music. Owen is bringing in extra staff, and we've hired a local band for the first half of the night before we switch to a DJ.

"This is going to be awesome," Jax says, clinking his beer bottle against mine. "The biggest party Skin & Ink has ever had."

"Let's hope nothing burns down this time," Claire adds with a wink.

"Accidentally setting a trash can on fire does not constitute burning something down," I say, rolling my eyes. "You're never going to let me forget that, are you?"

"Nope," Jax chimes in.

After finalizing the last details with Owen, I check my watch. It's just shy of eight o'clock. Hanging out with my friends made time fly.

"I should head out." I slide off the stool. "Got an early client tomorrow before we close up shop for the party."

Claire gives me a quick hug. "Make sure you bring your girl tomorrow. I can't wait to meet her."

"We'll see," I grunt, knowing I have every intention of showing Noia off.

The ride home takes longer than usual with Friday night traffic. You would think a small town in the mountains wouldn't have that problem, but you'd be wrong.

By the time I pull into the driveway, my shoulders are tight with exhaustion. An unfamiliar blue Mazda is parked next to Noia's SUV and I suddenly remember her friend Sasha is visiting this weekend.

Great. Just what I need. An audience for our slow-burn standoff. Guess I'll have to take it down a notch while she's around.

The house is quiet, but I can hear muffled voices and occasional bursts of laughter coming from upstairs. I recognize Noia's melodic giggle, followed by another woman's throaty laugh.

In the kitchen, I pour myself two fingers of whiskey and down it before pouring another, the liquor easing some of the tension from my shoulders.

Another round of giggles erupts from upstairs, followed by a hushed "Shhh!" then more giggles.

Wanting to give them and myself some space, I grab my

glass and head to my bathroom for a much-needed shower. The hot water pounds against my back as the steam clears my head.

After toweling off, I put on a pair of boxers and collapse onto my bed with a groan. Goonie appears almost immediately, jumping up beside me and settling into the crook of my arm with a contented purr.

"Looks like it's just you and me tonight, pudge," I murmur, scratching behind his ears.

The warmth of his soft body against my side is oddly comforting, and I find myself drifting into the soft darkness of dreamless sleep with Goonie's steady purr as my lullaby.

I HOLD UP THE TINY PINK PAIR OF PAJAMA SHORTS, scanning it with a critical eye. If Ryder plans on slow-burning me this morning, I might as well start things off with a bang.

Sasha always takes a shower right after she gets up; it's the only way she can get her ass in gear. So, while she's up here? I'm going to go down there and slow-burn his ass first.

Rummaging through my top drawer, I find a thin, white, practically see-through, tiny cutoff tank. I pull it on and turn to check my profile in the full-length mirror.

Nipples pebbled with excitement, my areolas are a little on the dark side, so I can just make out the circular rim through the fabric.

I run my hands through my hair to give it that 'just rolled out of bed' look, then pinch my cheeks for a little color. Perfect. With one last glance in the mirror, I head downstairs.

Ryder is sitting at the kitchen island with his broad back facing me. Only wearing a pair of gray sweatpants, his muscular shoulders and tattooed arms are on full display. His attention is focused on the book I picked for him, per his request at the bookstore.

Damn. Men that read are so fucking sexy. And men that read romance? A whole other level.

I take my time, making sure to stretch a little higher than necessary as I reach for a mug from the cabinet. This causes my tank to ride up, exposing the under part of my boob. Cool air brushes against my skin, making goosebumps rise across my flesh.

Thankfully, the coffeepot is still hot and I pour myself a cup, take a small sip and let out a soft, satisfied moan.

Behind me, I hear a low growl and mentally give myself a fist bump before slowly turning around.

Ryder is staring me down, eyes full of fire.

His gaze drops to my chest, then quickly back to my face before he drags it from my toes to my tits. The intensity of how he is studying me makes my nipples tighten even harder against the thin fabric.

"What do you think you're doing, kitten?" he growls.

His voice is rough and dangerous and I have to fight not to clench my thighs together in response.

Forcing the shiver away, I give him an innocent blink as I take another sip of my coffee. "Whatever do you mean, Rye?"

His jaw flexes as he slowly closes the book and sets it aside.

Rising from the stool, he rounds the island with predatory grace, keeping his eyes locked with mine.

As he stands before me, he's so close, the fresh scent of his sandalwood body wash assaults my nose. His storm gray eyes are dark and his pupils are blown, with a fire burning in their depths that practically turns my legs to jelly.

His voice drops to a murmur as his fingers brush against my bare arm. "You know *exactly* what I mean."

I swallow hard, doing everything I can to maintain my composure. "I'm just having my morning coffee."

"Dressed in *that?*" His eyes flick down to my barely there outfit again. "Where's your robe?"

Ignoring his last question, I ask, "What's wrong with what I'm wearing?" I flutter my lashes, attempting to feign innocence, all while fighting to keep my breathing steady.

"Nothing," he answers, taking the mug from my hand and setting it on the counter away from me. The movement brings him even closer. "In fact, I think it's perfect."

My breath catches as his hand comes up, fingers tracing the curve of my collarbone, then slowly trails them down my arm, leaving a riot of goosebumps in their wake.

The shower turns on upstairs and Ryder's eyes flick up, then back down to mine. A slow smirk pulls at his lips.

Then his hands grip my waist, and before I'm able to process what is happening, he effortlessly lifts me up and onto the counter. My bare thighs hit the cool marble, making me gasp.

"You think you can just come down here and pull a slow-burn on me?" he murmurs as his fingers start tracing light, maddening circles on my thighs.

His touch sends sparks of electricity up my legs and straight to my core, making my breath hitch. "I don't know what you're talking about," I squeak.

He leans in until his lips are a whisper away. "Two can play, kitten."

Oh, *shit*.

Then his mouth, hot and demanding, crashes down on mine. His tongue forces its way past my lips, claiming my mouth as he explores.

What started out as gentle circles, turns to fingers digging into flesh as he shoves my legs wide open and steps between them.

Just as I thread my fingers through his hair and arch into

him, he breaks the kiss, leaving me gasping, my lips tingling as my body aches for more.

Then, without warning, he bends down and hoists me over his shoulder.

"What are you doing?!" I yelp.

Blood rushes to my head, and all I can see is his firm, muscular ass. The only response I get is a grunt as he secures one arm tight around my thighs.

Palming his other hand on my ass, he squeezes, then gives it a smack, forcing another yelp from my throat as he takes the stairs, two at a time.

When we get to my bedroom, he stalks inside and deposits me unceremoniously on my feet in the middle of the floor.

Disoriented from being suddenly upright again, I can only stand there and wobble as his eyes rake over me, blazing with heat and something along the lines of triumph.

His sweats ride low on his hips, showing off the vee in the middle of his tapered waist. And he's hard.

"Get dressed, Noia," he orders, voice low and controlled as he shoves a hand through his already disheveled hair.

Then he turns and walks out, closing the door firmly behind him.

Mouth open in shock, my heart pounds as my body continues to thrum with need.

"What the... Jerk!" I finally sputter, stomping my foot in frustration.

The shower down the hall shuts off, and I hear Sasha humming to herself.

Shit! I need to pull myself together before she sees me like this.

Stalking into my closet to grab the first thing I can find, I pull on a sports bra—which will force my nipples into submission—then tug on a pair of jeans and a light blue sweater.

Damn if giving me a taste of my own medicine didn't work perfectly. Now *I'm* the one left wanting again, my body still tingling from his touch.

By the time Sasha knocks on my door, I've managed to tame my hair and somewhat calm my breathing.

"Come in!"

"Was that Ryder I just saw stalking down the hall with resting murder all over his face?" she asks as she steps into the room.

Eyebrows raised, she has her hands on her hips. "And why does your face look like it just got caught with its nose in the cookie jar?"

I smooth my hands over my jeans, trying to regain my composure. "He just... We were just... Ugh!"

Sasha's eyes pop. "Oh. My. God. You pulled a slow-burn on him while I was in the shower, didn't you? You little slut monkey!"

"Maybe." I collapse onto my bed. "And it was working too—until he turned the tables on me, again."

"Details."

With an exasperated sigh, I let 'er rip. "I put on a skimpy pair of shorts and a tank top that was virtually see through and went down to mess with him. But he just lifted me onto the counter, kissed me senseless, then literally through me over his shoulder, carried me upstairs, dumped me in the middle of the floor and growled at me to get dressed."

I groan. "Then he left."

Grabbing a pillow, I bury my face in it. "This slow-burn game is torture."

"Isn't that the point?" Sasha laughs, sitting next to me on the bed. "All I know is that this is the best form of entertainment I've had in months. Maybe my whole life, actually."

"I'm so glad my sexual frustration *amuses* you," I mutter into the pillow as I flop back onto the bed.

"Oh it does. It definitely does," she grins as she flops onto the bed beside me. "But I'll bet he's just as frustrated as you are." She barks out a laugh. "Pretty sure I saw just how frustrated he is, too. Caught a glimpse of... Well, let's just say... Congratulations?"

I toss the pillow at her head. "Fuck's sake, Sash."

She swats it aside. "So, what's the plan now? Because from where I'm sitting, it hella looks like he's winning."

ryder

Fuck. Fuck. Fuckit-y. Fuck.

Chest heaving, I slam my bedroom door closed and slump against it, cock hard.

When I looked up and saw what Noia was wearing, I nearly fell off the stool. The image of her in those tiny shorts and that effing see-through tank is now burned into my retinas for all of eternity.

The way her nipples pebbled beneath the thin fabric, and how her skin flushed even before I touched her—it took every ounce of self-control I possessed to walk away after I dumped her in her room.

This shit is just going to keep getting harder, and I still have some other stuff planned for next week before I let myself take her again.

"Goddammit," I growl, yanking open the dresser drawer with almost enough force to pull it all the way out and onto the floor.

I grab the first clean shirt I find and pull it over my head, then snatch my leather jacket off its hook. I need to get out of here before I march back upstairs and finish what we started, friend visiting or not.

Grabbing my keys and wallet, I storm through the living room and out the front door. The cool morning air does nothing to calm the fire raging like lava in my veins as I climb onto my motorcycle.

The engine roars to life, the vibrations between my thighs only intensifying my frustration. I tear out of the driveway, riding faster than I should on the winding mountain roads.

By the time I arrive at Skin & Ink, my breathing has evened out, but the tension in my body is still coiled tight. The shop is quiet when I walk in, with only Claire at the front desk.

"Whoa," she says, taking one look at my face. "Who pissed in your oatmeal this morning?"

"Not now," I toss out as I head straight for my station.

"Your client called. She's running about twenty minutes late."

Perfect. More time to stew in my sexual frustration.

I busy myself setting up my station. The methodical process helps ground me only for a few minutes before thoughts of Noia and her perfect nipples attempting to cut their way through her tank top take over again.

When my client finally arrives, I slip right into professional mode. The familiar buzz of the tattoo machine drowns out everything else as I lose myself in my art.

It's a small tattoo, so I'm able to finish within a couple of hours.

After sending my client off with aftercare instructions, I clean up.

"Ready to head over?" Claire calls from up front. "Jax texted. He and Lizzy are already at The Brew getting things set up."

"The party doesn't start till eight."

"Yeah, and there's a shit-ton to do before then." She raises a brow. "Unless you have somewhere better to be?"

Images of Noia in those tiny shorts flash through my mind, and I almost groan out loud. "No. Let's go. Just let me grab my jacket."

Tossing my gloves in the trash, I roll my shoulders, trying to release some of the tension.

"You still haven't told me what's got you so wound up lately," Claire says as she locks up the shop.

"Seriously," I grunt. "It's nothing you need to worry about."

The walk to The Brew is short, but Claire manages to interrogate me the entire way.

"So, this writer friend of yours... is she coming tonight?"

"Her name is Noia," I sigh, shoving my hands into my pockets. "And yes, Cee Cee, she's coming. So is her best friend, Sasha, who's visiting for the weekend."

"Perfect. More witnesses for when I embarrass the hell out of you with stories from your apprentice days."

Despite my mood, her laugh is infectious.

"You wouldn't dare."

"Try me, Blackwood."

When we walk into The Brew, the place is already buzzing. Staff members are arranging tables and setting up the bar while Jax directs a couple of guys hanging a massive "10 Years of Skin & Ink" banner across the back wall.

Lizzy is standing on a ladder, stringing up fairy lights along the exposed beams. Her blue-tipped hair is pulled up into a high ponytail, and she's wearing ripped jeans and a tank top that shows off her colorful tattoos.

"Thank god you two are here," she calls down when she spots us. "Jax has been driving me crazy with all his micromanaging."

"I heard that!" Jax shouts from across the room.

Claire chuckles and heads toward the bar to check on the alcohol delivery while I make my way over to hold the ladder steady as Lizzy steps down.

"Thanks," she says breathlessly, wiping her hands on her jeans. "These lights are a bitch to hang."

"They look good." I glance around, impressed by how much they've already accomplished. "Need help with anything else?"

"Yeah, actually. Owen just dropped off the centerpieces. They're in those boxes over by the DJ booth. Could you start setting them up on the tables?"

I nod and make my way over to open a box. Each centerpiece is a small, vintage tattoo machine surrounded by black and red roses, which was Claire's idea.

As I work, I wonder what Noia is going to think about all this. Will she feel comfortable around my friends and colleagues? Will they like her? Fuck... will she like *them*?

Just the idea of those two parts of my life colliding is more than unnerving.

noia

"You know what?" Struck with inspiration, I sit up. "I'm starving and I really need to get out of this house before I lose my mind. There's this cute little diner right across the street from Ryder's tattoo shop. We could grab some breakfast."

Sasha's face lights up with mischief. "You want to do a reconnaissance mission on your fictional-turned-real boyfriend's tattoo parlor? I'm one hundred percent in."

"He's not my boyfriend." But my protest comes out weak.

"Honey, the man carried you over his shoulder like a caveman. Sounds like boyfriend territory to me." She turns to head upstairs. "Besides, I want to see the place where all the magic happens."

"The magic happens here," I correct her, then immediately blush when I realize how that sounds.

"I mean his *tattoo* magic," she snickers down at me from the top step. "But clearly your mind is elsewhere. Give me five minutes to finish getting ready."

Twenty minutes later, we're in Sasha's car heading toward town. I direct her through the winding roads until we reach

Main Street, where most of the small businesses are clustered together.

"That's it," I say, pointing at the building to my right. "And the diner is just there, across the street."

Sasha pulls into a parking spot in front of the diner and cuts the engine. "Perfect location for spying."

"We're not spying," I insist, my stomach fluttering with nervous excitement. "We're just... having breakfast in a strategic location."

Rise & Dine is exactly what you'd expect—red and white checkered floors, black vinyl booths, with the smell of coffee and waffles saturating the air. We grab a front booth by the window that provides a clear view of Skin & Ink Tattoo.

"So that's where he works," Sasha muses. "It looks... nice."

"What did you expect? Some little shop in a seedy back-alley with a flashing neon sign?"

"Kind of, yeah," she admits with a laugh. "Given how you described him as broody and dangerous."

A waitress comes over and hands us menus. "Morning, ladies. Welcome to Rise & Dine. What can I get you?"

After we both order the Belgian waffle special, I steal a glance across the street.

"You know, it's so weird. Even though I'm the one who thought him up, he's got this whole other life now that has nothing to do with me," I say, stirring cream into my coffee. "Friends, a business, clients who know and trust him."

"That's what makes this all so fascinating." Sasha leans forward, resting her arms on the table. "He's becoming real in every sense of the word. Pun intended," she grins and I roll my eyes.

"You know how he's been taking me on day dates for inspiration?"

"Yeah."

"He took me for a ride on his motorcycle up the coast to this little seafood place. It was..." I pause, searching for the right words. "It was actually perfect."

Sasha leans back, looking impressed. "Damn, girl. That's romantic as hell."

"I know. And that's what makes me nervous. It's like he understands exactly what I need, sometimes even before I do." I stare out the window. "Each date is designed to push me just far enough out of my comfort zone that I feel... inspired to write."

"And that's bad because...?"

"Because what if this is temporary? What if once I finish my book, he just... goes poof?" My voice drops to a strangled whisper. "I don't think I could handle that, Sash."

She reaches across the table and squeezes my hand. "Has there been any indication he's becoming less real?"

"No, the opposite, actually. First his truck shows up, then his clothes, now his motorcycle..." I wave at the building across the street. "...the tattoo shop." I take a deep breath. "His past is starting to fill in too—memories, friends, his whole life story."

"Then stop worrying about the future and just enjoy what's happening now."

"Also, Goonie has all but abandoned me for him. And yesterday, Ryder didn't look so good. Almost like he hadn't slept in days."

Sasha taps her fingers thoughtfully against her coffee mug. "Maybe he had a nightmare? PTSD is a big part of his backstory, right?"

Guilt washes over me as I nod slowly. "I didn't even think about that. God, I'm so selfish! I've been so focused on my own issues, I didn't even think to consider that as a factor."

"Hey, this whole situation is uncharted territory for both of you. Cut yourself some slack." She tilts her head. "Cats are very intuitive, you know. Maybe Goonie is picking up on what he's feeling."

"Yeah. I think you could be right."

Our food arrives, and I cut into my waffle.

"What's our plan for getting ready for tonight?" Sasha asks around a mouthful of food. "This party tonight sounds like a big deal."

"I'm nervous," I confess. "Meeting all his friends and colleagues *is* a big deal."

"Don't worry. I'll be there for moral support."

"You just want to see if Ryder has any hot friends."

"Possible bonus," she grins, then her expression sobers. "But seriously, I'm glad this is happening. The universe picked up on what you needed and literally made it appear."

After paying the bill, we head out into the crisp morning air. When we reach the car, Sasha grabs my arm.

"Wait a minute." Her eyes light up with a dangerous gleam I know all too well. "We can't go to this party without proper ammunition."

"Ammunition?" I raise an eyebrow. "What kind are you talkin'?"

"You said you wanted to up the ante on his slow-burn game, right?" She waggles her eyebrows and jingles her keys. "We need to go shopping. Get you something that'll make his eyes pop out of their sockets."

"Sasha—"

"I saw this boutique a few blocks back." She looks at me over the hood as she unlocks the car. "The window display had this little black dress that would look phenomenal on you."

"I don't need a new dress," I protest weakly as I climb into the passenger seat.

"Oh, honey," she laughs, starting the engine. "This isn't

about need. This is about psychological warfare—and we're going to make sure you're armed with something nuclear."

Twenty minutes later, I'm in a dressing room surrounded by dozens of rejects. Still, Sasha keeps passing more options over the door, each one skimpier than the last.

"Try the red one next," she says through the door. "Red is the color of passion. And revenge."

"I'm not trying to get revenge," I mutter, but slip it on anyway.

When I step out, Sasha's jaw drops. "Holy shit. That's the one."

The deep crimson dress hugs every curve, ending mid-thigh. The neckline dips just low enough to show a good amount of cleavage, while the back features a large diamond cutout that exposes most of my spine.

"It's... a lot," I say, running my hands down the silky fabric.

"It's fucking perfect," Sasha corrects. "You look like sex on legs. He'll take one look at you in this and completely forget about any kind of slow-burn and jump straight into shoving his hands up your dress and into your panties."

I bite my lip, considering.

"We're getting it." She crosses her arms and gives me a quick, decisive nod. "And those black strappy heels we saw in the window."

By the time we leave the boutique, I'm the proud owner of not just the skimpy red dress and heels, but a matching set of black lace lingerie Sasha insisted was 'essential battle gear.'

FOR THE REST OF THE AFTERNOON WE VEG OUT IN FRONT of the TV with Goonie, watching movies and eating snacks.

Just after five o'clock, I get a text.

RYDER: *Change of plans. Need to stay at The Brew to help finish setting up. Party starts at 8. Meet me here?*

I hold the phone up for Sasha to see. "Looks like we're meeting him there instead."

"Perfect!" Sasha claps her hands together. "Plenty of time to get you looking even more irresistible."

I text back a quick 'That's fine' before tossing my phone aside.

Suddenly nervous, I mutter, "I'm starting to rethink this whole dress situation."

"No way." Sasha grabs my arm and pulls me off the couch. "You're wearing that dress, and it's going to make him regret this entire slow-burn thing."

Two hours later, I barely recognize myself. The dress makes my waist look tiny and my hips deliciously full. Sasha has worked her magic on my hair, styling it in loose waves that cascade down my back, and my makeup—dark smoky eyes and deep red lips to match the dress—is sultrier than anything I would normally wear.

"Holy shit," I whisper, smoothing my hands down my hips.

"I know, right?" Sasha appears behind me. Hair down, she looks stunning in a short black dress with a plunging neckline, and a silver pair of heels. "We look hot as hell."

I look at the clock and realize it's five minutes to eight. Guess we took a little more time getting ready than we planned.

My phone buzzes again.

RYDER: *You on your way?*

"We're running late and he's getting impatient," I say, feeling a flutter of anticipation in my stomach.

"Good. Let him wait." She grabs her purse and tosses me a small tube of lipstick. "For touch-ups. You're going to need it after he sees you in that dress."

At 8:05, we're climbing into Sasha's car.

"Ready?" she asks, eyes gleaming with mischief.

I let out a shaky breath. "God, I hope so."

With the way Sasha drives, it takes less than fifteen minutes to get to town, but it still feels like forever.

The Brew looks completely transformed when we pull up. Strings of twinkling lights hang over the entrance, and I can see a crowd already starting to form inside.

"Deep breath," Sasha says, squeezing my hand as we walk toward the door. "Remember, you're the 'Queen of Steam.' You can do this."

The moment we step inside, the energy hits me hard. The music is loud, the bass is thumping, and the space is packed with people—most of whom are heavily tattooed.

"Now we just need to find your man," Sasha shouts over the music as she scans the crowd.

I spot him before she does. Standing at the bar, he's wearing dark jeans and a tight black T-shirt, talking to a woman with vibrant purple hair. Even from across the room, his presence is magnetic.

Then, just like in the movies, he turns in slow motion, eyes darting around the room until his eyes land on me.

ryder

One minute I'm talking to Claire and the next, something shifts in the air, forcing me to turn around.

The world around me disappears, the music fading to a dull thrum as the crowd blurs into insignificant shadows. Even Claire's voice sounds distant to my ears as my eyes lock onto Noia standing across the room.

Holy. Fucking. Christ.

Wearing a crimson dress that hugs every curve of her body as if it was painted on, the neckline dips low enough to make my mouth suddenly go dry. Hair falling in golden waves around her shoulders, her toned legs are highlighted by black heels that make her look like she just stepped out of one of her own novels.

My eyes lock with hers and the next thing I know, I'm striding across the room.

I stop just close enough to catch the subtle scent of her perfume. My hands itch to touch her, to verify she's real and not some sexy figment of my imagination.

Right. Like I'm one to talk.

"You're here," I manage, my voice rough.

Her lips, painted the same deep red as her dress, curve into a smile that nearly brings me to my knees.

"I am," she answers with a hint of nervousness in her voice. "Is this okay? The dress, I mean."

"Okay?" I can't help the incredulous laugh that escapes. "Kitten, you look fucking incredible."

The woman beside her clears her throat dramatically. "And apparently, I'm invisible."

Tearing my eyes away from Noia takes all that I've got, but I manage to offer my hand to her friend. "You must be Sasha. I'm Ryder."

"Oh, I know exactly who you are," she says with a knowing smirk, shaking my hand. "Noia has told me all about you."

"Has she?" I glance at Noia, whose cheeks are now flushed my favorite shade of pink.

"Don't worry," Sasha winks. "Only good stuff. Well, mostly."

Before I can respond, Sasha narrows her eyes and leans in close, studying my face with an intensity that almost makes me take a step back.

"Huh."

The sharp smack of her palms when they connect with my face echoes loudly enough to turn a few heads. Pressing her fingers firmly into my skin, she kneads and squishes my cheeks like they're made of fucking Play-Dough.

"You really weren't giving me shit, were you? He *is* real," she says to Noia, eyes wide with disbelief as she continues massaging my face.

"Jesus, Sash." Noia shifts awkwardly and sighs. "Of course I wasn't."

The initial shock takes about another ten seconds to wear off. "You 'bout done?" I ask, my question coming out muffled from between my squished lips.

Sasha's eyes go wide before she quickly drops her hands and takes a step back. "Oops. Sorry."

"It's fine," I say, rubbing my jaw. "Last thing I expected was an impromptu face massage."

"Had to make sure." Sasha looks a little dazed. "I mean, Noia told me everything, but seeing is believing, ya know?"

"Right. Well, now that we've established I'm real and not just a figment of anyone's imagination," I say dryly, "how about I buy you ladies a drink?"

"God, yes." Noia looks mortified. "Something strong."

"Come with me." Placing my hand on the small of her back, I guide her toward the bar. The moment my fingers touch the bare skin exposed by the cutout in her dress, my dick gets hard.

Jesus.

Sasha follows behind us, but when we reach the bar, her eyes snag on something across the room. "I think I'm going to explore," she announces. "You two kids catch up."

Noia's friend disappears into the crowd, leaving us alone in our little bubble amidst the chaos.

"Your friend is..." I search for the right word.

"An incorrigible smart ass?" Noia grins.

"Something like that."

"Sorry."

"Don't worry about it."

I glance over Noia's head to see Sasha making a beeline straight for Jax, who's leaning against the wall near the DJ booth scrolling through his phone. She flips her red hair over her shoulder, and even from where I'm standing, when he glances up, I can see his eyes widen with sudden interest.

"Well, would you look at that," I murmur, nodding in their direction. "Your best friend just found mine."

Noia turns to follow my gaze, her eyes widening slightly.

"Oh shit. That's your best friend? Sasha's going to eat him alive."

"Jax can more than handle himself," I chuckle, signaling the bartender. "Two whiskeys, neat." I glance at her. "Unless you'd like something else?"

"No, whiskey's perfect, thanks."

The bartender pours our drinks, and I shift closer. I let my fingers drift in slow, deliberate circles against her spine, loving how she shivers beneath my touch.

"You wore this dress on purpose, didn't you, kitten?" I ask, my voice dropping to a low rumble only she can hear. "To drive me crazy."

I feel more than hear her breath catch, smirking when she tries her best to maintain her composure. "You're reading too much into it. It's a party, so I dressed up."

I smile against her hair, keeping the slow torturous circles swirling over her lower back before dipping my fingers just slightly beneath the fabric. "Liar."

The bartender slides our drinks across the counter. I hand one to Noia, making sure our fingers brush as she takes the glass.

"To slow-burns," I wink, clinking my glass against hers.

"And whoever gives in first," she says before taking a sip.

"That's gonna be you, kitten."

With a snort, she takes another sip, eyes locking with mine over the rim. When she lowers the glass, there's a perfect imprint of her red lips on the edge and all I can do is imagine the same imprint smudging the base of my cock.

It's at that moment Claire chooses to appear. "This must be the famous Noia!"

Reluctantly, I drop my hand from Noia's back. "Noia, this is Claire. Manager, mentor and a royal pain in my ass."

"Charmed," Claire says, looking Noia up and down with

open approval. "Well done, Ride. This one's definitely way out of your league."

Noia laughs, extending her hand. "It's nice to meet you. Ryder's told me a lot about you."

"All petty little lies, I'm sure," Claire winks. "We've all been dying to meet the woman who's got our boy here walking around with his head in the clouds."

"I do not have my head in the clouds," I growl.

"Sure, buddy." Claire pats my shoulder. "It's not like you haven't been spacing out for days, checking your phone every five minutes."

Noia's eyes dance. "Is that so?"

"Don't listen to her," I mutter, taking a long sip of whiskey. "She's full of shit."

"Oh, I'm definitely listening," Noia grins, leaning in close. "What else has he been doing?"

Claire's smile turns wicked. "Well, there was that time he was so distracted he accidentally tattooed 'No Ragrets' instead of 'No Regrets'—"

"That never happened," I interject, glaring at Claire. "Now she's making shit up."

With a grin, Clair raises an eyebrow, then turns back to Noia. "But seriously, it's great to finally meet you."

"Nice to meet you too."

"Come on." I gladly place my hand on the small of her back again. "Let me introduce you to some other people before Claire starts making more shit up."

"Oh, yeah. There's much more where that came from!" Claire calls after us as I quickly guide Noia through the crowd.

"Everyone is staring," she whispers, pressing closer to me.

"Can you blame them?" I murmur against her ear, wrapping my arm around her waist. "You're the most beautiful woman in the room."

Her cheeks flush pink again, and it's all I can do not to drag her into a dark corner and show her exactly what that dress is doing to me.

I introduce Noia to Lizzy and Owen, who immediately make her feel welcome. Lizzy, in particular, is thrilled to meet her.

"A romance novelist?" she gushes. "That's so cool! I've always wanted to write a book."

"You have?" I ask incredulously.

"It's not as glamorous as it sounds," Noia laughs. "It's mostly just me in my pajamas, drinking too much coffee and talking to my cat."

"Still, how cool would it be to create whole new worlds and characters," Lizzy sighs dreamily.

When I catch Noia's eye, something unspoken passes between us. If Lizzy only knew just how real those characters could become.

"It has its moments," Noia says softly, her eyes never leaving mine.

The temperature in the room seems to spike about ten degrees. I'm about to suggest we step outside for some air when Jax shows up, Sasha in tow.

"Jax," I nod, noticing how comfortable he and Sasha look together. "I see you've met Noia's best friend, Sasha."

"We've been getting acquainted," Sasha grins. The mischievous glint in her eye tells me everything I need to know about what direction they're heading tonight.

"You're Ryder's partner?" Noia asks.

"Co-owner," Jax corrects with a grin. "Equal partners in ink and crime."

"And bad jokes, apparently," I mutter, which earns me a punch in the shoulder.

Sasha's expression turns coy as she swirls her cocktail. "Jax was just telling me about your apprentice days. Something about you passing out during your first piercing?"

I shoot Jax a death glare.

"What?" He grins at me maliciously. "It's a good story! Big, bad Marine gets taken out by a needle and a little blood."

Noia's eyes widen with delight. "You passed out?"

"I did not pass out," I growl. "I got lightheaded." I shoot Jax another scowl. "There's a difference."

"He hit the floor like a sack of potatoes," Jax stage-whispers. "Pretty sure Claire has it on video somewhere."

"That video better miraculously disappear," I warn, with no real heat behind it. The way Noia is laughing, eyes bright, makes it impossible for me to stay annoyed.

"I'd pay good money to see that," she teases, running a finger down my arm.

The simple touch has me leaning in, lips nearly grazing her ear. "Keep touching me like that and I might have to whisk you off into a dark corner somewhere, kitten."

Her breath catches, but she recovers quickly. "Promises, promises."

"We should go get another round," Sasha announces, grabbing Jax's arm. "You two want anything?"

"We're good," I answer, eyes still locked on Noia's.

The moment they walk away, I slide my hand around to the small of her back. Tucking my fingers into the lower part of her dress, I tug gently on the hem of her panties. "Dance with me."

With a shiver, she nods and allows me to guide her to the dance floor where the DJ has slowed things down.

THIRTY-FIVE

THE MOMENT RYDER'S ARMS WRAP AROUND ME, everything and everyone else in the room disappears. His big hands settle on my hips, pulling me in close. As we sway to the music, the heat from his body seeps through the thin fabric of my dress, making my skin tingle.

"You're playing with fire wearing this dress," he murmurs, breath hot against my ear.

I tilt my head back to look at him, trying to maintain some semblance of control even as my body melts into his. "Maybe that's what I want."

His gray eyes darken, and his grip on my hips tightens. "Careful, kitten. You're about to find out exactly how hot things can get."

The song shifts to something more sensual, and Ryder pulls me even closer. My breasts are smashed against his chest, and I can feel the rapid thrum of his heartbeat. His hands drift lower, fingers tracing the edge of my ass, making me shiver.

"You're not playing fair," I pant.

"Neither are you," he growls back, his lips brushing against my temple. "The way you look tonight should be illegal."

"A little heavy on the cliché's tonight, aren't we?"

But he just keeps looking at me like I'm the only woman in the world as everything around us fades away.

"Rye," I breathe, not sure what I'm asking for.

"I know," he says, and I know he can hear the need in my voice. "Not yet."

The song ends, but he doesn't let go. Instead, he takes my hand and leads me off the dance floor, past the bar and into a quieter corner.

"Having fun?" he asks, voice tight.

"More than I thought I would," I admit, smoothing down my dress with shaky hands. "Your friends are great."

"They like you." He takes my hand and starts tracing circles on my wrist with his thumb. "Pretty sure Claire has already come up with a plan to adopt you."

My laugh comes out breathless. "She's protective of you."

"Yes. They all are." His expression grows serious. "This..." He gestures between us. "...means something to them—to me."

Before I can respond, Sasha reappears with Jax, both looking slightly disheveled and grinning like a couple of teenagers.

"Having fun?" Sasha asks, though her attention is clearly divided between me and the tall, dark-haired man beside her.

"Sure am," I say, doing my best to ignore the way Ryder's thumb is still stroking my wrist.

"Good," Jax grins. "Claire's about to give her speech, and then the real party begins."

As if summoned, Claire appears on the small stage at the front of the room, music fading away as she taps the microphone.

"Ladies and degenerates," she smiles. "Welcome to Skin & Ink's tenth anniversary party!"

Cheers erupt, and Ryder's hand squeezes mine.

"Ten years ago, two young idiots with more talent than sense decided to open a tattoo shop," Claire continues. Her gaze finds Ryder and Jax in the crowd. "One a former Marine with anger issues who couldn't watch someone get their ears pierced without fainting—"

"For fuck's sake," Ryder mutters with affection in his voice.

"—and the other was a college dropout who couldn't even tattoo a fucking dot."

Laughter ripples through the crowd as Jax nods and grins, raising his beer in affirmation.

"But somehow, against all odds, these two knuckleheads managed to build something special. Something that's become more than just a business—it's family." Claire's voice softens. "I've watched these two grow from talented but clueless apprentices into artists who change lives with their work. Amazing humans who help people to reclaim their bodies, tell their stories, and heal."

The sincerity in her voice makes my throat tighten. These people, this place, what they've built together—what Ryder has built—is as real as it gets.

Claire raises her glass. "To Ryder and Jax, who turned a dump into a dynasty. To our clients, who trust us with their stories. And to ten more years of tattoos, inspiration, and insanity!"

The room erupts in cheers as everyone raises their glasses and Ryder slides his arm around my waist, pulling me close as he tips back his drink.

"Speech!" someone shouts from the crowd, and soon the entire room is chanting, "Speech! Speech!"

Ryder groans. "I hate speaking in public."

"Go on," I nudge him. "You've got this."

With a resigned sigh, he squeezes my hip before making his

way to the stage. The crowd parts and I watch, mesmerized, as he takes the microphone from Claire.

"I'll keep this short," he says, voice deep and commanding. Then he clears his throat. "I'm not big on speeches."

The crowd laughs, and I see his shoulders relax.

"A little over ten years ago, I was in a really bad place. Angry. Lost." His eyes find mine across the room. "Claire took a chance on me when no one else would. Jax believed in me when I didn't even believe in myself."

He pauses, clearing his throat. "Skin & Ink isn't just a business. It's home. It's family. And every person in this room has been part of that in some form or another."

The sincerity in his voice makes my chest ache. This is a side of him I've never seen—vulnerable, grateful, humble.

"So, thank you," he continues. "For trusting us with your stories, your skin, and your friendship. Here's to ten more years."

The crowd erupts in applause as he hands the microphone back to Claire and steps off the stage. When he's back by my side, I can't help but smile up at him.

"That was beautiful," I say softly.

"It was fucking terrifying," he huffs, but his lips quirk up at the corners.

I look back at the crowd moving back onto the dance floor as the music starts up again.

My neck tingles and I glance up to find Ryder watching me.

"What?" I ask, suddenly self-conscious.

"I'm just... I'm glad you're here."

The simple honesty in his voice makes my heart stutter.

"Me too," I whisper.

"Come on," Ryder says, his voice dropping to a lower register, making my insides turn to liquid. "Let's play a game."

His hand engulfs mine, and before I realize what is happening, he's leading me through the crowd to the back of the room where a line of dart boards are mounted along the wall.

"I've never really played darts before."

Ryder's lips curve into a slow, dangerous smile. "Perfect. Then I can teach you."

The way he says it—like he's planning something wicked—makes my pulse race.

Plucking four darts from the board, he weighs them in his palm as he turns to me. "It's all about stance and follow-through."

"I'm wearing heels," I protest weakly.

"I noticed." His eyes rake down my body, lingering on my legs before flicking back up. "Trust me, they're not going to be a problem."

He positions me in front of the line marked on the floor, then moves behind me. The heat of his body engulfs me right off the bat as his chest presses against my back, allowing me to feel every hard plane of muscle.

"Now. You're going to hold it like this," he murmurs, his breath hot against my ear as he places a dart in my hand. His fingers close around mine, adjusting my grip. "Not too tight."

I swallow hard, trying to focus on the weight of the dart and not his proximity.

"Now, pull back..." One hand guides mine, while the other settles on my hip. "And release."

I throw the dart, but I'm so distracted that it veers wildly off course, missing the board entirely, bouncing off the brick and falling to the floor.

"Oops," I laugh nervously.

"Let's try again." He shifts but doesn't move away. If anything, he presses in closer, aligning his hips with mine.

The dart flies out of my hand, landing nowhere near the bullseye. I barely notice, too distracted by the way his thumb is now making slow circles on my hip.

"Again," he orders, his voice a rumble vibrating over my body.

He hands over another dart, but this time when I pull my arm back, his lips brush against the sensitive spot just below my ear, and I almost drop it.

"Focus, kitten," he chuckles, his stubble grazing my neck. "Keep your eyes on the target."

When his hand slides from my hip to splay across my stomach, pulling me even tighter against him, I can feel his rigid cock pressing into my lower back.

"Ryder," I breathe, my voice embarrassingly shaky.

"Mmmm?" His innocent tone doesn't match how his thumb is tracing the underside of my breast through my dress.

"You're slow-burning me again."

His low chuckle sends another wave of heat straight to my core. "Is that what I'm doing?"

I try to turn, but he holds me firmly in place, tightening his grip.

"Ah, ah, ah," he warns. "We're not done with your lesson quite yet. You'll get your reward soon enough."

The next dart flies even wider than the others, clattering to the floor as my concentration completely dissolves under his touch.

"Pretty sure I'm a lost cause," I sigh dramatically, leaning back against his solid chest and turning my head slightly so I can look up at him.

"Never," he growls, sliding his hand to rest just above the hem of my dress. "You just need more practice."

His gray eyes are dark with desire, pupils blown wide. For a moment, I think he's going to kiss me and end this exquisite torture, but he steps away instead.

"How about you take a turn?" I ask. "Maybe I can learn from watching how you do it."

Ryder takes his position on the line. It's clear he's done this countless times before. He rolls his shoulders, muscles flexing as he narrows his eyes at the target.

Shifting his stance, he raises his arm and throws.

The first dart strikes the bullseye with a soft thud. One after the other, he throws the second, then the third in rapid succession, each one landing somewhere inside the inner ring.

Damn, that's hot.

In an attempt to refocus, I scan the room for Sasha and realize she's disappeared. I search the bar, the dance floor, even the corners where people are chatting, but there's no sign of her flaming red hair anywhere. Come to think of it, Jax is missing, too.

I grin to myself. They've probably snuck off together.

Ryder's voice cuts through my thoughts. "What're you grinning about?"

"Sasha's gone," I say, glancing at him over my shoulder. "And so is Jax."

A knowing grin spreads across his face. "Called that one."

"You don't think they..." I trail off, though the evidence is pretty damning.

"Oh, absolutely." He steps closer, his body radiating heat. "Your friend works fast."

"Hey!"

He shakes his head. "I didn't mean it like that."

"Fine. So does yours, apparently." I laugh, but it catches in my throat as Ryder grabs my hand.

"Your turn," he says, voice rough as he hands me the darts.

The challenge in his voice lights a spark inside.

When I turn to face the dartboard, I arch my back, knowing the move makes my ass curve up in the tight dress. I take my time lining up the shot, bending forward just enough to give him a perfect view.

When I glance back over my shoulder, his mouth is drawn into a tight line, hands fisted at his sides.

"Like this?" I ask innocently, wiggling my hips as I adjust my stance.

"Fuuuck," he mutters under his breath.

I release the dart, and by some miracle, it actually hits the board this time. Not the bullseye, but close enough to count as a victory.

"Look at that." I spin around with a triumphant smile. "I guess I'm a natural, after all."

But my celebration is short-lived. Ryder's eyes are blazing as he stalks toward me, full of predatory intent.

"You think you're clever, don't you?" he smirks.

The next thing I know, he's grabbing me by the hand and pulling me across the dance floor, down a dark hallway and into an employee restroom.

Back pressed against mine, he walks me inside, then shuts the door and locks it, leaving us in total darkness.

Immediately on alert, all my senses, other than touch or sound, automatically shut down.

"I was going to give you a reward, but after the show you just put on, I'm not so sure." His voice is gravel in the dark, hot against my ear. Without warning, he pushes me up against the wall and yanks my dress up to my waist.

The cool air hits my newly exposed thighs as his large hand pushes between my legs, sliding up the center of my lace panties.

"Jesus," he hisses. "You're soaked."

I gasp, my head falling back against the wall as he slips his fingers beneath the lace, teasing along my slick folds.

"What do you think you were doing, bending over in front of me like that?" His free hand tangles in my hair, tugging my head back to expose my throat. "Hmm?"

His teeth scrape along my neck, making me shiver. "Did you think I wouldn't notice how every man in that room was looking at you when you did that?"

His fingers circle my clit, and my hips buck against his hand. "I—I didn't—"

"Didn't what?" he growls, pressing his rock hard length against my hip. "Didn't think about how that would make me want to bend you over and fuck you right there in front of everyone?"

My breath comes in shallow pants and my words get stuck in my throat as his fingers slide, circling my entrance.

He chuckles darkly. "You're such a little fucking tease."

Then he slides two fingers inside me, curling them to hit the one spot that makes stars explode behind my eyelids. "Let's see how *you* like being teased."

"Oh, god," I moan, clutching his shoulders.

"Quiet," he husks, his thumb circling my clit as his fingers start to pump. "Unless you want everyone to know what I'm doing to you here in the dark?"

The idea of being caught, of someone walking in and finding us like this—me with my dress bunched around my waist, his hand between my legs—only heightens my arousal.

My inner walls clench at his words and he chuckles low.

"You'd like that, wouldn't you?" he whispers. "For someone else to see how desperate you are for my fingers right now?"

His fingers move faster, harder, ruthlessly driving me toward the edge. My legs start to tremble as pressure starts to build low in my belly.

"*Please*," I whimper, not even sure what I'm begging for anymore other than release.

"Please what?" he demands, his voice rough with desire. "Use your words, kitten."

"I need to come," I gasp, shameless and desperate.

His thumb presses harder against my clit, his fingers pumping inside me a few more times before he suddenly pulls away.

"Maybe later."

"What?" I gasp, stunned, as my body throbs incessantly with its denied release. I can hear him sucking my arousal from his fingers, followed by a low, satisfied groan.

"That... that wasn't slow-burn! That was torture!" I protest, my voice quivering with frustration as I grip the wall behind me for support.

His chuckle is dark and delicious. "Exactly. A little edging never hurt anyone. And now we're even."

"Even?" I sputter-hiss, trying to smooth my dress down with trembling hands. "That wasn't fair."

"Who said anything about fair?" He's close, breath hot against my cheek. "You've been teasing me all night in this fucking dress. And then you all but bend over in it? Tsk. Tsk."

As I open my mouth to argue, his mouth, hungry and demanding, crashes down on mine. The taste of myself on his tongue sends another jolt of heat through my veins. But just as quickly as it began, he breaks away, leaving me breathless—again.

"We should get back before anyone notices we're missing,"

he murmurs, his hand finding mine in the dark. "And I could really use another drink... or four."

"You can't be *serious*." My voice sounds painful and needy as I jerk my hand away. "You're just going to leave me like this?"

"Yep." I can hear the smirk in his voice as he unlocks the door, letting in a sliver of light from the hall. "Don't worry, kitten. I'll make it up to you... eventually."

"You're evil," I whisper, squeezing my thighs together to ease the ache.

"Just playing by your rules. Don't you dare make yourself come. Cuz' I'll know."

Then he's gone.

I manage to find the light and switch it on. The harsh glare has me blinking against it as I make my way to the mirror.

My lips are swollen and smudged with red, cheeks flushed, hair a wild tangle from Ryder's hands. My pupils are blown, and my dress is wrinkled where he'd bunched it up around my waist.

"Jesus," I mutter to myself.

Grabbing a paper towel, I swipe at my smeared lipstick and smooth my hair with trembling fingers. The flush on my chest is harder to hide, but I fan myself vigorously, willing my body to cool the fuck down.

Finally, I adjust my dress, and after a few deep breaths, I reapply my lipstick from the tube Sasha insisted I bring.

"Guess I'm gonna need a drink or four as well."

noia

BACK IN THE MAIN ROOM, THE PARTY IS IN FULL SWING. I make a beeline for the bar, desperate for something to cool my rage.

"Whiskey," I tell the bartender. "Make it a double."

Ryder is on the other side of the room, leaning against the bar, looking far too pleased with himself as he talks with Jax and a couple of other guys I don't recognize.

I take the shot glass set in front of me and throw it back. The liquor burns its way down my throat, a welcome distraction from the throbbing between my legs.

"There you are!" Sasha rushes up to stand beside me. "I've been looking everywhere for you."

"Oh, yeah?" I raise an eyebrow, taking in her disheveled appearance. "And where have you been? You disappeared earlier."

Her cheeks flush almost as red as her hair. "Just... having fun. Hanging out with Jax."

"Is that what the kids are calling it these days?" I snort, signaling for another shot.

"Oh, hell no." Sasha grins and bumps her hip against mine. "What about you? Your neck is all flushed."

Downing the other shot, I huff out a laugh. "Ryder took our slow-burn deal to a whole other level."

My bestie leans in with a grin. "What did he do now?"

I signal the bartender for another drink, this time for a Whiskey Sunrise. Can't get drunk too quick. Gotta keep myself in check.

"He took me into the bathroom and... edged me. Then told me he would 'make it up to me eventually'," I tell her with air quotes.

"Oh no, he didn't."

"He sure as fuckin'-A did."

Sasha's eyes narrow as she leans close. "What are you going to do about it?"

"Honestly?" I take my drink from the bartender with a thank you and take a sip. "I have no idea. This slow-burn shit is driving me absolutely insane. Every time I try to turn the tables on him, it backfires. He always gives way more than he gets."

I scan the room, and my gaze lands on Claire and Lizzy sitting in a booth across from the bar, deep in conversation.

"Let's go get to know his friends a little better, shall we?" I say, feeling a spark of inspiration as the alcohol starts singing in my veins.

Sasha's eyes light up with mischief. "Oh, I see where you're going with this. Get the dirt on him from the people who know him best."

"Exactly." I smooth down my dress and toss my hair back. "Time to level the playing field."

Navigating through the sea of tattooed bodies, we make our way across the crowded room. I can feel Ryder's eyes tracking me, but I keep my focus on my intended targets.

We make it across the room in record time and sidle up to the booth. "Mind if we join you?"

Claire's face breaks into a wide grin. "Not at all. We were just talking about you, actually."

"All good things, I hope." I slide in next to Lizzy while Sasha takes a seat beside Claire.

"Of course." Lizzy says, moving over to make room. "We were just saying how refreshing it is to see Ryder interested in someone for more than just a minute."

"Oh?" I casually take another sip of my drink. "Is that unusual? Him being with me?"

"Unusual?" Claire snorts. "Try unprecedented. I've known that man for years, and I've never seen him look at anyone the way he looks at you."

My heart flutters traitorously in my chest. "And how does he look at me?"

"Like you're the light in his dark," Lizzy quips.

"Or like he wants to devour you whole," Claire adds with a wicked grin. "Which, based on the smudge of lipstick on your chin, he might have already done that."

Heat rushes to my cheeks as I swipe at my face.

"But it's nice to see him happy," Claire sighs. "After everything he's been through, he deserves it."

Genuinely curious now, I ask, "What exactly has he been through? He doesn't talk much about his past."

Claire and Lizzy exchange a look.

"It's not really our story to tell," Claire says carefully. "But let's just say his time in the Marines left some deep scars—and not just the physical."

Lizzy fiddles with her glass. "Has he told you anything about his time in the Marines?"

"He has, but not in too much detail." I take a tentative sip of my drink. "I think he's been having nightmares, but he hasn't said anything."

Resting her arms on the table, Claire leans in. "Just let him know you're there for him and you're okay to listen. That's all that matters in my book. He'll confide in you when he's ready. Just the fact that he's been with you this long tells me he trusts you. Give him some more time to open up."

"Thanks, Claire."

"Of course. I like you, Noia. You're good for him. I can feel it."

Lizzy leans in. "I might have had a crush on him when I first started working here, but he made it clear we were just colleagues. Now he's like a big brother to me, so if you hurt him..." She narrows her eyes. "I'll make you bleed."

I hear Sasha suck in a breath and my eyes go wide.

"Fuck's sake, Liz," Claire mutters.

Lizzy throws back her head and laughs. "Just kidding. I wouldn't make you bleed. Much."

I'm still trying to decide if Lizzy is joking when I hear the sound of deep laughter coming our way. I look up to see Ryder and Jax approaching our table wearing Cheshire grins.

Ryder's eyes lock with mine. "You ladies having fun?"

I notice Jax giving Sasha a slow once-over, his lips curving into an appreciative smile. My best friend returns his gaze and I grin inside.

Definitely going to get all *those* details later.

Turning my attention back on Ryder, I manage a casual smile, still pissed at him for edging me. "So much fun."

He narrows his eyes, clearly catching the sarcastic edge to my voice before he nods and flashes a smile. "Party's winding down. I gotta stay tonight to help clean up. You two gonna be okay getting home? You can stay and wait if you want."

Before I can respond, Sasha pipes up. "I've only had a couple drinks, so I can drive us back."

"You sure?" I ask, relieved that I won't have to call us a rideshare.

"Absolutely." She sets her glass aside. "I switched to water an hour ago."

Jax looks disappointed. "Leaving so soon?"

"Some of us have to drive home tomorrow," Sasha says with a wink.

I say my goodbyes and slide out of the booth, careful not to stumble on my heels.

"I'll walk you out," Ryder says, his hand finding the small of my back as we make our way through the thinning crowd.

"Thank you for coming tonight," he murmurs as we reach the exit. "It meant a lot having you here, meeting my friends."

Despite my frustration, I soften at the sincerity in his voice. "I had a good time. Your friends are great."

"They are," he agrees, looking pleased.

Outside, Sasha hangs back, giving us a moment of privacy as she digs through her purse for her keys.

Ryder tugs me closer, eyes dark with promise. "About earlier..."

I raise an eyebrow.

"I meant what I said." His voice drops into that damn gravelly register, instantly making my knees go weak. "I *will* make it up to you."

"When?" I challenge, unable to keep the frustration from my voice.

His thumb brushes across my bottom lip. "Soon. I promise. I have another date planned for next week. We'll see how things go then."

Before I can protest, his mouth captures mine in a hard, quick kiss, leaving me breathless for the millionth time tonight.

"See you in the morning. 'Night, Sasha. Thanks for coming."

"Thanks for having me. You've got some talented friends."

I bark out a laugh.

Ryder just shakes his head with a grin and heads back inside.

"Subtle much?"

"What? Jax is his best friend. No doubt he knows every detail about what went down."

"Guess we should head home," I sigh, watching Ryder's fine ass disappear back into The Brew. "I'm exhausted."

As soon as Sasha pulls onto the main road, she clears her throat.

"There's something I've been meaning to tell you since I got here, but the timing never felt right."

The seriousness in her tone makes me sit up straighter. "What is it?"

"Eric's been asking around about where you are."

My stomach drops. "Seriously?"

"He showed up at my studio last week wanting to know where you'd disappeared to. Said he's been trying to reach you for a while."

"Well, I blocked his number as soon as I found out he wasn't going to show up for our wedding," I snap. "What the hell does he want?"

"He said something about explaining himself. I told him to go fuck himself, obviously."

I rest my head back against the seat and sigh. "After all this time, what could he possibly have to say that matters now?"

"That's basically what I said." I suck in a breath and grab the door handle when Sasha takes a curve a little too fast. "Sorry. Just... he seemed pretty desperate."

"Did you tell him where I am?"

"Of course not!" she gasps, offended. "You know I would never do something like that. But I wouldn't put it past him to come here looking for you."

My heart races at the thought of my ex-fiancé showing up at my door. "Shit."

"Yeah. I wanted to give you a heads-up. Just in case."

I stare out the window into the dark. "I can't believe he thinks he can just waltz back into my life after humiliating me!"

"Men are assholes," Sasha offers helpfully.

"Not all of them," I murmur, thinking of Ryder.

"No." A small smile plays at her lips as she tips her chin. "Not all of them."

We drive in silence for a few minutes, my mind racing with thoughts about what went down that day. Suddenly, I realize I'm not sad anymore—far from it, in fact.

Now I'm just pissed. "Screw him."

"Exactly. And you know what?" Sasha says suddenly. "If that asshole does show up, you've got a six-foot-something tattooed former Marine living with you who looks like he could snap Eric in half without breaking a sweat."

That makes me laugh. "True."

"Plus, Eric's soft, pasty ass has always been intimidated by anyone with actual muscle. He'd take one look at Ryder and hightail it right outta there."

"God, you're so right." I laugh, tension easing from my shoulders. "What was I even thinking when I agreed to marry him?"

"You were thinking with your head instead of your heart," Sasha says gently as she shuts off the car. "But now you know better."

"You hungry?" I ask as we shuffle inside.

"Always." Sasha kicks off her heels with a grateful sigh as I do the same. "These shoes are killing me."

The moment I close the front door, Goonie struts into the room, winding around my legs, meowing loudly.

"Hey, baby," I coo, scooping him up. "Did you miss me?"

He purrs against my neck, and I'm struck by how normal everything feels—coming home late after a night out, hanging with my best friend, snuggling my cat.

I pour us each a generous glass of wine and start grabbing stuff out of the fridge to make omelets, while Sasha collapses onto the couch.

Fifteen minutes later, I'm handing her a steaming plate.

Settling beside her, I tuck my legs under me and dig in. "So. You and Jax?"

Her cheeks flush. "He's... fun."

"Fun?" I snort. "Sasha, you disappeared for almost an hour. What happened?"

"We just talked," she says, but the way she's biting her lip tells me there's a lot more to it.

"Bitch, spill it."

She takes a bite of her omelet, then sighs. "Okay, fine. We may have made out a little in the alley behind the bar."

"Just a little?"

"A lot," she admits with a grin. "Like, a lot a lot. He's a really good kisser."

By the look on her face, I'm pretty sure I know what happened next, but I ask anyway. "What else?"

"Then... he fucked me up against the wall."

"Sasha!"

"I know! Then he asked for my number, but I told him I live an hour away and I'm not looking for anything serious right now."

I study her face. "But you wanted to give it to him." I snicker. "Your number, I mean."

She rolls her eyes. "Maybe." She shrugs. "But you know me

—I don't do long-distance. And I really don't do what we did more than once with the same guy. Too complicated."

"Sometimes the best things in life are complicated," I murmur, thinking about Ryder's stormy gray eyes.

"Speaking of..." Sasha says. "What's up with your Ryder sitch? I mean, long-term."

Her question catches me off guard. "I... I don't know. I guess I'm trying not to think too far ahead."

"But you're falling for him."

There's no point in denying it. "Yeah. I am."

"Good. 'Cause you deserve to be happy."

noia

It's just past 2 a.m. when I hear the front door open and close.

Ryder's back.

After tossing and turning for over an hour, I'm still wide awake, my body still humming with frustration from him edging me earlier.

His heavy footsteps move through the house. The refrigerator door opens and closes before I hear the water running in the kitchen sink. Then his footsteps head down the hall toward his bedroom.

Silence falls over the house again.

Thirty minutes later, still unable to sleep, I slip out of bed. My heart hammers against my ribs as I tiptoe down the stairs in nothing but a tank top and sleep shorts. The steps creak beneath my feet, and I freeze, but the house stays quiet.

I make my way down the hall to Ryder's bedroom. The door is open a crack with a sliver of moonlight spilling through the gap.

Pushing it open just enough to slip inside, I quietly close the door with a soft click and lean back against it, heart thundering in my chest.

Sprawled across the bed, he has one arm thrown over his head, the other resting on his stomach. The moonlight streaming through the window bathes his tattooed skin in silver, highlighting every dip and curve of muscle. Wearing nothing but a pair of black boxer briefs, the sheets are tangled around his ankles.

Breath catching, I step further into the room. Even in sleep, he looks powerful, dangerous.

Then I have a wicked idea.

Careful not to disturb him, I move to the edge of the bed and slowly climb onto the mattress, my weight barely shifting it as I crawl between his legs.

Still a little drunk, I bite my lip to hold back a giggle as I reach out and lightly trace my fingernails up the length of his shaft through the fabric. To my delight, his dick responds immediately, thickening and growing hard from my touch.

I glance up at his face. His breathing has deepened, but his eyes are still closed.

Feeling even bolder, I hook my fingers into the slit of his boxers and gently pull his cock free. When it springs up, fully erect, I have to stifle another giggle.

I lower my head and take him into my mouth, sucking gently on the tip.

Ryder draws in a sharp, shuddering breath, but doesn't wake.

Slowly, I suck him deeper into the back of my throat, watching his face as I do. When he groans low in his throat and grows even bigger in my mouth, I can't help but smile around him.

Just as I'm getting into a rhythm, enjoying the taste and feel of him, I find myself pinned to the mattress with Ryder looming over me, eyes blazing into mine.

"What the hell do you think you're doing?" he growls, voice rough with sleep and arousal.

"I couldn't sleep, so I wanted to see if I could make you give in first? But since you don't seem to be into it..."

I try to get up but he quickly lowers his body on top of mine so I can't move.

Trapping my hands above my head, he spreads my legs with a knee and begins to thrust, rubbing his cock against my clit.

"I can make myself last a lot longer than you can, kitten."

He keeps thrusting, his breaths becoming labored.

"Oh, *fuuuck*."

"That's right." He tucks his mouth against my neck and begins to suck. Hard.

Pleasure ratchets through my body and I moan, but when I realize he's giving me a hickey, my eyes fly open.

"Ryder! Stop!"

His mouth leaves my neck with a pop and he rolls off me, panting hard. "Go back to your room, Noia," he growls.

Feeling somewhat ashamed, I rise shakily from the bed. When I reach the door, his voice cuts through the dark from behind me.

"You're not going to win this war, kitten. Unless you beg, I'm not going to fuck you or let you come."

Mentally beating my vagina into submission, I go back upstairs and flop onto my bed. It feels like forever before I'm able to drop off to sleep.

My heart hammers in my chest as I stare at the ceiling. Noia's scent still lingers in the room and my cock is still painfully hard, throbbing from the ghost of her hot, wet mouth.

"Fuck," I sigh into the dark.

When I woke up to Noia sucking my cock, it felt so fucking good, I nearly lost it right then and there. The feel of her kneeling between my legs, full lips wrapped around my dick, was erotic as fuck.

I feigned sleep as long as I could before I pushed her away and flipped her onto her back. Then it took every ounce of self-control I had not to rip off her shorts and bury myself deep inside her.

But I can't give in. Not yet.

I've been planning our next date for days now—something special that'll push her boundaries in all the right ways before I finally give in to what we both have been craving. If I cave now, all that anticipation, all that delicious tension we've been building, will be wasted.

I drag a hand down my face, willing my erection to subside.

"Goddammit," I growl, throwing an arm over my eyes.

Sleep is impossible now. I can still taste her, feel the soft skin of her neck against my lips. Marking her had been instinctive, primal—a need to claim what's mine.

Mine.

The thought slams into me. When did I start thinking of Noia as mine?

Goonie jumps onto the bed, settling himself on my chest with a disgruntled meow.

"Yeah, I know," I mutter, stroking his fur. "I'm a glutton for punishment."

Kneading my chest with his paws, he purrs in agreement.

"What am I supposed to do, huh?" I ask him quietly. "Just a couple of more days. That's all I need to hold out."

Goonie yawns at me, then closes his eyes, unimpressed with my current dilemma.

I let out a sigh and continue petting him. It calms me enough that after a few minutes, I'm able to fall asleep, dreaming of Noia's soft blond hair and her full red lips wrapped around my cock.

THE NEXT MORNING, I WAKE TO THE SOUND OF LAUGHTER drifting down the hall and the smell of coffee and something sweet.

Noia and Sasha are up.

I drag myself out of bed, pull on a pair of jeans and a T-shirt, and head down the hall, bracing myself.

When I walk into the kitchen, Noia is at the stove stirring eggs. Wearing jean shorts and a tank top, her hair is piled on top of her head in a messy bun, exposing the curve of her neck.

Seeing the dark purple mark I made only hours before makes my cock jerk.

Something primal and possessive stirs in my chest, but it's immediately interrupted by the sound of Sasha's chirpy voice. "Morning, sunshine."

"Morning," I grunt, making my way to the coffee pot.

I can feel Noia's eyes on me, but I keep my eyes to myself. If I look at her, I might just haul her over my shoulder and take her back to bed.

"Sleep well?" she asks innocently, but there's a challenge in her eyes.

"Like a baby," I lie, taking a long sip. "You?"

I look up and see her cheeks flush pink as her hand automatically goes to her neck, fluttering over the mark I gave her.

Her voice comes out as a squeak. "Fine." She clears her throat. "We're making breakfast. French toast and eggs."

"Sounds good." I take a sip of my coffee and lean against the counter, ogling her ass as she moves around the kitchen. "What time are you heading out, Sasha?"

Sasha's eyes dart between us, clearly sensing the tension. "After breakfast," she says as she grabs plates from the cabinet. "I should start packing. My drive back is going to take longer with Sunday tourist traffic."

"I'll help you after we eat." Noia scoops the eggs onto the plates before turning back to the stove to flip the French toast. "I was thinking of driving back with Sasha for a few days. Maybe do some shopping in the city."

My mug freezes halfway to my lips. "What?"

She turns to face me, expression neutral. "Just for a couple of days. I need to pick up some things, and it would be nice to have a change of scenery. For inspiration."

My jaw clenches and my hand tightens around the mug. She's running. "I thought I was helping with your inspiration."

Sasha glances between us, then suddenly becomes very interested in her breakfast. "I'll just... take this upstairs and go pack."

As soon as she's gone, I set my mug down and move to stand over Noia. "What's going on?"

"Nothing," she sighs, flipping another piece of French toast onto a plate. "I just need some space."

"Space," I repeat flatly. "This is about what happened last night."

"No. Well, yes." She tries to run a hand through her hair, but only manages to dislodge a few strands from her bun. "This whole slow-burn thing is driving me crazy, Ryder. I think some distance might help me... us... reset."

I step even closer, backing her against the counter. "Or maybe you're afraid you're going to lose our little bet."

Her eyes flash. "I'm not afraid of anything."

"Prove it," I challenge, dropping my voice into a low rumble. "Stay."

Her breath catches, and for a second, I think she's going to give in. Then she shakes her head. "I already told Sasha I'd go."

"Fine." I take a step back. "When will you be back?"

"A couple of days. Wednesday at the latest."

Three days without her. The thought makes my chest pull tight.

"I have something planned for us on Wednesday," I say, trying to keep the disappointment from my voice.

Her eyes soften. "I'll make sure to be back by then."

I take another long sip of my coffee, studying her over the rim. "So, this is your strategy now? Running away to avoid temptation?"

"I'm not running," she protests, the flush creeping up her neck proving otherwise. "I just need a break from..." She waves a hand in the air between us. "This."

"From me, you mean."

Her shoulders slump slightly. "From the sexual frustration. From wanting you so bad that I can't think straight. From waking up in the middle of the night aching for you."

The raw honesty in her voice makes my cock throb.

Unable to resist, I set my mug down on the counter and crowd into her again.

"You think distance is going to help with that?" I trace a finger along the mark on her neck, feeling her pulse jump beneath my touch. "You think you won't still see this and think about what you did?"

She swallows hard, eyes darkening. "At least it will remind me not to sneak into your room again."

"That was a dirty move, by the way," I whisper, leaning in and brushing my lips across her ear. "Waking me up like that."

"You weren't complaining at the time," she whispers back.

"Trust me, kitten," I chuckle. "I'm not complaining at all."

The air is charged with tension, and her breath hitches as I step back, eyes locked with hers.

"If that's what you need, then go." Shoving my hands in my pockets, I clench my fists. "I'll be here when you get back. And Noia? Our next date? It's going to push you over the edge."

"We'll see," she counters, her voice lacking conviction.

"All packed!" Sasha says as she stomps down the stairs.

"Great," Noia says, voice bright. "Let me just grab a few things and we can head out."

As she brushes past me to head upstairs, I grab her wrist. "Don't forget what I said."

Her eyes meet mine, dark with want. "Believe me, I won't."

noia

THE DRIVE TO PORTLAND TAKES JUST UNDER AN HOUR, most of which I spend staring through the windshield, my mind replaying every interaction with Ryder since I found him standing half naked in my kitchen.

Before I know it, I'm pulling into the underground garage, parking my SUV next to Sasha's Mazda in the extra parking spot.

Her apartment building is one of those sleek and shiny modern high-rises housing condos with floor-to-ceiling windows.

I grab my overnight bag from the back seat with a sigh and follow Sasha into the lobby. A doorman nods as we pass, and she leads us into the elevator, pressing the button for the twentieth floor.

"Do you think I'm doing the right thing," I groan, leaning against the wall. "Am I a coward?"

"Fuck no," Sasha says firmly. "Sometimes you just need to distance yourself to help figure shit out. Besides, it's only for a couple of days."

The elevator doors slide open, and we step into a hallway. Her condo is a corner unit at the end of the hall.

When she unlocks the door and ushers me inside, I'm hit with the familiar scent of coconut and cedar.

"Home sweet home," she announces, tossing her keys into a ceramic bowl by the door. "Make yourself comfortable. You know where the guest room is."

I drop my bag next to the couch and wander over to the windows. The view of Portland's downtown skyline from up here never ceases to amaze.

"Thanks for letting me come hang out." I look over my shoulder and give her a small smile. "I just needed some time to... breathe."

"I get it." She flops onto her couch. "That man is intense. In the best possible way, but still."

"You have no idea." I collapse next to her. "Every time I'm around him, it's like I can't seem to think straight. I feel like I'm losing control."

"You're scared."

"Yeah. But I'm more apprehensive than anything. I'm used to controlling the narrative. But with Ryder..." I trail off, searching for the right words.

"He's writing his own."

"Something like that."

"Don't worry." She pats my knee. "This will all work itself out. In a couple of days I have no doubt you'll think of a way to move forward with whatever's going on between you two."

Sasha pushes herself up from the couch. "I think this calls for some wine. Stay right there."

I sink deeper into the cushions, listening as she rummages through cabinets in the kitchen, returning a couple of minutes later with two glasses and an open bottle of merlot.

"Here." She pours a generous amount into the glass and hands it over. "A little liquid strength."

I take a long sip, savoring the rich flavors as they burst over my tongue. "Thanks. I didn't realize how much I needed this until now."

Sasha sits beside me, tucking her legs underneath her. "So, I've been thinking about something, and this weekend kind of cemented it for me."

"What's that?" I ask, watching the wine swirl in my glass.

"I'm considering opening a Summit Studio in Lakeside."

My heart skips with excitement, and I flick my gaze up to meet hers. "Seriously?"

"Yeah." Her eyes light up. "The market there is completely untapped. No dedicated yoga studio and just the one small gym. I fell in love with the town."

"That would be amazing!" A surge of joy hits me at the prospect of having Sasha close by.

"There's more." She takes another long sip. "I'm thinking I might even move there... permanently."

"What?" I sit up straight, nearly spilling my wine. "Are you being serious right now?"

She nods, grinning. "I've been feeling stuck here in Portland for a while now. Too many people, too much noise. This weekend reminded me of how much I love small-town vibes. There's a vacant storefront right on Main Street next to Rise and Dine that I know would be perfect."

"Sash, that would be incredible! We'd only be twenty minutes from each other!"

"Exactly." She nods. "I could come over for dinner, and we could go back to having wine and movie nights."

"And you could crash at my place like you used to in college," I laugh, feeling lighter than I have in days. "When are you thinking?"

"I'm going to be talking with a realtor next week about the space. If it works out, I could be operational within the next six months." She refills our glasses. "What do you think? Would I be cramping your style if I moved to your little hideaway town?"

"Are you kidding? Having my best friend close again would be the best thing ever."

"I just need to find a place to live, and I'll be set. But I'll worry about that later."

As much as I would love Sasha to stay with me, I know she prefers having her own space, so I don't offer. I'm just glad she'll be close to me again.

I clink my glass against hers. "To new beginnings."

"To new beginnings," she echoes, taking a drink.

We sit in comfortable silence for a bit before I bring up another important subject. "So... speaking of new beginnings. What are you going to do about Jax?"

Sasha coughs. "What do you mean?"

"Oh, come on. You two hooked up! We both know you don't like commitment, and it's a small town. The space you're talking about is literally across the street from Skin & Ink Tattoo, so you're going to run into him. A lot."

Sasha's cheeks flush. "It's not like that. I hooked up with him, sure, but it was just one night. I'm a grown woman who can handle running into a man I slept with."

"In an alley," I add helpfully.

"Yes, in an alley, thank you for the reminder," she snorts, rolling her eyes. "Look, Jax is hot and a fantastic fuck. But I'm not looking for anything serious, and I'm sure he isn't either."

"You don't know that," I counter, back to swirling my wine.

"Oh, god," she groans. "Please don't start matchmaking. Besides, if I do move to Lakeside, I'll be focused on getting the studio up and running. That's it."

I decide to let it drop for now, but the wheels in my head are already turning. Jax and Sasha had obvious chemistry, and I can't help but think there's something more to it.

"Fine," I concede.

"Let's talk about what you're going to do about your slow-burn sitch."

I groan and sink deeper into the couch. "I don't know. Part of me wants to just give in and beg him to fuck me senseless again. The other part is too stubborn to let him win."

Sasha snorts. "Honey, you both win if you end up back in bed. Maybe it's time to stop thinking about it as a competition."

The next couple of days fly by. During the day, while Sasha's running her fitness studio empire, I set up camp at her dining table with my laptop.

To my surprise, the words pour out. Maybe it's the distance, or maybe it's because I can finally think without Ryder's intoxicating presence clouding my judgment, but my characters are back to practically writing themselves.

FORTY

ryder

"Looks like it's just you and me now, pudge."

Goonie meows softly before jumping down from the windowsill and into my lap.

Picking up the Highlander novel I got at the bookstore, I settle in and start to read.

The next couple of days go by surprisingly fast as I manage to keep myself busy. The shop is slammed with walk-ins on Monday, and Tuesday I have a full day of appointments, including a complex back piece that takes over eight hours to complete.

When I'm not at the shop, I spend my time working out, reading and setting up our next date. The anticipation of seeing her reaction to what I have in store keeps me going—I miss her more than I'd care to admit.

Wednesday afternoon, I'm sprawled out on the couch reading a book when I hear Noia's car pull up in the driveway.

My heart rate kicks up when her car door slams shut. Goonie, who's been napping on my chest, raises his head and blinks sleepily.

"She's back," I murmur, my pulse pounding in my ears.

I force myself not to rush to the door like some lovesick teenager. Instead, I stay put and flip to the next page in my book, feigning nonchalance as the front door swings open.

Noia looks windblown and beautiful. Cheeks flushed, her hair is loose around her shoulders, and she's wearing a simple, cropped white T-shirt and jeans that hug her curves in all the right places.

"Hey," she says, dropping her bags by the door. Her eyes find mine, and for a moment, we just stare, the air crackling between us with three days' worth of pent-up tension.

"Hey yourself." I close the book and set it aside.

Goonie abandons me immediately, trotting over to wind around Noia's ankles.

Bending down to scoop him up, she laughs. "Did you miss me, troublemaker?"

"He not the only one," I say, rising from the couch. I move toward her slowly, giving her space, and myself time to gauge her reaction.

Her cheeks flush and she buries her face in Goonie's tummy before setting him down on the floor. "How were things while I was gone?"

"Quiet." I take a step closer, close enough to catch the subtle scent of her coconut lotion. "How was your time away?"

Her gaze darts to my mouth, then back up to meet mine. "I got some writing done. And the change of scenery helped a lot."

"Good." I want to touch her, but I shove my hands into my pockets instead. Come to think of it, I've been doing a lot of that lately when she's around. "I know you just got back, but you need to pack another overnight bag for our date."

Her eyebrows shoot up. "What kind of date?"

"We're going camping."

Her mouth drops open. "Camping? Like, in a tent? Outside?"

"That's generally what camping means, yes." I can't help but grin at her shocked expression.

"I don't camp," she says flatly.

I let out a frustrated breath. "You practically live in the woods, Noia. I was planning on taking it easy on you and I figured since you live out here, that you must've been camping before."

I think for a minute, then shrug. "Testing your comfort zone a little more won't hurt." I step back, crossing my arms over my chest. "Unless you're scared?"

Her eyes narrow at the challenge. "Nope."

"Good. Pack warm clothes. It gets cold in the mountains at night, even in summer. We leave in thirty."

"Thirty minutes?"

"Twenty-nine now," I say, tapping my watch. "Tick tock."

She mutters something that sounds suspiciously like 'bossy ass' as she grabs her bags. I watch her go, enjoying the view as she stomps up the stairs.

"And don't forget your hiking boots!" I call after her. "If you don't have any, tennis shoes will work!"

The only response I hear is a frustrated groan that makes me chuckle.

While she's upstairs getting ready, I load my truck with the camping gear I picked up the day before—tent, sleeping bags, cooking equipment, and enough food for a night.

I chose a spot by a secluded lake about an hour's drive into the mountains. It's accessible by a dirt road up to a certain point, then we'll have to head out on foot for about twenty minutes before we get there.

Yesterday when I was thinking through options of where we should go, the memory of it came back to me. It's a place I used to stay quite frequently after I got out of rehab and I've never brought anyone out there with me—until now.

Noia comes out of the house wearing jeans, a long-sleeved flannel shirt over a band T-shirt, and a pair of tennis shoes. Carrying a small duffel bag, the look on her face says she's being marched to her execution.

"I can't believe I'm letting you do this to me," she mutters as I take her bag and toss it in the back of the truck.

"I'll be fun, I promise." I open the passenger door. "And trust me, this is nothing compared to what I'll be 'doing to you,' if you behave."

Her brows hitch as she gives me a skeptical look before climbing into the passenger seat.

noia

THE DRIVE THROUGH THE MOUNTAINS IS BEAUTIFUL AS THE roads wind through dense forests and past rushing streams. Ryder's truck handles the rough terrain with ease, and despite my initial protests, I find myself pretty relaxed.

"So where are we going, exactly?" I ask, watching the scenery blur past.

"A place I used to go when I needed to clear my head."

One of his large hands is resting on the steering wheel, the other on the gear shift. When he shifts, his forearm flexes.

I squeeze my thighs together.

"It's peaceful and private." His lips curve into that maddening smirk. "Perfect for what I have in mind."

The way he says it makes heat pool low in my belly. "And what is that?"

"You'll see."

After about an hour, he turns onto a narrow dirt road that's barely wide enough for the truck to get through the trees without scratching it up. The truck bounces and lurches over rocks and roots, and I have to grip the door handle to keep from sliding around.

"Jesus, Ryder. Are you sure this is actually a road?"

"Relax, kitten. We're almost there."

Finally, he pulls into a small clearing and cuts the engine. Aside from the sound of wind through the trees and birds chirping, the silence is instant and overwhelming.

He climbs out of the truck and grins. "From here, we hike."

I jump down and follow him around back where he starts grabbing the camping gear. "How far is it?"

"About twenty minutes. So not too bad." He shoulders a large backpack before handing me the smaller one. "This is for you to carry. Just water and snacks."

The trail is well-worn but steep, winding through towering pines and over rocky outcroppings.

After the first ten minutes, my legs start to burn, but I refuse to complain.

Ryder is about ten feet ahead of me, occasionally looking back to make sure I'm keeping up. "You doing okay back there?"

"Perfect," I pant, wiping sweat from my forehead.

Just when I'm starting to wonder if I'm going to collapse, the trees open up and I gasp.

The alpine lake is pristine. Its surface shines like glass reflecting the surrounding peaks. The water is so clear I can see smooth stones sitting on the bottom. The whole scene looks like something from a freaking postcard.

"Holy shit," I breathe. "This is incredible."

"Told you."

Ryder drops his pack and starts setting up camp while I just stand there gawking at the view for a couple minutes before moving to help.

The tent goes up quickly, followed by a small camp stove and a circle of stones for a fire pit.

"How did you find this place?"

"Trial and error. After I got out of rehab, I needed somewhere to go where I could think. Figure out who I was without the pills." He tosses the sleeping bags into the tent. "I'd come up here for days at a time, to breathe in the silence."

"That must have been lonely," I say softly.

"It was. But also necessary." He straightens, storm-gray eyes meeting mine. "I needed to learn how to be alone with myself before I could be with anyone else."

The raw honesty in his voice makes my chest tighten. This is the most he's ever opened up about his recovery.

"You're the first person I've ever brought up here." He glances up from where he's crouched by the fire pit. "This place is... special."

Before I can respond, he looks away and starts pulling items from his pack. "We've got a little over an hour before dark. Want to explore a bit?"

I nod, not trusting my voice. The fact that he's sharing this sacred space with me feels monumental.

We spend some time hiking around our side of the lake. As we walk, Ryder points out different rock formations and wildlife. He's surprisingly knowledgeable, and I find myself hanging on his every word.

When we find a fallen log by the water's edge, we sit.

"I used to come up here when the nightmares got bad," he says quietly. "Something about being this far from civilization, this close to something bigger than myself... it seemed to help."

"You still have them, don't you? The nightmares?"

"Sometimes." He stays quiet for a few moments. "They're not as frequent as they used to be, but..." He shrugs. "PTSD doesn't just go away."

"I'm sorry," I whisper. I want to reach for him, but I'm not sure if I should. "Is that why you looked like you hadn't slept the other morning last week?"

"Yeah." He looks at me, eyes soft. "But even with that, they've been better since I've been living with you."

My heart stutters. "Really?"

"Really." He stands and holds out his hand. "Come on. Let's head back before it gets dark."

ryder

By the time we return to the campsite, the sun is starting to set behind the mountains, painting the sky in shades of purple and pink. I get the fire going while Noia unpacks the food.

"Please tell me you didn't just pack protein bars and beef jerky," she says, rummaging through the bag.

"Hey! Have a little faith," I grin, pulling a couple of foil packets out of a small insulated bag. "We're having hobo dinners. Potatoes, carrots, onions, and steak all cooked in the fire."

"Okay, color me impressed." She settles onto the log near the fire pit. "I was expecting hot dogs and s'mores."

"We've got those, too." I carefully shove the foil packets into the coals. "It would be sacrilegious to go camping without s'mores."

As we wait for dinner to cook, I pull out a bottle of wine and two plastic cups. "Here. Time to sit back and relax."

We sip our wine and look out at the lake. After a while, Noia shifts to look at me.

"Will you tell me more about what happened to you?"

I stare into the fire, watching the flames dance, debating how much to tell her. But there's a flicker inside that makes me want to tell her everything.

"I was on my second tour," I begin softly. "We were part of a routine patrol outside Kandahar. Me, Kade, and four others."

The memories instantly come flooding back—the oppressive heat, the dust, the constant awareness of danger lurking everywhere.

"Kade was my best friend. I'd known him since basic. We'd been through everything together." I take a long swallow from my cup. "We were checking out a village that had reported Taliban activity when we got word to pull back."

Noia's eyes, open and patient, stay fixed on me.

"On our way out, we got ambushed. Started taking fire from three different directions." My hands clench involuntarily. "We managed to find cover, but we were pinned down."

I swallow hard. "I remember Kade yelling at me to run, but there was an IED buried right in our path."

"Oh my god," Noia whispers.

"Kade..." My throat tightens.

The fire crackles, sending sparks up into the darkening sky.

"He was running with me to the Humvee and..." I close my eyes, the image of what happened next still so horribly vivid. "The blast threw me twenty feet. I remember it sounded like the world was being ripped apart, and then... nothing."

Noia grabs my hand and threads her fingers with mine. Her touch grounds me immediately.

"Next thing I remember was waking up three days later in a military hospital in Germany. They told me Kade didn't make it. That he'd taken the brunt of the explosion." My voice drops to a harsh whisper. "And that I'd almost lost my leg."

I set my cup down on the ground and roll up my pant leg to reveal the twisted mass of scar tissue running from my ankle to just below my knee. The skin is puckered and shiny, with deep gouges where chunks of flesh were torn away.

"Shrapnel tore through everything—muscle, tendons, even bone. The doctors wanted to amputate at first, but one surgeon was sure he could save it." I trace the line of the scar. "Took eight surgeries and a year of physical therapy before I could walk even close to normal again."

Our eyes lock. Noia's eyes are filled with tears as she looks at the scar and then back at me.

"May I?"

I nod, watching as she gently traces her fingers along the path of the scar.

"The physical pain was bad, but the survivor's guilt was even worse," I admit, loving how soothing her fingers feel on my skin. "I kept wishing it had been me who had died. Kade had a family, a baby on the way. I had no one."

I shove the denim down with a sigh.

"They had me on some pretty heavy painkillers," I explain. "At first, it was just about managing the pain. Then it became about numbing everything else."

I look up and she's still watching me in stunned silence. "I was a mess when I got back—angry and self-destructive. The pills were the only thing that made it bearable."

"You got addicted," she states.

"I did."

She squeezes my hand. "How did you get clean?"

"By hitting rock bottom. My neighbor found me overdosed in my apartment and called 911." I let out a bitter laugh. "Nothing like almost dying to force you to rethink your life choices.

"After I got out of the hospital, my counselor pushed me to join a support group. I fought against it at first, but it was either that or jail time since I'd been caught with too many pills."

My eyes scan the shoreline and I shift in my seat.

"I met Claire when she was assigned as my sponsor. She'd been clean for five years at the time. She was this loud, purple-haired force of nature who wouldn't take any of my shit."

Noia smiles softly. "I kinda got that impression."

"Yeah. She dragged me to meetings when I didn't want to go. Showed up at my apartment at all hours to make sure I wasn't using. Called me on all my bullshit excuses." I shake my head and chuckle. "I hated her at first."

"And now, not only is she your friend, she manages Skin & Ink."

"Even more than that, she saved my life." I check the foil packets nestled in the coals. "One night, about six months into my recovery, I was at a really low point. It was the anniversary of Kade's death and I was this close to using again," I say, holding up my thumb and forefinger a centimeter apart.

"Claire found me sitting in my car outside my dealer's house. She got in, took my keys, and drove for hours. We ended up at this all-night diner where she told me her whole story—things she'd never shared in group meetings. By the time the sun rose the next morning, I knew I wasn't going to use that day. And it was enough to help me get through to the next."

I pull the packets from the fire and set them on a flat rock to cool.

"A few weeks later, she introduced me to Jax. He was new to the program and dealing with his own demons. Not my story to tell, but we connected right away. Both of us were looking for something to focus on besides our addictions."

Noia tilts her head. "Is that when you got into tattooing?"

"Not exactly. Jax was already apprenticing at the same shop downtown where Claire was working. I'd go hang out there sometimes, just to be around people who weren't constantly talking about recovery. One day, she saw me sketching while I was waiting for Jax to finish up and she offered me an apprenticeship."

"Wait, you can draw? Like, really draw?"

The look on her face makes me grin. "Yeah, I've always been good at it. Used to sketch all the time when I was a kid, but I never dreamed it could be a career. Drawing is basically the backbone to tattooing."

"So you and Jax decided to open your own shop?"

"Eventually. We worked at that shop for a couple of years, built up our clientele and scraped together enough money to open Skin & Ink. Claire came with us to help manage."

A cloud of fragrant steam releases into the air when I open the foil packets, allowing them to cool while I dig through a bag for utensils.

I hand Noia a fork and one of the packets. "Careful, it's still pretty hot."

We dig into our meals, eating in comfortable silence until Noia takes a sip of her wine and clears her throat. "Claire mentioned something at the party."

Still chewing, I pop an eyebrow. "Oh, shit. What did she say?"

"She said she's never seen you look at anyone the way you look at me." Her cheeks flush behind the dancing shadows from the fire. "And you haven't been seriously involved with anyone for a long time."

I set my empty packet aside and lean back, studying her face. "She's right."

"Why?" Noia's voice is soft, hesitant. "I mean, you're..." She waves a hand at me.

"I'm what, kitten?" I can't help the smile tugging at my lips.

"You know." She rolls her eyes. "Gorgeous. Talented. Not completely terrible to be around."

"High praise, coming from you," I chuckle, then get serious.

"There was someone once. We were together for almost two years before my second deployment."

"What happened?"

I take a deep breath, surprised when I don't feel the once familiar twinge of pain at the memory. "Her name was Melissa. She sent me a letter while I was in Afghanistan telling me she couldn't handle the distance anymore, and that the waiting and not knowing if I'd come back or not was too stressful."

Noia's eyes widen and flare. "She broke up with you while you were deployed?"

"Yup. Got the letter three days before the ambush that killed Kade." I watch the flames dance. "I was distracted and angry. Not focused on the mission like I should've been."

Realization dawns on her face. "You blame yourself."

"I've always wondered if I'd been more alert, more present... maybe Kade would still be alive." I shake my head. "It's just another thing I've had to learn to live with."

"Oh, Rye." Her voice breaks as she sets her dinner aside and moves to sit beside me. "It wasn't your fault. You can't keep carrying that with you."

"I know that now." I put my hand on her thigh and squeeze. "After I got clean, I threw myself into my work. It was easier to focus on other people's pain than my own. Relationships seemed... unnecessary. Risky."

"What about now?" she asks, her voice barely above a whisper.

My eyes meet hers. "Now there's you."

The air thickens, filling the space between us. I reach up and brush a strand of hair from her face, letting my fingers linger against her cheek. In that moment, everything I've been holding back—all my control, all my careful planning—crumbles to dust.

"Fuck it," I growl.

Grabbing her around the waist, I pull her onto my lap.

She gasps, thighs straddling mine, hands automatically gripping my shoulders for balance. Her eyes widen, pupils dilating until only a thin ring of blue remains.

Before she can say a word, I capture her lips with mine. Hungry and desperate, a week's worth of pent-up desire unleashes in an instant. Her mouth parts on a gasp, and I take full advantage, sliding my tongue against hers as my hands grip her hips, pulling her flush against me.

She moans into my mouth, grinding on my cock, fingers tangling in my hair, the friction the best kind of exquisite torture.

"I want to come," she breathes against my lips.

"Show me how much," I growl, gripping her hips as she starts to move.

Her head falls back as she starts to ride, the pressure building with each roll of her hips. The firelight dances across her flushed skin. She looks otherworldly, beautiful beyond words.

"Ryder," she whimpers. "Please."

"Please what, kitten?" I ask as I tuck my hands under her flannel and slide it down her arms, leaving her in just her T-shirt. I trail my lips down the line of her throat, flicking the tip of my tongue against her fluttering pulse, savoring the taste of her skin.

"I need... I need..." Her breath hitches as I suck at the pulse point below her ear and shove my hand under her shirt.

She moans.

"Use your words," I demand, shoving her shirt up and latching my mouth onto her nipple.

"You," she gasps. "I'll do anything you want. Just let me come. *Please.*"

Her desperation pushes me past my breaking point. I stand, lifting her with me before setting her back on her feet.

"Take off your jeans."

Her eyes widen, darting around. "Out here?"

"There's no one around for miles," I remind her. "Just us, the mountains, and the stars. You just said you'd do anything to come. And I'm going to hold you to it."

She hesitates for only a second before she starts to unbutton her jeans.

Slowly, torturously, she peels them down her legs, revealing a pair of simple black cotton panties that somehow look sexier than any lace I've ever seen.

Once they come off, I sit back down on the log and pat my thigh. "Come here."

Confusion flashes in her eyes as her lips part in surprise.

"Lie face down across my lap," I instruct, enjoying the way her chest rises and falls with each stuttering breath. "Now."

Eyes never leaving mine, she takes two tentative steps before positioning herself across my lap on her stomach.

The fire casts flickering shadows across her bare legs, and I take a moment to appreciate the view—her perfect ass barely covered by those black panties and the smooth expanse of her thighs.

"Beautiful," I murmur, running my palm over the curve of a butt cheek.

She trembles beneath my touch as I map slow circles over her skin, gradually moving inward toward the edge of her panties. Restless, she wiggles her butt.

But I'm going to take my time, and in doing so, she is going to come—hard.

"Stay still," I command. Sliding my fingers under the waistband, I tug them down just enough to expose her ass. "I've been thinking about doing this to you for days."

My quick slap startles a gasp from her lips.

Rubbing in slow circles, I do it again, a little harder this time.

She moans again.

My cock is throbbing painfully, but I have to remind myself this isn't about me right now, it's about her.

Hooking my fingers, I slowly drag her panties down her thighs.

Once she's fully exposed, I run my palm over her bare ass, grinning at the goosebumps rising beneath my touch. "You've been driving me crazy for days, you know that?"

"You've been driving *yourself* crazy."

"Bad kitty," I chuckle as I push my fingers between her legs, finding her already slick and swollen. "Mmm, but always so wet for me."

I graze her entrance with my middle finger, barely dipping in before withdrawing again, making her whimper as she tries to push back against my hand.

"Stay still," I growl, landing another smack on her ass, making her gasp. "Or I'll stop."

"Ryder," she pleads. "Don't tease."

But that's exactly what I'm going to do.

I slide one finger into her heat, so slowly she trembles and lets out a shuddering breath. "I'm going to take my time with you, kitten. Make you feel every..." *Thrust.* "Single." *Thrust.* "Thing." *Thrust.*

With my finger fully seated inside her, I stop, feeling her inner walls pulse for a moment before I withdraw, slowly curling my finger and dragging it against her sensitive spot on the way out.

"Oh, fuck," she moans, fingers digging into my unscarred calf.

"You like that?" I ask, repeating the motion as I add a second finger.

Her only response is a desperate whimper as she lifts her hips, trying to thrust herself against my fingers.

Establishing a deliberate and torturous rhythm, I push in deep, curling my fingers to hit that perfect spot, then withdrawing completely. Each time she gets close, I slow down or stop, keeping her right on the edge.

"Oh, god," she begs, voice breaking.

My cock is so hard right now, I could come in my jeans just from watching her writhe in my lap.

"It's okay, baby. You can take it." I add a third finger, stretching her further. The firelight catches the slickness coating my fingers as I work her over, the wet sounds of her arousal making my dick throb.

Her thighs start to quiver, and I know she's close. I immediately slow my pace, keeping my fingers buried deep.

noia

"Ryder!" I'm practically sobbing his name by this point. "Don't stop!"

"Look at you," he murmurs, using his free hand to stroke my hair before tangling his fingers in it and giving it a tug. "So desperate. So beautiful as you beg me to make you come all over my fingers. I'm going to make you squirt so hard."

His fingers start to thrust again and this time he adds his thumb into the mix, circling my clit, pumping his fingers even faster.

My breathing turns ragged, my soft cries echoing across the water.

"Such a good girl," he encourages as my body starts to spark. "Don't hold back. I want to hear you scream my name so loud, you startle the birds from the trees."

The pressure is building fast, my body tightening around his thick fingers as he relentlessly works me over. I'm teetering on the edge of something massive, and it's like nothing I've ever felt before.

"Oh, god! Ryder, I'm—I—"

And then it hits me, a pleasure so intense my entire body literally convulses as the dam breaks. I feel a gush of wetness burst from my body, and I scream his name into the night as wave after wave takes over, blurring my vision.

"Goddammit, kitten," he growls, voice thick with satisfaction as he keeps slowly pumping his fingers. "That was fucking beautiful."

Panting and disoriented, all I can do is lie limp in his lap. I've never experienced anything that intense before—never knew my body was capable of it.

"Stand up."

My panties are still tangled around my ankles, but I manage with help from his hands gripping my waist.

"Take off the rest of your clothes," he orders, eyes burning with hunger as he unzips his jeans.

My legs are wobbly as I pull my T-shirt over my head and drop it on the ground, then my bra. The cool mountain air makes my nipples pebble even harder.

Transfixed, I watch with bated breath as he frees his thick, hard cock from the confines of his jeans.

"Come here," he rasps, stroking himself slowly.

Legs trembling, I step between his legs, mesmerized by how the firelight is playing across the veins of his shaft. The head is glistening with pre-cum and he's so fucking hard already.

"On your knees."

Heart thundering against my ribs, I sink down before him and look up at him through my lashes.

"Suck," he commands.

I moan, eagerly taking him into my mouth. His taste is intoxicating—sweet and salty, musk and male.

"Fuck," he hisses, threading his fingers through my hair. "That's it, take it all. Take me deep."

Hollowing my cheeks, I work him with my tongue as he guides my head, setting a pace that has me struggling to take all of him. My hands grip his thighs, and his muscles flex beneath my fingers as he fights to maintain control.

"God, your mouth is so hot," he groans, tightening his grip in my hair. "So. Fucking. Perfect."

I look up at him, watching his face. His eyes are hooded, jaw clenched tight, the tendons in his neck standing out as he watches his cock disappear into my mouth.

After a few more thrusts, he pulls away, his cock slipping from my mouth with a wet pop.

"Enough."

Standing, he spins me around and bends me over. Pressing a large hand between my shoulder blades, he holds me in position as he kicks my legs apart.

"Arch your back," he commands, and I comply instantly, presenting myself to him.

The cool night air caresses my exposed flesh, making me shiver with anticipation. The blunt head of his cock nudges my entrance, teasing me with shallow thrusts.

"Please," I whimper, pushing back against him.

"Words, kitten." His voice sounds strangled and rough.

"Please fuck me," I beg, beyond caring about anything but the need to have him fill me up.

With a primal growl, he thrusts, bottoming out in one powerful stroke. The sensation of being filled so completely makes me cry out, my fingers digging into the rough bark of the log.

"Jesus," he hisses, gripping my hips hard.

Each thrust is harder and deeper than the last. The sound of skin slapping against skin blends with the sounds of his ragged breaths and my desperate moans.

"Touch yourself," he orders, sliding a hand around to cup my breast, pinching a nipple.

My clit is so swollen and sensitive that the first touch makes my inner walls clench, drawing out a groan from deep inside his chest.

"That's it," he urges, increasing his pace. "Make yourself come. I'll be right behind you."

Pressure building rapidly, I circle my clit faster. His thrusts become more erratic as the dual sensation of his thick cock stretching me tight and my fingers circling my clit has me spiraling toward another orgasm.

I moan and my legs start to tremble.

"I can feel how close you are," he grunts, tightening his grip. "Come with me, Noia."

I scream as I fall, my inner walls clamping around his cock as my body convulses over and over again.

"Fuuuuck!" he shouts as he pulls out, squirting hot ropes of cum on my lower back and ass as he continues to work his cock, milking it for every last drop.

Panting, he pulls up his pants before collapsing onto the log. He cleans me up with some paper towels dampened from his water bottle before gently pulling me into his lap, cradling me against his chest.

Brushing sweaty strands of hair from my face, he kisses my forehead, then my lips. "You okay?" he murmurs.

I nod, still too dazed to form coherent words. The night air is cool on my sweat slicked skin, and I shiver.

"Come on. Let's get you inside before you freeze."

Still shaky and barely able to function, he helps me gather my scattered clothes, and leads me to the tent.

"Let me." He unzips the sleeping bags he zipped together, then helps me get inside the makeshift cocoon.

I let out a sigh as I slide between the layers, the fabric soft and smooth against my skin as he tucks it around me.

"Be right back." Pressing a kiss to my forehead, he ducks out of the tent.

I can hear him moving around outside—the splash of water and the hiss of the fire as he puts it out. The sounds of the night are louder now as crickets chirp and the water laps against the shore.

The tent opens to reveal Ryder, naked. Even in the dim light from the small lantern sitting in the corner, I can see every hard plane of muscle, every tattoo etched into his skin.

He slides in beside me, body radiating heat as he pulls me into his arms. I curl against him, resting my head over his steadily beating heart.

His voice is a low rumble against my ear. "Whatcha thinkin' about?"

"I'm still..." I search for the right words. "Processing."

His deep chuckle vibrates against my body. "That good, huh?"

"Shut up," I mutter, lips twitching. I'm too boneless, too content to manage giving him anymore shit than that right now.

"I've never seen anything as beautiful as you coming apart like that," he rasps, his fingers tracing lazy patterns on my back. "The way you..." He runs a hand down his face before pulling me tighter against him.

My cheeks get hot. "I've never... done that before. The squirting thing."

His voice is smug. "I could tell."

"Cocky much?"

"Whatever. You love it."

Since I can't deny it, I just huff and snuggle deeper into his arms. The sleeping bag is surprisingly comfortable, and Ryder's body is like a furnace against the chill of the mountain air.

"Thank you for bringing me here," I whisper. My brain fuzzes as sleep starts to take over. "For sharing this place with me."

His breath catches. "I've never told anyone the whole story before. Not even Claire."

"Why me?" I mumble.

"Because you're different, Noia," he says, voice dark and serious. "You have been since the moment I first laid eyes on you."

I'M PULLED FROM A DEEP, DREAMLESS SLEEP BY THE SUN filtering through the thin fabric of the tent bathing everything in a soft, golden glow. I'm still wrapped in Ryder's arms, my head on his chest, his steady heartbeat in my ear.

I blink the sleep from my eyes.

"Morning, kitten," Ryder murmurs, pressing a kiss to the top of my head.

"Mmm." I stretch against him like a cat. "What time is it?"

He shifts slightly to check his watch. "Just after seven."

"Too early," I groan, burying my face in his neck and breathing in.

His low chuckle vibrates through my body. "Time waits for no one. Besides, we should probably head back soon."

With a reluctant sigh, I untangle myself from his embrace and sit up with a wince.

"Sore?" he asks, a hint of smugness in his tone.

"What do you think?" I mutter. Unable to help myself, I grin.

We snack on granola bars as we pack up our gear. I'm

impressed with how efficient Ryder is, breaking down the tent and organizing everything with military precision.

The hike back to the truck is a lot easier walking downhill, though my thighs burn in a much different way than they did yesterday.

As we load the gear into the bed of the truck, I steal glances in his direction. His hair is still mussed from sleep and a day's worth of stubble darkens his jaw, making him look rugged and impossibly handsome.

"What?" he asks, when he catches me staring.

I quickly look away. "Just... thank you for last night. For everything."

His expression softens and he steps into me, tilting my chin up with a finger. "Trust me, the pleasure was all mine."

We climb into the truck and head out, back down the bumpy dirt road.

"So, what's the deal with your friend Jax?"

Ryder's lips twitch. "You mean besides the fact he fucked Sasha in the alley behind The Brew?"

My jaw drops. "How did you know?"

"Jax told me after you two left." He chuckles, shaking his head. "Apparently, your friend made quite an impression."

"She says she doesn't do long distance." I bark out a laugh. "But I think she likes him more than she lets on."

"According to Jax, it was her idea." He glances at me with a grin. "Something about wanting to check something off her bucket list?"

Hiding my face in my hands, I groan.

"It's probably for the best that she doesn't do long-distance relationships." Ryder's tone turns serious. "Jax is... well, let's just say he's not exactly boyfriend material."

I roll my eyes. "Figured as much."

"Hey. Don't get me wrong—he's my best friend and I'd take

a bullet for him, but Jax is what most women would call a 'fuck boy.'" Ryder shrugs. "He's never been with anyone for more than a few days, always looking for his next sexual conquest."

"Sounds just like Sasha." I sigh. "She's the same way. That's why she told him up front she wasn't looking for anything serious."

"And *that* sounds weirdly like they'd be perfect for each other," he laughs.

"Speaking of weird..." I grin. "What are some of the strangest things you've experienced as a tattoo artist? I bet you've seen some bizarre shit."

Ryder shoots me a glance, eyes crinkling as he grins. "I could write a fucking book with the shit I've seen and had to put up with."

I shift in my seat to face him better. "Tell me."

He's quiet for a moment, navigating a particularly rough patch of road. "Well, there was this guy who wanted me to tattoo his ex-girlfriend's face on his ass with devil horns."

"Definitely weird," I snort.

"Then there was the time a dude passed out and pissed himself in my chair," he says, shaking his head. "That was a fun mess to clean up."

I wrinkle my nose. "Seriously? Gross!"

"But probably the weirdest..." He pauses, a smirk playing at his lips. "There was this chick named Lisa who came in to get a tattoo on her hip. I think she was maybe in her early thirties."

"Okay..." I'm intrigued by the expression on his face.

"About halfway through the first session, I notice she's breathing kind of heavy, which isn't unusual—some people do that to manage pain. But then she starts making these... little sounds." His voice drops, like he's trying not to laugh. "At first I thought she was in too much pain, so I asked if she needed a break."

He pauses, his grin getting wider by the second.

On the edge of my seat, I wiggle in place as I wait for him to continue.

"She says no, keep going, she's fine. So I continue, and the sounds get... more intense." He glances at me and raises an eyebrow. "As a man I've been around long enough to recognize when a woman is about to—"

"No way," I gasp, my hand flying to my mouth.

"Yep." He nods, the expression on his face is not only amused, but somewhere along the lines of scandalized. "She had a full-blown orgasm, in the chair, right in the middle of me working on her tattoo."

"Oh my god!" I burst out laughing. "What did you do?"

"What *could* I do? I just kept working and pretended not to notice, even though it was obvious as hell. She was gripping the armrests so hard her knuckles were white." He shakes his head. "She came back three more times for different tattoos, always requesting me specifically."

"No!" I'm laughing so hard now my sides hurt. "Did she... every time?"

"Every. Single. Time," he confirms with a grimace, hitting the steering wheel, punctuating each word. "Jax started calling her 'The Moaner Lisa' whenever she'd book an appointment."

Tears streaming down my face, I start laughing even harder. "That's hilarious, not to mention horrifying."

"And do you want to know the worst part? She started bringing her boyfriend with her. He'd sit in the waiting area, watching, knowing exactly what was going to happen." He runs a hand through his hair and shudders. "The dude was getting off on it too. It was almost like they had some weird fetish thing going on."

"That's so disturbing." I wipe the tears from my eyes.

"He just sat there with a creepy smile on his face, watching strangers witness his girlfriend's... reaction."

"Ew! Please tell me you refused to tattoo her after that."

"Actually, yeah. After the fourth session, I told her she'd have to find another artist." He shudders dramatically. "Claire thought it was hilarious."

"I can see why," I giggle. "That's definitely going in my mental file of 'Things I Never Expected To Hear.'"

"What about you?" he asks, glancing at me with a mischievous glint in his eye. "Any weird fan encounters?"

"Well, there was this one guy who showed up at a book signing with a manuscript he'd written about us getting married. Complete with detailed descriptions of our honeymoon."

"Jesus," Ryder mutters.

"He kept insisting I read it right there at the table, in front of everyone. When I politely declined, he started getting loud, saying I owed it to him as a devoted fan." I shake my head. "Security had to escort him out."

"That's scary fucked up."

"Then he somehow found my home address and kept sending me copies of the manuscript for months afterward. I had to get a restraining order."

Ryder's jaw tightens. "Did he ever show up at your place?"

"Once. But I'd already moved to another apartment by then, so he just ended up at my old apartment building, harassing my former neighbors." I shrug.

"People are fucking crazy."

"So what's the weirdest tattoo you've ever done?" I ask, happily changing the subject as I settle back in my seat.

"There was this one guy who wanted me to tattoo a life-sized portrait of his pet ferret on his back. In full color. With a little crown on its head." Ryder grins at me. "Took four sessions."

"Please tell me you have pictures."

"I do. Actually, it's in my portfolio because it turned out awesome, even though it was... unique."

When we pull into the driveway, Goonie's furry, squished-up face is pressed up against the living room window.

"Looks like someone missed us," Ryder chuckles, cutting the engine.

"He's probably just pissed his food bowl isn't full," I say, smiling as I watch my cat's tail swish with excitement.

noia

As soon as we step inside, Goonie jumps down from his perch at the window to wind himself between our legs, meowing impatiently.

"Yes, I know. We abandoned you." I scoop him up. "It's not like I left you with extra food and your favorite treats or anything."

Ryder drops our bags by the door and stretches, his shirt riding up to expose a strip of tattooed skin above his jeans.

Memories of last night flood back with vivid clarity and I'm momentarily distracted.

"Noia."

"Huh?" My eyes flick up and he tilts his head with a knowing grin.

"I'll unpack the camping gear if you want to feed His Majesty," he says, nodding at Goonie purring loudly against my chest.

"Deal." I carry Goonie to the kitchen and set him down by his food bowl. "Sheesh. You'd think we left you alone for weeks instead of just one night."

After filling his bowl and refreshing his water, I head

upstairs to unpack. My inner walls and thighs ache as I move around the room, making me smile to myself.

I toss my dirty clothes into the hamper and step into the shower. When I get out, I smell something cooking downstairs.

Pulling on a pair of sweats and a T-shirt, I head back down to the kitchen.

Ryder is stirring something on the stove.

"Smells amazing," I say, coming up behind him to peek over his shoulder.

"Just some pasta with a quick marinara," he says with a shrug. "Nothing fancy, but I figured we could both use some carbs after last night."

Heat floods my cheeks when he looks down at me with a wicked grin.

"How 'bout I open a bottle of wine?" I ask, trying to distract myself from the way his shoulders flex as he stirs the sauce.

"Sounds good."

We move around the kitchen together like we've been doing it forever. I set the table while Ryder cooks, and soon we're sitting kitty-corner from one another.

"I've been meaning to ask you something."

"Hmm?" I twirl pasta around my fork.

"Why did you cancel your tattoo appointment?"

The question catches me off guard. "Um..."

"Jax mentioned it." He takes a sip of wine, eyes never leaving mine.

Suddenly nervous, I set my fork down. "I don't know. I guess I got cold feet?"

"About what? The tattoo itself or..." He hesitates. "Or because of me?"

"Both, maybe?" I sigh. "I mean, you remember. The appointment just popped up in my alerts out of the blue the same night your stuff showed up, and it kind of freaked me out."

"What did you want to have done?"

"A phoenix." I shrug, feeling a little self-conscious. "Rising from the ashes and all that. I know it's super cliché, but it felt symbolic after everything I went through with my mom, with Eric and where I am now."

Ryder nods thoughtfully.

"Now I'm thinking about getting something different." I play with my pasta, avoiding his gaze. "Something that represents this crazy thing called my life. Maybe a quote on my side, across my ribs."

"I could still do it for you."

"You could?" I blink in surprise. "I mean, of course you could, but—"

"Actually," he cuts in. "How about you come to work with me tomorrow and hang out? I've got an opening tomorrow after lunch. One of my clients had to reschedule." Intense and focused, his gaze locks with mine. "Let me do your tattoo."

My heart flutters. "Tomorrow? That's... so soon."

"I think it's perfect timing, actually." He grabs my hand, tracing slow circles on my palm with his thumb. "You said you wanted something that represents new beginnings. What better way to honor our unique situation and what we've been doing to help you get your mojo back? Could be good inspiration as well."

I hesitate, biting my lip. "I don't know..."

"Come on, kitten," he coaxes, dropping his voice to a low rumble, causing butterflies to take flight in my belly. "Let me put my mark on you."

The possessive edge in his voice sends a shiver down my spine.

Unable to resist the pull of his stormy eyes, I relent. "Fine. I'll come hang out and you can do my tattoo."

His lips curve into a victorious smile. "Awesome." Lifting

my hand, he presses his lips to my knuckles. "I can start working on the design tonight."

"Okay," I agree, suddenly excited. "But I get final approval."

"Of course." Standing, he moves around the table and pulls me to my feet. "You're going to love it, I promise."

Sliding his hands down to my hips, he pulls me against him. "And I promise to be gentle," he growls in my ear. "For your first time."

I roll my eyes and grin. "You are such an ass."

"Pretty sure we've already come to that conclusion," he grins wickedly before capturing my mouth in a searing kiss.

Later, curled up in bed with Goonie purring at my feet, I scroll through tattoo designs on my phone. Nothing seems quite right. They're all too generic, too universal, or just not... me.

With a sigh, I toss my phone aside and close my eyes, trying to visualize what I would want permanently etched on my skin. Something meaningful. Something that captures this crazy, unexpected chapter of my life.

The squeak of my bedroom door makes me open my eyes. Ryder, shirtless and barefoot, is standing in the doorway with a sketchbook in his hand.

My hearts skips when he leans against the doorjamb all sexy and shit. "Can't sleep?"

I shake my head. "Just thinking about tomorrow."

"I came up with an idea." He pushes off the frame and comes over to sit on the edge of the bed. "If you're interested."

Curious, I sit up as he opens his sketchbook and turns it toward me.

On the page is a beautifully rendered sketch of the Cheshire Cat from Alice in Wonderland, his enigmatic smile stretching across his face as he fades into wisps of smoke.

Beneath the image, in an elegant, flowing script, are the words:

We're All Mad Here

My breath catches. "Alice in Wonderland."

"I remember you told me it was one of your favorite books as a kid." His voice is soft. "And it seemed... fitting."

I trace my finger over the quote and something clicks into place. "It does kinda feel like I've fallen down a rabbit hole."

"Right?" He chuckles. "A man with a tragic past who appeared in your kitchen out of nowhere and a writer who creates fictional worlds—it is all a bit mad, isn't it?"

"It's perfect," I whisper as I study the intricate details.

The cat Ryder rendered is both whimsical and slightly dark. With intelligent eyes that seem to look right through you, they glint with mischief as his body dissolves into nothingness. Smoke curls and twists around the letters making them look as if they are floating.

"Did you just draw this?"

"Yeah." Rubbing the back of his neck, he almost looks shy. "I was thinking maybe here." Reaching out, he lifts up my shirt, brushing his fingers along my ribcage, just below my breast. "The cat could wrap around your side, with the quote following the curve."

His touch makes me shiver and my skin erupts in a riot of goosebumps. "Yes," I breathe. "That's exactly where I want it."

"I can adjust anything you don't like," he offers. His eyes stay locked with mine as his fingers continue to slowly caress my skin, but I shake my head.

"No. It's..." I search for the right words. "It's exactly what I didn't know I wanted."

Something intense and possessive flashes in his eyes. "Good."

I lean forward to kiss him and his tongue slides lazily along mine as his hand slides up my side, thumb brushing the under-side of my naked breast.

"Stay in my room tonight," I murmur against his mouth.

He pulls back, searching my face. "You sure?"

"Very sure." I scooch over making room for him on the bed.

With a groan, he sets the sketchbook on the nightstand and slides in beside me, pulling me into his arms. "Just to sleep," he says, pressing a kiss to my forehead. "You're going to need to save your strength for tomorrow."

I snuggle against his chest and breathe him in. "Thank you. It's better than anything I could have imagined."

"Just wait until you see it on your skin," he murmurs, his voice already growing heavy with sleep. "It's going to be beauti-ful. Just like you."

When I wake up the next morning, Ryder is already gone.

Downstairs, I find a note on the kitchen counter.

Sorry, kitten. Something came up and I had to go in early. Meet me at the shop at noon for lunch? -R

I WALK INTO SKIN & INK AT 11:45.

The shop is busy and I immediately spot Ryder sitting at his station, bent over a client's arm. The buzz of his tattoo gun is a steady rhythm that somehow feels oddly soothing.

Claire waves at me from behind the front desk. "Hey! You look... relaxed."

Heat floods my cheeks.

"Ryder's been humming all morning." She grins over at him, then looks at me. "And that man never hums."

When I glance back over, he's cleaning up his station while his client examines her fresh ink in the mirror with delight.

Claire follows my gaze and nods at the leather couch. "Why don't you grab a seat? Would you like some coffee?"

"Sure. Thanks."

I settle onto one of the leather sofas in the waiting area, watching Ryder work. There's something mesmerizing about the way he moves—confident and in his element—that makes my heart thump extra hard.

When he looks up and catches me staring, he flashes me a devastating smile and my stomach flips.

After his client leaves, Ryder strides over, leaning down to press a quick kiss to my lips. "Ready for lunch?"

"I am," I admit, standing up. "Where are we going?"

"Actually." His eyes twinkle with mischief. "I had something else in mind."

Before I can ask what, he grabs my hand and leads me toward the back of the shop and into a small break room. The space is cozy with a small kitchenette, round table, and a small couch.

"Jax picked up some sandwiches from the deli down the street," Ryder explains, opening the mini-fridge. "I thought we could eat here, and I can show you the final design before we get you into my chair."

My pulse quickens. "You finished it?"

"This morning." He sets the sandwiches and a couple cans of sparkling water on the table. "I couldn't sleep, so I came in early and worked on it."

There's something thrilling about the idea of Ryder permanently marking my skin, but it doesn't stop me from fidgeting.

"You good?"

"Just nervous," I admit.

"Don't worry." His voice is gentle. "I promise I'll take good care of you."

My heart is pounding with anticipation, my dick half hard as I lead Noia over to my station and gesture to the chair.

"Have a seat."

She hesitates only a moment before sliding onto the black leather.

The sight of her sitting in my chair, about to wear my art on her skin forever, sends a jolt of possessiveness through me that's so intense it makes my cock stiffen even more.

She's not the only one who's going to have to breathe through this.

"Nervous?" I ask as I adjust the chair.

"A little, but..." She gives me a shaky smile. "I trust you."

Those three words are a direct hit, and I swallow against a need so visceral I have to clear my throat. "You need to tuck your shirt out of the way so I can place the stencil. Or you can just take it off."

She snorts as she tucks the hem of her T-shirt up under her bra, exposing the smooth skin of her ribcage. The sight of her half-exposed while she sits in my chair makes my mouth go dry.

Focus, Blackwood.

Goosebumps rise on her skin when I clean the area with alcohol.

"Cold," she murmurs, sucking in a breath.

"Sorry." Rubbing my hands together, I get them warm before putting the stencil in place. "Hold still."

She inhales, body tense as I press the paper to her skin. When I peel it away, the outline is perfectly positioned along the curve of her ribs.

"Go check it out in the mirror." I pat her thigh. "Make sure it's exactly where you want it."

Noia slides off the chair and walks to the full-length mirror, eyes going wide as she takes in the purple lines.

"It's perfect," she whispers, tracing the outline with her fingertip.

"You sure? Once I start, there's no going back."

She turns, eyes bright as they lock with mine. "I'm sure."

"Good. Now. Back in the chair, kitten."

As she settles, I adjust my machine. When I turn the machine on to test it, a visible shiver runs through her body.

"This is going to hurt," I warn, pulling on my gloves. "Especially on the ribs. Deep breaths, okay? Try to stay as still as possible and let me know at any time if you need a break."

Eyes fixed on mine, she nods.

When I place my hand on her skin, the warmth bleeds through the glove and into my palm, forcing me to take a deep breath to steady myself. If I don't get my shit together, Jax is going to start calling me 'Moaner Ryder,' and I'll never live it down.

Fuck's sake.

"Ready?"

"Ready."

When the needle touches her skin, her breath catches and she flinches.

I pause. "You good?"

"Yeah, sorry," she sighs, licking her full lips.

Fuck.

"Keep going."

FORTY-SIX

THE PAIN IS SHARP, AND IT STINGS SOMETHING FIERCE, BUT there's also something strangely addictive about it. I keep my attention on Ryder's face as he works.

Deep in concentration, his dark brows pull together, eyes narrowed and focused. "You're doing great," he murmurs.

Eyes full of heat, he glances up at me, voice low and soothing as he wipes away the excess ink with a damp paper towel.

I give him a slow smile and bat my eyes.

He returns my smile with a wink and gets back to work.

I can't take my eyes off his hands. Those strong, capable hands that have brought me an insane amount of pleasure are creating something beautiful and permanent on my skin. There's an intimacy I hadn't expected, something almost more vulnerable than sex as he marks me, changing me forever with his art.

When the needle moves over a specific spot on my ribs, I suck in a sharp breath, the pain making my eyes water.

"Just breathe. You can do this." Ryder splays a hand firmly across my side to steady me, brushing his thumb back and forth.

His gentle touch helps to ground me, easing the sting. "Almost done with this section."

Gentle but firm, the side of his hand randomly brushes along the underside of my breast as he works. Each contact sends sparks through my veins, making it even harder to stay still.

The buzzing stops, and he leans back to examine his work. "How you holding up?"

"I'm okay," I say, surprised when my voice comes out in a needy sigh. "It hurts, but... not as bad as I thought it would."

His lips curve into a knowing smile. "Some people find it... stimulating."

My cheeks heat. "I wouldn't go that far."

"No?" His thumb strokes lightly across my ribs, just below the fresh ink. "Your nipples say otherwise."

I glance down at my hardened nipples, which are clearly visible through the fabric of my T-shirt. Looking up, I narrow my eyes. "It's cold in here."

"Sure it is," he chuckles. Lowering his voice to a sensual growl, his eyes darken as they rake over my breasts. "Ready for more?"

His double entendre goes straight to my clit and I have to swallow against the lust blooming between my legs. "More than."

The needle starts up again, and I watch his face as he works. It's more than magical being able to see him so at ease, doing what I know he loves.

"The words are going to hurt more," he warns as he shifts his position. "It runs right along the bone."

I nod, bracing myself as the needle moves to the sensitive area directly over my ribs. The pain makes me wince and grip the top of the chair.

"Easy," Ryder murmurs, his thumb stroking my side again. "Breathe, baby."

I focus on his touch, the way his hand splays possessively across my side, steadying me as he works.

"This is going to sound strange coming from me, but..." I close my eyes for a moment and the machine stops. When I look up, Ryder is watching me. "...I kinda get why 'Moaner Lisa' got off on this. Especially with the way you're touching me right now."

A low growl comes from deep inside his chest. "Not strange at all, kitten. I've been rock hard this entire time."

I suck in a sharp breath, my body responding instantly to the heat in his voice. "Rye..."

He shakes his head, jaw flexing as he forces himself to focus on the tattoo. "Don't say my name like that while you're in my chair, or I'm going to do something that'll give everyone here a show—and I don't share."

The needle starts again, and I bite my lip. The combination of pain and the feel of his possessive touch are intoxicating, making my head spin.

So I change the subject.

Kind of.

"By the way," I say, trying to distract myself. "There's something about the cottage I haven't told you yet."

Keeping his eyes on his work, he asks, "Oh, yeah? Like what?"

I bite my lip, my own Cheshire grin splitting my face, excited to see his reaction. "It has a few secret hide-y-holes."

The machine stops and his eyebrows shoot up. "Seriously?"

"I thought it might be fun to play a game when we get home." I lower my voice. "Hide and seek."

His pupils dilate, and his jaw tightens. "Fuck, Noia. I told you. Don't say shit like that while I'm trying to concentrate."

"Sorry." But I'm not sorry at all. "Just figured I'd give you something to look forward to."

He takes a deep breath and shakes his head, but the corner of his mouth is twitching. "Pretty sure you're going to be the death of me one day, you know that?"

I let out a long sigh. "Yeah, and I couldn't imagine a better way to go," I tease.

The needle buzzes back to life and he refocuses, but there's new tension in his shoulders. "Tell me more about these hidden *hide-y-holes*."

"Nope. Can't play hide and seek if you know where all the hiding places are."

"Fine." He glances up, giving me a quick glare. "But you're going to have to play my game while I finish this."

"What game is that?"

He smirks. "The quiet game."

"Almost done." Ryder's voice is strained. "Just a few more lines."

Sweat beads on my forehead as the needle traces the final curves of the script. When it finally stops, the sudden silence is deafening.

"There," he says, leaning back as he pulls off his gloves. "Done."

Body humming with adrenaline, I let out a shaky breath.

"Want to see?" He holds out his hand and I take it, letting him help me out of the chair.

Legs unsteady, I walk over to the mirror and suck in a breath.

It's even more beautiful than I imagined. Vibrant and colorful, the cat's mischievous grin seems to come alive on my skin, the elegant script flowing perfectly across my ribs.

"It's gorgeous." My voice is full of awe as my eyes lock with his in the mirror. "Absolutely perfect."

Something intense flashes in his eyes as he takes in my reaction. "I'm glad."

The possessive edge in his voice makes my knees weak.

Before I can respond, he turns me around. His hands come up to frame my face, thumb stroking my bottom lip. "Seeing my art on your skin... Knowing it's there forever..." He shakes his head, the look on his face almost pained. "You have no idea what that does to me."

"Me too."

He groans, pressing his forehead against mine, sliding his hands down to my waist, carefully avoiding the fresh ink. "But tonight..." He blows out a breath. "I'm going to show you exactly what it does."

A shiver runs through me at the promise in his voice. "Looking forward to it."

"You better be." He presses a soft kiss to my lips before stepping back. "Now. Let's get you bandaged up."

I HANG OUT FOR A COUPLE OF HOURS, TALKING TO CLAIRE and Lizzy while Ryder takes care of his next appointment.

He follows me home on his motorcycle.

When we pull into the driveway, my skin is buzzing, and my mind is racing about how our game is going to play out tonight.

Ryder parks his motorcycle beside my car and dismounts. The way he moves with predatory grace makes my heart stutter.

I fumble with my keys at the front door, hyperaware of him standing behind me.

When I finally get the door open, Ryder pushes in from behind, closes the door and throws the deadbolt. "We need to establish some ground rules for this game of yours."

"Okay." Needing some distance between us, I quickly move across the room and turn to face him. Fuck, my heart is racing. "Just like any other time, I hide and you seek. You have ten minutes. If you find me in the allotted time, you get to make me do whatever you want. And if you don't, then I get to make you do whatever I want—sexually speaking of course."

Ryder's eyes darken as he stalks toward me, his lips curving into a dangerous smile. "All right, kitten. I'm game. Let's play."

The intensity in his gaze sends heat rushing straight to my core. I take a step back. I already know where my hiding spot is going to be.

"I'll count to sixty." His voice is all heat and gravel. "Then... the game begins."

I nod. "One rule though—no going outside. Everything's fair game inside the house."

"Deal." Closing his eyes, he turns his back to me, shoves his hands in his pockets and starts to count. "One... two... three..."

Kicking off my shoes, I dart through the living room toward the stairs, careful to move as quietly as possible. My mind races as I consider the options. The cottage has several perfect hiding spots—places even Ryder, with all his tactical training, might not think to check.

"...twenty-five... twenty-six..."

When I reach the second floor, I pause, listening to him count.

The first hidden space that pops into my head is the one behind the bookcase in the guest room.

Nope, too predictable.

I head for the master bedroom instead.

"...forty-three... forty-four..."

I'm halfway across the room when I see my laptop sitting on the nightstand and suddenly get a crazy idea.

What if...?

Without thinking twice, I rush over, fingers trembling as I pull up a new document. If Ryder really did come from my imagination, maybe I still have some control over him. Maybe I can influence the game, make it even more exciting.

"fifty... fifty-one..."

I start typing frantically.

Ryder's senses sharpen like a predator on the prowl, stealthy and dangerous. The thrill of the chase awakens something primal inside him—the need to hunt, to capture, to claim.

My heart pounds as I hit SAVE. I close the laptop, unsure if it will even work, but the possibility makes my pulse race.

"fifty-nine... sixty! Ready or not, here I come!"

His voice sounds different—lower and more menacing.

A delicious shiver runs down my spine as I dash into the walk-in closet and push my clothes aside to reveal a small panel hidden in the wall.

Sliding it open, I crawl through the narrow passage and slide the panel closed.

Then, I set the timer on my phone and wait.

ryder

THE MOMENT I OPEN MY EYES, SOMETHING INSIDE ME shifts and tingles right before a primal hunger unfurls in my chest, making my blood run hot.

What the fuck?

Shaking my head, I try to clear it, but something feels off. I feel different. I feel... mean.

It reminds me of what it felt like the time Noia tried to force me back into her manuscript by making me kiss Lexi.

A feral growl rumbles from my throat. She did something to me, I know it.

Bad kitty.

All right, she wants to up the stakes by messing with my emotions? Now it's more than just a game—it's a hunt.

"I'm coming for you, kitten," I call out, my voice rough with anticipation.

I move silently through the living room, avoiding spots I know will creak. The soldier in me automatically catalogs potential hiding places—behind furniture, behind curtains, inside cabinets.

But Noia mentioned secret hide-y-holes, so that changes the dynamics.

For some reason, I *want* her to hear me coming, so I stomp up the stairs two at a time.

The upstairs hallway has three doors—bathroom, guest room, and the master bedroom. I check the bathroom first, pulling back the shower curtain.

Empty.

The guest room yields nothing—not even under the bed or in the closet. My eyes immediately go to the bookcase. Too obvious, but worth checking. I run my fingers along the edges, looking for a latch or switch.

Nothing.

That leaves her bedroom.

I pause at the threshold and my gaze lands on her laptop, sitting slightly askew on the nightstand. Proficient writer that she is, it's possible she had enough time to type something out.

When I think about what I am going to do to her after I find her, my cock thickens.

Adjusting my dick, I move methodically through the room, checking under the bed and in the bathroom. Nothing.

All that is left is the walk-in closet.

The door is open and I look around. Nothing seems out of place, but my instincts are screaming at me that she's close. Very close.

I run my hands along the walls, looking for irregularities. When I get to the back wall, I notice the clothes are pushed slightly to one side, unlike the rest, which are hanging neatly.

My fingers find a small seam in the paneling. A hidden door.

"Clever girl," I murmur.

But then, I have another I idea.

noia

THE CLOSET HAS GONE EERILY QUIET, AND THE SILENCE stretches as I strain to hear any movement on the other side of the panel.

I check my phone.

Time's up.

My heart races with triumph and I grin. I won!

Carefully, I slide open the hidden panel and crawl back into the closet. The oppressive silence makes me nervous, but also a little smug as I scan the interior of the bedroom.

Seeing no one, I step out of the closet and before I can take another step, a large hand clamps over my mouth from behind. I try to scream but only manage a muffled yelp as I'm yanked backward against a solid, muscular chest while another arm locks around my waist.

"I thought we talked about what would happen if you messed with my actions and emotions again, Noia," Ryder growls in my ear, voice sullen and dangerous.

He walks me forward, his body pressed tight against my back, and shoves me face-first up against the wall.

The hand over my mouth moves to wrap around my throat,

while the one on my waist slides across my stomach and shoves inside my jeans, into my panties.

All I can do is whimper.

"Looks like I win, kitten." His fingers slide through my folds to collect some of my arousal before sliding back up to circle my clit. "In more ways than one."

His evil chuckle sends heat rushing through my veins like molten lava.

"Why do I feel mean, huh?" His teeth graze my earlobe as his fingers continue their torturous exploration. "What did you do to me this time?"

"I—I just wrote..." I gasp as he slides a finger inside me. "I wasn't sure if it would actually work."

"You sure about that?" His grip tightens around my throat. "You thought you could control me, make the game more interesting, am I right? Hmm?"

A second finger plunges inside me, making me cry out.

"Fucking with things you don't understand," he growls, adding a third finger and curling them to hit that perfect spot. "When will you learn?"

My knees buckle, but he holds me up, his grip on my throat tightening even further.

"Funny thing is..." He starts to thrust. "It just made me want to punish you even more."

"The—the time was up," I gasp, bucking against his hand. "You didn't find me in time."

"Oh, but I did." I can feel his lips curve into a smile against the racing pulse in my neck. "I found your hiding spot with five minutes to spare. I just decided to wait and see what you would do."

I groan in frustration as jolts of pleasure ratchet up my spine.

"Tell me what you wrote." His thumb presses against my clit as his fingers pump in and out, making it hard to think.

"Just that—ah!—that you'd feel like a predator," I moan. I'm so wet I can hear what his fingers are doing to me. "That you'd want to hunt me down and claim me."

His voice drops to a sinister whisper. "You want to be hunted?"

"Yes," I admit as a gasp.

He spins me around, pinning me back against the wall with his body. Pupils blown, his eyes are black with desire, jaw tight.

"You want to be claimed?" His fingers are back working between my legs.

"Oh, god," I whimper, already so close to the edge. "*Yes*."

His thrusts slow to an agonizing pace. "Then your wish is my command."

With a growl, he withdraws his fingers, grips my wrists and pins them above my head.

Using his other hand, he unbuttons my jeans, tugging them down with my panties until they're tangled around my knees.

The cool air hits my exposed skin, making me gasp.

"Shhh." He rests his forehead against mine, breath hot on my face. "You lost the game, remember? Now you have to do whatever I want."

He releases my wrists, only to grip my waist and lift me, carrying me to the bed. He tosses me down on the mattress, then flips me onto my stomach.

"On your knees," he commands, and I instantly obey, heart hammering against my ribs as he pulls my jeans and panties off and tosses them to the floor.

"Is this what you wanted when you wrote those words?" he asks, his voice a dangerous rumble as he runs his hands down my back. "For me to lose control?"

"Yes," I groan, pressing my face into the mattress.

"You think you can control me?" His voice is a dangerous rumble as the blunt head of his cock nudges my entrance. "You think you can write my feelings, my actions? How do I know my actions have been mine? Have you been controlling me this whole time?"

"No," I gasp, desperate for him to fill me. "I would never do that. I'm sorry."

His palm connects with my ass in a sharp slap, making me yelp. "Not yet, you're not." And with that, he slams into me, burying himself to the hilt in one powerful thrust.

I cry out as the sensation of being filled so completely overwhelms all my senses. He doesn't even give me time to adjust, just sets a punishing pace that has me clawing at the sheets.

"This is what happens," he grunts, one hand gripping my hip while the other coils in my hair, yanking my head back. "When you play with fire."

Each thrust drives me closer to the edge, the delicious friction building so fast I barely have time to breathe. His fingers dig into my hip hard enough to leave bruises, marking me as his.

"Promise me you won't ever do that again," he demands, his pace relentless.

His thrusts are hard and deep, each one driving me further up the bed until I have to brace myself against the headboard, forcing harsh breaths and desperate moans from my throat.

"I won't," I groan, the pressure building to an unbearable level. "I promise."

"Damn right you won't." His hand tightens in my hair, pulling just enough to arch my back and change the angle of his thrusts, making the new position hit a spot inside me that makes my toes curl.

"Fuuuck. You feel so fucking good."

"Ryder, please," I beg, not even sure what I'm asking for at this point.

"Please what?" He slows his pace, drawing out each thrust until I'm whimpering.

"Harder," I gasp. "Fuck me harder."

He immediately complies, hips snapping against my ass as his fingers dig into my hips. Just the thought of wearing his fingerprints on my skin sends a fresh wave of heat through my body.

"You're such a dirty little slut for me, aren't you?"

The moan that bursts from my lips is barely recognizable.

"Promise you won't control me again," he grunts, pounding relentlessly.

"I—I promise." I pant, the words tumbling out without hesitation.

"I can't hear you." He reaches around to find my clit, circling it with a finger.

"Oh, god! Oh, fuck! I promise!" I cry out as pleasure builds, coiling tighter in my belly and tingling at the base of my spine.

"That's right," he growls. "And don't you fucking forget it."

The dual sensation of his cock stretching me and his fingers working my clit pushes me over the edge. My orgasm explodes, making my inner walls clench around him as I scream his name.

Following right behind with a hoarse shout, his hips falter as he empties himself inside me before he collapses, breath hot against my neck as we both gasp for air.

FORTY-NINE

Heart hammering against my ribs, I roll over. Noia lets out a contented sigh as I pull her against my chest, her body warm and limp with exhaustion. I press a gentle kiss to her forehead, watching as her eyes flutter closed.

"You okay?" I brush a strand of hair from her face.

"Mmm," she hums, already starting to drift. "Yes."

Within minutes, her breathing deepens and evens out. She's asleep, completely spent in my arms.

But the Sandman doesn't come for me.

My mind races as it replays the past twenty minutes. The way my emotions shifted and how the sudden predatory instinct took over, driving me to hunt her down. How the rush of possessiveness and the need to claim her felt much like my own desire, but also like something that had been forced upon me.

I stare up at the ceiling, a cold knot forming in my gut. She can still control me. With just a few keystrokes, she can change how I feel, what I want, maybe even who I am.

What if I never had free will at all? What if every decision I've made since I showed up here, every feeling I've had for her, was caused by what Noia was writing every day?

How much control does she actually have over me?

My stomach twists into knots when I think about all the memories that have been slowly starting to surface—my time in Afghanistan, meeting Claire, and opening the tattoo shop with Jax.

Were those real memories I somehow forgot, or just a convenient backstory she created to make me more three-dimensional?

The thought makes my skin crawl. I spent years clawing my way back from addiction, fighting to regain control of my life, my body, my choices. And now I discover that at any moment, she could potentially override all of that with a just a few keystrokes?

Christ, now *I'm* starting to question if I am real.

I glance down at Noia, peacefully asleep on my chest. Her lips are slightly parted, face completely relaxed. She looks so innocent, so unaware of the doubt and confusion she's triggered inside me.

She didn't mean any harm—I know that. Just playing, testing boundaries, trying to make the game more exciting. But still...

What happens when we disagree about something important? What happens if we fight? Would she use her power to make me bend to her will? Could she make me love her if I didn't already?

Do I even love her? Or was that the premise of my story from the beginning?

Carefully, I slide out from under her and pad quietly into the bathroom. Splashing cold water on my face, I look in the mirror. The man staring back at me seems solid enough—the stubble on my jaw, the tiny scar above my eyebrow, the tattoos covering my arms and chest.

I grip the edges of the sink. The thought of not being in

control of my own destiny makes my blood run cold. I've spent years fighting to regain control and just the thought I might never have had it to begin with is unbearable.

Moving silently back into the bedroom, I watch Noia sleep for a few moments longer. The moonlight streaming through the window makes her look almost ethereal.

I love her. That much I know with absolute certainty. But can I trust her with the very essence of who I am?

Grabbing my jeans from the floor, I pull them on and head downstairs. I need some air, some space to think.

Downstairs, I pace the living room, running my hands through my hair. Goonie watches me from his perch on the windowsill, tail twitching.

"What the fuck am I supposed to do with all this?" I mutter to myself.

I grab a beer from the fridge and step outside onto the porch. The cool night air feels good against my bare chest as I drop into one of the Adirondack chairs and stare out at the dark trees.

This whole situation is fucked up beyond belief. I'm falling for a woman who literally created me. A woman who can apparently still change who I am with just a few words. How can I trust anything I feel? How can I be sure *any* of this is real?

I take a long pull from my beer, letting the cool, bitter liquid slide down my throat. The moon is high and full, casting silver light across the yard.

I remember the look on Noia's face when she saw her tattoo for the first time—the wonder, the joy, the connection she felt to my art. That was real, right? It had to be.

And the way she trembled beneath me only a few minutes ago, the way she gasped my name as she came apart—that felt real too.

But now I'm questioning everything.

"Fuck," I whisper into the dark.

I've already survived so much. But this—this existential mindfuck—might be what finally breaks me.

With a frustrated growl, I stand and go back inside.

Maybe a ride will clear my head.

I hurry into my room and grab a Henley from the closet and pull it over my head.

Back in the kitchen, I scribble a quick note and leave it on the counter.

After closing the front door, I shrug into my leather jacket, shove my helmet on, and straddle my motorcycle. The engine roars to life, and I tear down the drive.

I ride until the first hints of dawn start to streak the sky, then turn back. By the time I pull into the driveway, I've made a decision.

I need to know for sure if my life is really mine now. And there's only one way to find out.

FIFTY

THE ROAR OF AN ENGINE JOLTS ME FROM A DEEP SLEEP. Disoriented, I reach across the bed, finding only empty space.

"Ryder?" I call out, my voice thick with sleep.

But the only answer I get is silence.

Throwing back the covers, I wince when the movement pulls at my tattoo. I grab Ryder's T-shirt from the floor and pull it over my head, then pad to the window just in time to see his motorcycle disappearing down the driveway.

My stomach knots with worry. Where is he going at this hour?

I check my phone: 2:37 a.m.

Goonie meows at me from the doorway, looking just as confused as I feel.

"I don't know why he left either," I tell him.

Scooping him up, I head downstairs.

The kitchen is dark, but when I flip on the light, I spot a piece of paper on the kitchen island. Heart pounding, I pick it up.

Needed to clear my head —R.

The note slips from my fingers.

"Shit." I sink onto a stool, hiding my face in my hands. "What have I done?"

Guilt crashes over me. I'd promised him I wouldn't write specifically about him anymore, wouldn't risk whatever strange magic that had brought him here. But I'd done it anyway, treating him like a character I could manipulate instead of a person with his own free will.

No wonder he left.

"I really fucked up this time, Goonie," I sigh, absentmindedly scratching behind his ears.

I drag myself back upstairs to where my laptop sits on my nightstand. Opening it, I pull up the document and stare at the words I wrote.

They're such simple words, but they manipulated him.

I think of all the pages I've written about everything we've done since he appeared—detailed descriptions of our thoughts, our feelings, our reactions.

Suddenly, I know that there's only one way to fix this.

"Shit."

With trembling fingers, I Control-A all the text—every word I've written about Ryder and about our dates since he appeared —and hover my finger over the delete key.

What if deleting everything about him, about us, makes him disappear altogether? What if this severs whatever magical connection that brought him here in the first place?

But I know I can't keep controlling him, intentionally or unintentionally.

He deserves better.

With a deep breath, I hit DELETE. The document goes blank, the cursor blinking at me accusingly from the empty page.

Closing my laptop with a sigh, I climb back into bed.

But I can't sleep. The thought of Ryder out there some-where, feeling manipulated and betrayed, keeps me wide awake.

I figure I might as well be productive, so I throw myself into cleaning—scrubbing the kitchen counters with more force than necessary, organizing the pantry, and doing three loads of laun-dry. Physical activity has always helped keep my mind from spiraling into worst-case scenarios. Too bad it never helped with my writer's block though.

By the time I've folded the last of Ryder's T-shirts, the sky has lightened from pitch black to a deep indigo. I carry the basket to his room, hesitating when I get to the door.

When I push the door open, the scent of sandalwood and leather envelops me immediately. I set the basket on the bed and start putting his clothes away in the dresser.

When I step into the closet, my heart stutters. All his things are still here—his boots lined up on the floor, his collection of Henley's. Relief washes over me in a wave so powerful it nearly brings me to my knees.

If his things are still here, it means he should still be here. He has to be.

With a renewed sense of hope, I head to the kitchen to start a pot of coffee and watch as the first golden rays of sun start peeking through the windows. The rich aroma fills the air as I pull eggs and bacon from the fridge, determined to have break-fast ready when he returns.

Just as I start cracking eggs into a bowl, I hear the distinctive rumble of a motorcycle coming up the driveway. My heart leaps into my throat, and I nearly drop the egg.

I hear the engine cut off. Then a few moments later, the sound of his boots hit the porch right before the front door opens.

With my favorite pink spatula clutched in my hand, I turn around.

Hair mussed from his helmet, his stubble is darker than usual and he looks tired.

My heart leaps. He's still here. Still real.

Afraid if speaking too loudly might somehow break whatever spell that's keeping him here, I whisper, "You're back."

Ryder shrugs off his jacket and hangs it on the hook by the door. "I needed to figure some things out."

"And did you?"

He crosses the room until he's standing right in front of me. Intense and questioning, his eyes search mine. "I need to know something first. Did you delete it?"

My breath catches. "How did you—"

"I just do, Noia." His jaw tightens. "Now answer me. Did you delete everything you wrote about me?"

I nod, swallowing hard. "Yes. Everything. I didn't want to risk controlling you anymore, even by accident. Even if it meant you would disappear."

Relief flickers in his eyes, softening the hard lines of his face. "I rode all night, trying to figure out if what I feel is real or if it was just you writing about us."

"But you..."

"I know it was my idea for you to write about everything. And I also know, except for what you did last night, it's not your fault if that's what's happening. Maybe the universe has other plans."

He runs his hand through his hair, letting out a deep sigh. "But I need to know if what I feel for you is real. I need to know if I'm the one making my own choices."

My hands are trembling so hard I have to set the spatula down. "What are you saying?"

"I think we need to spend some time apart." His voice is gentle but firm, his eyes never leaving mine. "Just to make sure that whatever this is between us is real and not just... fictional."

My heart plummets. "Time apart? But Rye—"

"It's the only way, Noia." He takes a step back. "I need to be somewhere you're not, somewhere I can assess my own emotions. Figure out if they're really mine."

Panic rises in my throat. "But where will you go?"

"I can stay with Jax." His expression softens. "He's got a spare room at his place."

"You don't need to leave," I argue. "I deleted all of it. I'm not going to write about you... us, anymore."

He shakes his head. "It's not just about that. It's about me figuring out who I am outside of... whatever this is between us. I need space to think."

"But—"

"I've already called Jax, and he's expecting me." It's obvious the decision is final by how his tone changes almost instantly.

I cross my arms in defense. "How long?"

"I don't know." He sighs again. "A few days, maybe a week."

"A week?" My voice cracks.

Instead of answering, he turns and heads down the hall. I follow him into his room, watching in shock as he pulls a duffel bag from the closet and starts to pack.

"This is crazy," I say, standing in the doorway. "You don't have to leave."

"Yes, I do." He keeps his eyes on the bag as he zips it closed. "For both of us. I thought you would understand. Or did you forget how you left me here alone so you could go have time to figure your shit out, too?"

Shit. Having what I did to him first thrown back in my face stops me cold.

I let out a sigh of resignation. "You're right. I'm sorry."

He gives me a slight nod.

Five minutes later, we're standing together at the front door.

Duffle bag over his shoulder, his face is blank, but his eyes tell a much different story.

All I can do is fight back the tears. Despite hating how vulnerable I feel and how much it hurts to watch him leave, I understand where he's coming from.

He steps into my space, cupping my face with his free hand, gently brushing his thumb along my cheek. "Give me a couple of days, okay? And then we can talk."

The tenderness in his voice almost breaks me and I just nod, not trusting myself to speak.

Pressing a soft kiss to my forehead, he turns and walks out the door.

I'm still standing in the doorway long after his motorcycle has disappeared down the drive and the sound of the engine has faded into silence.

Goonie winds around my ankles, meowing softly.

A single frustrated tear escapes, and I swipe it away. "Don't worry, pudge. He'll be back."

ryder

Jax's house is located on the outskirts of town. When I pull into his driveway, I cut the engine, and just sit on my bike.

Not only is my body heavy with exhaustion after riding most of the night, my mind is a fucked up mess of emotions.

The front door swings open before I make it up the walkway. Dressed in basketball shorts and a faded Metallica T-shirt, Jax's hair is sticking up in all directions like he just rolled out of bed.

"Dude. You look like shit."

"Fuck you." I shoulder past him into the house. "Thanks for the warm welcome, dick."

Jax chuckles.

His apartment is exactly what you'd expect from a single guy in his thirties—worn but relatively decent furniture, a massive 80-inch flat-screen mounted on the wall, and a couple of empty beer bottles still sitting on the coffee table.

I drop my duffel bag on the floor next to the couch and collapse onto it, scrubbing my hands over my face.

"Thanks for letting me crash."

"Not a problem." He eyes me suspiciously. "You gonna tell me what's really going on? You and your girl have a fight?"

He moves into the kitchen, grabbing a couple of beers from the fridge.

I blow out a long breath. "It's complicated."

"Complicated how?" He tosses me a beer before cracking one open for himself. "You two were all over each other at the party."

I tip my head back and stare up at the ceiling. How do I explain my current situation without sounding like I've lost my mind? There is no way I can tell him I'm actually fictional, and that until I showed up he probably didn't exist either.

"Yeah." I take a long pull from the bottle. "But it's... fuck, I don't even know where to start."

Jax flops down in the recliner across from me. "Start with why you're here instead of balls-deep in your hot writer girlfriend."

I shoot him a glare.

He just shrugs and grins before taking a swig of his beer.

"When I first moved in with Noia, it was just to help with her writer's block while my apartment was being renovated," I start, choosing my words carefully. "She'd been stuck for weeks after her asshole ex left her at the altar."

"Yeah, you mentioned that."

"Well, what I came up with to help, worked. She's been able to start writing again." I pick at the label on my beer bottle. "But somewhere along the way, things got... intense."

"You caught feelings," Jax states matter-of-fact.

"Yeah." I exhale slowly. "And now I'm having a hard time figuring out if what I'm feeling is real or if it's just because of our current situation."

"What situation?" Jax tilts his head. "You're living with a

hot blonde who writes smut for a living. Seems pretty straightforward to me."

If only he knew how far from straightforward my current situation actually is.

"I just need some space to figure my shit out," I say. "See if what I'm feeling holds up when I'm not around her all the time."

"Fair enough." Jax doesn't push, which is one of the many things I've always appreciated about him. "So what's the plan? Just hide out here until you get your head straight?"

"Pretty much." I finish my beer. "That a problem?"

"Nah, man. Stay as long as you need."

"Appreciate it."

"A little too early in the morning for this heavy shit." Jax stands up and stretches. "How about you go crash and when you get up, we can order pizza, drink beer and play video games the rest of the day?"

"Sounds good. Thanks."

"Guest room is all yours." Jax points down the hall. "Sheets are actually clean."

I grab my bag and head down the hall, my body practically screaming for sleep. The room is small but neat, with a queen-size bed, small nightstand and blue light-blocking curtains framing the window.

Shutting the door behind me, I drop my bag on the floor and close the curtains. Then I collapse onto the bed, not even bothering to take off my boots. The moment my head hits the pillow, I'm out cold.

WHEN I WAKE UP, MY MOUTH FEELS LIKE SANDPAPER AND my head is pounding.

I glance at the clock on the nightstand. I've been asleep for almost eight hours.

A quick knock sounds at the door before it opens.

"About time you rejoined the land of the living," Jax says from the doorway. "I ordered pizza. Large meat lovers with extra cheese and a couple sides of wings." He tosses me a cold beer. "Figured you could use this."

"I knew there was a reason I liked you." I crack it open and take a long swallow, the cold liquid soothing my parched throat.

The doorbell rings and when Jax leaves to go answer it, I haul myself up and into the bathroom to grab a quick shower. Throwing on a pair of sweats and a T-shirt, I head into the living room.

"Food's here," Jax says. "And I've got Call of Duty loaded up."

"Good. 'Cuz I really need to shoot something."

"Why does that not surprise me?"

The pizza smells like heaven, and my stomach growls in response. Grabbing a slice, I drop onto the couch and quickly scarf it down.

After downing the rest of my beer, Jax hands me a controller. "Prepare to get your ass handed to you," he grins.

"In your dreams," I grin back, already feeling better.

We spend the next several hours playing video games, talking shit, and demolishing the pizza and wings. It's easy to fall back into our usual rhythm, and for a while, I forget about everything else.

By the time we finish our sixth—or is it seventh?—beer, I'm pleasantly buzzed. The game ends with my character getting blown to bits, and I toss the controller aside.

"Fuck that shit," I mutter with a grin.

"Want another beer?" Jax asks, heading to the kitchen.

"Sure." I settle back against the couch.

Then it hits me. I wonder what Noia is doing right now. Is she writing? Is she thinking about me? Does she miss me as much as I suddenly realize I miss her?

"Hey. You good?" Jax asks, handing me another beer.

I take it with a grunt. "Just thinking."

"About your girl," he states.

"Yeah."

Jax studies me for a moment, then sets his beer down with a decisive thud. "Alright, that's it. We're going out."

"What? No, man. I'm good here."

"Nope. I'm not gonna spend the rest of the night watching you sit around and mope." He points in the direction of the hall. "Go get dressed. We're hitting The Brew."

"Fine," I grumble, pushing myself off the couch. "But just for a couple of hours."

Thirty minutes later, we're walking into The Brew. The place is packed, music thumping as we make our way across the room to where Claire and Lizzy are hanging out at the bar.

"Ladies," Jax grins, sliding onto a barstool. "Fancy meeting you here."

I nod at them and order a whiskey, wishing I was back at Jax's place. Or better yet, with Noia.

Claire slides onto the stool next to me, eyeing me carefully. "What's up with you? Where's Noia?"

"Not here." Shifting uncomfortably in my seat, I take a sip of my drink, bracing myself.

"Everything, okay?"

I shrug, this time downing half my drink.

Lizzy shoves Jax out of the way and leans on the bar next to me. Now I've got both women boxing me in.

"Why do you have sad puppy dog eyes?"

I glance over at Jax for help, but he just grins.

Asshole.

"I do *not* have sad puppy dog eyes," I growl.

"Oh, you definitely do," Claire agrees as she slides off the stool and grabs my arm. "Come on, broody. Let's go play some darts."

Next thing I know, she's dragging me over to a dartboard in the corner, Jax and Lizzy not far behind.

"So what happened?" Claire asks as she sets up the game.

She hands me the darts and I roll them over and over in my hand while I think about what to say. "It's complicated."

"Life's complicated," she says, lining up her shot. "Doesn't mean you should run from it."

Her dart hits the bullseye dead on.

Moving into position, I take my turn. "I'm not running," I argue, my dart landing just outside the center. Yup, definitely off my game, and in more ways than one. "I just needed time to think."

"About what?" Lizzy asks, perching on a nearby stool.

"Whether if what I'm feeling for her is real or not."

Claire's second dart hits the triple twenty. "You mean you're afraid you only like her because you're living in the same house?"

"Something like that," I mutter.

"Come on. You've been taking her out on these... adventure dates to help her with her writer's block, right?"

I nod and throw another dart, knocking one of Claire's off the board and onto the floor.

"Well, it makes sense with you spending all this time together that you'd start having some kind of feelings." Snatching the dart from the floor, she pins me with a look. "You've slept with her, haven't you?"

I nearly choke on my drink. " Jesus, Claire—"

"That's a yes." With a knowing smirk, she throws her final dart. "So, what's the problem? The way you two were all over each other at the party, it was pretty obvious."

"Yeah, we've slept together." I down the rest of my whiskey. "Multiple times."

"How was it?" Lizzy grins wickedly.

"Jesus Christ." I scrub a hand over my face. "I'm not talking about this with any of you anymore."

"That good, huh?" Jax chuckles.

I turn to glare at him. "Who the fuck's side are you on?"

"The side that wants to see you stop being a moody asshole." He signals the waitress for another round. "Look, man, I've known you for over a decade and I've never seen you like this about anyone."

I down the rest of my whiskey, reveling in the warmth as it burns its way down my throat. How do I go about explaining that I'm questioning my entire existence?

"Like what?"

"Happy," Claire cuts in softly. "For the first time since I've known you, you actually seem happy. Aside from tonight."

Her words hit me hard. She's right. I have been happy. Happier than I've been in years.

Lizzy pipes up again. "Are you scared?"

"Of course not," I snap. "Sorry. I just..." I rub the back of my neck. "I just need to know if my feelings are genuine."

"Why do you think your feelings aren't genuine?" Lizzy raises an eyebrow.

I sigh. "What if I only think I care about her because of our current situation?"

Claire throws her hands up. "Ride, that's literally how all relationships work. You meet someone, you spend time together, you develop feelings—especially now that you're sleeping together. You should've known that would take everything you're doing to a whole other level."

"But what if—"

"Nuh-uh," she interrupts. "You're seriously overthinking this. Do you miss her?"

I hesitate, then nod reluctantly.

"When you think about her, does it make you happy?"

Another nod.

"When you imagine your life without her, how do you feel?"

The question hits me hard. Just the thought of never seeing Noia again twists something tight and painful in my gut.

"Empty," I reply, my voice hoarse. "I feel fucking empty."

Claire gives me a knowing look. "There's your answer."

Several rounds later, the room is spinning. My head has taken on that pleasant, fuzzy feeling where everything is wobbly and soft.

"I think we should call it a night," Jax says, placing a hand on my shoulder to steady me when I start to sway on my barstool.

"Jus' one more," I insist, raising my empty glass.

"Nope. You're done." Claire plucks the glass from my hand. "Time to go home, big guy."

The thought of going back to Jax's place, to that empty guest room, makes me anxious. Then the back of my neck tingles, and I know where I need to go.

"My place," I blurt. "Take me to my apartment."

Jax frowns. "I thought your apartment was getting renovated."

I shake my head, immediately regretting doing so when my head feels like it's going to pop like a balloon. "Pretty sure it's done."

"You sure you don't want to stay with me?" Jax asks, concern written all over his face. "You can stay at your place tomorrow."

"I'm good."

"Okay," Jax sighs.

Claire and Lizzy help us out to Jax's truck. As soon as I'm in the front seat, I promptly slump against the window, the glass cool and soothing against my forehead.

"You're gonna feel like shit tomorrow," Jax mutters as he drives.

"Already do," I mumble.

After we park in front of Skin & Ink, Jax helps me out of the truck and up the stairs.

Fumbling with my keys, I drop them twice before Jax lets out an exasperated sigh and takes them away from me.

The door swings open, and I step inside. Every light is on, and the place looks... good.

Books fill the shelves lining the back wall, and a red throw blanket is lying over the back of a brown leather couch. A 60-inch flat screen sits on top of more bookshelves that are shorter than the others, lined up next to each other to form a makeshift entertainment center.

Framed posters and art hang on the walls. The floors look like they've been refinished, and the kitchen has been updated as well.

"Wow," Jax exclaims. "The place looks good, man."

Despite my inebriated state, somehow I knew this would all be here.

"Weird," I mumble, running my hand along the back of the couch. "This is exactly how I imagined it would look."

"Whoever did the renovation did a great job," Jax says, looking around appreciatively. "You want me to hang for a bit?"

I shake my head, surprised when the room doesn't spin as bad as it did before. "Nah, I'm good. Just need to sleep it off."

"You sure?"

"Yeah. Thanks for the ride."

Jax looks skeptical, but heads for the door. "Call me tomorrow."

"Will do."

As soon as the door closes behind him, I throw the lock, toe off my boots, and head into the bedroom.

Flanked by two nightstands, a king-size bed with a fluffy tan duvet sits on a large multicolored blue area rug up against the wall to my left.

In just a few strides, I'm across the room. I throw open the doors to the built-in closets and find they are no longer empty. All my clothes are hanging neatly inside—jeans, Henley's, T-shirts, my boots are lined up on the floor. There's even a couple of suits.

Swaying on my feet, I hear Jax's truck start up and pull away from the curb.

Making my way back through the apartment, I turn off all the lights. Back in my bedroom, I strip and collapse onto my new bed.

My last coherent thought before darkness claims me is of Noia's face and the hurt in her eyes when I told her I needed time and space.

noia

MORNING COMES WAY TOO FAST, FORCING ME TO ADMIT yesterday wasn't just a bad dream.

I reach for my phone on the nightstand and call Sasha, who answers on the third ring.

"Hey, babe. What's up?" Jeez, her voice is annoyingly chipper in the morning.

"Ryder left," I blurt, my voice cracking as tears threaten to spill over again.

"Whoa, back up. What happened?"

I fill her in on all of it: hide and seek, my stupid decision to control his actions, and how he showed up at the ass-crack of dawn after riding all night to tell me he needed space.

"He just... left?" Sasha sounds as stunned as I feel.

"Yeah." I swallow hard. "I deleted everything I wrote, even though I was scared he would disappear, but he came back. His stuff was still in the closet after he left."

"Have you checked again this morning? Like, are you sure his stuff is still there? Because the way his things have been appearing outta nowhere since he showed up makes me think things could disappear just as easily."

My heart stops. "Hold on."

Phone to my ear, I rush downstairs to Ryder's room.

The closet is empty.

All his clothes, his boots, everything—gone.

"It's all gone," I whisper, sinking to my knees. "Everything. Like he was never here."

"Okay, don't panic." Sasha's voice is calm and steady. "You need to call him. Right now."

"But what if he's gone for good? What if deleting everything I wrote about him made him and everything about him disappear?"

"Noia, listen to me," she says firmly. "Take a deep breath and call him. If he doesn't answer, leave a message and give him some time to call you back. Trust he's real and that he's not just going to vanish into thin air."

"Okay." My voice sounds small. "I'll call you back."

Taking a deep breath, I hang up with Sasha and call Ryder. It rings three times before it goes to voicemail.

The sound of his voice sends a sharp pang through my chest and I wait for the beep.

"Hey, Rye." My traitorous voice is shaking. "I just... I noticed all your things are gone, and I... Please call me back. Let me know you're still... here."

I hang up and sit on the floor of the empty closet, hugging my knees to my chest.

Goonie comes in, meowing and rubs against my legs.

"I really screwed up, pudge," I whisper. Using Ryder's nickname for him makes my heart twist. I pull him into my lap, burying my face in his tummy.

I have no idea how long I've been sitting here, lost in my own misery, when a loud, insistent knock at the front door startles me back to reality.

"Ryder?"

Heart pounding, I scramble to my feet, ignoring the pins and needles shooting through my legs as I rush to the door.

Halfway there, another knock comes, and then the doorbell.

"Coming!"

Hope blooms in my chest as I fling the door open, only to freeze in shock.

"Hey, Noia."

Perfectly groomed in his designer suit, reddish-blonde hair styled just so, Eric's smile is as practiced and polished as ever.

"What the fuck?" I grip the doorframe, suddenly light-headed. "What are you doing here?"

He has the audacity to look hurt. "I come to surprise you and that's how you choose to speak to me?"

I sputter, anger rising to replace shock. "Are you seriously asking me that? You left me at the altar without a word, and now you just show up at my door unannounced?!"

His smile falters slightly, but he recovers quickly. "I've been trying to call you for weeks. I know I have a lot to explain." He shifts his weight, looking nervous. "Can I come in? Please?"

Every instinct is screaming at me to slam the door in his face, but curiosity and a lingering need for answers, has me stepping aside.

"Five minutes," I say coldly. "Then you need to leave."

"Thank you." He steps inside and looks around. "The place looks good. Different than I remember."

I cross my arms over my chest, suddenly aware I'm still wearing Ryder's oversized T-shirt. Hope blooms in my chest again. Maybe he hasn't disappeared after all.

"Clock's ticking, Eric."

Eric's eyes narrow, gaze lingering on the T-shirt that clearly doesn't belong to me. "Look, I know I owe you an explanation."

"Then get to it."

He sighs, running a hand through his hair. "I messed up," he says finally. "Leaving you hanging like that... it was a big mistake."

I bark out a laugh. "You're a few months too late for that revelation. You left me behind and didn't even have the decency to tell me to my face."

"I know." He takes a step toward me, and I instinctively take a step back. "But I've been doing a lot of thinking. A lot of soul-searching."

"Soul-searching?" I repeat incredulously. "Since when have you ever been one to 'soul-search'? You don't give a shit about anyone but yourself. It just took you leaving for me to realize it."

"I deserve that," he says sheepishly. "But I'm here now because I want to make things right. I want another chance."

The sheer audacity almost leaves me speechless. "Are you being serious right now?"

He reaches for my hand, but I yank it away. "I panicked. I know it was unforgivable, but—"

"But what? What could possibly justify what you did?"

"I got scared." He shrugs. "Our relationship moved so fast, and suddenly there was a wedding and all these expectations..." He shoves his hands in his pockets. "I just needed time to think."

"What is it with men needing time to think?" I murmur to myself.

"What?"

"Nothing. Are you done?"

He takes a step closer, trying to close the distance between us. "I still love you, Noia."

Words that once would have sent my heart soaring, leave me feeling nothing. I study his face—the face I once thought I'd wake up to every morning for the rest of my life—and still feel absolutely nothing.

"Why are you really here, Eric?" I sigh, exhaustion taking over.

His expression shifts, and I catch a glimpse of something else in his eyes. "Your agent mentioned you've been having some... difficulties with the new manuscript."

And there it is. Eric works for my publisher, so either my agent or someone else must have filled him in.

Heads are going to roll.

"So that's what this is about," I say, voice tight with anger. "My book. Of course."

"It's not just that," Eric protests, taking another step toward me. "I miss you. We were good together."

I back up until the edge of the kitchen island presses into my back. "We were never good together. You just liked having a bestselling author on your arm at publishing events."

His expression darkens. "That's not fair. I supported your career."

"Oh, come on! It's obvious it was all just a business transaction."

He moves even closer, invading my personal space. "I made a mistake. People make mistakes."

"Back. Off," I warn, placing my palm against his chest.

He grabs my wrist. "Noia, please. Just listen to me."

In the distance, I swear I hear the rumble of a motorcycle engine. My heart leaps with hope, distracting me.

Seizing the opportunity, Eric lunges forward and smashes his mouth against mine.

"Mmph!" I struggle for a moment before I'm able to twist my head away. "Get. Off. Me!"

His hands grip my waist, pinning me against the island.

"Come on, Noia. I know we can fix this," he insists, trying to recapture my mouth.

Panic floods my brain and I shove hard against his shoulders, but he won't budge.

"I said no!" I screech, shoving my knee up into his balls.

Just as Eric doubles over with a high-pitched yelp, clutching himself, the front door crashes open with a bang.

FUCK MY LIFE.

My head is pounding, and my mouth feels like I've been chewing on cotton balls all night.

Groaning, I roll over and check my phone. It's just past noon, and I have three missed calls from Jax and a text from Claire, but nothing from Noia.

A little disappointed and strangely relieved, I drag myself out of bed and into the bathroom. My preferred brand of soap and shampoo are sitting in the shower niche and fluffy blue towels hang neatly on the towel bar.

I stand under the hot spray for a long time, still surprised at how my things suddenly showed up in my apartment. I had a feeling it would happen at the right time, but I never once thought it would be for the reason it did.

Wrapping a towel around my waist, I pad into the kitchen. The fridge is stocked with beer, almond milk, eggs, bacon, and other essentials. Coffee, cereal, and a few canned goods fill the cabinets as well.

It's as if the universe knew exactly what I needed.

I scramble some eggs and take a couple of aspirin. After

eating, I get dressed and head downstairs to the shop for my one appointment of the day.

My one o'clock is a long time client who wants a detailed sleeve using the watercolor technique—something that usually requires my full concentration. But halfway through the outline, I realize I've asked her to repeat herself three times because my mind keeps drifting back to Noia.

"Everything okay?" she asks as I wipe away the excess ink.

"Yeah, sorry. Just a little distracted today."

I force myself to focus, but it takes twice as long as it normally would. By the time we finish the session and schedule her next appointment, I'm mentally exhausted.

"Sorry about today," I tell her as she examines the outline in the mirror.

"No worries. It's looking amazing so far."

After she leaves, I clean my station meticulously, taking my time. With Jax out on a supply run and Claire handling paperwork in the office, the shop is quiet today.

Desperate for a hit of caffeine to help with my hangover, I head to the break room. The coffee machine gurgles as it brews a fresh pot, and I lean against the counter, rubbing my temples.

Suddenly, I realize I haven't checked my messages since I woke up. When I go to take my phone out of my pocket, it isn't there.

Shit. I left it upstairs in my apartment.

"Great."

I fill my mug and take a long sip, wincing when I accidentally burn my tongue. Setting the mug aside to cool, I decide to head upstairs to grab my phone, stopping abruptly when Jax walks in.

"Dude, what the fuck was that about last night?" he demands, blocking the doorway.

"Don't start with me right now, man. I'm not in the mood."

"Cut the crap." He crosses his arms. "You were a complete wreck, begging to go to your apartment. Then you don't answer my calls all morning?"

"Sorry about that. My phone was on silent."

"Seriously?" Jax narrows his eyes. "Claire and Lizzy were worried sick. We all were."

Spreading my arms wide, I force a grin. "As you can see, I'm perfectly fine."

Moving in closer, he lowers his voice. "Look, I don't know what's going on with you and Noia, but you need to get your shit together. You're not acting like yourself."

"I told you, I just needed some space to figure things out."

"And how's that working out for you?" Jax's tone drips with sarcasm. "Because from what Claire tells me about how you've been acting today, you're worse off than you were when you were drunk last night."

"Fine. I've been distracted today, okay? Is that what you want to hear?" I rake my hands through my hair. "Can you just lay off? How would you like it if I gave you shit about you moping around after Sasha left, huh?"

Jax's eyebrows shoot up. "I haven't been moping. It was just one night, no big deal."

"Yeah? And *that's* not what Claire told *me*." I push past him, heading for the stairs. "I need to get my phone."

"Fine," Jax calls after me. "But you're going to have to come to terms with what you're feeling eventually!"

Fuming, I take the stairs two at a time. The last thing I need right now is a lecture.

What I need... is Noia.

It's only been twenty-four hours and I miss her. Only been a day, and I already miss her smile, her laugh, the way she curls against my body at night.

I grab my phone from the night stand, heart skipping when I see she called and left a message right after I left this morning.

"Hey, Rye. I just... I noticed all your things are gone, and I... Please call me back. Let me know you're still...here."

She sounds scared.

Guilt floods my veins. She probably thinks I've disappeared completely, maybe even thinks she deleted me from existence.

Fuck. I have to go see her.

Without overthinking it, I grab my keys and race back downstairs. Jax is at the front desk when I burst into the room.

"I'm taking the rest of the day off," I announce. "Can you take me to your place to pick up my bike?"

Jax looks at Claire and she nods.

"Sure."

Ten minutes later, I'm tearing down the road toward Noia's cottage. The wind whips against my body as I lean into the curves, my heart pounding harder with each passing mile.

I should have called her back instead of just showing up out of the blue, but something in her voice made me panic. The fear, the uncertainty—it was all my fault.

When I pull into her driveway, I notice an unfamiliar black BMW parked next to her SUV. My stomach drops. Who the hell's car is that?

I cut the engine and take off my helmet. Through the front window, I can see movement inside—two figures standing close together in the kitchen.

Too close.

My blood turns to ice when I realize one of them is a man in a suit, and he's got his hands on Noia.

"What the fuck?" I snarl and climb off my bike, sprinting toward the house.

The front door is unlocked, so I don't bother knocking,

bursting through just as Noia drives her knee into the bastard's balls.

noia

I LOOK UP AND MY BREATH CATCHES IN MY THROAT.

Ryder, eyes dark with fury, chest heaving, is standing in the doorway, hands clenched into white-knuckled fists at his sides.

"What the fuck is going on?"

Still wincing, Eric straightens slowly. "Who the hell are you?"

"I could ask you the same question," Ryder growls, stalking into the room.

"I'm Noia's fiancé."

"*Ex*-fiancée," I correct, moving away from him.

Ryder's jaw ticks. "You're Eric."

"Yeah." Eric looks Ryder up and down with obvious disdain. "Again, who the fuck are you?"

"Your worst nightmare if you don't get away from her."

Eric's eyes narrow as he steps further away, eyes bouncing between us before he shoots me a glare. "Oh. I see. Didn't take you long to replace me, did it?"

"You replaced yourself when you didn't show up to our wedding," I snap.

"I think it's time for you to go," Ryder says, voice low and dangerous.

Eric snorts. "I'm not going anywhere until Noia and I finish our conversation." He turns to me with a sneer. "You can't just throw away what we had because you're screwing some biker."

"Watch me," I say, moving to stand beside Ryder.

Ryder puts his arm around my waist and pulls me against him, making Eric's face turn a bright shade of red I've never seen before.

"You don't know her like I do," he continues, voice rising. "We have history. We were going to get married."

"*Were* being the operative term," Ryder says, his voice deadly calm. "She's obviously moved on."

Eric's eyes flash with rage. "You think you can just waltz in here and take my place?"

"I'm not taking anyone's place." Ryder's grip tightens on my waist. "You gave that up when you left her without a word otherwise."

"That was a mistake—"

"Yeah, it was," I interrupt, finally finding my voice. "And it's not one I'm going to let you make again. We're done, Eric. We've been done since the day you walked away."

"You can't be serious!" Eric's face contorts with fury. "You're choosing this... this *lowlife* over me?"

And that's when Ryder's control finally snaps.

Releasing me, he lunges forward, grabs Eric by the lapels of his expensive suit and slams him up against the wall.

"Call me whatever you want," he snarls in Eric's face. "But you will show her the respect she deserves, or I'll make sure you regret it."

"Rye," I say softly. "He's not worth it."

For a moment, I think Ryder might ignore me and actually

hit him. Muscles coiled like lethal springs, rage radiates from every inch of his body.

But then he takes a deep breath, releases Eric, and takes a step back.

"Get the fuck out," he growls. "Now."

Hands shaking, face pale, Eric squares his shoulders and straightens his suit. "This isn't over, Noia."

"Yes, it is," I answer firmly. "Don't contact me and don't ever come back here again."

Eric's eyes dart between us one more time before he stalks to the door, throwing one last verbal jab over his shoulder. "You're going to regret this."

"Not even for a second," I toss back.

The door slams behind him, and a minute later his BMW starts up and tears out of the driveway.

"Are you okay?" Ryder's hands are gentle when they come up to frame my face. "Did he hurt you?"

I shake my head, suddenly overwhelmed. "No, I'm fine. Just shaken up."

"I'm sorry," he sighs, resting his forehead against mine. "I left my phone in my apartment when I went to work. I didn't get your message until right before I came over."

"Your apartment?"

"Yeah." Ryder takes a deep breath and steps back. He runs his hand through his hair and waves a hand at the couch. "Can we sit? I can explain."

My heart hammers in my chest as I follow him into the living room where he drops onto the couch. Shoulders hunched, he rests his forearms on his knees.

"Yesterday I went to Jax's and hung out," he begins, staring down at his clasped hands. "We ended up going to the bar and I got pretty wasted. I had this... feeling, so I insisted he to take me to my apartment above the shop."

"The one that's been empty since you got here?"

He nods, glancing up at me. "When I walked in, everything was there, Noia. All my stuff—clothes, books, furniture, everything."

Careful to maintain some distance, I sink down beside him. "So that's where all your stuff disappeared to."

"Yeah. And the feeling I had? It was like a tingle fluttering through my brain that had nothing to do with being drunk. Kind of like when my shirt appeared after you wrote it into existence."

"Like a sixth sense."

He nods and his gray eyes meet mine, full of mixed emotions. "I just wanted to make sure you were okay. Let you know I'm still here, but I still need time."

"Even after what just happened?"

"Especially after that." His jaw tightens. "Look, I came running because I was worried about you, and I'm glad I did. But it doesn't change the fact that I need to figure out what I'm feeling."

My heart is breaking all over again. "I understand," I whisper.

"I need to be sure what I'm feeling for you is real—that it's coming from inside me and not from whatever magic of the universe that brought me here." He reaches over and takes my hand, his thumb stroking my knuckles. "I care about you too much to not be certain."

I swallow hard, fighting back tears. "How long?"

"I don't know. A few more days, maybe?" His eyes search mine. "Can you give me that?"

Nodding, I force a smile.

He leans in and presses a gentle kiss to my forehead. "Thank you."

"Will you at least text me once a day? So I know you're still here and okay?"

"I can do that." He stands up, hesitating for a moment. "Are you going to be all right? What if Eric comes back?"

"I'll be fine," I assure him. "I can handle Eric. He might be a giant douche, but he would never hurt me physically."

Ryder's expression darkens. "Still. If he shows up again, call me immediately. Promise?"

"Promise."

He walks to the door, pausing with his hand on the knob. "I meant what I said, Noia. I care about you too much to not be certain."

After he leaves, I throw the lock. With my back to the door, I slide until I'm sitting on the floor, listening to the sound of Ryder's motorcycle fade into the distance.

Goonie meows, butting his head against my leg.

"You don't know the half of it." I scrub the tears from my face and pull my phone out of my pocket.

Sasha answers on the first ring. "Did he call you back?"

"No." My voice is still shaky as I push myself up off the floor. "He came over. But that's not even the craziest part."

Her voice turns serious. "What happened?"

"Eric showed up."

"No shit?" she barks. "What the hell did he want?"

I flop onto the couch and tuck my legs to my chest. "He just showed up out of the blue like nothing ever happened, talking about how he'd made a mistake and wanted another chance."

"Oh my god. The nerve of that asshole. Please tell me you slammed the door in his face."

"I wish. I only let him in because I wanted an explanation." I sigh, rubbing my fingers across my forehead. "Then he kissed me, and I kneed him in the balls."

Sasha's laugh is viciously delighted. "That's my girl! I hope you made the bastard cry."

"Then Ryder burst in like some avenging angel. You should have seen his face, Sash. He looked like he was going to murder Eric with his bare hands."

"Holy shit! That's awesome!"

I grin into the phone. "Fuck yeah, it was. So about his stuff. He told me it all showed up in his apartment above the tattoo shop last night. Said he had a feeling it would be there." I pick at a loose thread on my T-shirt—Ryder's T-shirt. "He came over because he got my voicemail and was worried."

"Oh, wow. I guess that's even more proof he's real and is going to stay. So what happened? Did they fight? Please tell me Ryder beat the shit out of him."

"He slammed Eric against the wall and threatened him, but he didn't actually hit him." An evil smile forms on my face. "Eric was practically crapping his pants by the time he left. And he was pissed."

"Good," Sasha says with satisfaction. "That's the least he deserves after what he did to you. So what about Ryder? Is he still there?"

My smile fades. "No. He said he still needs more time. Wants to make sure what he's feeling is real and not just... magic or whatever."

"Damn. I sure hope he figures it out soon."

"I hope so too."

noia

IT'S BEEN A WEEK SINCE RYDER LEFT.

A week of texts that say nothing more than "I'm still here," "Good morning," or "Sleep tight, kitten."

A week of staring at my laptop, unable to write a single word.

"That's it," I announce. Goonie, who's sprawled across my desk like a furry paperweight, chirrups up at me. "I'm done."

No more writing. No more obsessing over Ryder. No more waiting by the phone.

I need a break. From all of it.

Two hours later, I'm walking into Serenity Day Spa.

The receptionist greets me with a smile and checks her computer. "Full day package?" she confirms.

"Yes, please. Massage, facial, mani-pedi, the works." I hand over my credit card. "And any add-ons you've got."

"Excellent." Her smile widens. "We'll start with a detoxifying mud wrap."

By the time I leave the spa five hours later, I feel like a new woman—relaxed, pampered, and more centered than I have been in weeks. On the drive home, I stop at the bookstore to load up on some new reading material. Needing a break from romance, I grab a few mystery-thrillers.

The next day, I sign up for yoga classes at a studio the next town over. The instructor, a woman named Maya, welcomes me with a warm smile.

"First time?" she whispers as she helps me adjust my downward dog.

"That obvious, huh?" I grunt, doing my best to keep my heels on the mat.

She chuckles. "Everyone has to start somewhere. Just breathe through it and don't force anything."

Three days into my new routine, I'm sitting cross-legged on my yoga mat at home when my phone rings. It's my agent, Amanda.

"Hey! I've been trying to reach you for days," she says, exasperated. "The publisher is getting anxious about the manuscript. Are you almost done?"

Side stepping her question, I cut straight to the chase. "Did you tell Eric where I was?"

Her silence says it all.

"Noia, I—"

I barely manage to keep my voice calm. "You did, didn't you?"

"He was worried about you," she defends. "And the publisher needed updates."

"I trusted you." I take a deep breath and center myself. "You're fired."

"What? You can't be serious—"

"I'll be looking for new representation, and possibly a new publisher."

"Noia, please don't do this." Amanda's voice is high-pitched with panic. "You need me. You can't just walk away from your contract."

"Watch me."

A strange sense of freedom sings in my veins after I hang up and toss my phone onto the couch. I lie back on my yoga mat, staring up at the ceiling. The decision I just made should terrify me, but instead, I feel strangely liberated.

No more deadlines from publishers who only care about the bottom line. No more agents betraying my trust. No more writing what's expected of me.

Wait.

I pop up, struck by an idea so clear and perfect it almost takes my breath away.

"That's it!" I scramble to my feet, startling Goonie from his nap on the windowsill. "I'm going to start over."

I race into my bedroom and fire up my laptop. For the first time in months, new words pour out of me effortlessly as I plot an outline for a new series—a quartet of novels following four women who discover they have extraordinary abilities.

"No more perfect heroes with their perfect abs saving the day," I say aloud to myself as I begin to type. "I'm going to write about strong, complex, flawed women who save themselves— and maybe the world while they're at it."

My fingers fly across the keyboard. Kira is a former military pilot who discovers she can manipulate electromagnetic fields after surviving a plane crash caused by a lightning strike. She's fierce, flawed, and determined to use her new powers to protect those who can't protect themselves.

Three hours later when I finally come up for air, I'm shocked to find I've outlined three books and written the first chapter. My body might be stiff from sitting for so long, but my mind is alive with possibilities.

"Holy shit," I whisper, scrolling through what I've written. "This is really good."

I grab my phone and pull up the contact information for

Jasmine Torres, an independent publisher I met at a conference last year who specializes in fantasy and sci-fi with strong female protagonists.

Before I can second-guess myself, I hit call.

"Jasmine Torres."

"Hi, Jasmine. This is Noia Wilde. We met at the Salt Lake Book Festival last year? I was wondering if you might have time to discuss a potential new project."

Forty-five minutes later, I've scheduled a Zoom meeting for tomorrow morning to pitch my new series.

I dance around the kitchen, feeling lighter than I have in months. For the first time in a long time, I feel completely in control of my life.

JASMINE'S ENTHUSIASM DURING OUR MEETING THE NEXT morning takes me by surprise.

"I love this concept, Noia." Her eyes are bright with excitement. "Especially the idea of a series focused on women with extraordinary abilities who aren't defined by their romantic relationships."

"Thank you." I can't stop smiling. "I've been playing it safe for too long, writing what was expected of me rather than what truly inspires me."

"Well, I'm thrilled you reached out. I'd love to see more once you have it. Would you be comfortable sending me the first three chapters when they're ready?"

"Absolutely."

After we hang up, I practically float around the house. Even Goonie picks up on my mood, racing around the living room like a furry tornado.

"This calls for a celebration," I tell him, grabbing my purse. "I'm going to get us some treats."

I grab my purse and head into town. The weather is sunny with just enough breeze to keep it from being too hot. I roll down the windows as I drive, singing along to the radio at the top of my lungs.

The grocery store is first on my list, followed by the post office and the hardware store for some supplies to fix the leaky bathroom faucet.

My phone rings as I'm walking back to my car, arms loaded with bags.

"Hey, Sash." Juggling my phone and groceries, I unlock the trunk.

"How'd your meeting go?"

"Amazing!" I load the bags into the trunk. "Jasmine loved my pitch. She wants to see the first three chapters as soon as I'm finished."

"I knew she would." Her voice is full of pride. "I have a feeling this is going to be the fresh start you need."

"I haven't felt this excited about writing in… gosh, I don't even know how long." I slam the trunk closed and start walking down the sidewalk, eager to stop at the coffee shop for an iced latte before heading home. "It's like everything just clicked into place."

"Tell me more about this series. Super-powered women saving the day sounds badass."

I launch into an explanation, describing each of the four main characters and how their stories will interconnect.

"God, I love it so much," Sasha gushes. "It's so… you. The real you, not the one that's been trying to please everyone else."

"That's exactly how it feels."

"Any word from Ryder?"

I sigh, my good mood dimming slightly. "Just the usual texts.

But honestly? I'm okay. I mean, I miss him, but I'm not falling apart anymore. I've got my own life to live, you know?"

"That's my girl. Independent woman and all that shit."

There's something to be said about distraction, and love is definitely one of them.

I glance up and my heart stutters to a stop.

Across the street, Ryder is standing outside Skin & Ink.

My heart starts up again, skipping several beats as I take him in. He looks good wearing a white T-shirt that stretches across his broad shoulders and tight faded jeans. His hair is a bit longer, curling slightly at the nape of his neck.

As if sensing my presence, he glances up. Our eyes lock and the world seems to fade away.

"Noia? You still there?" Sasha's voice sounds distant in my ear.

"I gotta go," I say absentmindedly, never breaking eye contact with the man across the street. "I'll call you later."

Pulse racing, I hang up without waiting for a response.

A slow smile spreads across his face, and I answer it with one of my own.

Eager to close the distance between us, I start across the street. When I'm halfway across, Ryder's expression shifts to one of alarm as his eyes widen and he throws up a hand.

"NOIA, LOOK OUT!"

Confused, I turn my head to see a flash of red as the sound of screeching tires and the blare of a horn fills my ears before the pain takes over.

Then, voices, distant and distorted, start filtering through the black void.

"...need an ambulance..."

"...don't move her..."

"...bleeding from her head..."

Something warm and wet trickles down my face, and I try to open my eyes, but my lids are too heavy.

"Noia! Baby, can you hear me?"

A siren screams as Ryder's voice, frantic and broken briefly cuts through the haze. Someone is holding my hand and squeezing it.

"Stay with me, kitten. Please stay with me."

I want to respond, but my body doesn't want to cooperate. The darkness is pulling me under again.

The last thing I hear before I slip into complete darkness is Ryder's voice, thick with emotion.

"I love you. Please don't leave me."

ryder

Then...

RAIN IS COMING DOWN IN SHEETS. AS I ROUND A BEND ON my way back from Portland, I notice a pair of hazard lights flashing up ahead.

As I slow down, I can see a woman kneeling beside her SUV, struggling with what looks like a flat tire.

I pull over, grabbing my jacket from the passenger seat before stepping out into the downpour.

Approaching cautiously, I splay my hands out and away from me so I don't startle her. "Need some help?"

She looks up, blonde hair plastered to her face, blue eyes wide with surprise. "Oh, thank god," she says, relief more than evident in her voice. "I've been trying to change this stupid tire for like twenty minutes, but I think the lug nuts are over-tightened or something."

I crouch down beside her, water immediately soaking through my jeans. "Here, let me take a look."

"Thanks." She stands and takes step back. "I'm Noia Wilde, by the way."

"Ryder Blackwood." I offer my hand, which she takes. Her hands, warm and smooth, send a spark of electricity up my arm.

Inwardly shaking off the unexpected jolt, I kneel down in the mud and test one of the lug nuts. "Yeah, these are on pretty tight. Let me get my breaker bar out of the truck."

When I stand, I look over to see her shivering. "Here." I take off my jacket and hand it to her. "Put this on before you catch pneumonia."

"Thank you." She gives me a grateful smile and shrugs it on, sleeves hanging well past her fingertips. "You'd think being born and raised in Oregon, I'd be more prepared for this kind of weather."

"You from around here?" I ask when I return with my tools.

Watching as I position the breaker bar and apply my weight to it, she hugs my jacket tighter around her. "I just moved from Portland to Lakeside about a month ago. I'm a writer. Needed a change of scenery to get past some writer's block."

"A writer?" I grunt as I apply pressure to the stubborn lug nuts. "Anything I might have read?"

Her laugh, light and musical, goes straight to my dick and it swells to half-mast. "Maybe. I write smutty romance novels."

Damn, that's hot.

Now her name rings a bell. I pause and squint up at her through the rain. "No shit? One of my tattoo artists, Lizzy, reads your books. She's obsessed. Been talking about maybe writing one herself."

"She should." Noia leans against the SUV. "What shop?"

"Skin & Ink Tattoo." I move to the next lug nut, which turns more easily than the first. "Been there almost ten years."

"A tattoo artist." She sounds intrigued. "I've always thought about getting a tattoo, but I've never been brave enough to actually do it."

"What's really stopping you?" I ask, working methodically around the wheel.

"Fear of pain, mostly. And commitment issues." Her laugh is self-deprecating. "Once it's on there, it's on there, you know? Just want to make sure it's the right one."

I smile up at her. "The pain isn't as bad as most people think. And as for commitment..." I gesture to the intricate designs covering my forearms, visible beneath my rolled-up sleeves, "...sometimes the things that stay with you forever are the best things in life."

She studies my tattoos with open curiosity. "Those are beautiful. Did you design them yourself?"

"Most of them, yeah." I remove the last lug nut and pull off the flat. "What kind of tattoo would you get? If you ever worked up the courage?"

"Something meaningful. Maybe a phoenix?" She brushes a lock of wet hair away from her face. "I've been through some shit recently. The whole rising-from-ashes thing appeals to me, but it's overdone and seriously cliché. One of my favorite books as a kid was Alice In Wonderland, maybe something along those lines."

I nod in understanding as I position the spare tire. "I could draw something up for you. No pressure, just to see if you like it."

"Okay. That would be nice."

Two days later, nervous but determined, she shows up at my shop.

"I can't believe I'm actually doing this," she says, fidgeting in the chair as I set up my station.

"You don't have to go through with it if you're not ready."

She shakes her head. "No, I want to. I love the design you created. It's perfect."

The Cheshire Cat is whimsical, but with an edge of darkness.

During the four-hour session, we talk about everything—her writing, my time in the Marines, our favorite books, music and movies—even the douchebag that left her at the altar.

By the time I'm finished with the outline, I know I want to see her again, and it gives me an idea.

"How about I help you with your writer's block?" I offer as I bandage her fresh ink. "I could take you out on adventures, give you new experiences to write about."

Her smile is like sunlight. "What kind of adventures did you have in mind?"

"Maybe a ride on my motorcycle. There's also a bookstore the next town over that specializes in rare first editions we could explore."

Her lips curve into a teasing smile. "Are you offering to be my muse, Ryder Blackwood?"

"I'm offering to help you remember what it feels like to live in the moment." I hold her gaze. "See where it goes... no strings."

noia

Now...

MY EYELIDS FEEL LIKE THEY'RE WEIGHED DOWN WITH lead, but somehow I manage to force them open anyway. When I try to move, pain shoots through my body, making me gasp.

"Noia?"

I turn my head slightly. Fuck. Even that small movement sends daggers of pain through my skull.

Sasha is sitting next to me, and she looks tired.

My throat feels dry and scratchy. "You're here," I croak.

Relief flashes over her face. "Of course I'm here." She reaches for a cup of water on the side table and brings the straw to my lips. "Small sips, 'kay?"

The cool water soothes my parched throat. "What happened?"

"You were hit by a car." Her voice breaks slightly. "Some asshole was texting and driving. Didn't even see you until it was too late."

I vaguely remember what she's telling me.

"How bad?"

"Concussion, three broken ribs, and a lot of bruising." The smile she gives me is sad. "But the doctors say you're going to be okay. No internal bleeding, which was their biggest concern."

I try to nod, but the movement makes me wince.

"You've been unconscious for three days." Her voice is tight with emotion. "They had to put you in a medically induced coma because of the swelling in your brain."

"Three days?" I rasp. "Ryder..."

"He went to grab some lunch."

"He's here?"

"Of course. He was there when you got hit. I know you two were taking some time apart to figure shit out, but..."

Suddenly, it all comes rushing back.

My head throbs as two sets of memories compete for space—one where I found Ryder in my kitchen, and another where we met by chance one rainy day.

"Wait, that's not right." I struggle, trying to sort through the jumble of memories. "Ryder magically appeared."

Sasha's brow furrows with concern. "What do you mean?"

I shake my head, wincing again at the pain. I seriously need to stop doing that. "No, that's not... we met on the road? In the rain?"

Her eyes light up with recognition when she realizes what I am trying to say.

"Yes. You moved to your cottage permanently after... Eric. You got a flat tire driving back from Portland about three months ago, and Ryder stopped to help you."

Memories start to realign, forming a clearer picture. My head throbs as I try to force myself to make sense of it all.

"But my manuscript... He's the MMC in my new book... He came to life..."

Her expression grows more worried before recognition hits again. "Oh! You've been working on a romance novel about a book-boyfriend who comes to life, remember? But Ryder is real, Noia. Very real. And more than worried about you."

Before I can answer, the door opens, and Ryder comes in holding a paper bag and two coffee cups.

"Noia." Setting everything down haphazardly on the table, he rushes to my side. "Thank god."

When his hand touches mine, I feel the same electricity I felt that first day we met in the rain—the same warmth, the same connection.

"You're real," I whisper.

Ryder's eyes are bloodshot, jawline shadowed with stubble, and his dark hair is messier than usual, like he's been running his hands through it.

His brow furrows. "Of course I'm real."

"I'll give you two some time," Sasha says, rising from her chair. "I need to find the doctor anyway and let her know you're awake."

Once she's gone, he sits on the edge of the bed, careful not to jostle me. "You scared the hell out of me, kitten."

"I'm sorry."

"Hey, don't. It's okay." His grip on my hand tightens. "It's just... I thought I was going to lose you."

Fear and exhaustion are etched into every line of his face, raw emotion filling his stormy, gray eyes.

"I could hear you," I say softly. "When I was unconscious. I heard your voice."

A tear slips down his cheek. "Other than sleep and bathroom breaks, I haven't left your side. Not for a second."

"You told me stories about our adventures and said that you loved me."

He nods, bringing my hand to his lips. "I do. I love you, Noia. And I'm so sorry it took almost losing you for me to realize that."

"What about needing space? Figuring things out?"

"I had it figured out the morning of the accident, and when I saw you across the street..." His voice cracks. "I'm so sorry. All I know is that I love you, and I can't imagine my life without you in it."

Tears sting my eyes. "I love you too."

He leans forward, carefully pressing his lips to mine.

"Don't ever scare me like that again," he murmurs against my mouth.

"I'll try not to make a habit of getting hit by cars," I promise, managing a weak smile.

We break apart when a nurse bustles in. "Good to see you're awake, Ms. Wilde. How are you feeling?"

"Like I got hit by a car," I reply, wincing as I try to adjust my position.

Ryder fusses, helping me adjust my pillow while she checks my vitals and makes notes. "The doctor will be in shortly to go over everything with you. You're a very lucky woman."

"I know." I look at Ryder, who's gone back to holding my hand.

After she leaves, he brushes a strand of hair from my face. "Did Sasha tell you? Your mom called. She's catching the first flight out tomorrow morning."

I suddenly remember Tish has been away on vacation in Europe.

"Great," I groan. "Just what I need."

He narrows his eyes at me with a smirk. "She was worried."

"You talked to her?"

"I did. She was surprised when I told her who I was. You didn't tell her about us?"

"She had her suspicions, but I didn't clarify anything. If I had, she would've never stopped hounding me." I squeeze his hand. "Thanks for being here."

"There's nowhere else I'd rather be." His eyes grow serious as they fill with heat. "Actually, that's not true. I'd rather be with you at home in bed. I'm moving back in as soon as you're discharged. If that's okay with you."

"More than okay."

He smiles, some of the tension leaving his shoulders. "Good." His thumb traces gentle patterns on the back of my hand. "We're going to take this one day at a time. You focus on healing, and I'll be right there, taking care of you. Then you can get back to doing what you do best."

"And after that?"

"After that..." He leans in, resting his forehead gently against mine. "...we continue to live out our own story."

It's another week before they release me from the hospital. My ribs still ache and the bruises have turned a sickly yellow-green, but at least I can move without feeling like someone's stabbing me with every breath.

After I woke up and the fog lifted, my jumbled memories slowly started to adjust, becoming a more clear, coherent timeline.

While I never actually got knocked on my ass arguing on the phone with my agent, my brain inexplicably wandered down that path. Turns out my brain twisted what really happened with me getting hit by the car and a meeting I had with my agent about a month before I came to Lakeside.

Of course, Ryder never magically appeared in my house that morning. His truck, motorcycle, and clothes didn't actually materialize out of thin air. There was no book-boyfriend come to life, no fictional character stepping into my reality.

I'd been working on a fantasy novel about a romance writer whose fictional hero comes to life—that's where all my confusion stemmed from. The line between fiction and reality blurred when my brain was injured and they induced a coma. The doctor told me what I experienced is a known side effect of the drugs they use.

What actually happened was even better.

While I was in my coma, Ryder told me stories about our adventures—what happened at the hot spring, the day he took me to the seaside restaurant on his motorcycle and he told me about his past, our sexy trip to the bookstore and what went down after, and the camping trip where I learned even more about him—real memories.

We even acted out some of my ideas so I could make sure they were something that could work in my book—like hide and seek.

And Ryder's backstory? All his scars, inside and out, those are real, too. Very real.

And yes, Eric is real. Unfortunately. I'm so thankful Ryder showed up when he did.

The way Ryder and I connected was the real magic. How quickly we fell into each other's lives, how naturally we fit together—a whirlwind romance I couldn't have written better myself.

How he changed my flat tire in the pouring rain. How his jacket, smelling of sandalwood and rain, swallowed me whole. How he asked about what brought me to Lakeside and how he didn't flinch when I told him I wrote smutty romance. How my tattoo consultation turned into coffee, which turned into dinner, which turned into... us.

The smutty romance writer and the sexy, tattooed man who stopped to help a stranger in the rain.

epilogue
NOIA

One month later...

"Ready or not, here I come..."

I bite my lip to stifle a giggle when I hear Ryder's footsteps overhead, each heavy step making the old floorboards creak. My heart races as I curl tighter into the cabinet beneath the kitchen island, knees pressed to my chest. It's cramped in here, but worth it to see the look on his face when he finally finds me.

"*Kitten*," he calls, his voice deep and playful. "Where are you *hiiiiding?*"

I press my palm against my mouth, fighting back another laugh. After three weeks of healing, my ribs have finally stopped hurting when I breathe, and we've been celebrating my recovery in every delicious way possible.

The footsteps stop. I imagine him standing still, listening for any telltale sounds. Then they start again, moving toward the stairs.

"I'm coming for you," he sings, his voice growing closer. "And when I find you..."

The threat hangs in the air, sending a delicious shiver down my spine. My body tingles with anticipation, primed for what will happen when he finally discovers me.

His boots hit the bottom of the stairs, and I hold my breath. Through the small crack where the cabinet doors meet, I can see his feet as he moves through the living room, checking behind the couch and inside the coat closet.

"I know you're not upstairs," he muses aloud to himself. "Obviously there's no place to hide in the living room..."

I hear him open the door to the walk-in pantry, rummaging through it. Pretty sure he's trying to find another secret hiding spot. I've refused to tell him where they are just for this reason.

He moves back into the kitchen, and I shrink further into the shadows, pulse hammering in my throat.

Fuck, the tension is the most exquisite form of torture.

I bite my lip. I can hear him slowly circling the island, and my heart starts to thud in time with the pulse in my clit.

"I wonder..." His voice, a deep low growl, is now directly above me.

The legs of the stool scrape slowly across the floor, and there's an excruciating pause before the cabinet door flies open, and his triumphant face appears. "Caught ya!"

Before I can react, he grabs me by the ankles, pulling me from my hiding spot, making me squeal.

Latching his big hands onto my waist, he lifts me onto the island and steps between my legs, crowding me with his heat.

"That was fast," I pout.

"You think I don't know every inch of this house by now?" He trails his fingers along the edge of my shorts, sliding just enough underneath to make my breath catch with anticipation. "Every place you could possibly hide?"

I shiver as his fingers dance along my skin. "Maybe I just suck at this game."

"Or maybe..." His lips brush against my ear, breath hot. "I'm just that good at finding what's mine."

He grazes his lips along my jawline until his mouth hovers just above mine. "You know what happens now, right?"

"I have some ideas," I whisper, reaching for the hem of his shirt.

Grabbing my hands, he pins them behind my back. "My game, my rules."

"Tell me." My breath catches as he nuzzles into my neck again.

"First," he murmurs against my skin. "No touching until I say so."

I whimper as he releases my hands. Knowing I'm not allowed to reach for him only heightens the excitement pulsing in my veins.

"Second," he continues, fingers slowly working at the buttons of my shirt. "No holding back. I want to hear, every. Single. Sound."

My shirt falls open, revealing the black lace bra underneath. Ryder's appreciative growl sends a fresh wave of heat pooling between my thighs.

"Third," he murmurs. "You don't come until I say."

Sliding his palms up my thighs, he pushes them apart. Dipping his head between my legs, nose against the fabric, he inhales deep.

"Fuck, kitten. You smell so good."

The warmth of his breath against my center makes me squirm. He looks up at me with those stormy gray eyes, dark with desire, before hooking his fingers into the waistband, yanking my shorts down and off.

I gasp as the cool air hits my heated skin.

Leaving my shirt hanging open, he reaches for my bra, roughly tugging the cups down to expose my breasts. His mouth latches onto a nipple, sucking hard while his fingers find their way between my thighs.

"Oh, God," I moan as he slides two thick fingers inside me, curling them as he starts to pump.

His teeth graze my sensitive nipple as he works his fingers in and out, his thumb circling my clit with devastating precision. The dual sensation has me arching off the counter.

"Lie back," he commands, voice rough with need. He places his free hand on my sternum and gently pushes me down until I'm flat on my back.

"Such a perfect little pussy," he murmurs, withdrawing his fingers, but before I can utter a complaint, his hands are on my thighs, spreading them even wider as he lowers his head. The first swipe of his tongue makes my back arch as I cry out.

"That's my good little kitty," he growls against my flesh. "Let me hear you scream."

His tongue circles my clit before dipping lower, tasting me as his hands grip my thighs to keep me spread open for him. I thread my fingers through his hair, tugging when he hits a particularly sensitive spot.

"Rye..." I beg.

His only response is sliding his tongue inside me, his nose brushing against my clit. My hips buck against his face, chasing the pleasure that's building with every lick, every suck.

"Not yet," he says, voice rough with desire. "Remember the rules."

I whimper in frustration, my body aching for release.

"Look at me," he commands.

I lift my head to meet his gaze. His eyes are dark with hunger, lips glistening with my arousal.

"You're so fucking beautiful like this," he says. "Spread out on our kitchen island, so needy and wet."

He lowers his head again, but this time he sucks my clit between his lips, applying just the right amount of pressure. Then, he shoves three fingers inside me to continue their relentless rhythm.

"Fuuuck!"

His answering growl vibrates against me, sending shockwaves of pleasure throughout my body.

"So close," I gasp, tension coiling tighter and tighter with each swirl of his hot tongue as my hips buck against his face.

He pulls away only long enough to say, "Go ahead, kitten."

With his permission, I come with a scream, my body shuddering as waves of pleasure crash over me. Ryder doesn't let up, working me through my orgasm until I go limp.

When he finally lifts his head, his chin is glistening with my arousal, eyes dark and hungry.

Legs still trembling, he grabs my hips and yanks me off the counter. My feet barely touch the ground before he's spinning me around and bending me over.

Pressing his hand firmly between my shoulder blades, he pushes me down against the cool surface, kicking my feet apart.

The metallic sound of his belt buckle is followed by the rasp of his zipper. Trembling with anticipation, I'm already aching for more.

The blunt head of his cock presses against me before he slams inside, burying himself to the hilt. I scream, hands scrambling for purchase on the smooth countertop.

"Fuck, kitten," he groans, drawing back only to thrust hard again.

His hand comes down hard on my ass, the sting sending a jolt of pleasure-pain through my body. "You've dreamt about me doing this haven't you?" he growls, pulling almost all the way out before slamming back in.

I gasp as he smacks the other cheek, leaving what I know will be a perfect handprint. "God, yes!"

The pace he sets is punishing, each thrust driving into me harder and harder. His hand comes down on my ass again, pain blending with pleasure.

"You feel so fucking good," he pants, fingers digging into my hips as he pulls me back to meet each thrust. "Always so tight around my cock."

I can only moan in response, pushing back to meet each brutal thrust.

Quickening his pace, each stroke hits the perfect spot deep inside as the sound of skin slapping against skin mingles with our desperate moans.

"You take my cock so well," he pants, releasing my hair to reach around and find my clit. "Already close again, aren't you?"

I groan in response, his fingers working me as my second orgasm starts to build.

"Can you come for me again, baby?" His thrusts become erratic as he nears his own release. "I want to feel you squeeze my cock so hard."

Suddenly, I shatter, crying out his name. My inner walls clench, triggering his release as he drives into me, emptying himself with a hoarse groan.

Panting and trembling, we stay locked together for a few moments until he carefully pulls out and turns me around, gathering me into his arms.

"I love you so much," he murmurs against my hair, pressing soft kisses to my temple.

"I love you too," I say, melting into his embrace.

My legs are still shaky as Ryder scoops me up in his arms, cradling me against his chest.

"Let's get you cleaned up," he murmurs, pressing a kiss to my forehead as he carries me up the stairs.

I nuzzle into his neck, inhaling the intoxicating blend of sandalwood and leather that's become my favorite smell in the world.

My body is deliciously spent, every muscle relaxed as he gently places me on the bed.

After a quick trip to the bathroom for a warm washcloth, he returns to clean me up. Tossing the washcloth into the hamper, he slides in beside me. Pulling me against his chest, my back to his front, he drapes an arm protectively over my waist.

"Sasha texted me this morning," I say after a few minutes of contented silence. "She's decided to open one of her fitness studios in Lakeside and move here permanently."

Ryder's chest rumbles with laughter. "Jax is going to lose his shit when he finds out."

"Why? Because of what happened at the anniversary party?"

"Yup." His fingers continue their idle path along my arm. "He's been sexing up half the single women in town trying to forget her. Last week, he hooked up with that bartender from The Brew—Melody? I think that's her name. Anyway, the week before that, it was some tourist."

"Wait, seriously?" I turn to face him fully. "I thought they were on the same page. Sasha told me she was straight up about her intentions."

"For her, maybe. But Jax..." His fingers trace lazy circles on my hip, causing pleasant shivers to ripple along my skin. "He's been walking around like a lovesick puppy trying to pretend he doesn't give a shit. Which is kind of funny because before Sasha, he also lived by the one and done rule."

"Huh." I settle back, a smile playing on my lips. "Guess we're going to have to wait and see how their story plays out."

"You want my guess? With their chemistry?" He chuckles. "They're in for one hell of a ride."

THE END

Stay tuned for Sasha's and Jax's story.
Coming Spring 2026

dear reader...

Thank you so much for reading Hearts Fire. I hope you enjoyed Noia and Ryder's story.

If so, I humbly ask that you please take a moment to rate or leave a review on Amazon or Goodreads. Word of mouth goes a really long way for authors and would be greatly appreciated.

Happy Reading!

xoxo—Lara

about the author

Lara Bruni is an Award Winning author who lives in Salt Lake City, Utah. She writes paranormal romance and contemporary romance. In her down time, she loves to lose herself in the pages of a good book and enjoys watching rom-com and action movies.

larabrunibooks.com